The
PRINCESS
STAKES

AMALIE HOWARD

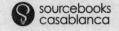
sourcebooks
casablanca

Published by Sourcebooks Casablanca, an imprint of Sourcebooks
P.O. Box 4410, Naperville, Illinois 60567-4410
(630) 961-3900
sourcebooks.com

Printed and bound in the United States of America.
OPM 10 9 8 7 6 5 4 3 2 1

*For my mom, who taught me to extend grace,
to use wisdom, and to be resilient.*

One

India, 1861

THE COPPERY SCENT OF SPILLED BLOOD COILED INTO Princess Sarani Rao's nostrils as she fled down the corridor toward the courtyard, her slippers soundless on the polished marble. She tugged on her maid's arm, hefting the carpetbag she'd stuffed full of jewels, weapons, and clothing over one shoulder. Bombay. They had to get to Bombay, and then find a ship. *Any* ship.

Her stomach roiled with nausea and nerves.

"Hurry, Asha," she whispered urgently. "Tej is waiting."

"Where are we going, Princess?" the maid cried when they stopped to make sure the second, less-used courtyard was deserted. Most of the noise had come from the front of the palace, which gave them a few precious minutes, and Sarani had sent Tej, her longtime manservant, with a hastily stuffed portmanteau to ready any transportation he could find. She was well aware that her life could end right then and there, just like her father's. This was a royal coup.

Sarani let out a strangled breath. "Anywhere but here."

She'd just seen her father—the Maharaja of Joor—lying on his bed and in his nightclothes with his throat slit. Bile crept up into her throat and she retched helplessly to the side, tears stinging her eyes. The distant sounds of shouting and the clang of steel filled her ears, the acrid smell of smoke permeating her nostrils.

She hadn't expected the attack. No one had, not even her father or his advisors, despite the fact that India, and in particular the princely state of Joor, had been divided in turmoil for years.

Things were becoming precarious with feudal nobility and hostile laborers fighting against British rule, annexation, and cultural practices, and the sepoys in the British army were getting restless.

But Sarani felt deep in her gut that this had been an assault from within. No one but family could get into her father's private quarters. Her cousin, Vikram, had the most to gain from eliminating the maharaja, and even if Vikram took power, he would always view her—the crown princess—as a threat.

The minute she'd found her father, Sarani knew that she would have to run if she hoped to get out of there alive. The only reason she hadn't been in her own quarters was because she'd snuck out with Tej to go down to her favorite childhood spot by the river. One last time, for memories' sake. To do something *normal* before she was married off like chattel the next day to Lord Talbot, the local regent and a decrepit English earl, whom she'd managed to thwart with an unnaturally long five-year engagement...until time had finally run out.

The single moment of whimsy had been the one thing to save her.

Sarani had known something was off as soon as she had returned. While climbing the trellised vine up to her chambers, she'd seen shattered glass on her father's adjacent terrace. And then she'd discovered him. Only her years of training with her weapons master had kept her from screaming or fainting at the sight of so much spilled blood.

Her room had been disturbed as well—sheets overturned, doors askew—as if a search had been made in haste. It had struck Sarani again that the assassin had known exactly where to go... exactly which suites had been hers and her father's.

She'd packed and woken her maid, blessedly unharmed in her own adjacent chamber. "The maharaja's been killed," she'd told Asha. "We have to go."

Tej was their only hope of escape. Locking down her grief and terror, Sarani searched the gloom for her loyal manservant, blood chilling with alarm, until she spotted him waiting with one of the smaller coaches a little way down the drive in the shadow of a cluster of banyan trees.

The boy waved, eyes wide from the driver's perch. "Get in! They're coming."

She and Asha sprinted down the drive and tumbled into the conveyance. It was moving before either of them could sit. Listening to the sounds of Asha's quiet weeping, Sarani forced back her own tears, her body tense with fear, as the carriage rolled off into the night.

Would they be followed? Had she left quickly enough? Would they be *safe*? If Vikram was the murderer—or had orchestrated the murder as she suspected—who knew what he might do? He would certainly not leave her alive. He might be a weasel of a coward, but he wasn't stupid.

The first leg of the journey took several hours. When they stopped to change horses, Sarani felt her dread start to ebb and stopped looking over her shoulder as often. No one chased them, and they'd made excellent time. After they were back on the road, the tears she'd been holding back came like the monsoon. They spooled hot and earnest down her cheeks, and she allowed herself to cry in the privacy of the carriage.

Asha offered her a lace handkerchief, sobbing quietly herself. "What will we do?"

"Go where they cannot find us." Sarani clasped her maid's fingers. "Asha, do you wish to come with me or stay? Tej has no family, but you do. We can secure lodgings for you in Bombay until you can safely go back to Joor."

"No, Princess, my place is with you."

With a sad nod, Sarani dried her tears and straightened her shoulders. They were on their own now and survival was tantamount. Money was no object—she had a fortune in jewels and priceless heirlooms in her portmanteau and carpetbag—but they would have to leave India until it was safe to return. A tiny voice inside acknowledged that could be never.

With the instability and political unrest, the safest place for her would be off these shores. As far away as possible…which left her with only one option.

Her mother's birthplace.

The thought of faraway London, known only from second-hand stories, made a knot form in her throat, but the alternative was much worse. If she stayed here, her fate would be the same as her father's. No, she would go to England and take on her mother's maiden name of Lockhart.

Pretending to be an English countess wasn't the worst thing in the world. She had fortune enough to last a lifetime. She had her wits. She had her training. And she was of aristocratic blood. Mostly.

She could do it…be English.

Sarani caught a hint of her reflection in the carriage window. A wild-eyed woman with dark-lined eyes and a bird's nest of black hair stared back at her, arguably more a mess of a girl than a high-born lady. She bit back a choked laugh. Her old French governess would be in a lather at the sight of her. Even with the aid of a bath and a comb, she wouldn't pass muster. Thanks to her mixed heritage, her complexion had changed throughout her life, and right now, it had taken on a brown glow from recent days spent outdoors. *She* might love it, but English aristocrats were more critical.

And they were quite dependably so…

Over the years, she'd witnessed many curious and disparaging looks by other English lords and ladies in her own court…ogling her as though she were an oddity. A princess of hybrid origins led to scrutiny, and not always the good kind. People saw what they wanted to see. Once, when she was twelve and sick of such intense observation, she'd hollered *boo* and made three visiting ladies spill Madeira all over themselves. Their reaction had been hilariously gratifying, but her punishment wasn't—she'd been forbidden from riding for a month.

Sarani blew out a breath. Plenty of Europeans had darker, olive-toned complexions. She would brazen it out if she had to. Besides, Lockhart was a common enough English name, and Sarani had been raised as a royal, if not a lady of quality. With an English earl for a great-grandfather, she had *some* claim on her mother's family—even if her half-Scottish, half-English mother, Lady Lisbeth Lockhart, had fallen in love with an Indian prince and renounced all ties with her home of birth.

The thought of England was daunting, but there was no one else she could turn to, at least not in Joor. Her father's relatives didn't accept her, not truly, and she couldn't put her trusted hand-maidens in more danger. And besides, she had no idea who her enemies were or who supported her cousin. Though she despised the fact that the British had barged into her people's lands like conquering heroes, ironically, to escape a murderer, Britain was her only hope.

Sarani inhaled a brittle breath, folding her hands in her lap. She could do this. She would get the three of them to safety.

She would just have to hide Princess Sarani Rao.

And not yell *boo* to any frail English ladies.

"Your Grace!"

Rhystan looked up from the length of sail he was inspecting aboard the *Belonging*, brushing a clump of sweat-soaked hair out of his face and squinting into the hot Indian sun. He scowled. Not at the person addressing him but at the use of his title. Two years and he still wasn't used to it. One would think as the youngest of three sons, he would have been spared the monstrosity, but no, sodding fate had had other plans. His scowl deepened as the identity of the man approaching became clear. The harbormaster.

"Thornton," he said, wiping damp palms on his breeches, one hand curling lightly over the end of the flintlock pistol tucked into his waistband. He walked to the edge of the rail and propped a booted foot onto the rigging. "What can I do for you?"

The man was red and sweating profusely when he came to a stop at the gangplank. Rhystan noticed a wiry local hurrying behind Thornton's bulk but did not recognize him. "It's of grave import, Duke."

"Captain," Rhystan corrected through his teeth and fought a sneer. The man was full to the brim with his own consequence, though he wasn't above taking extra coin to line his own pockets from time to time. "Spit it out then, this matter of grave importance."

"Immediate passage is required," he said. "To England."

"We will make it worth your while, sir," the boy standing behind Thornton piped up.

Rhystan frowned, his eyes on the harbormaster. "The *Belonging* isn't a passenger ship. And might I remind you that you have your own steamship, Mr. Thornton, which I suspect is much better equipped for comfort than this one."

"Not for me, Your Grace," Thornton spluttered, wiping a handkerchief over his perspiring cheeks. "For Lady Lockhart."

"Lady who?"

"Lady Lockhart, Captain," the small manservant replied. "She needs passage to England and can pay handsomely."

Rhystan frowned, racking his brain for a face to match the name, but none came to mind. Either way, the *Belonging* was no place for a lady. The ship was fickle enough as it was, having once been a converted auxiliary steam warship that had belonged to a dodgy American privateer, and the living quarters were less than lavish. Enough for him, of course, but nothing compared to the guest accommodations on the rest of his fleet.

He waved an arm toward the rest of the ships docked in the

harbor. "I don't care if she's the queen herself, I'm not taking any passengers. Find someone else."

Thornton shook his head. "None of the other packets are due to leave port tonight for England. Yours is the only one. She must depart without delay."

He glanced at the houseboy behind Thornton. "Why can't she leave tomorrow or the next day?"

"It's a matter of some expediency, sahib, sir," the boy stammered, and Rhystan frowned at the Eastern form of address he'd heard frequently when he'd been stationed as an officer.

"Who is your lady? Lady Lockton, you said?"

"Lady Lockhart, Captain."

The name sounded vaguely familiar, though he could not place it. Then again, he hadn't set foot on English shores in a while. All the names of the peerage sounded the same. "Tell your mistress to speak with Captain Brooks. He sails the day after next."

"That's too late."

"Why does she wish to leave so desperately?"

"There's been a death in the family. Your ship is the soonest on the ledger."

The reason struck an unexpected chord of understanding and sympathy within him. Death had a way of upsetting everything. This unknown lady was racing against time for closure, while he was doing the same, only he was trying to beat the clock to get to his purportedly ailing mother in time. Rhystan could empathize more than anyone.

The boy must have noticed his hesitation because he started forward and bowed deeply. "I implore you, sahib. Please, reconsider."

"Where are you from?" Rhystan asked, curious.

"Joor," the boy replied and then gulped as if it was something he shouldn't have disclosed.

But Rhystan was too stunned to dwell on his reaction. *Joor*. What were the odds?

Unwanted and unwelcome memories, long buried from Rhystan's

youth, rushed up to greet him. He shook himself hard and ground his jaw. What was in the past was in the past. He hadn't thought about Joor—or what had happened there—in years. And for good reason.

A feminine lilt rose in his head: *I'm yours, Rhystan.*

He throttled the recollections with brute force. Sarani Rao had never been his, not when she'd jilted him for an earl. Rhystan appreciated the irony, considering he now held the most venerated title of the English aristocracy, a half decade too late. Joor and that faithless princess were parts of his past that needed to remain dead and forgotten.

"Captain Brooks of the *Voyager*," he said to the servant, dismissing him and turning on his heel. "Tell him I sent you."

Sneaking onto a ship in the dead of night wasn't ideal. Or ladylike. Or sane.

Especially for one newly nascent Lady Sara Lockhart. But Sarani was desperate, and since the *Belonging* was the only one on the manifest leaving Bombay for England in short order, she didn't have much choice.

Tej had explained that the captain had been inflexible. Sarani would have gone herself to beg, cajole, or argue, but she was short of options and time. And she couldn't shake the sensation that one of Vikram's men had followed them from Joor.

"Where is the captain now?" she whispered to Tej.

"At the tavern with his men."

"Are you certain the ship is unguarded?"

Tej shrugged. "He's a duke. No one would be foolish enough to board this ship."

Except for them, clearly.

A half hysterical chuckle rose in her throat. She'd questioned Tej thoroughly, but the boy had been adamant that this was the only way if she wanted to leave Indian shores in short order.

"Won't those men waiting onboard stop us?" she asked as they crept up the footbridge where two deckhands were waiting.

Tej's pale teeth glimmered in the gloom. "I told them it was all arranged with the duke earlier and that he gave orders to settle you aboard in the meantime. I also learned that they were hired here for the journey so I convinced them to give up their places."

Sarani worried the corner of her lip. "And they agreed?"

"They'll live like kings with what you gave me to pay them," Tej whispered when the two men in question took their trunks.

Sarani winced. If this recalcitrant captain-duke found out that members of his recently added crew had absconded with a better offer, he'd be furious. He would be even more furious to discover his new, unwanted passengers. But Sarani hoped the ship would be long at sea before that happened. In any case, the amount of money she planned to settle upon him would be enough to convince him not to toss them overboard.

She hoped.

Sarani sucked in a breath, the briny waters of the harbor carrying a hint of salt on the wind. It smelled like rain. Though it was two months shy of the start of the monsoon season, if a cyclone was brewing, they would be stuck here for who knew how long and at the mercy of whoever had murdered her father. She shivered. No, this was the only viable alternative.

Then again, this duke might kill her, too, once he discovered the deception.

Sarani swallowed her fear and hiked her skirts. Better to beg forgiveness than ask permission.

The two scruffy-looking men led the three of them down into the hold and deposited them in a cabin the size of a closet. A lumpy bed took up one side, a small chest and a chair the other. The lodgings didn't matter. She and Asha could sleep together, and she hoped Tej would find a space in a hammock with the rest of the crew.

A frisson of doubt assailed her as she thought of the weapons she'd packed in the base of her bag: a brace of pistols, several daggers, a pair of polished sabers, and her precious kukri blades. All deadly, should she need to use them. And she might. Four months on a ship she had no right to be on and whose captain already sounded like an unforgiving sort.

Goodness, am I doing the right thing?

England was an entire world away, and fitting into life there would be a struggle. But she had no choice.

It was either that or die.

Two

"STORM'S IN THE WINDS, CAP'N!"

"All the more reason for us to outrun it, Gideon," Rhystan said to his quartermaster, standing at the helm while navigating their passage out of the harbor. "And save on coal while we can before we can put into port at St. Helena."

Gideon bellowed an order to hoist the sails.

"Give a hand with the moorings, Abe," Rhystan shouted to a nearby deckhand, who nodded and shot down the deck. "Raise the masts. Haul braces and sheets!"

"Aye, Cap'n!"

It didn't take long for the ship to be underway, the push of the incoming storm just enough to give them an extra boost once the sails were raised. Rhystan stayed on deck, keeping a close eye on the dark horizon. It was more difficult leaving port at night, but he didn't mind sailing in the darkness.

With the winds from the incoming storm at his back, they would make excellent time. And if they lost wind or ran into trouble, he'd drop the screw propellers. The ship was of a unique engineering design—half sail, half coal-fired steam—and the best of both worlds in terms of speed and function.

The glimmering light of dawn had yet to stretch across the sky, giving shape to the storm that chased their heels. Cyclones were rare but worse than a game of hazard. With any luck, the bad weather would blow past them. Squalls and storms were a necessary evil of being on the sea, and while Rhystan's ship was built to withstand them, cyclones were not pleasant to endure. Not even for the hardiest of sailors. He would prefer not to encounter one this early in the journey.

They'd been out in the Arabian Sea for several hours before he felt the insistent growl of hunger in his belly. Rhystan scrubbed at his sore eyelids. Visiting the dockside tavern last night hadn't been the brightest idea, but the crew had deserved a round of drinking and female company before the long trip. While he'd enjoyed a few tumblers of whisky, the latter hadn't been for him, however.

He'd spent one or two of his younger years in the company of enthusiastic spinsters and widows, but since he'd become duke, sating his desire wasn't worth the risk of wedlock—especially when those women invariably found out who he was and schemed to become the next Duchess of Embry. Now *that* was a trap he strove to avoid at all cost. Avoiding women altogether seemed to be a smart bet.

Rhystan scanned the horizon. "Right, Gideon, take the wheel. I'll head down."

A man of few words and even fewer expressions, his quartermaster grunted in answer. They'd been part of the original ship's crew together, and when Rhystan had purchased the *Belonging* from its previous captain to be the first ship in his shipping fleet, Gideon had chosen to stay on. A mountain of a man with part Turkish origins, Gideon kept to himself. He was a competent sailor, an even better fighter, and he was loyal. But beyond being an orphan and living as a deckhand on the high seas, he never spoke of his past.

That made two of them. Until the dukedom had crashed into his lap, Rhystan hadn't shared much of his past either. Where they came from did not make them who they were. If it did, he would be a sorry excuse for a man.

All over a woman who jilted him.

Rhystan frowned as he strode across the deck. Ever since he'd thought of Joor and Sarani earlier, he'd been unable to strike either of them from his mind. It'd been a lifetime ago. He'd been but a stripling himself in Joor. A third-born, cocksure, nineteen-year-old son of a duke, determined to make a name for himself and forge his own way.

"The army or the clergy," his father, the duke, had said on his seventeenth birthday. "Choose."

With the heir and the spare accounted for, Rhystan had chosen the Royal Navy to be contrary. After the navy, he'd joined the British East India Company because he knew his father wouldn't approve of any son of his dabbling with the working classes. Though tied to the British Crown, it was a trading company—an unscrupulous one as he'd later discovered—and much too pedestrian for a duke's son, even the bad egg of the family. He'd toed the line of being disowned until his father had practically ceased to acknowledge his existence.

When the accidental fire caused by a blocked chimney had consumed the hunting lodge and killed his brothers and father during the duke's fiftieth birthday celebration, the ducal estate had fallen to Rhystan, along with the care of his remaining family: a mother who resented him, a nearly grown sister he'd never known, and a sister-in-law and two nieces he'd briefly seen at the funeral. And so, the precious mantle had fallen to him.

The pressure. The responsibility. Everything he'd run from.

You should have been there, a voice taunted.

Rhystan rubbed his temples, a surprising amount of guilt and bitterness pouring through him. He hadn't been plagued with so many thoughts of his past in years. First, his pathetic first love, and now, his dead father and brothers. The title was cursed. *He* was cursed. Cursed in love, cursed in life. The only thing he hadn't been cursed with was a lack of fortune.

He stopped in the kitchens to wolf down his ration of food before making his way to bed with a bottle of whisky in hand. *A dreamless sleep*, he thought. That was what he needed. Not thoughts of his freedom slipping away or of hot, fragrant nights filled with laughter and adolescent vows.

Sarani.

The beautiful, headstrong daughter of the Maharaja of Joor. His first love. His *only* love. He'd learned quickly from that disaster.

He hadn't thought of her in years. Rhystan would have assumed the passage of time would have lessened the ache, but he was wrong. His chest contracted painfully. She'd been sixteen and stunning. He'd fallen head over heels for her and thought she'd felt the same, until he realized she didn't.

Rhystan came to a halt at the entrance to his quarters as the phantom scent of jasmine assailed his nostrils. He must be tired. Jasmine had no place on a ship like this. *She* had smelled like it, the soft skin at her throat and wrists delicately fragrant. He'd kissed them enough to know. Buried his face in her glossy waist-length hair. Stolen her kisses and shared more. He'd been intoxicated. So much so that the scent of jasmine haunted him to this day.

Slamming the door to his cabin, he tipped the bitter whisky up and gulped it down. He would exorcise thoughts of her from his mind even if he had to drain the entire bottle.

―――――――――

Sarani came awake with a start, clutching her pistol with a shaking fist. That noise had sounded too much like a gunshot. Had the assassin found her? Had she been followed? Discovered?

No, *no*.

She was on a ship. Secure in a shoebox of a cabin with the door shut. Shaking the webs of sleep from her head, she forced herself to release her death grip on the pistol. They'd been careful. They were *safe*. And from the soft sway beneath her, the ship was moving, which meant they were already at sea. Thank goodness for that, then. Her eyes flicked to Asha's motionless form. The loud bang Sarani had heard hadn't disturbed her maid's rest.

A tight fullness shot through her bladder when she uncurled herself from her cramped position, hunched over the chair. She glanced around the room for a chamber pot and found nothing even remotely resembling a receptacle for personal needs. Not even a bucket. Clearly, the cabin hadn't been prepared for guests, though she had no right to complain. Tej had said as much.

The ache became more insistent when she stood, and Sarani resigned herself to trying to find a pail. Or the head, as the sailors called it in her books. Urinating at the front of a ship would be an adventure, though the mechanics of it for a woman might be a smidge more complicated than for a man. Sarani was convinced petticoats were the devil's armor.

If only I'd been born a boy…

That old wish had been a constant during her childhood, and though she'd learned to do things as well as any boy—climb trees, shoot guns, fence, and wield a sword—she was still a woman. Living in a man's world. On a man's ship. Without a chamber pot.

Cracking open the door, Sarani peered down the gloomy corridor. No one was in sight. She crept out and slunk down the hallway, freezing when the murmur of voices filtered down to her but faded after a minute. Well aware she could be seen at any moment, she continued her search and almost wept with relief when she spotted a bucket and mop leaning against one wall. Snatching the former, she retraced her footsteps and came to a dismayed halt at the sight of several identical doors.

Her cabin was on the right, but she couldn't recall which one it was. Tiptoeing to the first, she pressed her ear to it and was greeted by the sound of loud snoring. That wasn't it, not unless her maid was impersonating a steam locomotive. The second was quiet; so was the third. There was no help for it—she would have to try both.

Sarani was deliberating cracking open the second door when more voices came from the stairs. Growing louder and heading her way! Discarding the hard-won bucket, she opened the door and closed it just as three men breached the corner.

Goodness, that was close. Her relief was short-lived, however, as her gaze adjusted to take in the shadowy details of a large cabin that was clearly not hers: the velvet drapes, the large desk covered with cartographer maps, a bookcase crammed with books, and the bed that was at least twice the size of hers...which was presently occupied by a man lying sprawled facedown upon the mattress.

Long, lean, and sculpted.

And shockingly *bare*.

Sarani's pulse throbbed. For a breathless moment, she was stunned into wonder by the taut, tanned lines of those broad shoulders, the muscled planes descending into the scooped hollow of his spine and tapering to a narrow waist cinched into snug breeches that left precious little to the imagination. Unperturbed by her flagging morality, her curious eyes traced over the firm rise of his buttocks and sinewy, splayed thighs encased in black fabric, and her mouth went dry while other parts of her went mortifyingly damp.

Gracious! She hadn't had such a visceral attraction to a member of the opposite sex in, well, ever. Not since...

No. She wouldn't think of him.

Not that a boy from her youth could compare. This was a *man*. A very large, very broad, and clearly very powerful man. She couldn't see his face, but his overlong hair was a sandy sun-streaked brown. Idly, Sarani wondered what he looked like and whether his front would match the back. Perhaps he would be old and weathered. His sun-bronzed back gave little idea of his age, but his face would.

She had a sudden, indescribable urge to see it.

A bottle rolled into view from beneath the bed as the ship rocked, amber liquid sloshing around inside of it. The bed's occupant groaned and flung one hand up over his head. Sarani didn't dare breathe as lucidity and understanding of her situation rushed back to her woolly brain. She should have been trying to hide instead of mooning over some half-naked—albeit put-Adonis-to-shame kind of naked—sailor.

"Cap'n, are you awake?" a voice said, footsteps stopping just outside the door, and Sarani's heart plunged to her toes as she shot a wry glance at the dozing man. She bit back a groan. Of course this had to be the captain…a duke, no less. It couldn't have been the cook or the surgeon or someone without the power to toss her overboard.

"Should we wake him?" the same voice asked.

No, no, for heaven's sake, don't wake him. He's dead to the world, and I need him to remain that way.

"We 'ave to 'cause Crawley found a stowaway," a hushed voice said.

A stowaway? Sarani clapped a distressed hand to her mouth. Had they discovered Tej? It was only a matter of time, she supposed, but at the rate they were going, she'd be discovered next…trespassing in the captain's quarters. When the voices grew more heated, arguing about what to do, she glanced around for a place to hide.

But as large as the cabin was, there was nowhere she could escape detection. The desk, more of a table, offered no hiding room beneath, but on the far side of the bed, there was a wardrobe and what looked like a door that led to a privy. She could probably hide in there.

The only problem was…she would need to clamber over the sleeping man to reach it. Not insurmountable, but not easy either. He was so tall that his feet hung over the edge of the bunk, propped upon a pair of trunks that blocked the way and were stacked too high for her to climb safely. There was no help for it. She would have to creep over him and hope that he was foxed enough to stay asleep.

"Sod it, I'll do it," one of the men said and scratched at the door. "Cap'n?"

With her heart in her throat, Sarani darted toward the bed and hiked her skirts, hopping onto the wooden bed rail. It creaked. She froze midstep as the captain let out a snore but didn't move. He was enormous, like a slumbering giant. Carefully, she moved to the lower rail at the end of the bed and then lifted one foot over his feet, nearly kicking over a heap of books beside it and toppling the topmost one. It made a soft thump as it fell open, but the captain didn't stir.

A sheaf of what looked like translated literature from the Royal Asiatic Society drew her eye. Poetry, if she had to guess. Other volumes in the stack caught her eye, including *Vanity Fair: A Novel without a Hero*, a book by Thackeray that had sparked many an impassioned discussion once upon a time with said boy from her past.

"The Sedleys are selfish bigots," she remembered telling him. "They don't care if their son is happy, only that he marries the right pedigree."

He'd nodded. "That's the way of the nobility."

"That might be so, but my parents made a love match. And what about poor Miss Swartz? It's revolting, such hypocrisy. They were willing to accept her money, but not her, simply by virtue of her Jamaican heritage. How is that fair?"

"It's not. And your parents were a rare exception to the rule."

"I want to dismantle the rules!" she'd growled.

The look on his face had been one of awed admiration. "If anyone can do that, you can."

Sarani blinked away the memory. What were the odds?

And why was she thinking about *him*?

Move, Sarani. Now's hardly the time to reminisce.

Giving her head a frustrated shake, she'd just made it to the other side when the tapping stopped and the doorknob turned. Her heart pounding, Sarani dove behind the privy door just before a head of carrot-red hair appeared in the opening.

"Cap'n?" the redhead whispered and tiptoed to the bed. "He's dead asleep, lads," he said, creeping back to the two others waiting in the corridor.

After a few more seconds of frantic argument, they shut the cabin door. Sarani stayed put, taking in the small water closet and then the empty chamber pot. She was fit to bursting. It wouldn't hurt to relieve herself, would it? The captain wouldn't be the wiser, and she'd rather not soil herself. Making quick work of it, she gathered her skirts and did her business with no small amount of relief before cracking the door and peeking around it.

Her breath caught. The duke was still sound asleep, but he had turned and now lay on his back. The arm that had curved around his head lay flung over his face, hiding it from view. A chiseled chest dusted in crisp hair rose and fell with deep, even breaths. Her dread didn't allow her to appreciate the frontal view of him— she was only intent on escape. Muttering an oath under her breath, Sarani blew out a breath.

Easy does it, she told herself.

Retracing her steps with her skirts in hand, she climbed up on the bottom bar and stretched out her left leg toward the bunk rail. She made the mistake of looking down in her precarious and admittedly lewd position—she was *straddling* the man, for heaven's sake—and nearly toppled over. Everywhere her eyes fell, she saw nothing but acres upon acres of masculine perfection. If his back had been delicious, his chest was a veritable feast. A slow ache took up residence in her belly and then spread like hot oil elsewhere.

She might be in a hurry, but she wasn't dead!

This man did not look like he had an ounce of excess anywhere on him, unlike most indolent aristocrats she'd met in India. The scattering of bronzed hair on his broad chest tapered into a trail that arrowed between the carved muscle of his abdomen to narrow hips. He was not given to indulgence, this man. Sarani gulped and suppressed a shiver at the dormant predator sleeping beneath her. If he woke, she'd be done for.

Then for heaven's sake, you henwit, stop bloody looking.

Sarani had almost swung all her weight over when she realized the soft sounds of breathing had ceased. There was no noise in the cabin at all. Chill bumps spread over her flesh, her sense of danger heightening unnaturally. She spared a glance down and almost shrieked as his hand descended from his face and came to rest on her stockinged ankle, lodging her in place.

Her gaze flicked back up, and Sarani couldn't move, not because he was gripping her with loose fingers. But because every bone in her body had stilled in horror, her eyes locked on his face—proud forehead, an imperial blade of a nose, and a bearded, square jaw framing lush, parted lips. Lips that had been seared into her memory.

This was the duke?

No, it wasn't possible. It couldn't be. Not *him*.

She had to be hallucinating. But those slanted eyebrows and bold cheekbones were distinctive. Taken together, his features were enough to make her heart leap and quail in equal measure, battering against her rib cage with a force that would leave internal bruises. Her lungs ached but breath wouldn't come.

"Dreaming…" he mumbled and inhaled deeply. "Devil… jasmine."

His raspy voice galvanized her into action. Her breath sawing out of her lungs, she almost managed to nudge her foot out of his slack grasp when his fingers tightened. Sarani could hardly take in any air, and her survival instinct kicked into action. *Flee. Flee. Flee.* She had to get out of there before he woke.

Too late! A pair of devastatingly familiar gray-blue eyes, the color of salt and storm, opened and fastened on her. They were very awake and very lucid.

His fingers convulsed on her ankle. "Sarani?"

The low rasp of his voice murmuring her name was too much to bear. Shock and stunned recognition flared in his gaze, emotions swiftly followed by such a fulminating hatred that she recoiled from the blast of it. He had every reason to loathe her, after all.

Breaking from her own horrified trance, Sarani wrenched her leg from his gasp and scrambled over him. She dove for the door handle, yanking it open. But he was faster, moving like the wind for such a large man. The door slammed shut, and he caged her between his arms, all burning rage and brimstone.

Trembling, Sarani turned to face him, her throat working. "Hullo, Rhystan."

Three

THE FIRST TIME HE SAW HER, RHYSTAN COULDN'T BREATHE.

Rising like a water sprite from a wide bend in the river, she was the most gorgeous girl he'd ever beheld in his life. And he'd seen a few. With his lineage and his looks, he'd never lacked for female company, not at Eton, at Cambridge, or as a naval officer. But no girl had ever made him feel like he'd run face-first into a wall.

"Who is that?" he asked, almost toppling from his horse in an effort to keep her in view.

The former commodore of his ship, Sir Edward Blankley, peered at him. "No one for the likes of you, Huntley," Edward said. "That girl's father, if I'm right, is the Maharaja of Joor."

Rhystan blinked, the knowledge that she was royalty and clearly out of his reach doing little to deter his interest or the sudden heated rise of his body. Though that could be because he hadn't been with a woman in months. He and Edward were on leave from the Royal Navy, having spent the last eleven months in the Baltic and Black Seas detaining smugglers, then ferrying them back to port in St. Helena for criminal sentencing. He should have gone back to England, but he wasn't finished seeing the world.

Or avoiding his tyrant of a father.

He felt a spurt of guilt at the stack of letters in his saddlebags. His eldest brother and the duke's heir, Roland, had recently written about the birth of his daughter. Even so, Rhystan had no intention of returning to England. It had taken him two years to earn his rank and to carve his own path without the Huntley name looming over him. Going back was tantamount to telling his father he'd won. And Rhystan would be damned if he ever gave the duke the satisfaction.

Tinkling laughter reached him again as the now heavily veiled young woman made her way up the hill surrounded by a bevy of handmaidens and guards. From what he'd seen before, the girl's hair was jet black, a sleek inky rope that reached her waist, and her skin, covered now, had been a glistening rosy-gold from her swim. He couldn't determine the color of her eyes from the distance, but he guessed they might be dark like that silken braid his fingers itched to deconstruct. He wondered what she would look like up close.

"She's beautiful," he murmured.

"I told you. She's not for you."

Rhystan scowled at his tone, but he was too mesmerized to care. "Why not? Too good for me?"

"The opposite. You're a *duke's* son," Edward said. "You'll be expected to marry according to *your* station. Which means an Englishwoman with an English pedigree. You toffs have to breed the next generation of blue bloods."

"Trust me, the Duke of Embry has two other sons to provide him with the bluest-blooded little ducal heirs. Roland is well on his way."

Edward sent him a dry look. "I'm certain if any of Embry's sons took up with a chit like that and brought her into the family fold, he'd care. So would the Dragon Duchess and all her toadies, I imagine."

"A chit like *that*? Like what exactly? Do you speak of all women like this?"

"I'm being honest."

"No, you're just being a prick."

"Heed me and set your sights elsewhere, lad," Edward said, turning his horse and steering it toward the village. "By all accounts of the local gossip, Princess Sarani is a handful and a half, and her father is in the middle of negotiations with the British East India Company. Find a diversion somewhere else."

Rhystan drew a breath. *Sarani*. Even the lyrical sound of her name made his chest clench. He would meet her, he vowed, no matter what he had to do.

As it happened, a few short weeks later, when Edward mentioned the ongoing treaty negotiations with the resident maharaja, Rhystan saw his opening. He would offer to transfer under Vice Admiral Markham, the Crown's representative overseeing discussions.

"You're not thinking, Huntley," Edward had warned. "And besides, the East India Company has a reputation. Their practices are corrupt."

Rhystan had shrugged. "I'll handle the Company."

"Don't do this. You're forgetting who your father is."

"I never forget who he is."

A disapproving Edward had left, and Rhystan had stayed on. It was at the next state dinner and ball celebrating the end of the treaty negotiations that he came face-to-face with her.

A goddess in opalescent silk.

Nothing in his wildest imaginings could have prepared him for the reality of her.

Like most of the attending nobility, the princess was dressed in European clothing—in her case, a becoming gown that made her sun-kissed complexion glow. She shone, pure and simple. Rhystan held his breath when he was presented to her, the proximity making him feel like his feet weren't firmly planted on the ground.

"Commander Rhystan Huntley," his reporting officer, Vice Admiral Markham, intoned. "Maharaja Devindar Rao, and his daughter, Princess Sarani."

From a distance, she had been beautiful. Close up, Rhystan was struck speechless. Other names were said, he was sure of it. He heard none of them. Somehow, he managed to bow and mumble a tongue-tied greeting, though he felt his neck heat with embarrassment.

A hint of deviltry curled the corner of the princess's lip, but it was gone before he could take stock of its appearance. She nodded regally, and then it was over, thankfully.

Disgusted with himself, Rhystan held up a pillar after the dinner concluded and the dancing began. The princess swirled past in a froth of silky skirts, her gaze touching him for a moment in what felt like a tangible caress.

God, those *eyes*.

He'd been lucky not to have seen them before. On the surface, she might have been the perfect royal jewel—pristine demeanor, elegant features, graceful bearing. But those expressive eyes of hers had told a different story. Something fierce had spun in their green-flecked brown depths, reminiscent of a free, defiant spirit undaunted by the trappings of nobility. It called to something equally untamed in him.

"Why haven't you asked me to dance?" a voice like cool velvet on hot skin asked.

Rhystan whirled, the scent of jasmine curling around his already overheated senses as the princess came into view. Several guards hovered behind her, ever vigilant. His jaw slackened as she laughed softly at his expression. He was still struggling to take in the honeyed rasp of her voice, to deal with the musical, chest-tightening sound of her laughter that followed. "Apologies, I assumed your card would be filled."

"It is," she said. "But I dance with whomever I please."

Once more, she laughed, causing him to fixate on her lips. They were perfect, a dark rose pout that curled in amusement. Gulping, he took in the rest of her face, from those entrancing eyes and strongly drawn nose to the golden freckles dancing over a pair of sweeping cheekbones. By God, she had to be one of the most stunning women he'd ever seen. His tongue felt thick in his mouth even as his heart raced.

"Are you naturally quiet?" she asked after he escorted her into the first turn of the next dance. "Or just shy?"

"I'm in awe of your beauty."

She sniffed and tossed her head. "A woman's worth is not only in her looks, sir."

Rhystan forgot about their audience and suddenly wanted to sample that saucy mouth, see if it was as tart as it sounded. "What other attributes should I be looking for?"

"Her intelligence, her compassion, her knowledge, her wit, her strength."

"I see no lack thereof, but then again, we've only just met. You could be a coldhearted, book-burning, humorless harpy for all I know," he teased, his chest leaping at the delighted curl of her lips.

She threw a dramatic palm to her heart and blew out a breath. "Take that back, you rascal! I love books, more than people, in fact."

Rhystan grinned, the flash of a mischievous pair of dimples in her cheeks making him want to tease them out again. They parted in a swirl of skirts and came back together. "Besides reading, what else do you enjoy doing, Princess?"

"I am fond of simple pleasures, Commander Huntley."

"Rhystan." It was the only word he could safely say after the word *pleasures* fell from her lips and his mind was blanketed with all manner of wicked things. Like kissing. Kissing her senseless, specifically. Sweat beaded under the collar of his uniform. This girl could be the end of him. He cleared his throat. "I mean, my name is Rhystan."

"Calling you by your given name in public would not be proper, Commander."

His voice lowered. "In private, then."

He expected her to slap him. To lift up the voluminous silk of her skirts and flounce away in indignant rage. But a thick fringe of jet lashes lifted as those storm-bright hazel eyes caught his, wicked mirth in their depths, her whispered cadence matching his. "In that case, you may call me Sarani. In private."

And in that moment, Rhystan was lost.

From that day onward, he spent every available moment he could in her presence. If an opportunity came up to accompany the princess, he volunteered for it, and if his commanding officer was noticing his obsession or disapproving of it, Rhystan didn't care. She was as intoxicating in intelligence as she was in beauty, and he was utterly lost.

However, he should have known it couldn't last, and after a few months, Vice Admiral Markham summoned him to his quarters.

"End it," he said without preamble.

"End what, sir?" Rhystan asked.

Markham did not look up from his papers. "This unpalatable distraction you have with Rao's daughter."

Rhystan stiffened. "*Unpalatable?*"

"We need to reduce tensions with the natives, and she's one of them."

Rhystan suppressed his growl of rage, knowing he was toeing the line of misconduct by challenging the man. He'd expected it from Markham, whose prejudice against the locals was obvious, but in recent weeks, Rhystan had become acutely aware of the hypocrisy of other officers in the British regime, particularly the Company, taking what they wanted without consequence and trampling the rights of the locals with impunity. They wanted the lands and the riches, but scorned the people who lived there. Including the maharaja and his daughter.

After spending so much time with Sarani and seeing things through her eyes, the duplicity dug at him. He'd seen those underhanded treaties for what they were—cheating local princes out of power and autonomy, while their lands were pillaged. Rhystan had even cast aside his pride and written to his father, hoping his and Sarani's concerns might be aired in chambers, but he should have said more. *Done* more. He blinked at the vice admiral and frowned. Had his letters even been delivered?

"May I ask on whose authority, Vice Admiral?"

Cold eyes met his. "The Duke of Embry."

Hearing his father's name was a blow. Rhystan's mind raced. How would the duke have learned about his relationship with the princess? Edward was the only one who had been privy to his interest in the girl, but the duke also had many connections in India, including the vice admiral.

"It's not that simple," he admitted. "I care for her."

What looked like disgust tinged the officer's features as a sneer appeared. "She's a half breed."

The slur to her mixed origins made Rhystan see red, but before he could launch himself across the table and grab the vile man's throat in his hands, two soldiers stepped forward to restrain him.

"She's bloody royalty," Rhystan growled, abandoning the hold on his temper.

"You forget your place, boy." The vice admiral rose, his revulsion clear now. "I've watched you for months casting pearls before swine. You're a disgrace to the entire British regiment." He nodded to his men, his lip curling. "Get this sorry sack of shit out of here, and make sure he's on the next convoy bound for London. Let his father deal with him."

Sarani rose from her bath, jasmine-infused water dripping down her skin as her handmaidens rushed forward to enclose her body in warm drying cloths. Her thoughts, as usual, centered on Rhystan... the handsome young commander who had stolen her heart.

Though in all honesty, she'd thrown it at him enough times herself in the past weeks. She wanted to throw more, including her body. Love made people stupid, evidently.

Is it love?

She'd devoured enough Sanskrit mythology to suspect it very well could be. The *Mahabharata*, the *Ramayana*. Her people loved their epic romances, and their gods and goddesses were renowned for celebrating life, devotion, and fertility. At the last, she flushed and bit her lip, her cheeks hot as the handmaidens dressed her in her flimsy nightclothes.

She wished she had someone to talk to, someone to confide in, but her mother had died from a mysterious stomach ailment a few years before. The doctor had said it was caused by diseased water, though Sarani had had her suspicions. A woman didn't go from being perfectly healthy to deathly ill in the space of one day unless she'd been poisoned.

Someone had wanted her dead.

Assassination wasn't a stretch. Some of her distant cousins in line for the throne had always scorned her mother. They worried she would birth a son. But mostly they resented her. She wished they didn't, but she understood why...she was an outsider. Her mother had taught her to judge people on their internal merits rather than their exterior appearances, but most people did not think like that. Not some of the locals, and certainly not the self-aggrandizing British who swarmed her father's palace.

Even with her status as a princess, Sarani wasn't truly accepted by the hundreds of English officers and their wives currently occupying Joor. They afforded her respect, of course, because of her station, but she wasn't immune to their whispered remarks and snide comments hidden behind fans and sugary smiles.

Sarani sighed. Only Rhystan had treated her as if her mixed bloodlines didn't matter. He reminded her so much of her mother in the way that he approached things—with fairness and an open mind. He had strong opinions about the corrupt agenda and actions of the East India Company and had ideas to dismantle them from within.

"I'll write to my father," he'd told her.

"Is he powerful?" she had said and then frowned. "But you don't speak to him."

His eyes had shuttered, but he'd nodded. "He has connections, and this is important."

Not that one man could fight the will or the arm of the British Crown, but her mother had once said that one stone could still cause ripples in the largest sea. The fact that Rhystan was willing to approach his estranged father based upon what *she* had shared with him spoke volumes. The truth was, the more time she spent with him, the more compromised her heart and mind became.

"Thinking about your handsome young suitor?" her maid, Asha, teased from where she was braiding and brushing Sarani's hair.

"No." But her fierce blush gave her away.

Asha smiled, her brown nose wrinkling. "Will you marry him?"

The innocent question threw her. Other than a few furtive kisses and stolen touches, Rhystan hadn't signaled his intentions. What were his plans? Would he stay in Joor? Go elsewhere? Sarani knew he was of good birth. His education, diction, and bearing certainly supported the notion that he was of aristocratic lineage, and his service record was unsullied. But he'd never mentioned returning to England, and the curt way he spoke of his home there suggested a painful history.

Her father would not throw out such a match if it made her happy, but she was his only child. She worried the inside of her cheek and squashed the suddenly uncertain direction of her thoughts. "Perhaps one day," she replied, noncommittal.

After dismissing her handmaidens, Sarani had just climbed into her bed with a book when a handful of tiny pebbles struck her shutters. Her heart leaped with joy and excitement. She and Rhystan had snuck out on many an occasion after such a signal. Vaulting up, she only had time to put on a pair of slippers before the shutters pushed open and a disheveled Rhystan tumbled in.

"What are you doing?" she hissed, eyes darting to her inner door. Rhystan had never come into her chamber before. She had always climbed down to meet him after dark in secret in the gardens. She frowned, taking in the details of his torn clothing and his wild hair. "What has happened?"

"Markham," he growled.

"The vice admiral?" She blinked.

"It doesn't matter. He doesn't matter. Only you do." Those striking gray-blue eyes met hers in the candlelight. "Do you trust me, Sarani?" The way he said her name sent shivers down her spine to her toes. She nodded, her throat thick. "Good, then listen carefully. I want to be with you. But we have to leave Joor."

Her heart jolted. He did want her, and then the rest of his words sank in. "Wait, what do you mean 'leave'?"

"Sarani," he said, his fingers coming up to stroke her jaw. "There's nothing for me here or back there. Don't worry, I'll take care of you. I swear it."

An oozing cut on his lip drew her eye. "Did someone hit you? Are you in trouble?" He rubbed his mouth and then raked a hand through his short golden-brown hair that also looked darker in patches in the flickering light. She frowned, squinting. Was that more blood? "What's going on, Rhystan?"

"I've been discharged from service," he replied. "Tomorrow, I'll arrange passage on a ship for us, and we can go wherever you wish to go."

Sarani felt the floor tilt beneath her feet. "Passage on a ship?"

"Yes," he said, gathering her close. "Do you love me, Sarani?"

She huffed a breath. "You know I do."

"Then trust me."

He kissed her, cupping her face with his large hands. Her fingers wound around his neck and into the silky short strands of hair at his nape. She craved the way his mouth settled on hers, but what she felt went much deeper than physical passions. She belonged with him. This was love, wasn't it? Before she died, her mother had told her that if and when she found it, she should never abandon it. Oh, no, her *father*. Would he understand?

"Meet me at the inn two nights from now. At the Flying Elephant. You remember?" He'd taken her to the rowdy tavern one night, both of them heavily disguised as Royal Navy landsmen, and she'd had the time of her life. "The owner's name is Sanjay. Ask for him and wait until I get there. Speak to no one else." His voice grew harsh. "No officers of the Company, no soldiers. No one. Do you understand?"

"Are you in some kind of trouble, Rhystan? My father can help."

A defeated look crossed his face. "He can't, not without offending important people. Agents of the Crown. My bloody father. And right now, those people hold all the power."

She recoiled. "*My* father is a *maharaja*."

"Under English law, Sarani," he growled. "Open your eyes. How long do you think that will last once the British get the control they want over Indian lands and assets? They're in power, not the princes, no matter what these treaties say. The princes are figure-heads, and you know it. It makes me sick to say it, but your father will not be able to protect us."

She bit her lip. Rhystan was wrong. Her father would go to the ends of the earth to protect her. But she also wasn't stupid or ignorant to the discontented mumblings in court. She understood the political game of which he spoke, and she, too, knew that all the power the East India Company was accumulating couldn't be good. Already local resentment was on the rise. Sarani couldn't blame her people—this was their home and it was being violated.

Rhystan cupped her face. "I won't come to you again. It's too dangerous. If you don't hear from me, be at the tavern two nights hence. Please, Sarani. This isn't what I planned for us, but I need you with me. Say you'll stand at my side."

Her heart could no more refuse him than it could stop beating. "I will. I promise."

Rhystan kissed her again before leaving the way he'd come.

After a restless sleep, Sarani passed the next day in a fugue. Nothing could hold her interest, not even her books. She'd half expected armed officers from the Company to be waiting in the palace courtyard, but there was no disturbance of any sort. Despite her suspicion that Rhystan was neck deep in trouble, she distracted herself with a grueling horseback ride after her studies were finished.

"Princess," a breathless groom said as she rode, wind-blown and red-cheeked, into the courtyard. "The maharaja commands your presence immediately."

Without stopping to change her riding habit, Sarani dismounted and made her way to the throne room. Her gaze scanned the occupants of the room, hoping that Rhystan might be there although he'd said he'd been discharged, but his lanky frame was nowhere in sight. Disappointed, she approached the dais, where her father sat.

Sarani curtsied. "You wanted to see me, Father?"

The fact that his normally stern face didn't break into a smile as it always did when he saw her should have been her first warning. The second was the distant expression in his eyes. "You are of marriageable age, and I have given my consent for you to marry the regent."

Everything whirled to a violent stop. *Marriage to the regent?* Sarani's jaw unhinged, her gaze flicking to the man in question. The regent, Lord Talbot, was an earl, one of the British Crown's agents assigned to monitor local nobility. He was an aging Englishman who had always sent her lecherous stares that had made her skin crawl. His vile opinions on the locals was sickening, and she knew he viewed them—and her as well—as less than property to be claimed.

"But Rhystan..." She faltered, flushing. "Commander Huntley—"

"Has left for England," Vice Admiral Markham said, stepping

into view, his eyes touching on her, a sneer in his tone. She didn't like the way he regarded her as though she were a stain on the edge of his cuff and not a princess a far step above him.

"He wouldn't leave," she said.

"I had him put in a convoy headed to Bombay myself."

Clenching her fists, she met the vice admiral's hard, scorn-filled eyes. "Why?"

"He assaulted me."

The words jumbled into a nonsensical rush, but something like satisfaction in the vice admiral's tone rubbed her raw. He was enjoying this. She recalled the blood in Rhystan's hair and his split lip and smothered her cry. Likely, the vice admiral's men had beaten him bloody for whatever crime they'd accused him of.

"He would never do that," Sarani said, her heart in her throat. "Why would you send him away? Because of me?"

"You?" the vice admiral scoffed, his pitch lowering to a vicious whisper for her ears only. "You dress like us and talk like us, but you will never be one of us. You're *nothing*."

Her eyes widened with shock. "How dare—"

"That is enough," her father cut in.

Though his face was dark red with suppressed anger, he did not say anything else. Sarani waited. Surely, he wouldn't stand for the man's insult! But then her eyes met his, and when she saw the resignation in them, her heart tumbled to her toes. Perhaps Rhystan was right, after all. Her father didn't have any power. Not with men like Markham speaking on behalf of the powerful British Crown. Their wardens. Their smiling oppressors.

"Papa?" she whispered, forgetting herself and her place.

"You will be wed to Lord Talbot," her father said, a note of regret in his voice.

Sarani gaped. "And if I refuse?"

"You will cease this nonsense."

Flinching at the harsh whip of her father's command, she

pinned her lips between her teeth and clenched her fists. He had never spoken to her like that before. *Ever*.

Tears filled her eyes when he beckoned her close and dismissed the rest of the people in the room. "You would sacrifice me to him?"

"Sacrifice, Sarani?" The words held so much sadness, so much pain. For the first time, he let some remorse show, though it did nothing to reduce her ire. "We are rulers. Sacrifice is a necessary part of duty. He is a British earl. You will be an English countess by marriage. What could this discredited Huntley offer you? He is nothing and no one—a third-born, soon-to-be-disowned pauper. We cannot risk the ire of the English or the agreements in place. You are a princess of Joor." His voice hardened, his dark eyes showing the merciless streak he was reputed to have. "Your duty is to your people."

She lifted a blazing gaze. "You speak of duty? Is it our duty to give in to tyranny? Because that is what this is, and you cannot see it. These men are nothing but pirates plundering in disguise. Look at what they did to Bengal. They are our enemy, can't you see that?"

Fear burst in his eyes at her heedlessly hissed words, and she knew then that her father would not listen. "Quiet, daughter."

"Silence has never done any woman any favors."

Her father didn't stop her when she ran from the room and closeted herself in her bedchamber, her body racked with hard sobs. She would have to let Rhystan go and marry a man three times her age. Duty would always come first.

Duty, and the will of powerful men.

She was no more than a pawn...a piece to be played on a board. Such was her fate.

Her very hollow future.

Why *shouldn't* she run? She could leave with Rhystan and never look back. But what if Markham was telling the truth and he was already gone? Her heart battled with her head, reason warring with impossible dreams. But in the end, Sarani knew she couldn't abandon her people, not when she had any shred of power left in her. She had a voice and she would use it, even if her new husband tried to muzzle her.

Quelling her protesting heart, she reached for a piece of parchment and a quill before hesitating. It was not the done thing for an unmarried lady to write to a gentleman, but Sarani couldn't bear the thought of Rhystan not knowing why she hadn't come, if he did show up to the inn. She had to explain why she'd broken her promise to meet him. Perhaps it was in the face of her own sorrow or perhaps it was because, deep down, she felt like she'd wronged him somehow. But he had to know the truth, even if he'd already been sent away for good. Her message might never reach him, but she had to try.

She asked her houseboy Tej to deliver the note in secret to Sanjay at the Flying Elephant, in the event that it would get to Rhystan. It was short and precise, conveying nothing of her inner heartbreak.

Commander Huntley,

I am to marry an earl, a peer of the realm, at my father's behest. Please understand that this is my duty. I wish you peace upon your return to your home. Be happy, Rhystan.

Sincerely, Sarani Rao,
Princess of Joor

She agonized about how to sign it. *Yours* had come to mind. But she wasn't his. She didn't even belong to herself.

She belonged to Joor.

Four

HULLO, RHYSTAN.

Two whispered words that felt like lead ballast and shot him five years into the past reverberated in his whisky-soaked head. The melodious hum of her voice prickling over his skin hadn't changed. Nor had its effect on him, clearly. Her jasmine-scented skin was pure opium, threatening to suck him down into its dark, sultry depths. Rhystan knew where that road led—he'd been there, and it had nearly destroyed him. He fought the pull with everything in him.

What the devil is the bloody Princess of Joor doing here?

"I'm sure you're wondering why I'm here," she said. Dimly, he debated whether he'd bellowed the question. He lifted an eyebrow in expectant silence, and she ducked beneath his arm to put some space between them. "I'm Lady Lockhart, you see."

He blinked, turning. "Lady who?"

"Lockhart. My manservant came to see you yesterday. About passage to England?"

Fighting past the fog in his brain, Rhystan recalled the boy who had offered him money. He distinctly recalled telling both Thornton and the servant *no* in no uncertain terms.

"I told Thornton and your servant that I would not take any passengers."

She cleared her elegant throat, those high cheekbones staining rose. "Yes, well. There was a misunderstanding. You will be compensated, of course."

Rhystan's eyes narrowed and he pushed off the door. He didn't miss her flinch or the fact that she'd moved to insert the desk between them. "I also made it clear that no amount of money would sway me."

His mocking gaze swept her trim form. Sleek tendrils of ebony hair escaped the loose knot of her coiffure to toy with the perfect oval of her face. Her beauty had not dimmed with time. He did not let his gaze drop to the decadent, dusky bow of her lips, knowing they'd always been his undoing.

Instead, he let his mouth curl into a slow, derisive smirk. "I assume then that you have some other form of compensation in mind?" The insinuation was far from veiled.

"You are a brute."

"And you are a beautiful woman, despite everything."

"You hate me, remember?" she tossed back. "Or have you forgotten your correspondence outlining my transgressions in such foul detail?"

His face tightened. He hadn't forgotten the response he'd sent from Bombay after receiving her thin excuse for a letter, delivered by Markham himself, but he hadn't waited around to find out whether she'd received his reply. Had she spoken to the tavern owner? Heard about the wretched state in which he'd been beaten and taken? Or gotten one of her lackeys to report back on what had happened to poor, naive, heartsore Commander Huntley?

She and whichever bootlicking earl she'd married had probably had a good laugh at his expense. His letter was the least of what she deserved.

"Everything above my waist does," he said with a pointed look. "Doesn't mean my cock agrees. Ask any of the men on this ship. Holes are holes."

Her face flushed red. "You are—"

"Yes, yes, a brute." Rhystan waved a careless arm. "We've already established that, Princess Sarani or Lady Whatever-The-Fuck-Your-Name-Is."

Ignoring her flinch at his oath, he sauntered to the near side of the desk while swiping the half-full bottle of whisky from the floor and taking a liberal swallow. Leaning on the edge of the desk, he crossed one foot over his ankle. The casual stance belied the latent rage coursing through his veins.

"So shall I call you Countess or Princess?" he drawled. "Which title is worth more, do you think?"

Her mouth tightened imperceptibly, her spine going stiff. "I should think duke trumps both of those, Your Grace."

Rhystan laughed without mirth. "Ah, the trap springs. You wish to set your sights on a loftier peer. I hate to disappoint you, my clever stowaway, but I'm not in the market for a wife." His mouth turned into a smirk. "Or a shipboard doxy."

"What happened to you?" she blurted out, a slender hand going to her throat.

His brows cinched in disbelief. "You have to ask?"

"Rhystan—"

"As you have so cleverly discerned, Countess, might I remind you that the appropriate form of address is 'Duke' or 'Captain.' And you were about to tell me what you were doing on my ship." His frown deepened. "Are you alone?"

"No, of course not," she said.

He pushed off the desk, rolling his shoulders. "Please don't tell me that Lord Liverhart is somewhere on this ship, or I will be forced to ferret him out and cast him overboard."

His unwelcome guest worried the corner of her mouth between her teeth in a gesture that made him desperate to kiss her once upon a time. Now, it only made him want to throttle something. He chose the bottle instead and lifted it to his lips to take another long swig. He then turned to lean over the desk, narrowing the distance between them.

Her eyes lowered to his bare chest and jerked away as if scorched.

"For heaven's sake, can't you put on a shirt?" Her cheeks flamed with bright spots of color. "You're indecent."

"You are in my cabin, Sarani dearest, on my ship." He smiled and flexed his pectoral muscles. He'd fantasized for years about how he'd receive her if their paths ever crossed, and while this wasn't one of the creative ways he'd imagined, he still took perverse delight in her maidenly discomfort. "And I was sleeping until you decided to climb into my bed."

"I didn't climb into your bed. I simply mistook the cabins because your men were outside," she snapped. "And it's Sara now."

"What?"

"My name is Sara."

He smirked. "So English. So tepid. Decided to deny your heritage, have you, Countess?"

"Desperate times," she said flatly.

Something in her voice made his eyes clash with hers, but he didn't care enough to delve further. At least, that was what he told himself. He was curious why she was running from India, but he would rather castrate himself than ask.

"You have yet to explain why you're here and whether I need to feed your earl to the sharks."

"I have…no husband." She sucked in a breath. "I'm here with my maid, and you've met Tej."

Rhystan blinked, his thoughts momentarily derailed. No husband? If she went by Lady Lockhart, did that mean she was a widow? He frowned. There'd only been a handful of titled English peers in Joor—a few earls and barons—but he hadn't cared to make their acquaintance or learn their names. No, the only obsession that had consumed him stood not a foot in front of him.

"Where is he then?" he asked and wanted to kick himself.

"Why does it matter?" Sarani—*no, Sara*—answered. It would be best for him to get used to thinking of her as that. A stranger. One who had conspired to wheedle her way aboard. He supposed he shouldn't be surprised. She was a master of artifice. He should know—she'd claimed to love him and then left him in the space of two days.

"You're right, it doesn't." Rhystan took another draught. "How did you get on my ship?"

"Tej paid two of your new crew to take their place."

His eyes narrowed. "Take their place?"

"You hired new men. We offered them more."

Rhystan couldn't control the rise of fury. The sheer arrogance of her. Buying off his crew? A logical voice in his head reminded him that they weren't truly his men, merely deckhand replacements he'd employed in Bombay, but he was too angry to listen. Shoving off the desk with a force that nearly broke it from its moorings on the floor, he strode to the door, grabbing his discarded shirt at the foot of the bed and yanking it over his head.

"Sorry to disappoint you, Princess, but I won't stand for it. I am turning this damned ship around."

"I can pay you." Her voice shook. "Whatever you want."

He halted, his shoulders stilling, and turned to rake her person with a contemptuous gaze. "You have nothing on this earth to offer, Lady Lockhart. Nothing I would ever desire in this entire fucking lifetime."

Sarani pressed a hand to her throat, feeling her fluttering pulse as the door crashed into its frame. That could have gone worse. She was still in one piece. For now.

She'd never expected to cross paths with *him*, not in a thousand years.

This duke was nothing like the boy she'd known. Apart from the physical likeness, that laughing, earnest boy no longer existed. In his place was a rugged, hardened man who had no soft edges, no compassion whatsoever. And no laughter in sight.

He'd grown taller, if that were even possible, towering above her, and he'd broadened, too. Significantly. Five years ago, she'd seen him without a shirt and the view had been incredible. The view now was brain-melting. His physique was sculpted to warrior-like perfection by what she guessed would have been years of hard labor on his ships, and his skin had been baked to a mouth-watering hue by the sun. But the biggest change was in his eyes. Those stormy ocean eyes had been unreadable. They'd become hard and unfeeling.

Unforgiving.

She was in dangerous territory.

His awful letter five years ago had been clear in his opinion of her, and Sarani had no doubt in her mind that he reviled her with a fire that still simmered under his skin. The missive had been laced with hurt, which she had understood, but the cruel intent had struck hard. It had delivered the bitter words of a cold, contemptuous stranger.

The man she saw now.

Sarani shivered, rubbing her own clammy, chilled flesh. Half expecting to see the captain's lumbering form lurking outside the cabin, she scooted to the next door and darted in. Asha was no longer asleep but unpacking their sparse belongings.

Her gaze fell on Sarani's pinched face. "Are you well, Princess?"

"Yes." She huffed a scattered breath. "It's Lady Lockhart from now on, remember." The address made her heart clench. Though it had been her mother's name, it wasn't surprising by any stretch that Rhystan had assumed it was the title of the earl she'd married. That had been clear from the way he'd spat it out like a mouthful of poison. "Try to get some sleep. It's still early yet. You can finish that in the morning."

Asha rubbed her eyes and nodded. "Will you not sleep?" she asked when Sarani moved back to the door.

"As if I could," she muttered and then forced a reassuring smile. "I need to speak to the captain."

"The captain?" Asha's eyes widened with fear.

She nodded. "He knows we are here."

Somehow she would have to convince Rhystan to help and not to turn the ship around. He hated her, that much was clear. But in most cases, love and hate were inexplicably twined emotions. The greater the love, the greater the hate. Perhaps love was stretching it, though Rhystan had had tender feelings for her in the past. Maybe those weren't all gone.

Or maybe she had skeins of wool in her brain.

Who are you fooling? The man loathes the air you breathe.

Just five years ago, loathing had been the opposite of his feelings. He'd adored her, his eyes alight with so much affection. Sarani forced herself to keep from being caught up in the images of a different, younger, less jaded Rhystan that filled her desperate brain.

She would do well to remember that that boy no longer existed. And the man in his place was a cold, hard, cynical brute who had an ax to sharpen at the grindstone. Regardless, she had to convince him somehow.

At any cost, even her morals.

She made to leave just as the cabin door crashed open and Asha cried out with a shriek, burying her head beneath the thin woolen blanket. Sarani's heart slammed into her throat at the looming sight of the windblown captain crowding the doorway. Anger and frustration brimmed in his eyes, and a part of her wanted to join her maid in cowering under the covers.

"Don't worry, Asha," Sarani soothed the girl. "There's nothing to be afraid of." With a glare, she walked to where the silent, seething duke was waiting, his harsh features unreadable. "Was that necessary? You scared her half to death."

"My ship, my rules, my doors."

"Your poor temper, too, clearly," she shot back.

His mouth tightened. Sparing the maid the obvious confrontation, Sarani followed him into the narrow corridor, crowded by his bulk. Another even larger man with a shaved head waited at one end, blocking the way. She blinked. Did Rhystan think she would run? Flee overboard?

A sudden heave of the ship had her careening toward him, and rough hands reached out to steady her. She felt the leashed strength in his fingers, smelled the sea on his clothes, and forced herself to look up. His lips were flat, those steely eyes guarded. Neither of them spoke, a thousand hours of raw memory ricocheting between them.

Sarani's entire body hummed with awareness.

Gracious, he only had to touch her and she was ready to launch herself into that solid chest. Strip herself bare and throw herself at his mercy, though a hard man like him would have none to spare. He would use her thoroughly. That dissolute thought made her burn hotter.

The captain shook his head, droplets of water catching her face. One flicked to her lips, and she tasted salt. Swallowing hard, she raised her eyes to his damp hair. "You're soaked," she murmured.

He blew out a breath and released her, a muscle beating in his jaw. "You've won."

"Won?"

"There's a cyclone on our heels," he gritted out. "If we turn back now, we'll be blown off course. So you get your wish, Princess. Passage to St. Helena at least."

She blinked. "St. Helena? The shipping port?"

"When we stop at the coaling station there to refuel," he said, "you'll find alternate passage, I'm sure."

It was more than she'd expected. "Thank you."

He scowled. "Don't thank me yet. You've cheated me of two of my much-needed men, and you will need to take their place. It's a long journey, and we need every sailor onboard to pull his weight."

Disbelief replaced relief. "I'm not a boatswain—"

"Clearly," he said. "But you owe me. An eye for an eye. A man for a man." Rhystan smirked. "Or woman as the case may be. You'll have to get those delicate hands of yours dirty."

"I'm not afraid of hard work."

His hand rose toward her, and Sarani held her ground. His thumb swiped across her cheek in an unbearably soft stroke, wiping away the stray drops of seawater that had landed there. She wanted to lean into that wide palm, remember the way he used to cradle her jaw, but she kept still, reminding herself that this wasn't the same man she knew. He hated her, scorned her, thought her a jezebel. He'd written as much.

She let out a breath. "What do you expect of me?"

"One of the men was supposed to be my new cabin boy," he said. "I'm sure we'll come to a suitable arrangement, Lady Lockhart."

The carnal smile that slid across his lips was decidedly predatory. Sarani couldn't hold back the shiver that chased down her spine, but she straightened it until it felt like the bones might snap. He might be the captain here, but there were still rules of decorum that needed to be followed. She was a lady…and he was a duke. Modesty would have to be maintained, for both their sakes. She might be at his mercy for the moment, but she was *not* his plaything.

Or a helpless pawn.

She made her voice as haughty as possible, stepping out of reach of the palm resting against her face. "I am not a boy. And my body is not for your consumption." Not that she hadn't been above offering up said body in her private thoughts a few minutes ago.

Heat flickered in his gaze, his hand poised in midair between them. "I am well aware. Don't worry, my lady. I won't ask you to do anything that breaks with civility. Much."

Holding her gaze, he raised his thumb to his lips and sucked the salt water he'd gathered from her cheek. The act was blatantly sexual, and transfixed by the lush lick of his tongue, Sarani felt her mouth go dry. She felt that decadent swipe right at her core and squeezed her legs together beneath her skirts. Though he couldn't see that reaction, his lip tilted in a smirk as if he knew exactly how flustered she was. Goodness, was it sweltering in here?

"Then I consent to these terms." She gulped.

"Unless, of course, you desire it. Consumption, that is." His voice was reduced to husky gravel that made her nipples tauten and push through the silk of her gown. Rhystan's eyes dipped to them, his hot gaze as palpable as if he'd yanked down her bodice and dragged his tongue over them. Sarani bit back the moan that crept into her throat.

"I will never desire it. You. Anything." The lies tasted bitter in her mouth.

He knew it, too. His smile widened.

"Sweet dreams, Princess," he said, turning on his heel toward the deck ladder at the far end. "Don't catch a chill."

Sarani frowned. "What?"

"You're soaked through, too."

His filthy meaning didn't reach her until he was at the end of the hallway. She took off her slipper and threw it at him. It bounced harmlessly off the wooden walls, missing him by an inch. She snarled in frustration and stamped her foot.

"Such temper, Lady Lockhart. Not befitting a proper English countess at all."

"Go sod yourself, Hunt."

"I do, daily. You should try it."

Mocking laughter echoed in his wake, and Sarani was left alone, furious, overheated, and ferociously aroused. That bloody insolent bastard was right as she clamped her trembling thighs together—she was drenched.

Five

THE PROBLEM WITH HAVING THE LAST WORD IN A BATTLE OF sexual innuendo was dealing with the provocative images that said words produced. Namely that particular woman doing as he'd recklessly advised—fingers lodged between her soft, sweetly scented thighs—and bringing herself to swift, heated completion.

Rhystan had seen the arousal in her overbright eyes. If he'd delved under those skirts, she would have been slick with it. Hell, he was at full mast himself. An hour later at the helm, outrunning a persistent bitch of a storm and sodden to the bone from rain and ice-cold sea spray, his erection had not diminished. Nor had thoughts of her touching herself.

Therein lay the problem.

"Conquered your frustrations yet?" his quartermaster yelled through the wind.

"Fuck off, Gideon."

"That's what she said, and what did that get you?"

Rhystan scowled. "When this storm turns, I'm going to thump that shit-eating grin off your face."

"You can try if it will make you feel better," Gideon remarked, folding thick arms across his chest and propping a boot on the rail as if the wind wasn't howling like a wild animal between them. "But I suspect it won't."

Rhystan's fingers tightened on the wheel. If it were a live thing, it would have been strangled to death by that point. Gideon was the only one who knew scant details of what had happened with the woman he'd left behind in Joor.

The memories he'd been fighting came back in force.

He'd been hunkered down in a room at the Flying Elephant when the messenger had come from the princess, missive in hand and followed closely by Markham's mercenaries. Before he could receive the message, they'd overpowered him at gunpoint, thrashed him senseless, and tossed him unconscious and shackled on a convoy bound for Bombay.

As if being injured and starved wasn't enough, he had arrived plagued with malaria. Abandoned in the barracks, his fevered brain fought to stay alert. Was Sarani in trouble? Did she need him? The thought of her believing he'd left without her had gutted him. And then, weeks later, when the fever finally broke, Markham had come himself to take great pleasure in giving him the crumpled parchment and informing him of her marriage to the regent.

She had chosen another.

Wedded another.

It was Gideon who found him half drowning in drink and opium and convinced him to join the privateering ship leaving Bombay. Rhystan had kept the small miniature of her that he'd had on his person—inside a locket he'd intended to gift her—but before he left, he'd written a reply to the princess of perfidy herself. His sentiments had been less than kind, but he'd left the note behind with most of his Royal Navy trappings, not caring whether it reached her or not. Obviously, it had. That pompous, bigoted arse of a vice admiral must have delivered it to her.

Not that Rhystan had cared.

But now she was here. On his ship. As intoxicating as ever. She'd always held some mystical sway over him, though he was older now. And wiser. She'd had her chance and thrown him over for a marriage to a peer. Lady sodding Lockhart.

Once he outran the storm, Rhystan intended to get some answers. Namely why she needed passage so bloody quickly to England, why she was traveling only with a maid and a houseboy, and what had happened to her husband. Other burning questions like why she'd chosen to turn her back on him would never escape his lips.

She'd made her bed, and he'd made his.

Doesn't mean you can't share one now.

The sly thought made his raging desires flame anew. He thought of her straddling him on the bunk, the feel of her trim ankle in his fingers and the heated rise of her bosom. He'd been a hairsbreadth from yanking her down on top of him when he'd realized who she was. The comprehension had been like a bucket of ice-cold water to his brain. The rest of his sex-starved body, however, continued to march on, despite reason.

Even now, drenched in salt and frigid spray, he wanted her.

Perhaps he should have sought out willing female company before they'd left port that last night in Bombay and braved the consequences. Anything would be better than the lust eating away at him. Rhystan shoved a hand through the wet clumps of his hair, ignored the demands of his stiff nether regions, and focused on the matter at hand—steering them out of the path of the oncoming storm.

"You truly intend to put her to work?" Gideon asked, piercing his thoughts.

He ignored the man's tone. "Yes. They took the places of two boatswains. Everyone contributes onboard."

"She's a lady, not a servant."

Rhystan scowled. "She's a goddamned princess. But she came here under false pretenses, and she'll pull her weight like everyone else."

"And the men?"

He hadn't thought of them. For the most part, he trusted his crew, but he'd taken on half a dozen new men after a bout of malaria had culled his ranks. Two of them had taken bribes from her over honest work, which didn't say much for them. And the others were unknowns.

Rhystan knew he had a ruthless reputation, but even he couldn't have eyes on a lady and her maid every minute of every day. Two females onboard for several weeks could prove disastrous.

He speared Gideon with a grin. "Since you pointed that out, you're on guard duty."

The look on the man's face was almost comical, his large jaw gaping and big fingers clenching on the railing. Rhystan was sure they would leave splintered dents.

"I'm your quartermaster," Gideon said. "Not a wet nurse."

"You hired those greedy bastards, so you're equally at fault."

"Fuck you, Hunt."

Gideon stormed off, and Rhystan fought his laughter. "Get in line, my friend."

A handful of weeks later, well into the voyage, a tight-faced, patience-stretched-to-the-limit Rhystan wasn't laughing. He was almost ready to throw his replacement cabin "boy" over the side. In the first week, they'd managed to outstrip the storm by a hair when it veered out to sea, east of the Indian Ocean. And after two more weeks of rain and rough seas, it'd been smooth sailing.

Smooth on the seas, though not on the ship itself.

The storm brewing within its casing was one of gargantuan proportions, promising casualties never hitherto recorded. One black-haired, bright-eyed victim in particular. Rhystan let out an aggravated growl as he climbed down from the crow's nest after checking the rigging and headed toward his cabin.

Lady Sara Lockhart, also known as the bedeviled royal thorn in his side, would be the death of him. Locking her in her cabin would be far too easy. Giving up and assigning her elsewhere would make him an object of ridicule. The men had started making wagers on when he would concede and admit defeat.

The answer was never. Gideon already couldn't stanch his

snickers about the ruthless captain being tested and bested by a kitten. Little did his faithless quartermaster know that this kitten possessed the heart and claws of a tiger.

As vexed as he was with his additional duties, Gideon had kept an eye on the two women. He'd started escorting the lady and her maid up to the deck for twice-daily walks, which they loved, and the men had gathered from the quartermaster's hostile scowl that the ladies were not to be harassed.

Asha had taken to playing a type of bamboo wind instrument, called a *shehnai*, in the evenings. The crew flocked to her like children waiting for sweets, and Rhystan didn't deny them the musical entertainment. The discordant notes of the *shehnai* were mournful and beautiful in equal measure, and the maid's skill with the instrument was remarkable.

It reminded him of his time in Joor.

He suspected the same was true for Lady Lockhart, who usually watched from the side with an undecipherable expression on her face. Sadness? Nostalgia? If he recalled correctly, she played as well, though her talents also extended to the pianoforte and the harp.

Once more, the thought of her made him scowl.

The crafty little imp defied him at every turn. If he gave an errand or a job, she went out of her way to botch it, and when he confronted her about it, she was all doe-eyed innocence. Rhystan knew she was pulling one over him. No one could be that naive or clumsy or unintelligent. And he knew for a fact she wasn't.

He tasked her to mend his clothes, and she somehow managed to sew the sleeves shut. He ordered her to dust his cabin, and she managed to find a rag that the cook had used to wipe his hands while gutting fish. His quarters had stunk of fish entrails for days on end. He'd had half a mind to make them switch rooms and have her sleep in the stench she'd created, but he couldn't bring himself to give up the bed that had been built to accommodate his large frame. He'd borne the reek in grim silence until it had faded.

His precious collection of books had been rearranged by binding color and then size—nautical and scientific texts mixed in willy-nilly with volumes of Shakespeare and poetry. It'd taken him hours to find one with charts he'd been working on, lodged neatly between Thoreau and Brontë. If she hadn't boasted once upon a time that her own collection of books in Joor was meticulously arranged by *subject* and *author*, he would have thought it a blunder.

No, it had been intentional.

Rhystan supposed they were small acts of rebellion, considering how crudely he'd treated her that first day of discovery. But he hadn't escaped punishment either. Despite the tomfoolery, desire was a double-edged sword that cared little for its wounded.

Her constant presence wore at him, getting under his skin and driving him mad. Her jasmine scent lingered everywhere. Not a day went by that he didn't wake with an erection or go to bed without one, and his dreams were chock-full of erotic fantasies, all of which included her.

Not that he would ever admit that.

Once belowdecks, he summoned her to his cabin, intent on making his displeasure known and putting his foot down once and for all. He was the bloody captain, damn it!

"You rang, your lordship," she said with a jaunty bow.

Rhystan gaped at her appearance. Somewhere in the last day, she'd purloined a pair of loose trousers and a shirt, a patched coat, and a pair of scuffed boots. The overall look was better suited to a cutpurse on the streets of St. Giles than a lady. It was also disturbingly provocative. The woolen fabric of her shortened pants outlined the shapely lines of her legs to indecency, and the coat buttons strained in their moorings over the distracting swell of her bosom. None of her clothing did anything to hide those feminine curves.

"What the bloody hell are you wearing?"

"Clothes?"

The corners of his mouth drew down. "Not suited to a lady."

"If I have to run around your ship, this is better for mobility than a dress, trust me." She arched a dark eyebrow with a cheeky look that made him want to bend her over his knee. "Unless of course you plan to throw a ball anytime soon. Then, by all means, I shall rush to be garbed in all my best finery."

"You are a lady," he growled, ignoring her sass.

"But as you've commanded, I'm your cabin boy." She crossed her arms over her chest, the motion propping her bosom upward, and adopted a studious expression. Warning bells began going off in Rhystan's brain. "I've been talking to some of the boatswains, you see, and apparently I am expected to perform other duties as well. As cabin boy, that is."

Rhystan dragged his eyes from her breasts and focused on her eyes.

Mistake. They sparkled with mischief.

"Other duties?" he mumbled, the base of his neck tingling as it always did when he suspected trouble.

"Of the carnal variety. They used a specific word that I'm not familiar with. Bug—"

He choked and nearly fell out of his chair, the urge to commit murder flashing through his mind as he cut her off. "Who exactly have you been talking to?"

She waved an arm. "No one in particular. And I'm certain I couldn't remember their names."

Of course she couldn't. The little scamp was protecting their identities. And for good reason—he'd thrash the lot of them.

"This is not that kind of ship," he said tightly. "And my carnal needs are well in hand, thank you very much." Twin flags of color leaped into her cheeks, and Rhystan reminded himself that two could play at this game, despite the heavy, clamoring ache in his groin. "Unless, of course, you were volunteering your services, which is an entirely different proposition."

Her hands dropped to her sides. "Hardly."

"Then button those smart lips of yours and do your job."

"Yes, sir, yes!"

The added tongue-in-cheek salute made his jaw clench. "On that note, I think I will require a bath tomorrow evening. Tell Gideon to have the men use some of the rainwater we collected from the last squall." The expression on her face was so full of longing that Rhystan nearly cackled. "If you behave, you may have a bath as well."

She scrunched up her nose as if the thought of sharing his bathwater was beneath her but then shrugged as though her next thought was that beggars couldn't be choosers. The frown reappeared when she narrowed her eyes at him in sudden suspicion. "What's the catch?"

"What do you mean?"

"Why are you being so…generous?"

His smile was slow. "I consider it quite selfish actually. A beautiful woman bathing in my cabin? What's not to want?"

"You won't be anywhere in the cabin with me," she said tartly. "I'll forego the bath if I have to."

He grinned, feeling the odds finally beginning to tip in his favor. "Care to make a wager on that? Because trust me, Princess, you'll be begging for it."

Six

SARANI ITCHED EVERYWHERE. SHE HAD GRIME ON HER NECK, IN her armpits, behind her knees, in every imaginable bodily crease. And the more she thought of the proffered bath, the worse the itching became. It wasn't as though she was dirty. She cleansed herself from top to bottom with a cloth and water from the wash basin every evening, but the thought of actually submerging her body into clean water, even if it was only a hip bath, made her delirious with need.

Damn Rhystan for putting it into her head! Bloody man.

You'll be begging for it.

The five words became a taunting drumbeat to her pulse. By the time she'd consumed her simple meal of boiled beef, bread, and peas with Asha, she was a mess of want and anger and frustration. All over a sodding bath. One of the simple pleasures she'd taken for granted was now on her top list of coveted things. Not only was her temper holding on by a thread, but her vocabulary had taken on a distinctly unladylike slant. She had the boatswains to thank for that.

At first, they'd tried to curb their language, but when she didn't gasp in ladylike horror, they'd fallen back to old habits. Now she had a very colorful collection of oaths, some she'd employed more than once in the past day. Under her breath, of course. And usually always directed to one rotten soul in particular.

If that man thought she was going to beg, he was mistaken. Sorely. Completely.

She scratched at her ribs beneath the rough clothing and sighed.

Who are you fooling?

No one, really. She wanted the bath. Badly. *Blast it.* She would eat humble pie. She would devour it and beg for more. She didn't even care if Rhystan bathed first. He took meticulous care of his personal hygiene. She would know—she had to empty the used basin water from the small chamber in his quarters and refill it twice daily after his ablutions. Though he was a foul-tempered arse, he didn't make her empty his chamber pot, thank goodness. He had Tej do that.

A small mercy for which she was grateful.

Back in her cabin, where Asha was tidying the cramped space after patching a small mountain of men's clothing, Sarani had the thought that Asha and Tej did not look worse for wear. For the most part, her servants had been treated well, which gave her hope. Tej had been tasked with helping the ship's cook. He stirred oats and broth two times a day. And when he wasn't helping in the kitchen, he was mending sails, braiding ropes, and shoveling coal with the other deckhands, or emptying ducal chamber pots overboard.

She hadn't spoken to either of them about what had happened in the palace since they'd left, keeping her lingering fears buried. And her worry that her cousin Vikram had to have allies who'd been opposed to her father. Deposing him would not have been easy if her cousin didn't have support. Getting an assassin inside wasn't the issue, it was making sure that *he* would be championed by the British regent as the new maharaja. Sarani grimaced. Talbot undoubtedly would have been salivating at the thought of more control. Pockets would have been liberally lined...enough to commit regicide and enough to ensure Vikram's new station.

That craven, heartless bastard.

Though she mourned her father deeply, fretting about the past wouldn't help her now. Even though they were well on their way from India, Sarani couldn't be sure that trouble wouldn't follow them, especially since she'd involved the harbormaster in Bombay to help her secure passage. And to be truly safe, Sarani had needed to vanish. Without any trace.

The harbormaster was a trace. A loose end and someone who had seen her. And that worried her.

She hadn't been exactly silent in the past five years...sticking to her vow to fight where she could. She funneled every cent of her pin money to the local militia and kept her ears open for information. What she'd been doing was easily treason, but her people deserved a chance to fight for the freedoms that had been stolen from them. Even if they didn't trust her completely, they accepted the little she could do. Sarani had the sneaking suspicion that her father suspected her illicit rebellion, but he'd never done anything to stop her. He might have bent a knee to Britain's mercy to protect the people of Joor, but a man like Vikram, however, would be nothing but a self-serving lackey.

And he would want her dead.

Putting her worries aside, she washed up at the basin, grumbling to herself about dirt, and shrugged into her night rail and robe that Asha had set out. Though the maid's duties had changed, she still insisted on serving Sarani as she had in the palace. While Asha drew a brush through her heavy, lank hair, Sarani sighed and absently scratched at her torso. Even her favorite jasmine oil did little to mask the grime. Were there vermin in her clothing? Goodness, for the life of her, she could not stop dreaming of having a bath. If only to remind herself that she was human and to feel clean from her skull to her soles.

"What I wouldn't give for a bath," she groaned.

Asha's hand stilled. "Haven't you had one?"

"No, why would I?" Sarani's eyes popped, looking past Asha's wrinkled nightclothes to her freshly scrubbed skin that shone like polished umber and her clean, shiny hair. How had she not noticed that Asha was cleaner than she was? Because she'd been too busy scratching and being miserable, that's how. She blinked. "Have you had one?"

Asha blushed, her eyes downcast and full of guilt. "Yes, yesterday. I'm so sorry, my lady. I thought you would have as well, but His Grace mentioned that you were focused on your ship tasks and would have one later."

Snarling under her breath, Sarani shook her head and clenched her fingers. She could easily have had a bath as well. Rhystan had offered her lady's maid a bath before extending the same courtesy to her. Not that she begrudged Asha the bath. After all, she was more family than servant. But that devious, underhanded bastard had known exactly what he was doing!

This was just one more move on the chessboard between them. He wanted to torment her. To gain the upper hand. To make her beg. Several of those choice oaths she'd learned rose to her lips as she thought of his last words to her about begging and saw red.

She shoved open the door and crashed into Rhystan's chamber, intending to blister the hide off the man. And froze.

Good *gracious*.

It was the most seductive thing she'd ever seen in all her life.

For the love of all things holy, it was unseemly how light-headed she became at the sight of the long, narrow copper tub, shaped like a hollowed-out boat and full of steaming, scented water. A jar of soap and a washcloth sat on a nearby stool along with a pile of toweling.

Sarani glanced around the empty cabin. She stared at the mesmerizing scene and actually moaned. Glancing around, she didn't hear a sound. Perhaps Rhystan had been called above decks for some urgent matter. Would it hurt if she dipped in and out quickly?

She could be lightning fast.

Oh heavens, she couldn't!

Rhystan would know, though it would serve him right if she took the bath obviously drawn for him. Sarani scowled. That dratted man didn't deserve this glorious slice of heaven. The soft slosh of water nearly made her swoon as the ship rolled slightly. And that was all it took for her scruples to disappear like smoke on the wind.

Sod it!

Bolting the cabin door, Sarani stripped off her robe and night rail and climbed in, uncaring that the pernicious rotter of a duke could return at any minute. The minute her feet touched the warm water, she was past the point of reason or caring.

It was divine.

The water soaked in her salt-weathered, moisture-starved skin, and without a second thought, Sarani shimmied down and dunked her entire head beneath the surface. Bliss didn't even begin to describe what she felt. She'd died and gone to heaven.

As much as she wanted to luxuriate, she also didn't want to be caught sans clothing in the captain's bath, so she availed herself of the soap and scrubbed her hair and skin as fast as she dared. She threw a look toward the door, but it was still locked with the bolt thrown. It wouldn't keep an irate man from kicking it in, but she was hoping that Rhystan would still be a gentleman. Even if she'd broken in and stolen his bath.

Though given the strain between them, it was unlikely.

She hadn't exactly been the most obedient or accommodating boatswain. In fact, she'd gone out of her way to be contrary, plucking his temper like a master of strings. At first, it'd been to get back at him, but then it became a matter of mulishness. He was determined to break her with menial work, and she was determined to show him he couldn't.

Using the pitcher at the side of the tub, she rinsed her hair and washed the rest of the suds from her body. Throwing another quick glance back to the door, Sarani hummed her delight and rested her arms along the sides of the tub. Goodness, she could stay there forever.

Sighing with pleasure at the sudsy warmth, her gaze wandered the room. She had tidied it earlier, though she'd meant to fill his whisky bottles with water. She'd do that tomorrow. Her eyes touched on the polished brass bucket that stood upon the desk and then stilled. They swiveled back in shock at the strange shape that was reflected in its shiny surface.

Why did that resemble a person?

And *why* did its arms just move?

Squinting at the reflection, she flung a look over her shoulder and nearly screamed at the silent man who lounged just inside the doorway to the privy, his thick arms across his chest, one ankle propped over the other. The duke wasn't breaking down the sodding cabin door because he was already in the blasted cabin.

"Don't let me stop you," he drawled as their gazes collided, his eyes heavy-lidded and hers stunned senseless.

Sarani found her voice…and her modesty, clapping her arms over her exposed bosom and hunching down, despite knowing that he'd already seen all there was to see and then some. It hadn't been more than a handful of minutes before she'd dropped her drawers faster than a doxy on the wharves for a florin. A heated blush roared its way up her neck and onto her cheeks.

She bit her lip. "What are you doing in here?"

"This is my cabin," he pointed out. "And that's my bath."

"Why didn't you announce yourself, then?" she snapped.

He smirked. "And miss all the fun?"

Shoving off the frame, he prowled into the room. Sarani's gaze chose that inopportune moment to snag on his superbly bare chest and the rest of his body clad only in loose trousers. Her breath hitched, skin going hotter. She was equal parts panicked and aroused, her eyes gorging on that broad expanse of tanned skin and the fabric that stretched over bunched thighs with every step. Had he always been this enormous?

"Don't come any closer," she warned.

Horribly aware of her own nudity and the fact that the only things separating him from her were those thin linen pants that hid nothing—not even that thick bulge at a very grievous eye level— Sarani reminded herself to breathe. If she swooned, she'd never forgive herself. And if she kept ogling his groin, she'd have to kick her own arse.

She cleared her parched throat. "Turn around. I wish to get out."

To her horror, his hands dropped to the crotch of his trousers, unbuttoning the first button of his falls as he did so. "By all means, you can, but I intend to have my bath. With or without a saucy, mouthy urchin in it."

"I beg your pardon?" she spluttered.

"Stay or leave, the choice is yours."

He grinned at her and winked, his fingers popping another button. She gulped. The man's arrogance knew no bounds. But as he swaggered closer, she couldn't look away if she tried. She'd seen snake charmers in the village market, the cobras hypnotized, and she felt much the same—helpless to do anything but watch as his fingers flicked open another breath-stealing button. Sarani licked dry lips, a thoroughly shameless part of her wishing to see him in all his nude glory.

And judging from the snug-fitting fabric, it would be glorious.

Her breath refused to come, every nerve in her body screaming with tension as a lighter swath of pale skin was exposed where the sun hadn't bronzed him. When the last button unsnapped, the waistband loosened and rustled over his narrow hips, snagging on the deliciously flexing muscles that formed the shape of an arrowhead.

Pointing right to...

Sarani's breath fizzled.

"Like what you see?" he asked, his voice feathering across her overheated senses and jolting her into horrified action.

Mortified beyond belief—she was *so* going to kick her own arse later—Sarani reached over and grabbed a length of toweling, hurling herself over the far edge of the tub and averting her eyes just as he shucked those diabolical trousers to the floor. Lava-cheeked, she covered herself with the thin drying cloth and didn't look, not even when she heard the sounds of water being disturbed. That didn't stop the mental images from assaulting her.

She didn't know which was worse—seeing the reality or fantasizing about it. Her brain, as it turned out, was deviously creative. Not that those thin trousers had afforded any dratted modesty. His sex had been large and thick and long.

Holy heavens, why was she fixating on his *sex*?

There should be no thoughts of sex, parts or the act thereof.

No sex, not his sex, never any sex, she chanted in her head.

Desperate to make a hasty exit without further humiliating herself, Sarani snatched up her discarded clothing and dragged her night rail over her damp body, nearly strangling herself with the ties. She made the mistake of turning around and immediately wished she hadn't. Whereas the copper tub had almost hidden her from view, his bulk dwarfed it.

She tried not to look, truly she did. But holding on to any willpower was a lost cause, not when the duke sat like a pasha, in all magnificent indolence, his arms lazily draped over the edges and that powerful chest of his on mouthwatering display. Droplets clung to the hair there, dampening it to dark gold. One foot lay propped on the edge of the tub, the other beneath the water, exposing a thickly muscled calf.

Dear goddess of eternal fertility, why did he have to be so masculine? Five years ago, he'd been boyishly handsome, but now he was simply devastating…exuding leashed power and a raw virility that left her body in flames and her usually sensible mind in ashes.

As a sailor, couldn't he have had scurvy? Loose teeth and bulging eyes? Maybe a harelip or a peg leg? Was that too much to ask?

But no—his lips were perfect, his legs were in fine muscular form, and his storm-colored eyes...well, she'd never stood any lick of defense against them. Not five years ago, and not now, when he was hip-deep in a bath and bare as he was born, staring at her with a sensual smirk on his lips.

Those mercurial eyes of his glittered when her gaze finally returned to his. "Changed your mind on staying?" he asked. "I won't hold it against you if you did. Or I might, if you insist."

Sarani couldn't handle the playful lilt of his voice, much less make sense of his words, not while he was so...so dratted naked.

"Hold what against me?" she mumbled, her brain fighting to keep up.

"What you've been devouring with your eyes."

Her face scorched. "You are...insufferable."

"So I've been told by my very sassy cabin boy." He lifted a golden eyebrow, a smirk playing over his lips. "Speaking of cabin boys, did your gossiping cronies inform you that a traditional duty is assistance during a bath?"

Sarani's knees nearly buckled at the idea of touching him. Of putting her hands on those acres upon acres of glistening skin. She wanted her hands on him, her lips on him, her tongue... Gracious, her mouth actually watered at the thought. She wondered whether all those muscles were as hard as they looked. If it was a cabin boy's job, then it was her duty to do it, wasn't it? For the sake of devoted cabin boys everywhere. She'd turned and almost taken a half step back toward him before she came to her rioting senses.

Oh, get it together, you bean-brained hussy.

She should stand her ground. Cut him dead like the royal she was. Flay him alive with the whip of her tongue. But her stupid, shameless tongue had apparently decided to mutiny. It had other ideas instead of sensible speech...ideas that involved licking and sucking and a variety of lewd things that defied decency or morality.

Her mouth went dry at her wicked thoughts of tasting him *there*.

Squaring her shoulders, she met his stare. "I wasn't aware that you required washing like a helpless babe."

"Are you offering?"

"No."

A glittering gaze swept her. "You know you want to, or at least your body does."

"And what would you know of what my body wants, Your Grace?"

His hot stare fastened on her breasts. To her undying shame, her nipples were proclaiming their steadfast adoration, straining against the thin, dampened lawn of her nightclothes that had now become transparent. Sarani slapped her arms across her front, her cheeks on fire.

"So I'm cold... What of it?"

His smile was wicked. "Are you certain that's the reason?"

"For a duke, you're no gentleman."

"I never said I was." His smile grew teeth. "And you should know that I'm done playing games, so you had better get used to it, my little *apsara*."

The lyrical sound of the Hindustani nickname he used to call her—*water nymph*—rolling over his tongue did unconscionable things to her needy heart and already shaky willpower. She was weak when it came to this man. And here he was, throwing down the gauntlet.

He hates you and wants to punish you.

He's a wolf in sheep's clothing.

Don't trust him.

Gathering the shreds of her dignity, she tossed her chin high. "Play your games or don't. But I guarantee you, Captain, that the only thing you will do is lose."

Seven

"THERE'S A SHIP ON OUR TAIL."

Rhystan passed the spyglass to Gideon and shaded his eyes with one palm to squint at the horizon. It was no more than a black speck in the distance, but the vessel had been following in their wake for some time. Possibly since the storm they'd outrun in the Arabian Sea, though Rhystan couldn't be sure. He hadn't been preoccupied with it because he'd been more focused on what lay ahead than what was behind them.

Gideon shrugged and lowered the glass. "This is a common enough trading route. We see other ships all the time."

"Yes, but they either pass or disappear after a few days. That one has maintained the same gap. That's what worries me."

"You expecting trouble, Captain?"

Rhystan shook his head at his quartermaster. "Not that I know of, but keep an eye on it," he told him. "Best be prepared if it is."

Gideon actually looked elated at the prospect. Then again, after being stuck on a ship for weeks on end, a man tended to get restless. And a man like Gideon needed an outlet more than most. Normally, he and Rhystan sparred on deck once a day, but they'd both been busy.

In the Baltic Sea when they'd first sailed together, they'd dealt with many unsavory types on the ocean, including cutthroat pirates, whom Gideon had been merciless in hunting down. Given his lethal array of skills, he'd enjoyed putting his deadly scimitars to use. He'd been in the business of privateering for the carnage and the coin, but lately, actual physical combat had been sparse.

In that first year after leaving Joor, Rhystan had made it their business to disrupt the East India Company whenever they could. They sank ships in the dead of night, disrupted known opium trade routes, and repossessed valuable cargo, only to redistribute it to the locals it had been stolen from. He had taken great pleasure in compromising their shoddy practices and emptying their coffers.

The past four years, however, he'd spent more time in the West Indies, investing in infrastructure, trading goods, and doing what he could to better the lives of the people there. Handing over ownership of the former duke's plantations to the locals was the first thing he'd done as duke. It wasn't nearly enough to account for the crimes of the past, but it was a beginning—and a sign of how he intended to proceed.

Ironically, those choices had been because of Sarani.

Not that he would ever tell her that.

In Joor, she'd always been suspicious of the crown's motives. "They didn't come to settle or to integrate," she had grumbled once when they were at the river. "They came to pillage. Tell me that isn't true."

Rhystan remembered thinking of Markham's plans to subjugate the princely states under his rule. "I wish I could. In their eyes, more advanced civilizations have always explored lesser ones."

"*Lesser*?" Sparks had flown from her. "What makes their country more advanced than mine? Our art, our wealth, our cultural history cannot even be measured. One people's standards of civilization cannot be held to another's!"

She'd been right, of course, and in truth, he'd never looked at the expansion of the British empire in the same way. She'd made him open his eyes to the injustices being committed in full view.

Rhystan frowned at the thought of their now intersecting paths. Five years had passed in a blink and yet felt like an eternity. It was a miracle he'd even been in Bombay at all, but he'd received word of an enormous shipment of opium, arranged by none other than his old friend, Markham.

Had fate had a hand in his return?

In this unwelcome reunion?

With one hand on the wheel, Rhystan let his gaze rove the deck, over the handful of men swabbing the wood clear of seaweed and crusted salt, until it fell on one small figure. Sarani sat with Tej and Red, a man he trusted, braiding ropes. A cap was pulled low over her head, and the nondescript clothing she wore made her blend in with the others, but she could be clothed in a burlap sack and he'd still be able to find her.

He wasn't an enthusiast of her male attire, but Gideon had pointed out that she didn't draw as much notice from the men. Rhystan begged to differ. He'd prefer to see those slender legs obscured by yards of voluminous fabric, not encased in formfitting trousers. Then again, heaving manure from the livestock pen off the side of the ship while wearing a dress wasn't ideal. He scowled. The damned quartermaster had had a go at him for that, too.

"Mucking out the stalls, Captain? She's a lady."

"There are no bloody ladies on this ship, and it's a job. Her job for the man she replaced."

"Get the boy to do it," Gideon had said. "Put her in the galley instead."

The galley was a better place for her, true. A kinder place. Rhystan knew he was being harsh, but he couldn't be weak. Not after what she'd done. "Shoveling shit is what she deserves."

To his everlasting surprise, however, she'd borne the foul task without complaint. Grinning even, when she returned to see to his duties reeking to high heaven of filth and dung and tracking God-knew-what into his cabin. His scowl deepened. If it were up to him, she'd be sequestered in his quarters from sunup to sundown. Or off the sodding ship altogether. Between his marauding cock and his unraveling temper, his patience was at a new low.

Her presence rubbed him raw, mostly because it reminded him of things he needed to keep buried. Like speculating on whether the honeyed taste of her would still be the same. Or wondering if she was still ticklish on the sides of her ribs. That night in his cabin, it had taken every ounce of discipline not to drag her into the bath with him, and all the time he'd watched her, he'd felt like an interloping voyeur.

At first, when he'd come out of the privy, he'd observed her internal debate with amusement, waiting for the perfect moment to announce himself and offer her the bath, but then in seconds, she'd stripped. The power of speech left him, followed quickly by the power of coherent thought. He—a seasoned man of the world—had been knocked senseless by a mere slip of a girl.

Their handful of stolen kisses and furtive explorations in their youth had not prepared him for the sight of her unclothed—all that glorious, honey-hued skin and a pair of perfect dusky-tipped breasts, not to mention the mouthwatering swells of her buttocks and those never-ending slender legs that he instantly wanted wrapped around him.

He'd been hypnotized.

And hard as forged Damascus steel.

As the minutes went by, he hadn't been able to bring himself to move, not when every delicious feminine curve had been on display. He'd stood there in silence, jaw agape, guilt and desire warring inside him, and had wolfed down the sight of her. In his stupor, he'd realized two things. One, Princess Sarani was no longer a girl. And two, his body's reaction to her was much the same as it'd been five years ago.

Even now, as she sat on the foredeck, her ratty clothing did little to diffuse the memory of the damp, dewy skin hidden beneath it, and his body swelled. Rhystan adjusted the crowded crotch of his trousers discreetly, ignoring Gideon's smirk as he followed Rhystan's line of sight to where Sarani sat. The man's thick black eyebrows rose, but Rhystan pretended not to notice. Hell if he'd acknowledge acting like an oversexed greenhorn to his bloody quartermaster.

Sarani leaned in to hear something Red was saying and burst out laughing. The unaffected sound made his heart leap and his groin tighten further. Rhystan scrubbed a hand through his hair, yanking at the roots, and blew a frustrated breath through his teeth. He didn't have to look at the blasted man beside him to see that he was grinning from ear to ear.

"Why don't you just put yourself out of your misery?" Gideon asked. "If you want her that badly."

Rhystan shot him a glare. "I don't."

"Lie to yourself all you please, but the sexual tension between the two of you could propel this ship to the Americas and back again. Admit it, you want her."

"Why would I want a lying, conniving, silver-tongued, devious—" He broke off at the warning look in Gideon's eyes, but not before the object of his diatribe had joined them on the quarterdeck, carrying a tray with his midmorning pot of tea.

"Princess," Gideon murmured, though Rhystan had the sneaking suspicion he used the deliberate royal address to grind him instead of being proper. The quartermaster didn't give a lick about courtly etiquette or anyone's noble rank. It chafed at Rhystan's rapidly souring mood.

"Please, it's just Sara," she said, flushing and setting the tray down on the ledge next to the wheel. She masked the flicker of injury in her eyes with bluster when her stare met Rhystan's. "Don't you get tired of talking about yourself, Captain? Honestly, anyone would think you hate yourself, the way you carry on."

"I wasn't talking about me."

Her chin jutted up. "I'd hate to hear who was your unfortunate target. Though if that was directed at me, having Red spitting in your tea all these weeks will have been worth it."

Gideon guffawed, and Rhystan blinked. Was the chit jesting? Then again, he wouldn't put it past her. He *had* been awful lately. He frowned at the tea on the tray as though the trace of the boatswain's saliva would make itself known, and she smirked. "You should see your face."

"Don't you have ropes to mend?"

"Finished. I was heading to the fo'cs'le."

Rhystan's lips twitched. She even sounded like the rest of the crew now. She sauntered off the way she'd come, but not before his gaze snagged on the threadbare stretch of fabric hugging her taut behind as she climbed down the steps.

In a flash, he was hurled back in time into a memory of a much younger girl draped in a tunic and a near-transparent sari—a length of deftly draped and pleated cotton—climbing up the banks of the river one sweltering afternoon to collapse beside him on the grassy slope. The wet fabric had clung to her legs after her lengthy swim, hiding nothing.

As a gentleman, he'd averted his gaze from the slim outline of her legs and the gentle flare of her hips, though his lower body had already been at excruciating attention. He'd practically thrown his discarded coat over his lap to hide his raging erection.

When she'd entreated him to read a paragraph from his book to her, he had, though his arousal had not waned in the least as she gripped his sweaty palm in hers. Hand in hand, they'd stared at the clouds, him reciting the words and her listening in thoughtful silence, interrupting only when she had an opinion on the author's narrative.

Which was often with those particular volumes.

"Thackeray is a condescending cynic." She'd huffed in outrage, quoting him, "'To be despised by her sex is a very great compliment to a woman'? He doesn't seem to hold females in much esteem, does he?"

Rhystan had laughed. "His narrative is tongue in cheek. And

he does have some worthier gems, like 'Revenge may be wicked, but it's natural.'"

"Revenge is rather a waste of emotion and effort."

"Who said that?"

She'd shot him a plucky grin. "*I* did."

Even back then, she'd defied convention, not one to hide her quick, clever mind, unafraid to use her intelligence. She pushed every limit, exceeded every expectation. She'd lived according to her own rules. A laughing girl with mischief and fire in her eyes. The fierce, rebellious spirit who had stolen his heart. He'd thought he had hers in return. But that girl was gone. Just like the boy he'd been was long gone.

Perhaps nothing of either of them remained. Bitterness and betrayal had a way of doing that, he supposed, scouring away at anything good until it disappeared. He refused to let himself wonder what might have been…whether they would have been married with children by this point, though the thought of her carrying his child made something in his chest ache. Damn, he was a glutton for pain.

"Let me guess," a smug voice drawled. "You're lying back and thinking of England. Or is it India?"

He glared at Gideon. That wasn't what he'd been thinking, though it came damned close. "I'm thinking of wiping the deck with your face."

"Name the time, Captain."

Though he was spoiling for a fight, Rhystan's eyes tracked Sarani's movements as she headed toward the forecastle, only to be blocked by a handful of men at the entrance to the crew's quarters. He couldn't hear the conversation over the snarl of the wind, but he could see the immediate tension squaring her shoulders. Her hands drifted to her waist. He'd noticed the twin brace of knives there. If she was anything like the girl he'd met, those blades weren't decorative.

"Should you intervene?" Gideon asked with a frown.

Rhystan sighed, propping one leg up on the rail. "Watch."

Sarani calmly eyed the men surrounding her, not letting any apprehension or weakness show on her face. For the most part, she'd been left alone by the rest of the crew, with the exception of Red, whom she considered a friend, though she'd felt their stares, some more curious than others.

They knew she wasn't male, despite the men's clothes. But well, she couldn't muck out the pens in a dress, could she? She had Rhystan to thank for that foul duty. It wasn't too terrible, however. She'd insisted on taking care of her own stallion from time to time in Joor, though she'd never mucked out a manure-laden stall herself. In Joor, such a job wouldn't be acceptable for a royal, but that didn't mean she was incapable, especially not to prove a point to *him*.

Then again, she'd never been the usual type of princess.

Like most royals, her father had always wanted a son, and to her delight, she'd been educated and trained like one. Sarani suspected that her headstrong mother had had a hand in that, too. She'd wanted her daughter to embrace all of who she was, and her father had encouraged it. His pride in each of her accomplishments—from fencing to fighting to riding to her schooling—had never waned, even though other British nobles had turned up their noses, and until that day in the hall when he'd commanded her to marry the regent, he'd never treated her as any less because of her sex.

It was that strength she channeled now as she faced down her aggressor.

"What do you want?" she asked the man who'd blocked her way.

He had gold-edged, brown-stained front teeth, his blond hair was hanging in greasy clumps over his face, and his eyes devoured her body like a galley rat with a biscuit crumb. Red had said he was one of the new crew, hired in Bombay.

There was a tacit understanding that she was under the duke's protection, and most of the men wouldn't cross their captain, but these newer recruits didn't know the rules. Or didn't care. Twelve weeks on a boat could weaken the hardiest of men.

"Ta talk like."

Clearly, if talking meant something else entirely. She scowled. "I don't have time to waste talking. I have work to do, as do you. Let me pass."

Drawn by the din, more men crowded the way, but Sarani did not let her fear show. Her hands tightened on the hilts of her curved kukri blades tucked into her waistband. A gift from a Mughal emperor, they rarely left her person. Especially since she'd left Joor.

Tej appeared, his dark eyes wild, but Sarani shook her head in warning. He would get his young throat slit in a heartbeat. Her eyes slid over her shoulder to where she'd left Rhystan and the giant quartermaster, but she didn't let her eyes linger. She could call out for their help, but she preferred to take care of this situation on her own. Things would go better in the long run if she did.

Her weapons master had taught her that being aggressive and confident was half the battle. She straightened, making her small body seem bigger than it was. "I'll ask you again. Let me through."

The man licked cracked lips. "Give us a kiss first or show us yer tits under that shirt. Everyone knows ye're a woman."

He snatched at the collar of her shirt, and she batted his hand away. Tej lurched forward, murder in his eyes, but she forestalled him with a fierce glare. This was her fight. These men needed to fear *her*, not some man who came to her rescue. Otherwise, they would only come back when she was alone and possibly more vulnerable.

"Touch me again, and you won't be using that hand again."

The man sneered. "Ye mean ta fight me?"

She withdrew her kukri from their sheaths, hefting the familiar weight of them in her hands, and stifled a wince. Her palms were abraded and scabbed from her shoveling work, but that wouldn't affect her skill, not with this boor. She used the pain to settle her, drawing it in, her focus razor-sharp like the blades in each hand. Energy coursed through her, but she waited, eyes fastened on her target.

"Are you going to stand there all day?" she asked, lifting a mocking brow.

With a leer, he rushed at her and she spun out of the way, her arm flowing upward in a sinuous strike that sliced along his lower ribs. A line of red appeared on his stained shirt.

"Ye bloody bitch!" he snarled, pulling a cutlass from his belt.

He came at her again but she avoided his blows easily, wheeling and ducking, her own arms darting out to leave more scarlet stripes on his person. They were shallow, meant to taunt, not injure. Sarani wanted her skill to be recognized. She wanted the rest of the spectators to know that she was toying with her foe, that she had the upper hand. He realized it, too, rage burning in his eyes.

The man grabbed his crotch. "Ye'll like what I'm going ta do ta ye."

"If your skill with whatever's in there matches your skill with that cutlass, then I'll have to decline."

The watching crowd—larger now—guffawed. Her glance slid toward where Rhystan had been, but there was no sign of him now. That rat bastard. He didn't even care that she was in danger...not that she was in any, of course. Fighting her opponent was child's play. Still, his absence stung. Just one more hint that he simply did not care.

Well, she knew what Rhystan thought of her.

No matter, she didn't need him to save her.

But a second glimpse to the empty quarterdeck cost her dearly as a sneaky blow to her temple knocked her sideways. As she scrambled to fight the darkness crowding her vision, the man slammed into her body, taking them to the ground. He smelled worse than he looked, the foul stench of his breath blowing into her face.

"Got ye now, wench." His tongue snaked out to lick her cheek, and she gagged at the unwashed smell of him. His hands tore at her shirt, clamping over one bound breast and squeezing roughly. "I knew ye weren't a boy."

Sarani snarled in his face, shoving her arm down between their bodies. "And I knew you weren't a man." With a howl, he went still, and Sarani knew what he felt—the point of her blade jammed right into the soft flesh of his testicles. "Touch me again, and you'll be gelded, I promise you. Now, get the hell off me."

But before he could move on his own accord, he was torn away like a piece of fluff.

Rhystan stood there, chest heaving and eyes blazing, holding the man by the nape of his neck. The smell of blood and urine permeated the air as he handed him off to a silent Gideon.

"Cap'n, I didn't know she was yers, I swear," he blubbered.

"She's not mine," Rhystan growled. "She's not anyone's property."

He nodded at his grim quartermaster, and with one practiced flick of his wrist, Gideon flung the screaming man overboard. Sarani gasped, though she felt no sympathy for the blackguard. He'd shown her none. And if she'd been a weaker person without the means to defend herself, she could very well have been at his mercy. She stared at Gideon and swore she could see a twinkle and a glimmer of respect in those hardened eyes.

Or maybe it was pure, deadly delight. He scared her, but Asha insisted that he was a gentle giant. Though if her tenderhearted maid had seen him chuck a man over the side of a ship without batting an eyelash, she might reconsider her opinion.

Holding her shirt closed, Sarani propped herself up on one elbow, staring at Rhystan, who looked as though he was going to murder everyone. "I had it handled, you know." She grinned and caught sight of Red's mop of hair behind the captain. "By the— how do you say it again, Red?—ah, yes, the big, hairy ballocks."

Red cackled. "Not his. They were probably the size of peas."

Sarani rose and made a show of wiping the blood off her kukri on her pants and looked up to meet the wary eyes of the surrounding men. "I don't know if any of you were friends with that piece of filth, but I swear you'll sing like a nightingale if you come near me. I'm just as good with a pistol as I am with these. Steel or lead, your preference."

"No one will touch you," Rhystan snarled and then glared at the crew. "No one touches her. No one looks at her. No one sneezes in her direction, or you're shark bait if she doesn't gut you first. Understood?"

"Aye, Cap'n!"

"Now get the fuck back to work!"

They scattered like ants, until it was just a few of them standing there. Tej remained, but Sarani dismissed him with a quick jerk of her head. He left with reluctance, his gaze trained warily on Rhystan as if he didn't like what he saw. And no wonder. The duke was furious. Sarani opened her mouth and shut it at the ferocious thunderstorm brewing on his face.

"Sodding hair on the devil's arse, I should have turned back and braved the cyclone instead," he muttered, raking a hand through his hair before turning his glare to her. There was more lightning than anything else in those gray-blue eyes fastened on her, and a wary trickle slid down her spine when he advanced on her, stopping short of crowding her. "What on earth were you thinking to fight him?"

Sarani narrowed her gaze at him. "Are you saying that was my fault? That *I* provoked him into cornering me and groping me?"

"No, of course not!" He sighed and pinched the bridge of his nose. "But you are a woman on a ship full of men, and not all of them are good men."

"Clearly."

His lips tightened. "This is why the *Belonging* isn't a passenger ship. I can't have eyes on you all the time."

"You don't have to. I can take care of myself."

"And what if there's more than one?"

She met his livid gaze with cool hauteur. "There won't be."

"Sarani, don't be stubborn."

Her breath caught at the same moment as he realized his slip and the soft use of her given name. Those unreadable eyes softened for the briefest of seconds, and time fell away.

They could have been anywhere—the ship, the river in Joor, reading to each other on a hillside, dancing in the palace ballroom like they'd never left it, his eyes on hers and brimming with desire. Brimming with something other than bitterness. Sarani's ears felt hot, her brain a muddled mess. Ribbons of heat chased through her veins as an eternity of memory passed between them. An eternity of pleasure, pain, love, rage, promises, and betrayals. Ending in heartbreak.

The story of them. Told in a handful of heartbeats.

Rhystan exhaled, and time resumed. His eyes were pieces of flint. Empty of emotion, hollow of anything that had to do with her.

"I'll see to it you have a guard."

She shook her head to clear it. "That's not necessary."

"I'm the captain, Lady Lockhart, and this is my ship. Remember that. I've better things to do than worry about you, like dealing with the fact that we're probably being followed by the British navy. Or worse." He cursed softly as though he hadn't meant to divulge that, but then sucked air through his teeth. "My cabin needs scrubbing. See to it."

Without another word, Rhystan turned on his heel and walked away. But Sarani was too busy trying to calm her galloping heart as she peered out on the horizon to find the telltale speck in the distance. The minute she saw it, fear prickled over her skin.

It could be anything. A trading vessel. A navy ship. A passenger ship bound for England, just as they were. But she knew. She knew exactly who was on that ship.

And they were coming for her.

Eight

SARANI STOOD AT THE RAILING AGAIN, WISHING SHE COULD steal the captain's spyglass. It wasn't to memorize the sun's descent into the waiting cradle of the ocean or to appreciate the spectacularly gorgeous sunset that blazed across the sky and cast orange and pink swaths over the glasslike surface of the sea.

No, it was for the black speck on the horizon.

Was it her imagination, or was it getting bigger? She'd kept an eye on the ship for five days, and it was there every time she looked. The winds had died down, and the captain had resorted to steam for the rest of their journey to St. Helena. Though if that ship carried her enemy, it wouldn't matter if the *Belonging* was docked at the island.

St. Helena was a thriving port, but it wasn't England. Sarani wouldn't be able to hide there, not for long anyway. Rubbing clammy palms on her trousers, she almost jumped out of her skin when a large shadow loomed beside her. Her kukri blades were in her hands before she recognized the man.

The duke's laconic quartermaster.

"Planning to gut me from navel to nose, Princess?" Gideon asked.

She tucked the weapons back into their sheaths. Gideon was huge. She doubted she could reach his chin even with the tip of her blade. He looked like many of the men from her homeland, with rich dark brown skin that gleamed in the sun, but his huge height and blue eyes made her wonder if he was mixed with some kind of Nordic Viking. His bald head was shiny and dotted with sweat.

"No, and don't call me that."

"Why?" the large man said. "You are a princess. Pretending you are not serves no purpose."

It does when people want you dead.

"Regardless, it's just Sara now. Did Asha return to the cabin?"

"No, she wanted to watch the sunset."

Sarani turned her head to where Asha sat cross-legged on the deck, her lips rolled between her teeth, and stared out to sea. She'd just finished playing the *shehnai* and was now focused on the glimmering ocean.

The maid looked up, her eyes caught on the sky, her jaw sagging with wonder. "It looks like Joor," she said.

Sarani felt something tug on her heart, her eyes flicking to the sunset. It did look a little like Joor. An explosion of red, orange, and gold, like the sky was on fire. The slightest hint of a storm blackened the edges, adding an unusual depth to the striations of color. She drew a ragged breath, letting nature's beauty sink in for a scant moment, though the anxious pressure in her breast didn't abate.

By her count, they had a week left to get to the coaling port at St. Helena. She'd overheard Gideon saying that they'd caught some favorable winds, which had cut the journey short a few days, and the captain's judicious use of his steam propellers had helped. However, if that shadow of a ship caught up to them, she knew she would be bringing trouble to Rhystan and his men. She had to know what that ship meant, and what better time than the present to ask the man who could give her answers.

"Is that vessel following us?" she asked Gideon, sidling over to him.

Unreadable eyes met hers. "Why?"

"Rhystan, er, the captain said something the other day, that it might be the navy."

"Perhaps."

Sarani waited, but nothing more was forthcoming. She resisted the urge to kick the unhelpful giant in the shins. "Are you expecting trouble?"

"It's not for you to worry about."

Oh, you have no idea, you big, uncooperative lump.

She sensed she wasn't going to get anything out of him, at least not about that ship. Or anything about this ship. Or Rhystan, or why the British navy could possibly be tracking them. Or any useful information at all. Her eyes narrowed with sudden suspicion, recalling the crates in the hold that were sectioned off and padlocked.

"What cargo does the *Belonging* carry?"

Gideon grunted. "What?"

"If this isn't a passenger ship, what does it carry?"

The man had the audacity to smile, or offer what passed for a smile anyway. It was more of a grimace on that taciturn face. Sarani knew that whatever he was going to say was going to aggravate her even further. She wasn't wrong. "Ask the captain."

"Fine, I will."

Knowing Asha was safe with the ogre, even though Sarani wanted to kick him in his truculent shins, she decided to make her way down into the hold. Not to see the crates in question and assuage her curiosity but to feed the livestock and clean out the paddock. Anything would be better than thinking about what that ship on the horizon meant. Even shoveling piles upon piles of smelly dung.

She should have known Vikram wouldn't let her go so easily, not when he'd murdered a maharaja without a qualm. Sarani feared for Asha's family and the rest of her handmaidens—she hoped they were safe—and she worried for her people because Vikram would be looking out for himself, not them. Her father, for all his faults and concessions to the crown, had tried to keep Joor's interests at heart. Even her loathsome engagement to Talbot would have been a necessary evil.

Though it had only been a few weeks, she felt the loss of her father keenly. While she knew Western traditions of mourning meant she'd be garbed in black for months, her people treated death differently. Their cultural and religious traditions were tied up in rebirth, what they called *samsara*. She hoped her father would have been cremated—not even Vikram would provoke the gods, despite his certain hand in the maharaja's death. And initial mourning would have lasted thirteen days, whereupon she would have worn white, not black, to honor him.

Sarani glanced down at her stained clothing. Not that she had a choice now. She didn't have a garland of flowers or anything on her person, but she offered up a simple chant in her heart for him. Her moments with him had been precious, if few later on. As a child, she had memories of him carrying her on his shoulder, tossing her up into the air while she giggled and gasped for breath, and him pointing out the movement of the stars. Sarani stopped on the lower deck and caught the first glimmers winking in the distance. He'd taught her about the constellations, the positions of the planets, and their meanings from ancient Indian scriptures called the *Rigveda*.

"It's called science of light," he'd explained once.

Perched high on his shoulders, she'd wrinkled her nose. "Why, Papa?"

"The planets are constantly in motion, and on the day of someone's birth, their destiny is written. We offered water and light for blessings on yours."

"Papa, did my stars say I would be big and strong like you?"

"You will be a force, little one."

The memory made her chest ache as Sarani stared up at the darkening, purplish sky above the ship. She wondered if this journey—and his death—had been foreseen. "I miss you, Papa," she whispered.

With one final look to the brightening stars, Sarani swallowed down the lump in her throat and headed down to the pens where she grabbed her trusty shovel. Her shadow, Red, trailed her at a discreet distance, staying away as if sensing her morose mood. The cheeky boatswain had always accompanied her around the ship, but now he was extra vigilant. Her official guard, she supposed. Normally, Red was a chatterbox, but he hung back, content to keep an eye on her, and didn't intervene.

Sarani bit back a curse. No doubt, it was a command from Rhystan...that she had to perform her duties alone. It wasn't Red's fault. In fact, in his defense, he had offered before, but she'd always refused. She wanted to pull her weight for the sake of the crew.

Not their hard-headed, hard-eyed, hard-bodied captain.

With a groan, Sarani gritted her teeth, swallowing the foul oaths about the man fulminating on her tongue. If a little work was the price to pay for safe passage, she would do it. And she would do it without complaining. She wouldn't voice her murderous thoughts, but that didn't mean she couldn't enjoy the idea of punishing the captain with slow and gratifying delight.

In fact, as she started to shovel the fresh clumps of manure into a heap, she took great satisfaction in imagining his stupidly handsome face beneath it.

━━━━━━━

Rhystan consulted the cartographic charts on his desk and downed the rest of the whisky in his tumbler. His eyes burned from lack of sleep, but he was studying the maps to see if there was an alternate route, at least to see if the ship behind them would follow. But he needed fuel, and turning back toward Cape Town wasn't an option. He had sailed enough oceans to know that the other ship's identical course wasn't by chance.

And his gut had never failed him.

It wasn't a ship from the Royal Navy. That, he'd already ascertained. It was a private passenger ship, one that looked like an East

India Company steamship, but it was too far away to tell. It wasn't a trading vessel or he would have taken no small delight in blowing it to pieces. It was also too far away to determine if it meant them harm. In other circumstances, he would slow his pace and allow the ship to catch up. While most of the guns on the *Belonging* had been removed for the sake of weight and speed after her redesign, there were still a few, and they were kept in good working order.

He wasn't afraid to use them.

But with Sarani onboard, he couldn't risk endangering her life.

Slumping back in his chair, he poured another glass of whisky, letting the spicy burn of the liquor numb his brain. With continued luck, they would reach port in less than a week. The winds on the journey had been advantageous, and apart from the ship on their heels and the initial threat of the cyclone and a few smaller squalls in between, the voyage had been uneventful. Well, with the exception of one willful passenger.

Rhystan glanced around the spotless cabin. Everything was in meticulous order—the bed made, bookcase neatly stacked, his clothing laundered, folded, and put away. Even the furniture shone, polished to within an inch of its life. Something was on her mind. Normally, he would find telltale signs of rebellion, like watered-down whisky bottles, salt in his morning coffee, or barnacles in his bedsheets. That last one he was certain had been Red's idea, considering the boatswain was responsible for scraping them off the hull.

But the last couple of days, Sarani had been on task and quiet. Too preoccupied for pranks.

Stop thinking about her.

Willing himself to focus, Rhystan studied the charts again and gave up after a few minutes. Despite his mental exhaustion, he was restless, agitated. Mostly because of what awaited him in England and the fact that he had been urgently summoned by his mother, the Dowager Duchess of Embry, purportedly because of ailing health.

He had no doubt that it was yet another ploy to get him back to English shores. Marry some insipid, docile debutante. Beget an heir and a spare. Take control of the dukedom. Settle down. Become his blasted father.

Bile climbed into his throat. That was his worst nightmare. His eyes chased longingly over the map around the coast of Africa into the Atlantic Ocean. How easy would it be to replenish supplies and coal in St. Helena and change course? Head to France or Spain or even New York?

You want another family death on your conscience? Your mother's this time?

His inner demons were right, curse the lot of them.

He had no way to know if his mother was pretending or was actually on her deathbed, but he hadn't been there when his father and brothers had died. Despite his fractious relationship with his father, guilt over that had eaten away at him, mostly because of his brothers.

Though Roland had been a miniature replica of the duke, Rhystan had idolized Richard when they'd been children. He'd taken their deaths hard. All of them, even the duke's. At the funeral, the desolation on his mother's face had been a potent reminder of his failures.

Of the fact that he could never measure up.

On top of that, he hadn't seen his nieces or his own sister in two years. He had spared them a thought or two, but no more than that. Last he heard, Roland's widow had recently remarried and moved to Northumberland.

Clearly, Rhystan wasn't and would never be of ducal caliber. And his father had known that, drummed it into him. Fate had buggered them both, it seemed. Because once he returned to London, his mother, in her dubiously ill state, would probably waste no time putting pressure on him to marry and secure the future of the dukedom. His legacy.

Rhystan had almost written to her and said, "Pick one." He

knew it wouldn't matter to his mother who the future Duchess of Embry was as long as she was of the right bloodline and could carry the next ducal heir to term. His mother would have a list of eligible young ladies waiting for him, and then he'd be expected to do his ducal duty.

Hell.

Duty was an exacting master.

Rhystan loosed a breath, for the first time understanding what had possessed Sarani to marry another for the sake of court and country. It wasn't enough to forgive her completely, but he wished she could have trusted him. Given him a chance to offer his own suit, to use his eminent family name for their sakes. But she hadn't…because she hadn't known. Because he hadn't been honest with her from the start about who he was. Back then, he'd wanted nothing to do with the Duke of Embry.

Cursing, he slung back another two fingers of whisky, aware of the pleasant fog expanding in his brain. A vision of hair so black it absorbed light and a pair of laughing autumn-colored eyes danced in his mind's eye.

Her Highness, the Princess of Joor. Now, Lady Sara Lockhart.

His Grace, the Duke of Embry. Now, Captain Rhystan Huntley.

He wasn't unaware of the similarities between them. Both hiding behind other names and fleeing from their pasts, and now running into each other here on the high seas. He would laugh if it wasn't so absurdly tragic. A pointless Shakespearean tragedy, in which the real bedevilment was how bitterly ironic it was that the only woman he'd ever wanted to marry had been *her*.

And then she had let him go without a qualm.

She had never loved him. Not truly.

He rose, stumbling slightly, and made his way next door, only to halt at the hushed sound of arguing. The two women presumably, considering both voices were female. Rhystan didn't care that he was shamelessly eavesdropping.

"There's nothing you can do, Princess," Asha was saying. "If you are right, then we will have to face it when the time comes. Worrying about it now does nothing."

Sarani made a frustrated sound. "We need to act!"

"We are on a ship in the middle of the ocean," the maid said, her voice calm though she also sounded frightened. "What would you have us do?"

"I don't know! How can you be so calm when we're in danger? That could be Vikram's doing for all we know, sending his henchmen after us."

"I'm afraid, too, but the captain won't let anything happen."

"Don't be naive, Asha." Something that sounded suspiciously like furniture being kicked and a muffled screech and oath followed. "That. Heartless. Man. Does. Not. Care."

"I beg your pardon, Princess, but I think you're wrong." Asha sniffed. "Would he have allowed us to stay on this ship if he didn't care?"

"Correction, he does not care about *me*."

"Then why keep us?"

"He had no choice, Asha. There was a cyclone. And I'm not his guest. Everyone knows how little he thinks of me. Not much has changed." The words carried a deep undertone of bitterness. "We all have to work like wretched landsmen for our passage. Heaven knows I'm sick of shoveling dung for days on end."

Guilt flooded Rhystan at that statement, even though he sensed it was uttered in frustration. He didn't have time to hide as Sarani opened the door and came face-to-face with him standing there. Unabashedly listening.

He leaned against the ship's wall and folded his arms across his chest, refusing to admit that he was indeed guilty. Nostrils flaring, she tightened her mouth as she watched him, the sheen of tears in her eyes obvious. For once, she made no move to hide her vulnerability.

"Enjoying yourself?" she snapped.

"We need to talk."

She huffed and then sighed tiredly. "About what?"

"Come with me."

Without waiting to see if she followed, he made his way back to his own cabin two doors down. Instead of resuming his seat behind the desk, he rolled up the maps and waited, hips perched on the edge of it. He debated pouring another drink but decided he'd had enough, and he needed to be somewhat clearheaded in dealing with Sarani, considering the mood she was in. Though his current state of sobriety was debatable.

"If I have to come out there and get you," he warned, "you're not going to like it."

She entered the cabin a few seconds later, face defiant and hands clasped behind her back. Her sleek jet hair hung loose past her shoulders. Rhystan couldn't help noticing that she had donned a soft, green muslin dress. It was a simple morning dress, but it suited her. The color set off the green-gold flecks in her eyes and made her honeyed skin turn luminous. While the sight of her in trousers made his blood heat, he couldn't deny that she was lovely in a gown.

"No trousers?" he asked.

"They needed to be washed," she said. "I tripped in the paddock."

He clamped his lips together to keep from grinning. Red had reported that she had indeed fallen on her arse right into a steaming pile of cow shit while cursing up a storm, most of it directed at Rhystan. "You look nice."

"What can I do for you, Captain?" she asked. "I'm exhausted, and I'm sure you didn't summon me here to talk about my appearance."

"You told Asha you were in danger. What did you mean?"

A host of emotions crossed her expressive face. "You were spying."

"It's my ship."

She glared at him. "Yes, I'm well aware that a person can't be expected to have any privacy in your presence."

He arched an eyebrow, drumming one finger against the wood of the desk and holding her gaze in a silent battle of wills. Eventually, she sighed and her eyes fell away. They'd been full of wariness and vulnerability. He sensed her hesitancy, but he needed answers and he would have them.

"Sarani?"

She exhaled, hazel eyes flaring at the use of her given name, the words following in a rush. "The reason we left India is because my father was murdered. And I believe whoever killed him is on that ship that's been following us. With the intent of finishing what he started."

———

The confession wasn't as difficult as Sarani had thought it would be, though Rhystan was still blinking in stunned surprise as if he'd been expecting something else. She assumed that he would have thought she was running from a scorned lover or an irate husband. Not a murderer.

"What happened to Lord Lockhart?"

Her mouth fell open, even though she'd expected him to be thinking along those lines. "*That's* what you want to ask me? After I tell you the Maharaja of Joor, my *father*, was murdered and we're being tracked by his killer?"

"Answer the question, *Countess*."

Sarani rolled her lips between her teeth, but then shook her head. Telling him the truth would not hurt them at this point, and Asha was right that they were in the middle of the ocean with no options but what they had at hand. Which were Rhystan, *his* ship, and *his* men.

She walked over to the desk, poured herself some whisky, and took a healthy swallow, not even gasping when the liquor burned a hot path from her throat straight down to her quivering belly. She took another sip for good measure. For courage.

"There is no Lord Lockhart, not in the way you imagine anyway," she began, her gaze on the tumbler between her palms. Bringing up the past felt like picking at a nearly healed scab. "In Joor, as you know, my father ordered me to wed Lord Talbot, the regent. I put off the wedding for as long as possible with any excuse I could come up with. At first, it was because I was too young and wanted to wait. My father agreed. And then later, the rebellion and mourning for those who died. Anything to prolong the engagement." She didn't hide her shudder at the memory of Talbot—his ashen, almost skeletal features and those watery eyes that stripped her bare every time they fell upon her. "He was odious."

"Wait, you *didn't* marry? Markham told me that you had."

Sarani didn't miss the stunned rage that darkened his expression. She shook her head. "No. The wedding was supposed to be the day after I ran." She drew a breath. "When my father was assassinated, I knew it was only a matter of time before Talbot or the murderer would come for me. I suspect my cousin Vikram was behind it. He has the most to gain, though he would not have acted without Talbot's help." She lifted the glass, thought about it, and then set it down on the desk. She didn't need her mind muddled. "Tej got us to Bombay, so we decided to leave on a ship in the dead of night that just so happened to be yours."

"What are the odds?" he murmured.

Sarani was not particularly religious, but destiny—or karma as she learned from the *Upanishads*: the philosophical law of ritual action and its effect in the universe—did indeed seem to have a twisted sense of humor. Fate had decided to throw them together once more.

"Slim to none, rather." Sparing him a glance, she shot him a tiny, wry smile. "England was the only place I could think of where we could be safe. My maternal grandfather was the youngest son of the Earl of Beckforth, who married a Scottish countess. My mother had saved documents of the property she had inherited through my great-grandmother's title, and I decided to take her maiden name of Lockhart." She exhaled and reached for another bracing sip of whisky.

"Traveling as Princess Sarani Rao was much too conspicuous, and it's easier to travel without a companion as a widow. I just didn't expect to run into you." Sarani swallowed hard. "But then, once we were away from Indian shores, I thought we might be safe. Obviously, we're not. Whoever killed my father has followed us and means me harm. Or it's Talbot, coming to claim his due."

They stared at each other in silence, her hand rising to her pounding heart as she tried to catch her breath from the confession that had tumbled out.

"I am sorry for your loss," he said after a beat. "Your father was a good man."

"My father was undermined by those around him, just as you once said. In the last few years, he became nothing but a figurehead."

Rhystan dipped his head. "All the same, I'm sorry."

"I can't imagine what Vikram promised Markham and the regent. He could not have done this without their knowledge or support." She paused, tears gathering in her eyes. "Money, I suppose. And power."

"Markham had to have been desperate."

She blinked. "What do you mean?"

"I made it my business to ruin him. He was skimming money for years and profiteering off of unspeakable practices. I destroyed his dealings and revealed his behavior. From my last report, he'd been demoted."

Sarani let out a breath. Come to think of it, the vice admiral *had* been looking a lot worse for wear in the last year, but she had just thought it'd been because of local unrest. Despite the loss of the sepoys two years ago, the fallout had been significant.

"Desperate men are dangerous," she said.

Sarani lifted an anxious gaze to the duke. He was watching her steadily with no sign of distrust or skepticism, and the only emotion she could see was the flexing muscle in his jaw and his white-knuckled grip on the edge of the desk. Was he angry? Did he believe her? Would he turn around and tell her she deserved what she'd sown? Sarani could never tell with this new version of the boy she'd known, but she needed his help, more than ever.

His next words made her jump. "You think your cousin is behind it?"

"I don't know. Papa's"—a small sob escaped her lips—"throat was cut. It had to be someone who had access to the palace. Who *knew* the guards. With all the growing instability in the region, my father was careful about who he trusted and who he allowed into the family apartments. And yet someone still got to him. The fact that that ship has been on our tail for weeks can't be a coincidence. I'd rather be wrong than willfully ignorant."

"Where were you planning to go in England?" he asked. "To the Earl of Beckforth?"

Sarani shrugged. "That was the plan."

"And if that didn't work, what then?"

His cool tone irritated her. She was well aware that going there was a long shot. Her mother had been quite publicly cut off and the scandal had been the talk of the town for years, and given what Sarani had learned about Englishmen and their bigotry, it wasn't likely that she would be welcomed back into the family fold with open arms. But she'd been low on options—low being the understatement of the century—and she didn't even know which of her distant male relations was the current earl. Perhaps, whoever he was, he would be more open-minded.

One could only hope.

"I have money," she replied with some defiance. "I'll find somewhere to stay. Go to my mother's holdings in Scotland."

"And when your store of money runs out?"

Lifting an eyebrow, Rhystan folded his arms across his broad chest. Sarani had the sudden indescribable urge to be cradled against him and wrapped in his strong arms. Ever since the death of her mother, she'd been largely self-reliant—the maharaja being occupied with affairs of state—but the idea of leaning on someone else for a change had appeal. Not that Rhystan was offering. He was simply playing devil's advocate.

Though that didn't mean she had to *like* him poking holes in her plans.

She would be *fine*!

"I don't know," she snapped. "I can get work, I suppose. I can now add shoveling horse manure, being a maid, fetching food, heaping coal, and braiding rope to the list of things to recommend me." In a fit of frustration, she slammed her hand down upon the desk and shrieked in pain, cradling her injured fist to her breast. He was beside her in an instant.

"What have you done?" he demanded. "Show me."

"It's nothing," she replied, but the agonizing throb in her palm nearly made her see stars.

Despite her protests, he wouldn't take no for an answer, drawing her hands carefully to him. Slowly, she opened them, displaying their red raw, blistered surfaces and wincing. Half scabbed over, several of the plum-colored, oozing streaks looked angry and irritated, and they stung fiercely.

Rhystan swore. "Damn it, Sarani, what in hell happened?"

"The wooden shovels in the animal pens have splinters, and using my kukri earlier must have torn some of the scabs. When I fell, I caught myself with my hands. It made some of the older wounds reopen."

"They're bloody festering, you daft woman. You should have come to me."

She shot him a sour stare. "To whine?"

"Yes. No! This is not whining, you fool-headed imp." Rhystan leaned over to blow on the tender, aching skin, and something else crept into the edges of her pain. "Be sure to add bullheaded, stubborn, and contrary to your job-qualifications list." Propping her against the desk, he released her hands gently to get a clean strip of linen from a nearby chest and poured some of the whisky on it. "We have to clean it properly. I won't lie… This will hurt like the devil."

"I'm not afraid."

One thick eyebrow arched. "You've proven that time and time again. Ready?"

Sarani nodded and bit back a scream when he dabbed the alcohol-soaked cloth to her skin. Sending her an apologetic look, he blew a warm stream of air on her hands again and repeated the process. The second time hurt less, but not by much.

The next few times his breath gusted on her skin, however, she felt the tingle of it in her chest. The sight of his head bent over her was doing strange things to her equilibrium. His distinctive masculine scent wafted to her, and all she wanted to do was breathe him in. Lean into him. Obviously, it was a moment of weakness because she was in pain.

Memory leached into the present with scattered images of a different Rhystan, a younger Rhystan, head bent over her hands that had been decorated with mehndi in the Mughal tradition by one of her handmaidens. He'd kissed each of her red-stained fingers and the dotted sphere at the center of each palm when she'd explained that the stain had been made from the ground leaves of a plant.

"What is it for?" he had whispered.

"Blessings for luck, joy, and beauty."

His easy smile had been full of wicked promise. "I believe a man makes his own luck, and you already have the last one, so it shall be my earnest pledge to bring you as much joy as possible, Princess."

One of her handmaidens had piped up. "Also for marriage and fertility, sahib."

Sarani's blush had nearly matched the color of the dye on her hands, but Rhystan had only smiled a secret smile and continued kissing her fingertips. Until he'd approached her in her chambers that fateful night, she'd been hopeful of his intentions and a future between them. Marriage. Maybe even children someday.

But then duty had intervened and destiny had conspired to throw them apart. Only to hurl them back together. The symbolism of the current moment was not lost on her. Not that he was flirting or kissing her fingers. Even now, the memory of his lips on her skin was so fresh that a rash of gooseflesh broke out on her arms.

Huffing a shallow breath, she almost snatched her hand away.

"Does that hurt?" he asked, glancing up.

Sarani forced herself not to give away her roiling emotions or the lie that left her lips. "Some."

Reaching for more clean linen strips, he added some salve from a jar and expertly bandaged her palms. "There. Better?"

"Yes, thank you," she whispered.

Rhystan stood upright but made no move to step away, instead caging her with his arms on either side of her hips on the desk. Her newly bound and dressed palms sat cradled in her lap, a puny barrier to the tension that was unspooling between them. Had he been thinking about the last time he'd held her hands as well? Nothing showed in his expression—no softening in those hard, inscrutable eyes.

But still he stared.

Their breaths loud in the silence, the duke studied her face in wordless fascination while she did the same. Relearning him. Remapping his features. Taking in the maturity of his stern bristled jaw and the dissolute curve of his mouth. Oh, that *mouth*… It had known hers intimately. Tasted her skin, sipped at her hands, her neck, the slope of her cleavage.

With a blush, Sarani wrenched her eyes away to trace his strong, bold nose, the arch of his cheekbones, and those darkened, storm-hued irises. Silky blond-brown hair streaked gold by the sun framed his cheeks and curled into his brow, and her injured hands ached to sweep it away.

Her tongue darted out to lick dry lips, and his stare returned there. Within a heartbeat, the tension humming between them spiked and ignited, spreading like wildfire over spilled oil. Rhystan's sharpened gaze turned hot and desirous, scorching her, making her breasts tighten and lust settle between her thighs. Heavens, she wanted to be consumed. She wanted to *burn*.

Sarani didn't know if it was out of gratitude or desire or madness. She didn't care. She was hurt, scared, and she wanted comfort. She wanted him.

Shoving to the points of her toes, she collided her lips with his.

Nine

THE SCENT OF JASMINE BURNED LIKE INCENSE THROUGH Rhystan's senses.

Her lips. Her soft, lush, wet mouth. The subject of a thousand erotic fantasies. Breaking him apart like a hammer to glass. Sweetness and sin. Darkness and desire. Virtue and vice wound indecently together, addling his brain and hardening his body in equal measure. The divergent combination had always been his undoing—the wellspring of his strength and the secret to his ruin. It had always been her.

He'd made himself forget.

But the moment Sarani's lips touched his, five years of buried memory descended upon him like a hurricane. Five years of wanting. Of raw, unmitigated need.

Rhystan's hands wrapped around her, one at her nape and the other at her waist. They were greedy, too…desperate to remember the feel of her, the flare of her hip, the softness of her throat, the silken skeins of her inky hair. His fingers clutched and caressed, holding her close and desperate to take what she offered.

One kiss wouldn't hurt.

And yet one kiss could wreck him unconscionably.

Because he didn't want to just kiss her mouth, he wanted to kiss her everywhere. From the bend of her elbow, to the curve of her breast, to her stomach, her thighs, all of her.

Her teeth grazed his lower lip and sensation blasted through him, a groan rumbling in his chest. She tasted of heated spice, whisky, and pure lust. A part of him knew he should pull away, save himself from the destruction that would surely follow in the wake of this, but he couldn't. When that sweet, bold tongue crept past his lips to touch his, Rhystan stopped fighting and gave in. For *this* kiss, he'd take his chances with ruin.

With certain devastation.

Angling her head, he opened his mouth on hers, eager to reconquer lost territory and take charge. Thrusting into her, sucking, nipping, and then soothing. Letting her know that all wasn't forgiven. Reminding her that all wasn't quite lost to memory. Not one to stand by idly, Sarani put her injured hands awkwardly around him, a ragged moan escaping her parted lips. He took; she gave. He came undone; she brought him back together.

Their kiss wasn't gentle, but she submitted to his rough claim with equal hunger, willingly, receiving him as though he'd never left. Kissing him as though he'd never become a stranger. As if he weren't the hated enemy. As though she were still his.

Moments, or an eternity, passed, and they stayed joined at the lips, sharing heartbeats and breath, reluctant to relinquish the connection. The kiss was less frantic now, light nudges and licks over bruised, swollen lips. Violence had given way to something tender, infinitely sweeter.

And exceedingly more dangerous.

Anger, Rhystan was familiar with. He'd honed it, held it close for years, let it pummel him and shape him into who he'd become. But *this*…this feeling of intimacy, of fragile undone yearning, shook him to the core. Threatened the hardened armor of who he was. And that he could not allow. Fuck. *Fuck.*

Struggling for control, he tore himself from her clasp.

"Rhys—" Her voice was thick, clogged with sated passion.

He clenched his jaw. "Don't."

He needed to bloody think! And he couldn't with the heady scent of her in his nostrils and the sweet taste of her on his tongue. Every battered sense was reeling. All he wanted was to throw himself back into her embrace and lose himself in her. Drag those luscious hips to the edge of his desk, part her thighs, and drive into her body until they were both lost to pleasure.

He spared a glance to the wild-eyed, red-lipped woman standing inches away. Emotions chased across her face, and she pinned the inside of her cheek between her teeth. Sarani looked as staggered as he felt—stunned that the inferno between them had somehow managed to stay alive after all this time.

How had it? Because despite everything—betrayal, rejection, bitterness, and a half decade of hate—the attraction, the *passion*, was still there. Rhystan wanted her with a ferocious desire that had not abated in five years.

And she wanted him.

But regardless of the random flare of lust, they were over. Sarani Rao was in his past. She was female and he was simply a man with needs that had not been met in some time, as evidenced by the unrelenting pressure in his groin.

"Damn it," he muttered, raking a frustrated hand through his hair.

Dark lashes dropped over her eyes, hiding her thoughts from view, one bandaged palm rising to quell the shaky rise of her breast. "I'm sorry," she whispered. "I should go."

Rhystan scrubbed his face with one hand and took another step back, giving her a wide berth as she swept past him to his cabin door in case he did something infinitely stupid like try to stop her. She had to leave, and he needed to clear his head and stop thinking with other disorderly parts of his body.

With a shaking hand, he reached for the tumbler of whisky she'd left behind on the desk and drained it. The thought that her lips had been on this glass, too, made his bruised lips burn. Rhystan swiped at his mouth with the back of his knuckles, sucking in a breath at the residual tenderness. Recalling the sight of her red, swollen lips, he knew she'd given as good as she'd gotten.

But then, Sarani always had. In Joor, she'd lived and fought with passion, never giving ground, never conceding. Their first kiss had been a battle for position, for dominance. Surrender had never crossed her mind, and he'd loved it. He relished her fight, that fierce intensity that had always called to its likeness in him. Even with the illusion of submission, this kiss had mirrored its predecessors, and Rhystan wasn't sure who had emerged the victor.

He smiled reluctantly. She'd make love like a warrior. The image of a gloriously nude Sarani Rao riding him into the bedsheets filled his addled brain, and his knees nearly failed him.

Christ, he needed to have some bloody sense beaten into him. He was full of sap and spoiling for a fight. And he knew just the man for the job. Without a second thought, Rhystan made his way to the upper deck to find his quartermaster.

Gideon threw one look at him and raised his eyebrows. "Now?"

"Now," Rhystan growled.

Gideon grinned, the sight of which usually made grown men piss themselves, but Rhystan only stared back as the enormous man shed his belt, boots, and weapons without another word. He did the same, yanking off his boots and shirt.

Nothing like a bracing round of bare-knuckle boxing to get one's head sorted out. It didn't take long for a crowd of his older crew to gather, some pulled from their beds because no one liked to miss the captain and the quartermaster beating each other bloody—or miss out on the wagers. Bets and money were already changing hands as the men formed a loose circle.

"Rules?" Gideon asked, rolling his massive shoulders.

Rhystan scowled. "None. First to call it."

Gideon shot him a sardonic look. "That bad?"

Snarling, he answered with a nasty jab to the man's jaw, and the fight was on. It took every bit of his focus—thank God—to avoid Gideon's punches. The man was the size of a mountain and built of pure muscle, so getting hit by him was tantamount to getting hit by a train. Despite his bulk, he was also fleet of foot and moved like he was executing the most delicate of waltzes, with swift, beautiful, lethal precision.

But then again, so was Rhystan.

He dodged a thick fist swinging at his head and ducked to pummel Gideon's torso. Crowing, the man barely flinched at the attack and kicked out, catching Rhystan in the thigh. He swore he could feel his bone shudder from the blow, but managed to limp out of the way and jab his knuckles into the softer tissue of Gideon's throat.

They traded more savage blows, getting some in and missing others, and after a good while, Rhystan finally felt weariness start to creep in. For all his skill and size, Gideon was also looking a bit the worse for wear. Blood trickled from a cut at his eye and one on his lip. Rhystan was sure he looked much the same, feeling a stinging on his cheek and tasting the metallic tang of blood in his own mouth. He swiped a lock of damp hair out of his face and eyed his adversary.

They wouldn't stop until one of them was unconscious or called the fight.

Those were the rules.

"Had enough yet, Captain?" the bigger man drawled.

"I've got all night."

"Do you? Doesn't seem like you have the stamina. Or is it the ballocks? Then again, could be the stem, too." His quartermaster laughed, showing a row of bloodstained teeth. "Stem or berries, Captain?"

Rhystan's gaze narrowed. "Shut the hell up."

"Been a while since you had a woman, no? Can't figure out which end is up? Let me help you out there—it's the pointy end."

The men around them roared with laughter and hollered lewd insults. The rub to his masculinity was salt in an open wound, and Rhystan couldn't help feeling rage that he'd been reduced to a dithering greenhorn who'd fled from his own private quarters with his tail between his legs. After one blasted *kiss*.

Gideon was right. The current version of him wouldn't have hesitated to toss any willing bit of muslin to his bed or bend her over his desk, no matter who she was or who she'd been, and finish what he and Sarani had started. And she had been willing…desperately so.

Then why had he stopped?

As if his thoughts had conjured her, Rhystan caught a glimpse of Sarani hunkered down by the stairs, her stare trained on the fight. She didn't display an ounce of worry. She'd seen him spar before, though his style and technique had changed in the past handful of years.

Eyes as beautiful as the night sky met his. Arousal roared and churned anew through his beaten body. His desire had not waned in the least, not even with a man the size of a house giving him and his libido a thrashing. No, only one thing would satisfy.

The minute distraction allowed Gideon to get a blow into his chin that smacked his head sideways. Despite the crunch of bone, Rhystan followed with a ruthless jab to his quartermaster's gut that had the man stumbling back with an ugly wheeze.

Stretching his aching jaw, Rhystan smirked at Sarani, who had bolted to her feet, and he raised a mocking eyebrow at the look of admiration edged with concern on her face. Unsurprisingly, she shot him a crude finger gesture that made him laugh aloud. Which made him unable to dodge the ham-sized fist that came directly at his temple.

He was still laughing when he crashed down like the sorriest sack of shit this side of the ocean.

"Move aside, you lot!" Sarani swore as she shoved through the smelly line of bodies exchanging coin and other items to crouch at Rhystan's side.

Gideon stooped beside her and grunted through a split lip. "He's out like a blown lamp."

"I can see that, you great oaf," she growled, wincing at the swelling bruise that was already spreading on the duke's temple and cheek. "Did you have to hit him that hard? And why were the two of you brawling anyway? Fisticuffs isn't the way to solve disagreements."

"We didn't have a disagreement," Gideon said. "He needed to let out some sap."

"Sap?" she repeated.

His pointed look made Sarani blush.

Oh.

Their passionate interlude in the cabin must have sent him here to Gideon. It had very nearly sent her over the side of the ship into the frigid sea to cool her overheated blood, so she could empathize. But this? Choosing to be pummeled to oblivion? It seemed rather counterintuitive, not to mention barbaric.

Scanning his limp frame, Sarani winced at the bloodied state of the duke, tearing off a piece of her hem to wipe the blood away from the corner of his lip. Her fingers traced the edges of the sculpted lips that had devoured hers, and her breath caught, her own lips tingling in response.

She snatched her fingers away, fighting the tide of her blush with everything inside of her as her entire body started to hum with arousal…just from the one touch. She revised her earlier thought. Perhaps there *was* something to thrashing the lust out of one's body. Or in Rhystan's case, welcoming insensibility. She'd give anything to douse the emotions cresting inside her.

The attraction between them had always been their destruction, and so many years later, that appeared still to be true. Much like Rhystan, Sarani hadn't been able to shut her eyes after she'd left his cabin. Her every nerve had been on fire. So when the cheers and hoots from the crew had drawn her topside, she'd been grateful for the interruption.

Once she'd seen what was happening and who was fighting, however, she hadn't been able to move a muscle. Though his opponent's upper body had been bare as well, her greedy eyes hadn't strayed from Rhystan's glistening, chiseled, shirtless form. She'd seen many men brawl before, but nothing came close to Rhystan's predatory grace. While Gideon fought like a bear, Rhystan moved like one of the feral tigers native to Joor, all sinew and ruthless elegance.

She'd been mesmerized, reminding her of the times when she'd boxed with him in secret in Joor. In secret because her father would definitely *not* have approved of any man putting his hands on her person. While Sarani's unusual eastern and western upbringing allowed her some liberties, she was still a princess of Joor. Rhystan had found her arguing about pugilism with her weapons master in one of the training centers, and when her instructor had outright refused for fear of the maharaja's reaction, Rhystan had offered to demonstrate some basic strategies.

After showing her how to hold her stance, with feet shoulder-width apart and offering as little of her body as possible for a target, Rhystan had danced around her, fists raised to his chin. He hadn't been as broad as he was now, but he'd still towered over her.

"Go on, hit me," he'd goaded her.

Unable to resist, she'd thrown a few lackluster jabs. He'd evaded her initial strikes easily, but Sarani had used the time to watch his feet and track his movements, committing them to memory. With that unearthly grace of his, he'd spun and jeered at her.

"You're not even trying, Sarani."

"I *am* trying, you bully ruffian."

He'd laughed at her puny efforts. "Then try harder."

The scoundrel had taunted her until she'd gotten so angry that she'd watched and waited for the precise moment when his prancing feet had brought him close enough within range to punch upward with all her might. The contact had surprised them both.

Rhystan had had a sore jaw for days. It was a small-won victory that she'd gloated about.

Watching him fight Gideon, it was apparent that his pugilistic skills had only improved. The orchestrated grace with which he'd boxed before had gotten scrappier and more vicious. He still moved like a cat, but his new style was savage. And until he'd caught sight of her and been distracted, Rhystan had held the upper hand. Though admittedly, it'd been by the thinnest sliver of margins.

Sarani assumed she was to blame for that, too.

"Help me get him to his cabin," she told the quartermaster. "I'll see to his injuries."

It was the least she could do.

At least, that was what she told herself.

Ten

RHYSTAN'S EYES FLICKERED OPEN AND HE GROANED. *HELL.* IT hurt to blink. It hurt to breathe. Everything hurt. His head felt like it had gone straight through a wall, and his ribs squeezed like they were buried under a ton of stone. A wheezing breath blew out of him as he registered the familiar details of his cabin, lit by a single lamp. His eyes slid to the nearest porthole and the hazy gray-and-purple light shining through it.

How long had he been out?

He sighed, groaning slightly at the crushing pressure in his chest. His ribs were going to be sore for a while. Gideon hadn't pulled any punches this time. Nor was he going to live it down with his crew. It'd been an age since his quartermaster had bested him. Usually any fight between them ended in a well-earned draw, never in a loss on his part. This time, however…his thoughts had been occupied elsewhere.

He moved to sit up, only to be restrained by a firm but gentle hand.

"Don't," a soft voice commanded.

A cool cloth touched a cut on his forehead, and he hissed. Other details registered in his pounding brain, including the faintest scent of jasmine and the shapely silhouette of the woman tending to him.

Sarani.

The early-morning gloom in the cabin sheathed her in lamplight and shadow, as if she were some elegant, graceful nymph stealing into his dreams. She was the one who'd taught him about such spirits—celestial dancing nymphs, much like Muses, Valkyries, naiads, and nature spirits from other types of lore—when he'd teased her about her obsession with swimming. He closed his eyes and let memory wash over him.

"You're like a water sprite or a siren," he'd told her once when she'd convinced him yet again to sneak out to visit her secret spot at the river.

"I'll lure you to your death, shall I?" she'd teased back. "Like an *apsara*."

"A what?"

"A heavenly water nymph, skilled in the arts of music and dancing"—she'd thrown him a sultry look over her shoulder that was so full of promise that his knees had buckled on the steep slope of the riverbank—"and seduction. Sent to lure sages from their purpose."

"I'm already yours," he'd croaked, mesmerized.

"Are you?"

"As long as I draw breath, you will be the only *apsara* to tempt this wastrel's heart."

She'd laughed and floated in the pool then, the voluminous white folds of the traditional garb fanning about her, looking much like the divine nymph she'd described, and Rhystan had never been more grateful for the isolation of their secret spot than he had at that moment.

The small waterfall had been a short hike away from where the villagers usually bathed and washed their clothing, but it was worth it for the seclusion. There she was free of the trappings of her station and could speak her mind. There he could kiss her fragrant skin without recrimination, judgment, or censure. It had been their secret adventure.

The first time he'd shown her the pool, climbing through the sweltering bush hadn't deterred his fierce princess in the least. She was adept at sneaking out of the palace. She'd allowed her maid,

Asha, to accompany her for propriety's sake, though she'd refused a guard, insisting she could defend herself well enough should any need arise. And she could with those kukri blades of hers. Not that she'd needed them where Rhystan was concerned; he was already wholly at her mercy.

As the recollection dimmed, he licked dry lips. That was a more fitting name for her than the lukewarm Sara. His *apsara* sent to lure him from his purpose, from reason.

And now she had returned.

He ground his jaw. He was hardly the naive, lovestruck lad he'd been then, though he couldn't deny the attraction that still burned like an unchecked flame between them. His heart was already beating a resounding staccato in his chest. And other parts of him... Well, he'd been at half-mast for so much of the voyage that it had become his natural state.

A sorry state indeed.

Rhystan shook his head at his inability to control himself and winced at the ache that shot up his spine and between his bruised ribs. There was no doubt in his mind that she was dangerous, and not just to him. She'd already brought danger on his heels with this unnamed assassin, if her story about why she'd fled Joor and Indian shores was true. Now that his thoughts had settled somewhat, his brain had processed the information she'd shared.

She never married.

The thought flew into his brain like a fly to honey. But it didn't matter if she was unmarried or a widow. She wasn't his.

Why can't she be?

He almost growled at the supremely rational voice in his head. Theirs was not a story that could ever end in some unrealistic happily-ever-after. The court in Joor had been a small taste of what any union between them would face.

As vile as his behavior had been, Vice Admiral Markham would not be the only one in England to look down the length of his arrogant, prejudiced nose at Sarani. The truth of her lineage would come out sooner or later. London, with all its social rules and discrimination, was hardly the place for either of them.

St. Helena was still an option. He could rid himself of her once they put into James Bay. Though his gut clenched at the thought of leaving her in an island port without any means of escape. Would she be able to find passage on another ship? With another captain? One who wouldn't take advantage? His jaw clenched at the thought of any such unscrupulous man getting his hooks into her, having her at his mercy on the seas. With her blades, she could defend herself against one, but what about many?

She's not your problem.

She wasn't, and yet he warred between wanting to protect and punish her. But punishing her didn't mean abandoning an Indian princess at a random shipping port of call. The wolves would scent her vulnerability and be upon her in seconds.

A cool cloth dragged across his brow, and his gaze snapped open to his unwelcome nurse.

"What are you doing?" he growled.

She recoiled at the venom in his tone. "You're hurt. I wanted to help."

He didn't snarl that it was because of her that he was hurt, that she had driven him to seek a thrashing from the biggest man onboard. Because in truth, provoking Gideon had been his choice. He'd needed a release from the paralysis that had gripped him. He'd needed reason pounded into him. "You've done enough."

She sat back, her face contrite. "I'm sorry. If I'd known that this was your ship, I would have found another or told Tej to hide us somewhere else. I never would have—"

"Stolen onboard and bribed my crew?"

"Chosen this ship," she finished, a faint blush cresting her cheeks.

"But it is my ship and here we are," he said with a groan as he pulled himself to a sitting position. He licked parched lips and took the cup of water Sarani offered, wishing it were whisky instead. Anything to burn away the hint of jasmine seeping into his nostrils and making him desire impossible things. He swallowed and exhaled. "The current Earl of Beckforth is not the friendliest of men."

A surprised gaze met his. "You know him?"

"I've heard of him."

He blew air through his lips and thought back to what he knew—scant though it was, and it had only jogged his memory after he'd skimmed through the latest copy of Debrett's he had in his collection. Beckforth had inherited the earldom when the previous earl had died without male issue. The man was rumored to be close-fisted with money and a quiet sort of man with an aloof nature. Not exactly the kind of earl to welcome a half-blooded daughter of a disowned third cousin.

Not that it mattered.

Princess Sarani Rao would hardly be welcomed with open arms if the peerage discovered her identity. The scandal when Lady Lisbeth had left England—in defiance of her parents and on a ship bound for India with an Indian prince—might have died over two decades, but those poisonous harridans who had chased her from the *ton* and vilified her were still very much alive. And they would not hesitate to revive painful gossip and malign Sarani for being the issue of such a union.

It would take a miracle to protect her.

Or…marriage to a powerful peer.

His gaze snapped to hers, and she sucked in a breath, jeweled eyes going wide as if he'd laid his hands upon her person. A nervous pink tongue darted out to wet her lips, and once more, Rhystan felt his body stir.

Why *shouldn't* it be her?

He'd wanted to marry her once upon a time, and as he'd noted, he was still attracted to her. The pretense would be a believable one. It could be an arrangement, one that would be mutually beneficial: she would get her fresh start with the protection of a duke, and he would be freed of the parody of being paraded on display like a prize bull to hordes of matchmaking mothers. Especially to his own.

If he already had a fiancée, his mother couldn't very well force him to court any other without inviting ridicule, could she? And once he'd made sure the dowager was hale and hearty, he could leave without any attachments.

A smile drifted over his lips as he considered his new plan.

Who would have thought it—his cursed first love, now his unwitting saving grace.

Sarani didn't like the predatory gleam that had appeared in Rhystan's eyes as soon as his hunter's stare fastened on her. She could see the wheels in his brain turning, and instinctively, she knew that whatever he was thinking would decide her immediate future on his ship.

Her stomach flipped and soured. Goodness, would he turn her over to the assassin? Cut her loose in St. Helena? She was prepared for that option, though being stranded on an island with a killer on her heels wasn't ideal. And it would be impractical to hide within the small and no doubt tight-knit local aristocracy.

The newssheets mailed to the palace in Joor a year ago wrote of a short visit to St. Helena by Prince Alfred, second son to the queen, and the excitement of the local elite. Everyone knew everyone. She would hardly be able to blend in to avoid detection, and she wouldn't have much time to secure passage on another ship, but it wasn't an impossibility. She had money, and money could work magic in difficult situations.

Sarani did not need a man, much less a salty, mercurial sea captain, to save her. She could—and would—save herself.

Still, Rhystan's intense gaze unsettled her. And that sudden smirk did not bode well.

"Why are you staring at me?" she asked.

His blue-gray gaze slipped down to her bandaged palms, the tips of her fingers grasping the now-warm cloth in them. Sarani tossed it back into the bowl and straightened her shoulders, her belly tightening with dread. If he chose to, he could toss her overboard just as he'd done with the unfortunate fellow who had put his hands on her. Not that he would…but he *could*. He held all the cards here. Every instinct screamed that whatever fell from his lips would not be in her best interests. She held her breath when his mouth opened.

"Since you have injured yourself," he said, "I have to think up another suitable position for you to pay for your place on my ship."

"I can still work."

Rhystan smiled. "No, I've a better idea."

He couldn't mean…

Oh, good gracious.

Though a spark of desire ignited in the pit of her abdomen, Sarani shook her head wildly, backing away several steps as though reason would miraculously appear with more space between them. It didn't. "I refuse to be your 'shipboard doxy,' as you called it, or whatever insanity you've conjured in that head of yours," she burst out, waving a wild hand. "Regardless of what happened between us earlier"—she sputtered at the sudden gleam in his eye—"that's not going to happen, Your Grace."

A darkening gaze met hers. "Would that be so bad, Sarani? Being in my bed?"

Would it?

Parts of her body went instantly molten as her eyes slid to the very bed he was propped upon, visions of those fine sheets crumpled around a pair of naked, intertwined, writhing bodies. His. Hers. No end to where each of them began. Much like the carvings and sculptures she'd discovered during a trip with her father to a princely state where the temples of Khajuraho depicted *maithuna*—the coupling between a husband and wife.

Her maid, Asha, as wide-eyed as she, had been a veritable fountain of information. Hot-cheeked, Sarani had been riveted, gobbling up the wickedly erotic depictions of the Hindu god Shiva, the masculine aspect of divine creativity, and the Goddess Shakti, the feminine aspect of the power of creation. Her people saw the concept of physical desire as something sacred, and that sexuality was a symbol of unity and oneness. She bit her lip. What would such *oneness* be like with Rhystan?

No, no, no!

Hastily, Sarani blinked the provocative and categorically unwelcome imaginings away. Heavens, what was wrong with her? She was surely out of her mind. There was no future, sexual or otherwise, with this man. She must have inhaled rope fibers and they were clogging her brain, because she couldn't possibly be thinking that climbing into the Duke of Embry's bed wasn't remotely the worst conceivable idea in the history of existence.

Her body hummed its denial.

Not exactly the worst.

"Yes. No." She gave her head a rough shake. "Of course it would be. And my name is Sara. I'm not that girl anymore."

"No, you're not," he said quietly. He paused with a shadow of a smirk. "As diverting as it is to see you at such a stunning loss for words, that's not the offer I had in mind."

A breath rushed out. In relief? Disappointment? Sarani hissed to herself—definitely the former. "Oh. It's not?"

"No."

"Then what?" she asked.

"An offer of marriage." Before the word or its implication could properly sink in, he arched a bronzed brow. "To me."

Sarani blinked. "Why on earth would you—" She gaped, her

jaw falling open in indecorous horror. "Marry you? You have to be joking."

"Au contraire, I'm deadly serious. I'd like us to become engaged."

"One of your quartermaster's blows must have addled your mind, Your Grace," she said with a frown. "Might I remind you that you are a *duke*. An engagement to…me will never be countenanced by your *mother*, remember?"

"Talbot was a peer and you were engaged to him."

Disgust rolled through her. "Talbot was a swine, the bottom of the barrel, ousted from London. Marriage to me was a windfall for a man like him."

Sarani couldn't disguise the ripple of pain that threaded through her words.

Even Lord Talbot had reminded her on more than one occasion that *he* was doing *her* a grand service by offering her marriage. Oh, he'd desired her badly. Sarani had known it from the way he'd slavered over her body, his eyes wild with lust, but he had lorded his privileged male superiority over her like a cudgel. His close friend Markham had made no attempt to mask his contempt, and others had followed suit.

Especially the ladies; they'd been worse than the men.

It made her think of Thackeray's words that it was a great compliment to any woman to be despised by her sex. She still wasn't able to find it in her heart to agree. Women should lift each other up, given the barriers they faced on account of their sex alone and not having the same power as men. It had been what her mother had taught her and what her father had bolstered by allowing her to be raised as a son would be. Perhaps even to be esteemed as one would.

Until he'd traded her off like a goat, that was.

Marriage—the sole thing any highborn woman was good for. At least she and other Englishwomen had that in common. And here she was…crumbling like a house of straw at the duke's offer, because it had to be a joke. The memory of her broken heart was her undoing, the prospect of wedlock to him twisting her into painful knots. Marriage to Talbot would have been intolerable. Marriage to Rhystan would be the end of her.

"This is the answer for both of us," Rhystan said.

With the barest flinch, Sarani closed her eyes. "No. Not for me. I'd sooner go back to Joor."

Rhystan narrowed his eyes, tracking her like a hound scenting a fox. "You're telling me that you'd rather face your father's murderer than become engaged to me?"

In a heartbeat.

Nodding fervently, Sarani retreated several more steps until the cabin door pressed into the backs of her shoulders, halting her flight. It was by far the lesser of two evils. By a long shot. Her heart pounded against her ribs, her throat closing as buried memories surfaced, reminding her of what came with wanting too much. And the price that accompanied such arrogance. She had learned that lesson the hard way.

It had been drilled into her by men like Markham and Talbot: Someone like her did not belong with men like him. *Sons of dukes, brothers of dukes, or dukes themselves.*

She let out an agonized breath.

"Sarani." Her given name was a caress upon his lips, but his next words were a ruthless arrow to her heart. "Hear me out. You owe me that much."

Reaching behind her for the door latch, she fought the lance of guilt. "Even if I did, my answer will still be no. When we dock tomorrow, it's best for me to take my leave in St. Helena as planned."

Eleven

MARRIAGE.

Sarani had endured a restless sleep from the moment she'd left the duke's cabin after his preposterous proposition, and she'd tossed and turned all night, tortured by visions of her wedded to the man who'd stolen the heart of a starry-eyed girl all those years ago. Those dreams had been intertwined with more salacious fantasies of what came after the wedding…as in the bedding. And *that* had left her in a wicked, restless state that made further sleep practically impossible.

She stared up at the ceiling, fisting her fingers in the twisted bedsheets, her eyes flicking to her exhausted maid who had taken refuge in the armchair halfway through the night to avoid her mistress's constant thrashing. Poor Asha. Sarani had explained in a few short words what Embry had proposed and Asha's eyes had gone wide, though she had uncharacteristically, if wisely, not offered any counsel.

Sarani throttled a grunt of frustration.

Marriage.

The utter nerve of him. It was unconscionable. Absurd. Unthinkable.

But after several hours of indignation, her innately practical mind had slowed enough to consider both the advantages and the disadvantages. Despite their tumultuous history and the decisions that had pushed them apart, something had brought them back together. And if she put emotion aside, the duke could be the answer to her prayers.

A duchess would be unassailable.

The *ton* would accept her without question because she wouldn't just be Lady Sara Lockhart, returning mysterious heiress from India, she would be Lady Sara Lockhart, fiancée to the exalted Duke of Embry. By default, an uncontestable extension of him.

She would be safe from harmful gossip, but her identity would be swaddled up in that of yet another man. One whose motives weren't entirely clear.

Why would he offer to wed her?

What reason could he possibly have? With his fortune, looks, and title, he would have his pick of brides in England. Unless he wanted her specifically. He couldn't be that vengeful, could he? Wanting to exact retribution for her betrayal all those years ago? Her chest tightened. If anything, the past few weeks had taught her that the man Rhystan had become was capable of that and more. He was ruthless in the extreme.

Cold. Powerful. Exacting.

Sarani thought of the tender way he'd soothed and bound her hands, and then she remembered that he'd set her to work shoveling manure in the first place. She, a princess shoveling cow and horse shit, and one he'd proposed to nonetheless. It was beyond the pale.

A small giggle escaped her lips. When did Rhystan ever care about what was proper? And now he was a duke who could do as he pleased without fear of recrimination or punishment. As duke, no Vice Admiral Markham would have him tossed on a convoy. No man below his rank would dare put his hands on the duke or question his authority.

Sarani stilled.

Perhaps he was right. Or perhaps she was so weary she wasn't thinking straight.

It didn't matter. She was set on her course: she, Asha, and Tej would disembark and make their own way. With a determined breath, she rolled to the side of the bunk, performed her ablutions, and got dressed in her boy's clothing without waking Asha. Perhaps a round of exercise on deck would help calm her roiling thoughts. Palming her kukri blades and slipping them into their leather harness that crisscrossed her shoulders and hugged her hips, she immediately felt better.

She exited the cabin and climbed the stairs to the main deck.

The pale golden rays of the morning sun washed across the worn wooden planks of the ship, splitting through the rigging and the foremast and mizzenmast and glittering across the uncommonly glass-like surface of the sea. It wasn't like the usual chop of the open ocean.

A few men working the sails tipped their caps to her as she walked by.

As she climbed to the quarterdeck where the huge figure of Gideon stood, Sarani noticed other things through the sunrise haze. Like the tips of other masts glinting in the distance and what looked like the curve of land. Were they in a bay? Gracious, had they arrived at St. Helena already? She frowned when she reached Gideon, putting a hand to her brow to get a better view through the glare.

"Have we reached port already?" she asked.

His answer was a grunt that sounded like *aye*.

Something that felt like regret settled low in her stomach. It would be moments, not hours, that she would have to say her goodbyes. Gather her belongings. Formulate another plan of action. She huffed a breath, wondering idly where Rhystan was and feeling her sense of regret deepen. An ache began to build in her throat.

"I suppose I should thank you," she said to the quartermaster. "For all your help these past weeks." He gave another noncommittal grunt. "For what it's worth, you have my gratitude. I better get back belowdecks, wake Asha, and retrieve our things."

She retraced her footsteps, dimly registering that the ship's nose pointed out to open water. Within seconds, sails were billowing and they began to gather speed. The shapes of other ships became smaller and smaller, and she could no longer see the outline of land. Sarani halted, blinking her confusion. Shouldn't they be slowing?

"Gideon, do we not need more coal?" she asked, stalking back to the quartermaster.

Cold if marginally sheepish eyes met hers. "Already done."

Because they weren't putting into port...they were leaving port.

"Done?" The word emerged as a shriek. "But I'm to disembark."

"Too late."

Her mouth fell open. What did *that* mean? Had they somehow already refueled? Confusion was followed by awareness of the fact that they were leaving the shipping port—her only avenue for escape. "Turn this ship around! I demand it."

"Can't. Captain's orders."

Hissing a foul curse through her lips, Sarani grabbed the wheel, but the damned thing wouldn't budge beneath Gideon's hold. Not that she expected she could turn the blasted ship with a flick of the wrist, but she wasn't just going to stand there and be told she couldn't leave. She was a grown woman and she'd made up her mind, damn it to purgatory.

Damn him to purgatory. Captain's orders, her foot.

"Where is that insufferable horse's arse?"

In a fit of rage, she whirled and nearly collided with the broad, hard chest attached to the insufferable arse in question. Her gaze slid up to the smirk on his full mouth, and she very nearly punched it. "I wish to get off."

His smirk widened at her unfortunate choice of words. Blast it, was everything an insinuation with him? Rhystan planted his hands on his narrow hips.

"No."

"*No?*" she repeated, fury sparking. "You cannot keep me a prisoner on this ship. I demand to leave immediately." Rhystan's gaze slid to Gideon, and the man left after their silent exchange until she and Rhystan stood alone on the quarterdeck. Sarani's hands hovered over her blades, the meaning clear enough. "Explain."

His brow lifted infinitesimally at the threat, looking more amused than afraid as he took the wheel, and she scowled. But then he let out a measured exhale, steel-gray eyes capturing hers. "It's not safe, Sarani. I used the rest of the coal stores to get here under cover of night so that we could resupply and leave quickly. You should know that there are reports of a man looking for someone of your description and willing to pay heavily for information on your whereabouts."

Her anger instantly deflated. *Oh, no.* How had the murderer caught up to them? The winds had been favorable, but they would have been for his ship, too, and the route they'd taken would have led straight to St. Helena. She swallowed, her legs threatening to collapse.

"England is the safest choice for you," Rhystan said quietly. "I can turn this ship around if that is your wish, but I urge you to reconsider my proposal for both our sakes—an engagement for the sake of mutual convenience, no strings attached."

Her eyes fastened on him. "What do you mean?"

"If you won't marry me, then pretend to be my fiancée, Sarani. That's all I ask."

―――――――

Rhystan held his breath, watching the myriad of emotions play over her expressive face. He gave no quarter to the small but necessary lie he'd told. He had given the order to shorten the remaining distance to the port and to restock in the dark, which had cost him more than a pretty penny and a few favors, but they had been for his own plans.

He needed her.

The slight fabrication was simply a means to an end. The more his own strategy to avoid wedlock and the caprices of his mother solidified in his head, the more he needed Sarani to cooperate. Forcing her hand would not lose him any sleep. The lie he'd invented about reports of a man searching for her would be the clincher.

Sarani was clever and sensible; it was only a matter of time before she saw the benefits of such an arrangement. Once she got past the emotion, that was. He knew where her concern stretched from... He hadn't exactly won her friendship or loyalty. Or treated her with a modicum of respect or fairness. He had given her no reason to trust him, not with his recent behavior.

And she didn't. Rhystan could see it in her eyes.

But he didn't need her to trust him; he only needed to convince her to agree to what was on the surface a logical solution. Though he had to admit that a dark part of him was deeply elated at the idea of having her in his grasp under the guise of an engagement. To anyone who mattered in the *ton*, she would be his. And when it was all said and done and he'd gotten what he wanted, he would walk away...just as she had.

Two birds, one stone.

A pair of suspicious hazel eyes narrowed on his as though she'd sensed his train of thought. "What do you get out of a sham engagement?"

He debated telling her the truth and then shrugged. She would see through anything else. "My mother has grand plans to thrust me into ballroom upon ballroom of debutantes on my return. I'd rather avoid such torture if possible." He exhaled. "That's where you come in. If I arrive with a fiancée, it hinders her plots."

"You don't wish to marry?"

"I belong to a demanding mistress." Rhystan saw the stark confusion on her face before he waved an arm at the surrounding sea. "The ocean owns me, body and soul."

"But you're a duke," she said, a frown pleating her brow. "You have…duties."

"I have stewards to see to those duties, including my mother the duchess and her army of servants, who do a much better job than I could." He sucked in a breath. "I return to see for myself that the lady's health is hale, to check on my sister, and to offer gifts to my sister-in-law and my nieces. Then I intend to leave."

She blinked. "You have a sister?"

"Her name is Ravenna," he said. "The unfortunate youngest of four with three older brothers."

"Brothers?"

His heart squeezed with forgotten sorrow and guilt arced through him that he hadn't spoken of them to her…or to anyone. "Dead, along with my father."

"I am sorry."

Rhystan shoved the sentiment back where it belonged, down deep, and hardened his expression. "Your answer, my lady. Which is it? Do you wish to return to St. Helena? Or do you agree to my proposal?"

She bit her lip, her eyes glancing over her shoulder to the departing shores, her indecision clear. He still couldn't fathom that she would choose to face a killer over betrothal to him. She'd always been headstrong, but her intelligence had always been a dependable foil to her more impulsive ideas. He felt a stroke of admiration for her unshakable courage, as misguided as it was.

"Will it be in name only?" she asked. "This temporary engagement."

Rhystan fought back amusement. "Meaning?"

"No…er…kissing," she said, a blush rising up her neck. "Or inappropriate touching. Or any other things."

"No."

A shocked stare collided with his, hot color saturating those elegant cheekbones. Her lips parted on a gasp. "What do you mean, no?"

"Just what it sounds like," he said. "My mother will see through the subterfuge if it's not believable. You must allow me to touch you, and you must be willing to touch me. Though based on recent evidence, that will not be a hardship for either of us."

Desire and heat twined through him, and Rhystan willed his overeager body to behave. A cockstand at this juncture would not win him any favors. He glanced at her flaming cheeks. Or perhaps it would. He leaned on the railing, jutting his hips forward. Rhystan knew the moment her gaze dipped to the overcrowded area in question, when a strangled sound escaped her throat and her flush deepened to dark rose. "You are unspeakable."

"I'm a red-blooded male," he returned evenly. "You want me, and I want you. Ignoring the monster between us won't make it go away, Sarani."

She rolled her eyes at his innuendo. "Your ego is truly enormous, unlike that part of you. And my name is Sara."

"Sara, then," he conceded, resenting the shorter sound of it on his lips. He much preferred the lyrical sound of her whole name but would yield if it meant that much to her. "The duchess will ferret out any lie in a heartbeat. As my fiancée, you must act the part, because she has to believe it's a love match."

Her slender throat worked. "Why? Most gentlemen hardly marry for love."

"Because she is well versed on my vow never to marry. The fact that the ever prosaic, unsentimental duke has been brought low by Cupid will undoubtedly appeal to her female sense of romanticism." He didn't add that the Duchess of Embry did not have a romantic bone in her body.

Sarani narrowed her eyes, lips pursing. "Female sense? I didn't expect such a deeply elemental thing to be relegated to one particular sex or for you to describe it so."

His lips twitched, that tart rejoinder reminding him of their many vigorous discussions. From politics to literature to philosophy to science, they'd never been at a loss for topics of discourse, and she'd always argued her points passionately and with conviction. Those few times that he'd won an argument, she'd conceded with grace, willing to learn and widen her worldview. He'd never met another like her. Smart, articulate, and deviously clever.

Had she been born a man, she might have left revolution in her wake.

"Everyone knows women are hopeless romantics," he said, biting back his smile.

"A sweeping generalization," she said, eyes sparking. "I know of many men who would stake their fortunes on the value of a single romantic gesture."

"Let me guess, poets like Byron?"

She sniffed. "And Coleridge, Wordsworth, and other poets of English note while you're at it. Not all of the great poets hail from the west, you know. Jalal al-Din Rumi's evocation of divine love could be read as the most intimate kind of love poetry."

"I'm familiar with translations of his work. It might surprise you that James Redhouse is a distant acquaintance of mine." He smiled, seeing her brows pleat at the mention of the well-known literary translator.

"I thought I saw something from the Royal Asiatic Society in your bookshelf," she said. "I did not take someone like you to be a connoisseur of Rumi or a collector of peregrine literature."

"Why? Because I'm a humble ship's captain?" He shot her an arch look.

"No. Because you've…"

Changed.

He saw the moment the banter fled from her eyes and the wariness returned. Once more, she turned a desperate, panicked gaze to the shoreline. "I don't—"

"Sarani, you are not safe there," he interjected before she chose rashly and he had to resort to less pleasant measures to get his way. "I will protect you in London. You will have the safeguard of my family and my name. Once I conclude my business in London, we can end the engagement however you please. A public scene? A quiet send-off? It's up to you."

"You could have any woman you choose."

He nodded. "But with you, I would have an understanding. With you, this is a trade. An eye for an eye—we both get something out of it." He let out a measured breath. "It's your choice."

She was much too intelligent not to know it was merely the illusion of choice. St. Helena would be dangerous, not only for her but for her servants…whom she considered family. Rhystan could see the war waging in her mind. She'd always been fiercely independent, and that trait had not been tempered. It would gall her to accept his help, especially when her every instinct warned against trusting him. And she had every right to mistrust him.

"I don't rate as a wife for the son of a duke, much less an actual duke," she said eventually. "Your letter stated as much, so why the change of heart?"

He frowned, recalling the harsh lines of the letter he'd written five years ago. "I thought you didn't think I was high-ranking enough for you. You were a princess and I was a lowly, third-born son with little to recommend me. I was jealous and angry when I wrote that."

"That was obvious." She shook her head. "Your sentiments were more than clear."

He tilted his chin. "I was furious at what I thought you'd done—that you'd married another—though now I can hardly blame you for obeying your father's wishes, seeing as I'm to be put through the same paces for the sake of duty. Forgive me for being an angry, jilted man."

It still pulled, the old injury of losing her, like a scab that hadn't quite healed. Early on and believing her love false, he had yearned for vengeance, when every single memory of her had brought pain and fury in equal measure. But now he needed her—the one woman who had ever broken him. The whole thing stung of irony. And folly.

"I propose a peace," he said and then pushed a conciliatory grin to his lips. "No more barnacles in my bed, and no more mucking out stalls. I'll prove to you that I can be quite civil."

"We don't suit," she whispered, something like desolation flickering in her gaze. "You said it yourself. No one will believe that we are to be wed."

Pushing off from the rail, he shuttled the distance between them, noting the wild pulse in her throat and the immediate widening of her eyes. His brow lifted. "I counter that we suit rather well."

"That's lust."

"Lust is as good a basis for an aristocratic marriage as any," he said.

"But you said you wanted love."

Rhystan reached out a hand to tuck a loosened strand of hair behind one ear. Her lush mouth parted on a soundless sigh that she couldn't quite hide. "No, you misunderstand me. I require the *pretense* of love. Easy enough when one puts one's mind to the task. A glance here, a touch there. Whispered nothings and sentimental looks. Love is but a show, you see. You have to admit that Byron had the right of it—the man was a swindler of women's soft hearts."

He could see the argument push to her lips, then see her swallow it down with force. Oh, the rub that she still chose to believe in love nearly made him laugh out loud. Despite her strong opinions and unconventional views, his fierce princess remained quixotic at heart. Some things hadn't changed. He tucked that bit of information away to use later.

Worrying that temptingly plump lip of hers, she heaved out

a breath. After the barest moment of indecision, her shoulders straightened and she met his stare. "If I agree to your terms and I'm followed to England by my pursuer, will you agree to help me identify who wants me dead and why?"

Rhystan squashed the burst of triumph. "Yes."

"And Tej and Asha will both accompany me?"

He nodded. "Of course."

"And I can walk away once your business has concluded in town, ending the engagement?" She paused, lashing him with a guarded glance. "Without recrimination."

"Once our mutual goals have been achieved, yes."

Sarani closed her eyes, her proud frame hunching slightly. "Then I agree."

Twelve

THIS BETROTHAL IS A MEANS TO AN END.

The Duke of Embry is a means to an end.

Sarani repeated the mantras almost every hour of every day for the next few weeks. The fact that it was wedlock to the only man she'd ever wanted to marry meant nothing. The fact that she had broken his trust and lost his heart also meant nothing. It would not be too much of a stretch to pretend to love him. She had once, after all.

This was a mutually agreed upon decision that would benefit them both.

They were both adults; they could do this.

It was only when the *Belonging* had turned toward the English Channel that her nerves started to coil and knot with trepidation. Blast it, could she do this? London wasn't Joor. She wasn't a princess in her own palace…in her own *space*.

Not that that had earned her any favors with the British nationals there, especially over the last handful of years. Rhystan had been right. Less than a year after he'd been discharged by Markham, discontent had risen to the point of rebellion, and as Markham's and Talbot's influence had grown, her father's had diminished. His court, and his power as maharaja, had become little more than a mockery. As had her station in the palace. One English viscountess had had the gall to order her about like a servant and then complained to Talbot when Sarani hadn't obeyed her.

Her father had asked her to be reasonable.

She'd nodded dutifully and promptly sold off her bridal jewels, donating a significant fortune to the sepoy army.

It had taken Sarani months to armor herself, walking with her head held high. She'd let their cruelty bounce off like raindrops on a window and plotted in secret with those who wished to see their oppressors gone from her lands. Her father's hands might have been tied because of the crown's power, but hers weren't. And even in the aftermath of the rebellion, she'd made it her purpose to help those who had lost husbands and wives and children. She had lost loved ones, too.

One of her oldest friends, Manu, who had become queen of the princely state of Jhansi, had been a vocal supporter of the resistance. Her state had been reclaimed by the British under the doctrine of lapse and her adopted son rejected as ruler. Her death, after fighting for the freedom of Jhansi and then being cut down in Gwalior, had hit Sarani hard. Manu had died defending their people and what she believed in.

Unsurprisingly, most of the northern princes had remained loyal to the British. Earl Canning, the first Viceroy of India, had commended them on being *breakwaters in a storm*. In the end, despite heavy losses, the rebellion had led to the dissolution of the East India Company, and Queen Victoria's proclamation about obligations of duty had ushered in a new era. The queen's sentiments hadn't stopped power-hungry peers like Talbot from exerting his influence over her father and the vassal state of Joor, however, and life had changed.

There was every indication that life in London would be worse, and each nautical mile that shortened the distance to England's shores thickened the lump building in Sarani's throat. To fit in to the *ton*, she had to be unquestionably perfect. And so Sarani spent the remaining weeks of the journey brushing up on social customs and etiquette, acting the part of a proper English lady, and learning about the family tree of the Duke of Embry from the stack of books in Rhystan's cabin, including a copy of *Debrett's Illustrated Peerage*.

"How do you have this?" she'd asked him, sifting through the red and gold-embossed volume and wrinkling her nose. "Or better yet, why?"

Rhystan's stare had been measured, impossible to read. "When I became duke, my mother insisted that I refresh myself on my peers, meaning those worthy of a duke's attention, of course. It was a gift. She still hopes that I could aspire to be the sort of duke my father was." His tone had left little doubt of what he thought of the gift as well as walking in the shoes of the former duke.

"Things did not improve with the duke?" she'd asked, recalling the little he'd told her of him. She'd never even known he had siblings.

"No." The reply had been terse.

"And your mother?"

His face had tightened. "She has always wanted what was best for her children."

Even with such a vague answer, Sarani hoped to make a good first impression on the Dowager Duchess of Embry. It did not sound like it would be easy—*who gave their son a copy of* Debrett's *as light reading?*—but maybe she was overthinking it.

At Asha's insistence, Sarani was now careful to wear proper gowns and avail herself of an annoying parasol while on deck since her skin was wont to tan in the sun without too much effort. Though she loved when her skin deepened with color, in England, she knew from her mother and French governess that western ladies valued their porcelain complexions. And looking like a sun-burned, freckled hoyden would not earn her any favors, not with a haughty duchess thwarted in her plan to marry off her son to a pretty English rose of *her* choosing.

Still, it didn't stop her grumbling to Asha when she had held out the parasol.

"I'll look sallow," she'd complained. "Using this won't make me any paler. This is silly."

Asha had set her jaw. "It's what English ladies do."

"English ladies would envy a corpse!"

"Better than being an actual corpse if Vikram gets his hands on you."

Sarani had buttoned her lips and taken the dratted parasol, resisting the urge to crack it over her knee. At first, Red had laughed himself silly...until she'd produced her kukri blades from the hidden pockets sewn into her skirts and told him to laugh again. Wisely, he had refrained.

Asha and Tej had both taken the news of her impending engagement in stride, agreeing that it was for the best. She personally might not need a man to survive...but in the world of English aristocracy, society decreed that she did. A woman needed a husband to have value.

It was a concept that had always rubbed her raw. Even as the daughter of a maharaja and the inherent privilege that came with it, she'd worked on standing on her own merit in Joor. She fought for her people where she could, made up her own mind by considering the facts, not what was spoonfed to her. And it wasn't in her to withdraw or need to be rescued. But now she had no choice.

This was England...a different world entirely.

A different universe, if she was being honest. Admittedly, she was afraid, despite never having been cowed by anything in her life. Not when she'd been promised in marriage to Talbot. Not when the sepoy infantry had come guns blazing to their gates during the rebellion and Markham's army had made an equally vicious stand. But now...the fear gnawing in her gut threatened to cripple her.

All because of the threat of strange, foreign shores.

"Your best friend Manu died defending her people," Sarani hissed to herself while stirring broth under the watchful eye of the ship's cook. "The least you could do is hold your head high. You're a princess, not a helpless damsel."

In truth, she felt as though she were about to jump off a plank into shark-infested waters, only these sharks would be dressed to the nines in yards of silken finery while wearing smiles that hid their bloodthirsty, razor-sharp teeth.

"Well, you'll just have to make do then. You've handled worse," she told herself.

"Less talking, more working," the cook snapped, making her startle.

"Sorry," she muttered.

True to his word, the duke had ordered her to switch jobs with Tej, and now she spent most of her time helping in the galley: baking bread, stirring boiling pots, or sifting dried grain to separate from vermin. It was tedious, but at least she wasn't shoveling manure or forced to endure the duke's presence in a cabin that grew smaller by the day. Rhystan might have relented, but he was still short a boatswain thanks to her, and she would not make others shoulder her share.

Tej was Rhystan's primary cabin boy now, and though he was free with information on the captain's whereabouts—allowing Sarani to slip in unnoticed to borrow one of Rhystan's many volumes of poetry or novels to stave off boredom—a part of her missed their private interaction.

A stupid, cabbageheaded part of her.

She knew it wasn't because he was intentionally avoiding her. The entire crew, including their captain, had been busy. They'd faced some rough weather along the stretch of the Atlantic, then outraced a few suspicious-looking ships that a wide-eyed Asha had whispered were smugglers. A few warning cannons had been fired, and Red had told Sarani with a grin not to worry, that the captain had a reputation for being a *right mean bastard*.

Hunched near the gangplank leading to the quarterdeck, Sarani had glimpsed said mean bastard standing on the poop deck, shouting orders, hands clasped behind his back, legs apart, shoulders proud and strong, and didn't doubt Red's boast for a second.

Rhystan's face had been grim, his expression deadly. Power and danger emanated from him in spades, making her shiver. And yet the sight had also made a scalding heat distill through her body like ink through water.

Cabbageheaded was clearly too weak a description for her.

Despite his promises, Sarani forced herself to keep his letter etched in her memory. His words had been succinct, with the precision of a dagger set to remove a heart from its prey, and the letter had done its job, even if it'd been written in anger. Years later, those cruel words still bit like blades in her memory.

It didn't matter that he'd changed his tune.

Sarani wasn't so naive that she didn't know Rhystan had some other motive and that this sham betrothal would benefit him in another hidden way at her expense. The hard, intractable man he'd become didn't forgive or forget slights. So what *did* he want from her? Every instinct in her brain screamed not to trust him. But she'd had no choice then, and she had none now.

Like Odysseus, she was stuck between a monster and a whirlpool. Or like the boatswains said when they hung in the precarious bosun's chair to caulk the long seam that ran from bow to stern—that they were hanging between the devil and the deep. Neither scenario presented pleasing odds. With Rhystan in front of her and a killer behind her, the duke was obviously the lesser of two evils.

Or is he?

Sarani suppressed the clench of warning that gripped her spine. Now was not the time for doubts. She would use him to get settled in England, see Tej and Asha safe, and accept his help in determining the identity of the assassin if he tracked her to London.

Sarani repeated her mantras.

The betrothal is a means to an end.

The Duke of Embry is a means to an end.

Rhystan watched with a narrowed eye as Gideon expertly navigated the crowded Thames, the putrid stench of its riverbed climbing into his nostrils. He trusted his quartermaster's skill as they steered toward the fairly newly constructed six-year-old Victoria Dock. Collisions happened frequently given the volume of movement on the river, but pillaging by thieves was more predominant, which was why he and several of his men kept a keen eye out as they sailed past nearby vessels.

His throat tightened as a cold sensation settled over his shoulders, the mantle of duke thumping over his shoulders like a salt-crusted, waterlogged blanket. London—it was the only place in all the world he truly didn't want to be. On the sea, he was judged on his effort and worth as captain. Here, every step was measured, every action noted, but for the flimsiest of reasons. One wrong word and a goddamned scandal would be certain to ensue. He resented the charade with every bone in his body.

Scowling, Rhystan shook off his annoyance. The only solution was to make this visit as short as possible and be back out to sea where he belonged. He thought of his mother and sister, and guilt speared him. They'd done fine without him all these years. No sense changing something that wasn't broken.

"See that the cargo is unloaded," he shouted to Gideon once the *Belonging* was docked beside a massive steamship on the wharf.

The sale of the tea, spices, lace, and silks they carried would fetch a pretty penny. Fair trade was an important part of his shipping business, and though most of it was aboveboard with the Crown, Rhystan didn't wear his trousers down around his ankles either. The taxes levied on merchant goods was astronomical.

"See you at the tavern?" his quartermaster asked.

Rhystan scrubbed at the several weeks' growth of beard he'd acquired, knowing that he would have to break from their usual tradition. "Not today. I have to find my valet to make myself presentable and be off to Huntley House to make sure my mother isn't on her last breaths as implied by her letter."

"Is she?"

"You've met the lady," Rhystan said. "What do you think?"

Gideon's succinct opinion of the duchess, who had glared at him at the funeral as though she were facing him down at dawn, had hit the nail on the head—she was clever and manipulative to a fault, though her loyalty to her family was unquestionable.

"I think that she's as fine as a farthing fiddle," he said. "But I'm wagering she wants you to marry, settle down, and be duke."

Rhystan's mood darkened. "Precisely."

"I'll drink a pint to your sanity, then."

"It will take more than a pint." Rhystan sighed. "Put a round on the lads from me."

With that, he donned his coat. He'd sent word of his impending arrival to his own private residence a carriage ride away in Mayfair, but if anything, they'd put into London early. His coachman might not yet be there.

And then there was the matter of his…fiancée.

As if his thoughts had conjured her, Sarani—*blast*, he had to stop thinking of her by that name now that they were in town—Lady Sara Lockhart strolled from belowdecks, her two servants in tow. Rhystan blinked. Unlike him with his unkempt appearance, she was the picture of perfect aristocratic elegance, dressed in a modest but stylish mauve gown trimmed in lace, with her rich, dark hair coiled into a low bun and loose ringlets framing her exquisite face. A fetching, feathered bonnet completed the picture.

Lord but she stole his breath.

Rhystan sucked in a sudden gulp of air. He was not the only one so affected. Several of his crew gaped openly, and even stoic Gideon wore a slightly bemused expression. Rhystan didn't know which version of Sarani he preferred more—but whether she wore boy's clothing or a fashionable dress, she captivated.

"Your Grace," she said, approaching him and dipping into an effortless curtsy.

Inclining his head, he cleared his tight throat. "My lady, you look well."

"I've a part to play, don't I," she said, the words soft and only for his ears. "And if London is anything like my court in Joor, we can be sure that curious eyes and inquisitive minds are already reporting on the prodigal Duke of Embry's arrival, as well as the unexpected female passenger on his ship. Believe me, gossip will fly faster than a winter squall."

He almost smiled at the choice of words. She was right, of course.

In retrospect, Rhystan would not put it past his mother to have made some grand announcement in the newssheets about her son's anticipated return. Though she would not have known about Sarani or the fact that he would be arriving with a fiancée. The gratifying thought almost made him smile. A gleeful part of him could not wait to see his mother's face.

Speaking of, he'd better make haste before she found her way to him before he was properly groomed and attired…before the Duke of Embry's own costume was securely in place. His gaze scanned the clogged docks packed with dockworkers, wagons, coaches, and then traveled in reverse to stop on a handsome coach emblazoned with his ducal crest that was waiting a short distance away. He shouldn't have been surprised. Even with an early arrival, his very efficient servants would have had someone watching for his appearance.

With a deep breath, he offered his arm to his future bride. "Shall we, then?"

"As you wish, Your Grace," she replied, slipping a gloved hand onto his forearm.

Though he could sense her trepidation, there was no hint of it on her face. Her expression was serene, her chin held high. She carried herself with the easy elegance of a born aristocrat. Which she was. Hell, she was of *royal* blood, even though he knew some of the British nobility might not view it that way. Especially his mother.

Once more, he was struck by the similarities between the lives they led—both straddling two worlds in which neither of them wholly belonged. Both running from something. And they were about to pull off the coup of the season.

He was so engrossed in his own thoughts that he didn't realize she was speaking as they approached the waiting ducal carriage, where his coachman and tiger stood, dressed smartly in their crimson and silver livery.

"Thank you for doing this, Your Grace," she said quietly. "I shall endeavor to hold up my end of our bargain."

"As will I."

And he meant it. He would protect her if someone from Joor had followed her, though once they'd left St. Helena, neither he nor Gideon had seen any more of the ship that had been on their tail. There was the chance that it could have been pure coincidence. Either way, he would see Sarani safe and settled once they parted ways.

He had considered the fact that she could make the perfect wife for him. They could live separate lives—he on the sea, and she wherever she wanted. However, that solution would only be temporary, because eventually, there would be the matter of children.

His, to be specific. Despite his views on his father and the dukedom, he had a responsibility to continue the ducal line. And as much as he'd been at loggerheads with the former duke, Rhystan was deeply aware of his duty. He would need an heir.

And even though the idea of a tigress-hearted daughter with jet-black hair and fierce hazel eyes made his pulse leap, it was out of the question. Though a fake engagement and even a fake marriage were easy prospects, there was no way he would have a child with a woman he could never trust.

And Sarani Rao had broken his heart once.

He would never open himself to the possibility again.

Thirteen

It was astounding what a full bath, a shave and trim by a devoted valet, and a wardrobe full of expensive, fashionable clothing could do. Despite the prevailing preference for facial whiskers—and the *ton*'s laughable notion of masculinity and vigor—Rhystan chose to be clean-shaven, though he did keep his hair on the longer side. The only way the thick curls could be tamed out of sea-blown wildness was with some length to them.

Within the hour, the Duke of Embry, brushed, groomed, and buttoned to within an inch of his life, was officially in residence at his house in Mayfair, and judging by the stacks of invitations he'd seen on the mantelpiece in the foyer, just about everyone knew it, too.

Ignoring his valet's long-suffering look, he tugged at the narrow band of his necktie knotted and held in place with a diamond stickpin. "Must it be so tight, Harlowe?"

Giving one last look in the mirror and barely recognizing himself, he peered at his brother's old valet. Harlowe had come into his employ after Roland's death. Rhystan hadn't had the heart to dismiss the man after he'd been in service for so many decades to the Huntley family. He'd known the man as a boy, and his dedication to the family had never wavered. He'd been tasked with nothing but waiting for the new duke to return to London.

"It must, Your Grace." Harlowe squinted. "Unless you prefer a bow."

Rhystan scowled. "The stickpin will do."

The valet bowed. "Might I say how good it is to see you again and to have you home at last. The years at sea have been kind. You…" His voice broke as he fought to compose himself, the breach in decorum quite abnormal for a valet of Harlowe's competence. "You look so much like him."

It took Rhystan a moment to realize that the valet meant his brother, though he might well have meant the former duke, since both brothers favored their father in looks. He and Roland had resembled each other with their tawny hair and blue eyes, while Richard and Ravenna had taken the auburn hair and fair coloring of their mother.

With a trimmed beard and short-clipped hair, he would have been his father's mirror image. Hence the shave and the overlong mane. He'd much rather look like a dockworker with his sun-streaked hair than see the face of his dead father in the mirror. Not that he didn't hear the man's voice in his head, condemning his son's chosen lifestyle on a daily basis. It was a simple enough act of defiance, he supposed, now that he was the Duke of Embry. The old tyrant had finally gotten his way—Rhystan was well and truly in the ducal fold.

"Where is Lady Sara?" he asked Harlowe.

"She is in the gold room in the north wing, Your Grace."

Rhystan shot the valet a blank look. Was he supposed to know where or what that was? He assumed a bedchamber, but it'd been years since he'd spent any length of time at this residence. He'd bought the house years ago, once he'd had his first financial windfall in shipping, with the idea that he'd never have to set foot in Huntley House—his family's London home—or be forced to deal with the duke's everlasting displeasure.

Even now, he could feel the man's disappointment from the grave. Roland had been the heir, Richard, the spare, and Rhystan, ever the duke's despair. The rebellious son who would never fit the mold of what his father wanted, never abide by the rules of an aristocracy he deemed backward and insular.

"The lady's companion is in the adjacent blue room, Your Grace," Harlowe went on, brushing an invisible speck of lint from the sleeve of Rhystan's morning coat.

"Very good."

For the sake of propriety—inasmuch as they could stretch the truth—Sarani's lady's maid would also serve as her companion. Despite their engagement, fake or otherwise, a woman could not remain in her fiancé's residence overnight without a proper chaperone, and there was no way Rhystan was abandoning Sarani to the duchess at Huntley House. His mother, even on her rumored deathbed, would be ruthless.

He strode downstairs to his study and stared at the mountain of correspondence on his desk. Usually, he would receive a bundle of anything urgent at his château in France, but he hadn't returned to the Continent in months, having chosen to stay in the Americas before the most recent and unexpected voyage back to India.

Roland's man of business and longtime solicitor, Mr. Longacre, had done an excellent job of managing the various tenant estates. His reports were meticulous and detailed, and Rhystan had never had any reason to doubt the man's abilities.

"Where is Longacre?" he asked over his shoulder, knowing his ever-efficient butler was hovering in the foyer. "I sent word to his offices that I wished to see him."

Morton cleared his throat from the doorway. "He has just arrived, Your Grace."

A tall, twitchy, bespectacled man entered the room, carrying a pile of ledger books in his arms. After dumping the books on the edge of the desk, he attempted a clumsy bow. "Your Grace, welcome home. I have sent you letter after letter with no response. The estates are in disrepair, and I'm at my wit's end with the creditors."

Rhystan frowned at the outburst, gesturing for the harried man to sit. Disrepair? *Creditors?* "Since when?"

"The Dowager Duchess of Embry assured me that you were aware of the situation." He shuffled some papers in the pile and shoved one of the ledgers toward Rhystan, cracking it open to the last page. Rhystan was good with numbers, but even he had a hard time calculating the staggering losses accounted in one of the columns. He thumbed through the book, eyes scanning pages upon pages of meticulously itemized costs and sums in the negative.

His frown deepened as he reached for another ledger and flicked through the accounting. "How did this happen?"

"Lord Roland was in debt up to his ears, Your Grace. He and Lord Richard had several bad railroad investments go wrong when the railway company up and disappeared with their money. It was a secret that only came out after his death when his many creditors came calling. The dowager duchess ordered me to leverage the earnings of the ducal holdings and to increase tenant taxes. Many of the farmers have left, and the country staff has been culled significantly." His face flamed with obvious embarrassment. "I, too, am owed several months of wages."

Rhystan blinked in dumbfounded surprise—he'd known none of this. The duchess could have reached him at any time, but for whatever reason, she'd chosen to keep the state of their finances from him. Roland, the favored son, had thoroughly decimated the family coffers.

Why hadn't he asked for help?

Pride, Rhystan supposed. Pride and stubbornness. No one wanted to ask the purported prodigal son of the family for a farthing, even if said son had enough fortune to share. The former duke, if he'd been aware of the misfortune, would have forbidden it for sure. His mother hadn't let anything slip of the decline, and if it wasn't for Longacre, Rhystan would never have been the wiser.

Was this behind her ploy of illness?

He released a breath. "Don't worry, Mr. Longacre. I have more than enough funds to cover the debts and pay any outstanding wages." With another longer glance to the totals in the columns, he wrote out a check to his bank, Barclay & Co., in London for a significant amount of funds to be paid to the bearer. "There, that should cover it. If you need more, do not hesitate to return."

"Thank you, Your Grace."

"And, Mr. Longacre," he said as the man gathered his belongings. "Thank you for your discretion and long-standing constancy. In the future, please direct any and all financial or fiduciary concerns to me."

"Of course, Your Grace." Coloring at the unexpected praise, the solicitor paused at the door. "Do you intend to stay in London, then?"

Rhystan pinched the bridge of his nose with his fingers and nodded. "For now."

At least until the state of the dukedom was sorted out.

And God knew how long *that* was going to take.

Sarani sighed with sublime delight as Asha brushed and dried her hair in front of the fire. She had just taken the longest, most decadent bath known to humankind. The bedroom she'd been shown to was tastefully opulent, but the sumptuous bathing room was what had knocked the wind from her lungs—all rich wooden paneling and hand-painted porcelain tiles, and almost as large as the connecting bedchamber.

It had lacked for nothing, including modern plumbing for not just cold but hot running water. The massive claw-foot tub had been designed with an ingenious gas heating device.

Sarani hadn't been able to get out of her fine clothing fast enough, nearly ripping buttons in her haste. She'd languished in that gorgeous tub in the piping hot water until her skin had begun to protest and had only gotten out when Asha had murmured that His Grace would be expecting her shortly.

She hadn't seen Rhystan since their arrival, and he had been mostly silent in the coach, a brooding expression on his handsome face. She suspected that being in England did not sit well with him, much as it didn't for her, though for other reasons he had yet to share.

If he ever would.

In hindsight, she realized just how little she knew of the duke's origins, other than that he was a well-born gentleman who'd been an officer in the Royal Navy once upon a time and was now a rich, powerful duke who captained a ship. Who clearly did not want to be in London.

His stilted behavior in the lavish coach on the way to his residence had indicated as much. Sarani had known Rhystan had deep pockets, given he owned his own ship, but the sight of the ducal crest emblazoned on the lacquered coach had been her first inkling that he didn't exactly lack for fortune. Rather, if the luxurious coach and its liveried servants had been any signal, he was rather well-off.

"This is fancy," she'd told him once they'd left the wharf to settle into the plush confines of the fine carriage.

A hint of color had brushed his cheekbones. "It was my father's."

"It's very nice." That had been an understatement. "Where are we going?"

"To my residence in Mayfair."

She'd bitten her lip. "Is that…proper?"

"We are engaged," he'd replied. "But if you are worried, Asha can assume the role of your companion and chaperone. Problem of respectability solved."

"Even I know that a lady's maid won't pass muster as a companion, at least not according to the rules of etiquette here."

Unreadable eyes had met hers across the carriage. "You are engaged to the Duke of Embry."

"You say that as if anyone in the *ton* will refrain from gossiping like fishwives at market. If decorum is not observed, the shame will fall upon me, not you."

To her surprise, he'd nodded after a beat of scrutiny. "Very well. I will retire elsewhere tonight. Once I meet with my mother and introduce you, perhaps you can stay at Huntley House. My sister should also be in town for the season. She's a few years younger than you, just now eighteen."

"What's she like?"

A fond smile had curved his lips, making her heart hitch an unexpected beat. Seeing any kind of emotion on his face that wasn't lust, loathing, or some combination thereof was a bit of a shock. "Demure, sweet, dutiful."

The opposite of her, clearly.

He didn't have to say it, but the implication had been more than obvious.

They'd passed the rest of the journey in silence. And then, as they'd driven through the bustling streets of Mayfair, not even Rhystan's sourness could detract from her fascination with the clean lines of the architecture, carriages pulled by matching teams of plumed horses, and the neat groups of sedately dressed lords and ladies. It was the antithesis of Joor, lacking the joyful chaos, intricate architectural styles, and broad palette of bright color she was used to. It was all so very...structured.

She'd smoothed nervously at her skirts, drawing Rhystan's stare as they'd pulled up in front of a gorgeous town house.

"What's the matter?"

She'd swallowed, not sure why she suddenly felt panicked. "I didn't expect it to be so pristine. Even the cobblestones are freshly scrubbed."

"Don't let the exterior fool you," he'd murmured. "Beauty is only skin deep. After all, the loveliest of smiles can mask the cruelest of intentions, can't it?"

Her eyes had flashed to his, drawn by the harsh, bitter note in his voice, but he'd already returned his attention to the signet ring on his finger.

Now, Sarani's nerves returned in full force while Asha combed and styled her hair into a low chignon with looped ringlets over her ears. She gave herself a critical look in the mirror when Asha was finished. The remaining weeks of travel after St. Helena that she'd spent cooped-up belowdecks had been effective in making her look like an English corpse bride. She pinched the apples of her cheeks, making them flush with a dusky hue. There, that was marginally better.

Now she didn't look quite so sallow. Sarani glanced at Asha in the mirror whose brown skin practically glowed next to hers. Unlike her, Asha had been parasol-free and soaking up the sun for days. Sarani swallowed her envy and grimaced at her reflection. She wished she could line her eyelids with liberal amounts of kohl—it always made her eyes pop like jewels—but that would set her apart even more, and the goal was to fit in…not stand out.

She was beginning to feel an acute sense of pressure.

"Do you require face powder, Princess?" Asha asked.

Sarani wrinkled her nose. She hated the stuff, though blending in was the point, wasn't it? But when her gaze slid to the translucent dust in its decorative dish, everything inside of her suddenly choked. Did blending in mean becoming invisible? The parasol was one thing, but this was one more step of erasure.

"No, not tonight." *Not ever.* She lowered her voice, glancing over to where the undermaids were bustling about the antechamber. "And it's 'my lady,' don't forget. And remember, you are to play the role of my companion as well, so you must act accordingly."

Asha nodded. "Of course, my lady."

After donning a bottle-green gown from her portmanteau, Sarani gave herself one last look. A tepid English rose stared back at her. Perfectly coiffed hair, freshly scrubbed skin, and elegant clothing combined to groom her into the future Duchess of Embry.

All except for her eyes, which blazed. They burned with fire, defiance, and pure, unadulterated ferocity. As if to say: *How dare you give in? How dare you become this parody? How* dare *you?*

Sarani gulped, her throat tightening, and lowered her lids. Now was not the time for her inner tigress to come out fighting, claws first. It was a matter of necessity if she was to survive. There were rules that had to be heeded, modesty that needed to be minded. She had to be perfect.

"Ask His Grace's valet about an available modiste," she said to Asha. "I will require a full wardrobe befitting a future duchess. Money is no object." It would not be, with a raja's fortune in gems in her carpetbag. "And ask Gideon to look into how I can sell some of my jewels."

"Yes, my lady."

Sarani inhaled and exhaled, risking a final peek at her eyes. The fierce gleam there had calmed, thank heavens. Eyes could reveal so much about a person if one knew how to read them. She'd learned that as a girl in her father's court. They often gave away when a man was lying or revealed what he truly desired. Smiles, expressions, and words could be easily faked, but the eyes rarely lied.

Markham's disdain beneath his official bearing had been obvious. Talbot's lust had shone through his gentlemanly reserve. The ladies of the court had envied her while they derided her. Back then, even Rhystan had been transparent, his affection shimmering in those blue-gray eyes. Now, not so much. These days, he was near impossible to read between the irregular bursts of anger and desire, which meant that she had to tread carefully.

"Beggin' yer pardon, milady," a young maid said at the door, "but His Grace is inquiring whether you are ready to depart for Huntley House."

Canting her head, she stood and smiled graciously at the maid. "Thank you. You may inform His Grace that I'll be down shortly."

Sarani pasted a demure smile on her lips and clasped gloved

hands together at her waist, channeling the many lessons her mother and her stalwart governess had imparted about English high society. Such lessons of comportment were also part and parcel of being a princess, but what was needed of her now as Rhystan's future bride would require a strategic touch. She elongated her spine, angled her chin a smidgen downward, and held herself with impeccable poise.

A line from Rumi's poetry struck her: "Be the rose nearest to the thorn that I am," and she let a serene smile touch her lips.

Time to be the rose.

Fourteen

HUNTLEY HOUSE WASN'T MORE THAN A FEW STREETS AWAY, but the duke had insisted on taking the carriage. Restlessly, Sarani twined her fingers into her fine skirts, her nerves on edge. She would have preferred to walk—at least to get rid of some of the tension coiling in her limbs.

But apparently, walking was out of the question, at least for the distinguished Duke of Embry and his betrothed. It'd been on the tip of her tongue to quip that London made a man weak in the knees. But delicate, well-bred ladies did not mention parts of men's bodies. Nor did they tease gentlemen, nor poke at their masculinity. They sat and simpered, smiled when they were spoken to, and pretended to be objects of voiceless decoration.

Sarani had never been any good at sitting still or staying quiet. Words were powerful, and she had no intention of being cheated of hers. Not by anyone, not even the man pretending to be her future husband.

Despite being born in Joor and honoring the traditions of her people, Sarani had also been raised by a strong half-Scottish mother whose opinions did not match those of her peers, which was why she'd eloped with the love of her life in the first place. She'd taught her daughter to think for herself and to be resilient and relentless in her goals. That unusual approach had given Sarani an outlook unlike any other woman of her acquaintance.

Unlike proper English ladies.

Then again, most *proper* girls probably would not have leaped like a freedom fighter into the trenches…spied for a militia, lied through their teeth to avoid an arranged marriage to a jackal, and sent all their pin money to fund their best friend Manu's efforts against the British.

Maybe that was why Vikram was coming for her.

Treason was punishable by death, wasn't it?

Sucking in a breath, she lifted her surreptitious gaze to the somber man sitting opposite, wondering for the dozenth time whether she was out of her mind for putting her faith in him. Rhystan wasn't a friend. He wasn't even an acquaintance. He was just someone she'd known once, perhaps loved in the most innocent of ways. Someone she might have married under different circumstances.

Had she made the right choice?

It was a loaded question. Before, she'd chosen duty over love, but a part of her always wondered what would have happened if she'd run with him. If she'd said no to her father and asked Sanjay from the Flying Elephant to help her get to him. What would their life have been like? Would they have been happy? Would he have become the same hard, guarded, intimidating man he was now?

The duke's formidable presence fairly crowded the spacious coach. A pair of gloves along with a satin-trimmed top hat rested on the sliver of bench beside him. His attention remained on the signet ring on his small finger, though she could tell that he was quite distracted by whatever held his thoughts. Judging by the downturned curve of his mouth, it wasn't good.

Sarani took the rare opportunity to study him.

Inasmuch as the windblown guise of the sea captain suited him, this look of the London gentleman suited him even more. His finely milled, charcoal frock coat fit his broad shoulders to perfection, and contrasting dove-gray trousers hugged the length of his long, muscled legs. Polished Hessian boots peeped out at the hems. He was every inch a duke, and she could not deny that Rhystan wore wealth and elegance well.

Even when he was fastidiously clothed, no one could question the duke's raw virility, nor the power that lay coiled beneath all those pressed yards of fabric. Danger curled from him in a way that made her blood heat. He was a wolf in sheep's clothing, a hardened pirate disguised in gentleman's trappings. Her eyes trailed back up, her mouth going unreasonably dry as her stare collided with his.

A smirk tugged at a corner of his full lips.

"Enjoying the view?" he asked.

Swallowing her mortification at being caught, she lifted her chin on a small huff of air and let a bit of her captive tigress loose. "Shouldn't I? After all, this isn't a look I've seen before."

"Look?"

She gestured to his person. "The Duke of Embry, in the flesh."

"I was a duke on the ship."

"You were captain on the ship," she corrected. "This is different. It's like you've put on a costume and you're about to go on stage."

"All life's a stage, my lady."

Her heart gave a thump at the possessive caress over the last two words. "This isn't a performance, Your Grace. At least not for you. This is real life. You're a duke now, and you have responsibilities."

His mouth tightened as he gave a humorless laugh. "Trust me, Lady Sara, I'm well acquainted with your position on the matter. For you, duty is the death of anything that matters, isn't it?"

The words cut like daggers, despite being the truth. Though she'd rebelled in small subversive ways, she'd always been a servant to her position. With him. With Talbot. With anything that had been required of her. At least on the surface.

"When one is a princess," she ground through her teeth, "duty is the *only* thing that matters."

"You were a princess."

Her burning gaze collided with his. "I beg your pardon?"

"You *were* a princess. You're an English lady now on hallowed English soil. Daughter of a Scottish countess. Fiancée of an English duke. The only duty you have is to me as your future husband."

His mouth widened into something that could hardly be counted as a smile, his eyes remaining cold and slyly calculating.

Sarani felt like a mouse being toyed with by a lion, and she did not like it one bit. Her gaze slid to the door latch. She could end this right now. Open that carriage door and leave. Find her own way out of this mess somehow. Her emotions crashed and jumbled, spinning wildly.

"Have second thoughts already?" the duke asked, watching her. "Might I remind you of the dangers you're facing, Princess." His use of her defunct title was a mockery. "You need me, remember? You have no home, a family that might not welcome you, no connections, an assassin on your heels, dwindling funds, and nowhere to go."

The perfunctory list slammed the wind from her sails. When he said it like that, her problems sounded insurmountable. Sarani gathered her anger, cloaking herself in it. She refused to feel powerless, even in the face of such miserable odds. With a hiss, she reminded herself that he needed her as well.

"I have money," she snapped. "And you need me, too, my lord duke. You have no marriage prospects, a mother who expects you to wed for the sake of the dukedom, and no way out of your predicament but for me to pretend to be your fiancée. People in glass castles should think before casting stones."

A bark of laughter burst from his lips. "Good thing we're trapped in this glass castle together, then."

"You and your castle can get buggered." She gasped as the vulgar oath left her lips, a hand flying to her mouth. Blast those foul-mouthed boatswains…and blast her ungovernable temper where the duke was concerned.

"So crude, Lady Sara." Rhystan tutted, though something flashed in his eyes before it disappeared. Heat? "Surely, you don't expect anyone to believe you're a demure English lady when such filthy sentiments fall from such pretty lips."

"This is never going to work," she muttered. "How can I be

your fiancée when you make me want to tear my hair out by the roots? I can't pretend to…care for you when all I want to do is stab you with a shard of glass from your stupid invented castle."

"Ouch," he said, his mouth twitching. "That hurts."

"The truth always hurts."

He stuck out his hand. "I propose a truce, then."

"A what?"

"Truce. A cease-fire. Temporary amnesty."

She glared at him, ignoring his hand. "I know what truce means, you jackanapes. No one, least of all your mother, is going to be convinced that we are a love match. This is foolish. She'll see right through this. Through *me*." Her feeble confidence dissolved as panic set in. "I have a feisty tongue, made worse by weeks spent with your crew. I despise being told what to do. I couldn't possibly make you or any Englishman a dutiful, *proper* wife. This is impossible."

"You gave your word."

Sarani clenched her jaw as the carriage rolled to a smooth stop. The sounds of the coachman descending from his perch reached her ears. Within moments, he would be opening the door in front of Rhystan's childhood home, and then there would be no turning back. "Why don't you want to be duke?"

The brief hint of humor evaporated, shutters closing down over his face. "What does that have to do with anything?"

"It just does. Answer the question."

He went silent for a long moment, but then he spoke, his voice dripping with coldness. "Because I'm not fit for it."

———

Rhystan stared at Sarani, his throat like a vise. Hell if he ever wanted to admit that to her of all people. But as she'd so eloquently pointed out, he needed her as much as she needed him if he had any hope of thwarting his mother. And the only answer he could give to her question was the truth. The ugly, pathetic, awful truth.

"I don't understand," she said. "It's your birthright."

"No," he bit out. "I wasn't even the spare. It was only by a horrific accident that this fell to me. They died in a fire. I didn't." His breath sawed out of him in short bursts. "Because I wasn't there. I was never part of this life. It was never supposed to be me—the ne'er-do-well third son. The rotten egg."

"You're still the son of a duke," Sarani said after a beat, reaching out to touch his sleeve and then pulling back as if uncertain of its welcome. "What happened to your father and brothers was tragic. We can't always choose our paths. Sometimes, they're chosen for us. And you're not rotten."

"Because you know me so well?" He laughed, the sound harsh in the confines of the coach. "You met an idealistic boy, one who had the naivete beaten out of him, and it taught me one thing: I carve my own path, Princess."

The coach door opened then, and he took the opportunity to hop out, his soles making a clapping sound against the cobblestones. Sarani looked like she had more to say, but as her eyes swept outward at the exterior of the ducal residence, apprehension flooded them.

Taking his hand, she stepped down and took in a clipped breath at the bottom of the stairs. Oddly, Rhystan wanted to comfort her, but he buried the impulse. She would not welcome it, and he would not open himself up to being spurned in the middle of the street.

Inside the foyer, the duchess's butler took their outer trappings, and Rhystan scanned the familiar space. Not much had changed despite their apparent astronomical decline in fortune. The furniture was polished, the marble floors shone, and familiar paintings hung on the mahogany-paneled walls. He half expected to hear his father's and brother's baritones in low conversation. A knot of emotion formed inside him.

"Rhyssie!" The high-pitched screech was the only warning he got before a whirling devil in skirts crashed headlong into him. He braced as a pair of wiry arms wound around him with no regard for propriety, squeezed, and then released. Despite being a good foot shorter than he was, his baby sister scrutinized him down the length of her pert nose. "Good Lord but you've turned into a mountain! And your arms are like slabs of granite."

"Ravenna," he said with a fond grin. "You've grown, too."

And she had. The last time he'd seen her for the funeral, she hadn't been so tall. Or so pretty. It'd only been two years, and she'd gone from girl to woman in a blink. Coiled loops of auburn hair framed a narrow, heart-shaped face, and there was a distinct look of coquettishness in her eyes.

Rhystan frowned. Wasn't she still twelve or some such? *Eighteen*, a voice in his head reminded him. He scowled at the revealing bodice on her gown but was saved from growling his displeasure when his sister turned an appraising gaze to Sarani, who was standing quietly at his side.

"Who's this, then?"

He touched Sarani's elbow, keeping the fond smile on his lips firmly in place. "Allow me to present Lady Sara Lockhart," he said. "My fiancée."

"Your *what*?" Her shriek could probably be heard all the way to Piccadilly.

"You heard me," he said with an exasperated look. "Lady Sara, this is my apparent hellion of a sister, Lady Ravenna, who evidently has forgotten her manners and not to scream like a banshee indoors."

Sarani's brow rose infinitesimally as she shot him a look that said: *Demure, sweet, dutiful*? He felt heat crawl up his neck. Perhaps he had exaggerated slightly in his description of Ravenna. Then again, the last time he'd seen the little minx, she'd been barely out of the schoolroom…and maybe a bit intimidated by the drifter-turned-duke brother she hadn't seen since childhood.

"I don't know, Your Grace," Sarani said, her rich, melliflu-ous tone curling over his senses. "I, myself, can be a hellion on occasion. It's rather liberating." She inclined her head and offered a conspiratorial smile to the incorrigible chit. "It's a pleasure to make a fellow hellion's acquaintance, my lady."

His sister's grin lit up her entire face. "If we are to be sisters, I insist you call me Ravenna."

Sarani smiled back. "Ravenna, then. And I'm Sara."

Remembering her forgotten manners, Ravenna ducked into a hasty curtsy, eyes gleaming with sudden mischief as her bright copper-colored gaze returned to Rhystan. "Now this is a surprise. We expected you, but not two of you and certainly not a fiancée. Does Mama know?"

"No," he said. "Not yet. Is she at home?"

Ravenna grinned. "She's been at home ever since word arrived that you'd put into port. You are in so much trouble, you naughty boy."

He rolled his eyes. "I'm a grown man, Ravenna."

"As you say, Your Disgrace." She stuck out her tongue and lifted one shoulder in a shrug. "She's in the drawing room. Come along before she sends reinforcements."

"Reinforcements?"

She gave an unrepentant grin. "Your harem of female suitors."

Rhystan felt his jaw drop. "I beg your pardon, did you just say 'suitors'?"

"Oh yes, she's been interviewing them by the handfuls—who wants to be the next Duchess of Embry? It's been the rage for weeks all season." She leaned in and lowered her voice in a stage whisper. "I've heard from the servants' grapevine that the wagers at White's are through the roof. Lady Penelope is the favorite so far, though I find her a tad…conceited for my liking."

Her gleeful gaze slid to Sarani, who, to her credit, hadn't said a word despite her rapidly twitching lips…which indicated she was either going to scream or burst into laughter. Rhystan grimly suspected the latter.

"She's the daughter of the Duke of Windmere and quite an

heiress," Ravenna went on, quite oblivious to her brother's brewing frustration. "A splendid catch, the papers are all saying. Well, bully for them. Because Lady Sara from"—she paused and frowned at Sarani, wrinkling her nose—"wait, where are you from?"

"India."

Ravenna's eyes went wide, her scrutiny sharpening on Sarani's face and clothing with newfound appreciation. "Truly?"

"By way of England and Scotland," Sarani added hastily. "A relation to the Earl of Beckforth."

"Oh, lovely. I don't believe I'm acquainted with him."

Rhystan nearly swore under his breath. He saw the same aggravated look cross Sarani's face as if realizing what she'd just admitted out loud. It wasn't a calamity per se, especially if Ravenna didn't share it with the duchess or any other nosy members of the *ton*. But it could not be taken back, not without drawing more attention. And Ravenna, as devoted a sister as she was, was still a girl at heart. Juicy secrets had a way of getting out…and Sarani's truths were hers to share.

"Come along," Ravenna said, striding along the corridor. "I wasn't jesting about the reinforcements, though it will likely be Fullerton. He's our exceedingly proper butler. He's new. Don't worry, Brother dear, none of your prospective brides are here. I was teasing."

"Thank God for that," Rhystan muttered, his brain muddled by her incessant prattling. He spared Sarani a glance. Despite the earlier glimpse of humor at his predicament—which seemed to grow darker by the second—she hadn't said a word. His hand grazed the small of her back, his voice lowering. "Are you well, my lady?"

"Very well." She peered up at him, eyes glittering with a glee to rival his sister's. "Honestly, I'm quite excited to meet your harem. Assess the competition, if you will."

Ravenna's laugh trilled back toward them. "Oh, Rhyssie, I do like her immensely. Please do marry her."

Rhystan bit back a sigh. The two of them together spelled

trouble, but it was too soon to dwell upon it as he caught sight of his mother, ensconced in a divan in the drawing room, her back resting upon a mound of cushions. He narrowed his eyes at her complexion, checking for signs of illness and finding none. She was as hale as anyone; he'd bet his fortune on it.

Not that he expected her to be ill—not if she was busy interviewing a harem of prospective future duchesses.

"Mother," he said in greeting.

"Embry, darling," she said softly as if it pained her to speak, and Rhystan almost rolled his eyes. "How wonderful to see you."

"And you," he said, moving to kiss her outstretched hands. "You look rested."

She smiled. "I'm much recovered, and better now that you are here." Her gaze shifted to where Ravenna stood with Sarani, and he could see the widening of her pupils and the suspicion that instantly filled them. "I thought I heard voices in the hall. Who, pray tell, is your guest?"

"Mother, may I present Lady Sara Lockhart." He reached back, pulling Sarani to his side and leaving his mother in little doubt of their familiarity. "Lady Sara, my mother, Her Grace, the Dowager Duchess of Embry."

Her eyes panned between them, incisive, cold, and ever assessing, falling for an instant on the place where his hand gripped Sarani's elbow with possessive ease. A sharp intelligence glimmered in her gaze, followed by an imperceptible tightening of her lips.

"Who, exactly, is she to you?"

"Why, the future Duchess of Embry, of course." Rhystan couldn't quite curb the smug note in his voice. "Do be the first to offer us your blessing."

He should have been prepared, because honestly, it was to no one's surprise when the duchess fell back to her cushions in a dead faint.

Fifteen

A WEEK LATER, AN ANXIOUS, JITTERY STOMACH HAD BECOME the bane of Sarani's existence. For every pristinely appointed London home she'd set foot in—one assembly, one musicale, and two soirees—the roiling sea of nerves never seemed to get any easier. In fact, the bloody fretfulness had worsened to sickening proportions. Unease was her constant companion.

At first, she'd thought that maybe it was a premonition or an instinct for danger. Had her cousin's assassin found her? But Rhystan had insisted that Gideon and a few of his men were watching the harbor for a ship resembling the one that had been tracking them, and nothing out of the ordinary had been reported. That ship had to have been coincidence.

But Sarani couldn't shake the feeling that something was off. Perhaps she was sensitive to the foggy airs and false humors of England. It was a distinct probability.

Because, goddess alive, she missed Joor more than she'd thought possible.

She missed the vibrant splashes of color, the singsong chattering of people in the market, the smells of simmering spices. The hot breezes dancing over her skin. The river and secret waterfall. She missed swimming and staring up at the clouds. Even though she didn't have many friends or extended family, Asha and her other handmaidens had kept her company. She missed their jokes and their palace intrigues with the guards. But most of all, she missed being herself and not having to observe some breath-strangling English drawing room rule every sodding second.

Sit this way. Stand that way. Don't have an opinion.
Simper. Flutter your eyelashes. Sip overwarm punch.
Be the rose.

She hated the dratted rose—it symbolized everything she could never be. And that had been made evidently clear by the most perfect of roses herself: the Dowager Duchess of Embry.

After reviving from her faint upon hearing of their betrothal, the dowager duchess's disposition had not improved. She'd looked upon Sarani as one would a bothersome flea when they'd first been introduced, and now Sarani had the distinct impression that the dowager duchess suspected far more than she was letting on. She was much too clever to be tricked.

And that terrified Sarani to no end.

She had been prepared for an explosion after the duchess recovered, but the woman had handled it with remarkable poise, a cool if dignified felicitation falling from her thinned lips. The call for champagne had surprised Sarani, given her swoon, though the coldly appraising look Rhystan's mother had leveled across the rim of her flute had not.

A keen judge of character, Sarani guessed that the dowager would be a formidable enemy, and already after only eight days—having been swiftly ensconced at Huntley House for decorum's sake—she felt the knife edge of disapproval. A huff here, a curl of a lip there. The keen glances at Asha, who had accompanied Sarani while Tej had stayed on with Rhystan under the kindly eye of Harlowe.

None of it was ever in view of her precious son, of course. No, her smile was practically painted on for her dear duke of a boy. With him, her subterfuges were much more practical.

Embry, dear, don't you want to wait to make an official announcement? You've only just arrived.

Or Sarani's favorite: *At least allow me the dignity to save face before you're taken off the marriage mart. Surely you don't wish to embarrass me, given the soirees I've held on your behalf?*

And by soirees, she meant interviews for her son's future wife.

Of course, Rhystan had diplomatically agreed. The farce of their engagement had been only for his mother's benefit, after all. Though his acquiescence didn't seem to have deterred her efforts in the least. No, the competition was still fierce. Ravenna had been delighted to show Sarani the popular London newssheets, which were calling the contest for Rhystan's hand the Duchess Duels.

The Duchess sodding Duels.

Like that arrogant devil was some spectacular prize to be won. On paper, he was, considering his title and fortune, but if his head were to grow any bigger with self-importance, he'd float away to the moon.

"It's ridiculously brilliant," Ravenna had giggled one evening after she'd snuck into Sarani's chamber, a regular occurrence that Sarani didn't mind. Unlike the duchess, Ravenna had been a breath of fresh air in an otherwise suffocating space. The girl's dry sense of humor, unfailing honesty, and clever mind were things that Sarani appreciated. Admittedly, at times not so much the *unfailing* honesty. Especially with respect to her brother.

Ravenna spread out the *Times* and pointed to a ridiculous caricature of galloping women on a racecourse. "They've likened it to the Gold Cup during Ascot week. See here. Lady Penny is two leagues ahead of Lady Margaret. They're the two favorites and have the best odds." She'd jabbed at the drawing, nearly poking a hole in the paper. "And here's Lady Clara. Sadly, she's at the very back of the pack with no hope unless a miracle happens. She's my friend and not interested in the Duke of Disbelonging in the least, but her mother is making her. She's on her second season with no prospects."

"Duke of Disbelonging?" Sarani had snorted. "That's not a word."

Her grin had turned impish. "Do you prefer Duke of Dashing Desire?"

"Hardly," Sarani had protested.

Ravenna had giggled and waggled her eyebrows. "When Rhystan isn't looking, you stare at him like he's a juicy plum pudding you can't wait to dig your spoon into and get to the warm fruity, gooey center."

Sarani's face had heated to boiling, though she'd be a liar to deny it. Seeing the man sweep through ballrooms like a disguised predator made her faithless heart kick up a notch. Something about him polished to perfection and dressed in formal wear made him seem more dangerous, as though he were a wild, savage beast in a crowd of house-trained pets waiting to pounce. Sarani couldn't deny that she stared her fill of him…whenever he was not aware, of course. The fact that Ravenna had noticed her staring, however, filled her with alarm.

"You're sorely mistaken. I loathe plum pudding," Sarani had said and steered the subject away. "And you, have you had a season?"

"This was meant to be my first." The girl had tried to hide the flash of disappointment behind careless bravado. "But after mourning for so long for Papa and my brothers, Mama wished to wait until Rhystan returned. I suppose she knew he'd be back this season, because I was presented to the queen after Easter along with a hundred other girls, so I'm officially *out*. But who needs parties anyway? All you get are stuffy ballrooms, silly smelly sirs, and warm lemonade."

Sarani had blinked, more pieces of the puzzle falling into place. So the dowager duchess had intended her son to return. The timing of Ravenna's presentation at court as well as the interviews of potential brides were part of a meticulous scheme to see the Duke of Embry settled. After all, any enviable match of a duke would only help his unmarried younger sister. An odd feeling had squeezed against Sarani's ribs.

Was it pity? For Rhystan, Ravenna, or herself?

"Silly smelly sirs?" she'd asked, shaking off the strange reaction.

"Have you ever noticed how gentlemen think that bathing means dabbing oneself with copious amounts of perfume and calling it done?" Ravenna had wrinkled her nose with an affected huff of disgust. "It's bloody awful. Like putting rose water on a pile of refuse and expecting a perfectly clean lady to dance with it."

Sarani had burst into laughter, though a part of her had wondered whether Ravenna's marriage prospects had all been put on hold because of Rhystan. He'd been gallivanting who-knew-where while his sister languished in a state of painful limbo, waiting to be presented to society by her only remaining brother, the duke. And he had not been there.

Then again, Rhystan had been running from his own demons. From expectation.

Daughters and sons of the aristocracy were pawns to be played at will—to increase fortunes, to gain a title, to strengthen an alliance. Even she had not been spared from the crushing weight of duty, until she'd had no choice. She had run from Talbot and Vikram, unwilling to be prey either to a smarmy rotter or an underhanded assassin.

Rhystan had run from his birthright and mother.

That didn't mean she trusted him, just that she empathized.

Swallowing past the growing lump of nausea in her throat, Sarani stood at the threshold of the staircase of the dowager duchess's home leading down into the lavish ballroom, her stomach in its usual knots. This "intimate" welcome home party was yet another ploy by the duchess to make her son come to his senses and select a woman of her choosing. Sarani could feel it.

She hadn't seen Rhystan in days. Apparently, he'd been busy dealing with some estate issues with his solicitor. Though he hadn't shared anything with her, she could see the strain of it in his features whenever she did see him. Admittedly, the burden of the charade was wearing also on her. Pasting a smile on her face, she approached Fullerton.

"Lady Sara Lockhart," the butler intoned as she descended.

She felt the gazes flock and settle on her as though she were some circus oddity or breed of rare creature that the Duke of Embry had brought back from his travels. It was India, for heaven's sake, she wanted to scream, not some uncivilized hellhole. Even as she thought it, she almost laughed. Most of these narrowminded people likely viewed her birthplace and home as worse than that.

Propaganda…it was a dangerous weapon.

Though the people in this room might not suspect her mixed origins, she knew they had already judged her harshly for having been raised in the colonized east…a place full of murderous heretics, according to the *Times*, which would undoubtedly have tainted her somehow. British news commentary denounced colonial society everywhere, often portraying its people, even in their own colonies, as mad and promiscuous.

Now walking among these hubristically superior English nobles, Sarani had never felt more like Miss Swartz in Thackeray's *Vanity Fair*. Even now, she could see the author's written words in her mind's eye: *"Marry that mulatto woman? I don't like the color, sir."*

Gracious, if they only knew the truth…

Would they snub her as well?

Sarani held her head high, catching the eye of the dowager duchess, who stood surrounded by fawning admirers. The ice in the woman's glare did not dissipate, and Sarani felt the scrape of it like a blade. Resisting the urge to roll her eyes and leave, she approached and bowed her head in greeting, curtsying elegantly.

"My lady," she murmured.

Haughty brows vaulted to the dowager duchess's hairline. "The proper address is Your Grace, but I suppose you should be forgiven considering where you're from. The wilds, truly."

Sarani felt her cheeks heat with shame as the entire entourage twittered behind their fans. Of course, she *knew* how to address a duchess, but nerves had twisted her tongue. The dowager's venom was hidden behind a patronizing, sugary smile, but Sarani would not fall prey to such an obvious trap. The woman clearly wanted to establish how unsuitable Sarani was as a match for her son in her eyes, royal or not.

"As you say, Your Grace, my apologies," she replied sweetly. "Though some of the Indian princes would beg to differ with that assessment."

"Oh, have you met many Indian princes, my lady?" a young blond-haired woman blurted out. "I've heard that their clothes are studded with rubies and emeralds."

Sarani held the dowager duchess's eyes for an extended beat before smiling gently at the girl who had spoken and then gone pink as though she'd crossed some unforgivable line. Perhaps she had from the looks of the other ladies. Sarani gave a wide smile. "Yes, and they do. They're quite ostentatious, truly, some of the displays of wealth. Rubies as big as one's fist and emeralds the size of plums."

"I cannot even imagine!" the girl exclaimed.

"They are uncivilized," another lady scoffed with a look of affront. "*Truly*, I do not know how my father expects me to mingle with heathens from the colonies. It is insufferable."

Sarani detected the scorn in the woman's tone and the tangible derision in her pale eyes. Undeniably pretty, she was dressed in a gorgeous gown, her heart-shaped face twisted into a sneer. Sarani would put money on this being one of her so-called rivals.

Lifting one shoulder in an elegant shrug, she straightened her spine, her brow lifting in an arch that would rival the Dowager Duchess of Embry's. "I am certain we have not been introduced. Do remind me, since I have been in the *insufferable* colonies, what is the proper etiquette again?"

The lady went red, opening her mouth to spew some scathing retort, but closed it as her eyes flicked—along with everyone else's—to the ballroom entrance.

Sarani did not have to turn. She *felt* his presence like a palpable force. A wash of goose pimples spread across her skin, the fine hairs of her neck lifting in instant response.

"The Duke of Embry," the majordomo intoned.

All at once, the chatter died as every lady with a pulse, even the married ones, smoothed her dress and patted her coiffure. Sarani forced herself to remain still, even when she felt the duchess's gaze flick coldly toward her. Sensing Rhystan's approach, she turned slowly, her blood thickening to molasses in her veins at the breathtaking sight of him dressed in raven black from head to toe.

Sweet merciful heavens, he was sin on a stick. Her hitherto dry mouth watered indelicately.

"Duchess." He greeted his mother with a quick nod of his head and then turned to her. "Lady Sara," he said, his deep voice washing over her as he lifted her gloved hand and kissed it. "How lovely you are."

"Thank you, Your Grace," she mumbled with a curtsy, the whole of him assaulting her shaky senses on every level. Sight, smell, hearing, touch. The only thing missing was taste. Her traitorous tongue darted out to wet her lips.

His gaze slid there, a smirk forming as if he knew exactly the effect he had on her.

Could he sense that she wanted to do unspeakable things to him? That she wanted to claim that sinful mouth without a care for decorum like the heathen she was accused of being? Releasing a ragged breath, she pinned her tingling lips between her teeth, and his smirk widened. And now, her cheeks were positively on fire.

She cleared her throat. "You are, too. Lovely. Er, handsome. Drat, you know what I mean. You look well."

Gracious, she was a lackwit. Queen of the Lackwits.

He smiled as the musical strains of a new set began and offered her his right arm. "Will you dance?"

Sarani hoped her knees would not fail her. "I am yours to command, Your Grace."

———————

Rhystan was well aware he was causing a scene by ignoring everyone else, given the glowers coming from the thin-lipped visage of his mother. Yet even she wasn't aware of just how close he'd come to throwing propriety to the wind, flinging Sarani over his shoulder, and hauling her from the room like a Neanderthal at her husky, provocative reply.

I am yours to command.

Did the minx know what she was doing to him? The flash of unguarded pleasure and then the unhidden hunger in her gaze as he'd greeted her had nearly brought him to his knees. And then, the likely innocent response that had lewd fantasies of him commanding her elsewhere—in bed and without clothing—had sent his brain into a frenzy of lust.

Rhystan knew he was practically dragging her to the ballroom floor, but he did not care. He needed her in his arms. From the moment he'd set his eyes on her, his body had leaped to attention, but something within him had also settled.

It was a kind of calm a ship would see in the middle of a hurricane.

He'd been drawn to her the moment he'd entered the crowded ballroom—gleaming like a vibrant lotus flower in a garden of lackluster blooms. His eyes had narrowed when he'd seen her in the company of his mother, but she had not been intimidated, not his tigress. Her spine had been ramrod straight, her shoulders back as she took a simpering debutante to task. He didn't have to hear the exchange. From the look on the other girl's face, Sarani hadn't been cowed in the least.

He knew he had been absenting himself from her too much. The situation with the ducal estates was grimmer than he'd expected, and according to Longacre's projections, it would take a ludicrous amount of money to make them financially stable. Money, which he had, thanks to his many investments, but it wasn't a quick or easy fix, which meant he would have to be in London much longer than he had anticipated.

But now, he didn't want to think about the estate or its solvency. He wanted to think about the woman in his arms and the strange sense of well-being that had slid through the marrow of his bones, tethering him to her. Everything else had fallen away—his mother, her schemes, Longacre, his financial burdens…all of it.

There was only Sarani.

"You look beautiful," he said as he guided her into place for the waltz.

A blush stained her cheeks. "Thank you."

Her gown—it had to be new—was a bold topaz color that made her changeling eyes lean toward brownish-gold and her cheeks glow. It was fashioned in the current style with an embroidered bodice that left the tops of her elegant shoulders tantalizingly bare, hugged the length of her torso to her waist, and then flared out in a bell shape to the floor. Long ivory gloves, matching the blond lace accents on the dress, covered her from fingertips to upper arms.

She looked magnificent, outshining every other female in attendance.

A princess among peasants.

Rhystan wanted to trace his mouth along those elegant collar-bones, scrape his teeth along that beautiful expanse of honey-rich skin, and mark her in the most carnal of ways so that everyone there would know she belonged to him.

She's not yours.

The thought was a harsh reminder of the game he was playing—that they were both playing. They weren't true intendeds. They weren't even friends. They were temporary allies, and she was a means to an end. But that reasoning didn't negate the fact that it felt like the first time he'd been able to breathe in days as though she were his very air.

He tensed, waiting for the familiar resentment to rise, but it wasn't there.

His gloved palm tightened against her trim waist as they twirled into the first rotation. His swift pivot brought her upper body within inches of his, the crinoline beneath her skirts crashing into his hips. She gasped, her fingers clutching for purchase on his shoulder, and he grinned at her vexed expression.

"Stop that," she hissed. "Everyone's watching, and your mother's glare might set fire to the entire ballroom. I'm already objectionable in her eyes. She'll think I can't dance."

"If anyone can't dance, it's me," he joked. "I've practically forgotten how."

She huffed a small laugh. "I seem to recall you acquitting yourself quite well in the palace several years ago. What you lacked in confidence, you certainly had in skill."

Her eyes widened as though she hadn't meant to bring up the past, but for the first time in years, the thought of them in Joor did not gut him. He remembered his scattered thoughts and the challenge in her stare when she'd reprimanded him for not asking her to dance.

"I was too busy trying to count the measure in my head so as not to brutalize your royal toes," he said easily. "I wanted so terribly to impress you."

Her eyes dipped for a moment and then raised back to his, her reply so soft he almost missed it. "You succeeded."

It was on the tip of his tongue to ask why she hadn't fought harder for him, but he swallowed the bitter question. Rehashing *that* was only a recipe for misery. Falling into silence, he distracted himself with their avid audience. His gaze caught on Ravenna as she stood to the side. Guilt slashed through him. She'd practically turned into a woman overnight, and a beauty by all accounts. It would also be up to him to see her properly settled before he left.

His guilt doubled as an unpleasant thought cut through him that he was doing exactly as his mother was—finding and selecting a spouse for Ravenna—when he was so violently opposed to her doing the same for him. Rhystan shoved aside his discomfort; the rules were different for men and women. Women of quality were bred to marry well.

That doesn't mean they relish being traded like heads of cattle.

The voice in his head sounded like Sarani.

He blew out a breath…better for him to choose a match for Ravenna than his mother. Unlike him, she couldn't gallivant on a ship, nor could she be husbandless, and Lord knew what kind of man the duchess would approve for her—some old goat with an even older title who would only quash her bright spirit. Rhystan frowned. She was eighteen. Did she have any suitors? Was she sweet on anyone? It was curious that no gentlemen had sought her out where she stood, nearly invisible in white chiffon against the marble pillar.

"She's charming, your sister," Sarani said, following his stare. "I've enjoyed her company. At least she doesn't want to shove me on the first ship back to India."

He smiled. "I've missed the ship, you know," he said as they executed yet another libido-torturing turn, his voice low. "And you tending to my needs."

A smile lit her face, despite the underlying innuendo. "You mean you miss me sewing your sleeves shut and setting barnacles in your sheets?"

"I thought you emphatically declared that second one was Red's doing."

She flushed. "He was the bosun who scraped the things off the devil."

God, the sound of ship's lingo on her lips fired his blood. It was just like her to know that the curved seam on the hull was called the devil. The memory of her standing on the quarterdeck, black hair lashing into her face in those tawdry, formfitting breeches and with kukri blades in hand, had him stiffening in a second. It didn't escape his notice that she was equally at ease on the bow of a ship surrounded by lowborn sailors as she was in a ballroom filled with the upper crust of English society. She'd been that way in Joor, too—a kindred spirit with the locals at the river and a princess with the peers at court.

It had been one of the things that had drawn him to her.

He'd never known anyone like her, not then and not now. No one had ever fit him as she had. In nautical terms, she was the true north to his south. His forgotten heart kicked stupidly against his ribs at the thought, and then that cold voice in his head chimed in, reminding him of what had happened the last time he'd felt this way about a girl. The burst of pleasure unspooling within him withered and died.

Damn, he was an idiot.

He might have impressed her with his dancing, but in the end, she'd agreed to marry someone with a title, handpicked by her father. Regardless of how well she felt in his arms or how well he felt in hers now, he needed to remind himself of that. She was a tool, nothing more.

Their agreement was only fake, after all.

Rhystan ended the dance abruptly, ignoring the flash of hurt surprise on her face as he deposited her where he'd found her and swept his mother's favorite into the next set.

Distance was best.

Sixteen

"TELL ME THE TRUTH, EMBRY, SHE'S THE GIRL, ISN'T SHE?" THE dowager duchess demanded.

Rooted in her tracks en route to the morning room where she was to meet Ravenna, Sarani felt her skin go hot and then icy cold. Her Grace's voice was hard and insistent, drifting from the open door of the study. Sarani wanted to cover her ears and flee. She abhorred eavesdropping, but her stubborn feet refused to move.

"I don't know what you're talking about," she heard Rhystan say, his voice laced with irritation. "What girl?"

"The one from Joor," came the acidic reply. "Lisbeth's colored daughter."

Sarani flinched, though she was more than familiar with such a descriptor. She'd heard them all at some point or another. More importantly, though, the duchess *knew*. Or suspected, rather. After all, one did not show up with a female of unknown origins on one's ship returning from India and declare that one was to be married to said female. Especially when one was a duke.

"You are mistaken." Rhystan's voice was hard.

"I am not. Do you know what this will do to our family? The scandal it will cause? How could you bring her to London? Bring her here as your *bride*?"

Sarani's heart clenched, the familiar bitterness wrapping its barbed fingers around her. She'd known the duchess could be brutal, given that Sarani was ruining her grand plans, but that didn't make it any easier to hear the obnoxious sentiments.

"Rhystan, be reasonable," the duchess went on. "You are a duke. She is not suitable."

"Enough!" And then more softly. "Enough, Mother."

They did not speak for a long moment, and Sarani had almost coaxed her limbs to respond when a masculine throat cleared.

"Why did you not tell me about Roland's and Richard's debt?"

Dead silence ensued, but Sarani frowned, listening for the duchess's reply. "It was not your burden to bear."

"I'm not duke only when it pleases you, Mother. If you had informed me, the interest alone on the defaulted loans could have been avoided. Hundreds of thousands of pounds."

"Which is why you need to marry an English heiress. Restore our name, not drag it through the mud. A woman of her character cannot—"

Suddenly, Sarani could not take any more. Cursing her uncooperative feet, she ran toward the back of the house and into the gardens beyond. The slight chill in the morning air was bracing enough to douse the heat billowing through her veins. She did not stop until she came to the large elm buttressing the perimeter wall at the very back of the garden.

How dare the duchess impugn her character? She was *not* a woman of poor integrity or lacking in moral fiber. She was proud of who she was. Her exterior—or happenstance of birth—she could not control. And besides, that should not bloody matter!

Sarani bit back a sob, covering her mouth with a fist. She wrapped her arms about herself, remembering how precious she'd felt last night at the ball. How magical it had been for a handful of moments—until Rhystan had left her without explanation and proceeded to dance with every unmarried female in attendance to the gloating smugness of his mother. Sarani's heart had shriveled.

She'd been on the verge of falling for a fantasy.

Because it *was* a fantasy, wasn't it?

Oh, she would *not* cry. Not for that poisonous woman. Not for

Rhystan, not for anyone. She'd shed enough tears mourning circumstances she could not change. Like many others, she had not picked the life she'd been born into. Yes, she had privilege, but that privilege came with many other traps. Traps of belonging and erasure. Traps of never feeling like she was enough.

You are the product of love, my little bee. Never doubt how much you are loved. Her mother's voice echoed in her head.

It'd been after some of the children at court had excluded her from their games, calling her Paste Princess. They'd tripped her in the courtyard, muddying her new dress and mocking her with other ugly names until she'd run away weeping. Her mother had cleaned her face, wiped her tears, and told her that she should hold her head high, rise above small-minded people, and never allow herself to be reduced by others.

It was a struggle, but she'd learned to tuck those feelings of inadequacy away. She could not control others; she could only control herself. But some days, like today, her courage and those lessons failed her. Some days, she wanted to disappear.

Sarani had never doubted she'd been cherished by her parents. They had defied expectation, propriety, and everything and everyone for love. But where had love gotten them? Spurned, criticized, and eventually murdered...with their daughter left to pick up the pieces in a world that had no place for people like her.

A tear of self-pity slipped free, marking a hot path to her chin.

"Princess, are you well?"

Hastily, Sarani swiped at her damp cheek and turned to see Asha approaching, a concerned look on her face.

"Yes, Asha," she said tiredly, unable...or unwilling to correct her on the address. Sarani shook her head, the truth spilling out of her. "Though I admit, it's not what I expected."

"What isn't?"

She waved an arm. "England. Here. Being Lady Lockhart. I am not my mother."

"We had no choice, did we?" Asha said softly. "We left to save our lives."

That was true. She glanced at the maid. "Are you happy here?"

"My feelings do not matter, Princess. I am here to serve you." She took a breath. "But if you are asking whether I am content, I have a roof over my head, food to fill my belly, and a safe, warm place to lay my head. Everything else is hullabaloo."

Sarani frowned. "Hullabaloo?"

"My *nanijan* used to say, 'Sticks and stones can crack your bones, but words are as light as air.'"

"They can still hurt."

"Sometimes," Asha said with a shrug. "The other servants may view themselves as my betters and gossip when I walk past, but my only duty is to you, Princess. I remind myself that there are others in much worse situations. Survival isn't anything to be ashamed of. It takes great courage to lift one's feet and step forward."

The maid's quiet words were exactly what Sarani needed to hear. Not caring who might be observing from the many windows of Huntley House, she gathered Asha into an embrace. "Thank you, my dear friend. Your counsel is invaluable."

"You are welcome, Princess Sarani." Asha smiled, dark eyes crinkling with affection. "Tej and I are off to the market. His Grace has requested you join him for a ride in Hyde Park this afternoon. I've pressed your green riding habit."

Sarani felt the constriction in her chest ease and loosen.

Perhaps a ride was exactly what she needed.

Rhystan watched as Sarani commanded the mare with a light, firm touch on the reins. Even sitting in a lady's sidesaddle, which she'd never much liked, she rode with such grace. She'd always been an excellent horsewoman, and that had not changed in the last five years. A vision of them racing across the plains beyond the palace in Joor darted into his brain. Even then, he'd rarely been able to beat her. And he'd tried. She'd been fearless and skilled—a winning combination.

"Do you still race?" he asked, steering his stallion to trot abreast with her.

Sarani glanced at him, her eyes glittering with pleasure. That was better than how solemn she'd seemed earlier when she'd met him at the mews. "On occasion. The races have grown in popularity with the princes. However, they particularly did not like losing to a woman, and my father forbade me from entering."

He arched a brow. "You let that stop you?"

"Hardly," she teased, her lips curving into a wicked smirk that shot straight to his groin. "I dressed like a man and took their money that way."

Rhystan couldn't help it; he laughed. "Minx."

"I prefer 'impresario,'" she tossed back. "I rode until I took a bad fall a few years ago that weakened my spine. The doctors said I would never ride again, and yet here I am. Though I confess, I'm not as hell-for-leather as I used to be."

Rhystan wasn't surprised in the least. She'd always been dauntless. The girl he knew would never let something as life-altering as an injured spine slow her down, nor would she let anyone tell her she couldn't do anything. His mouth bowed into a reluctant smile.

"Why is that?" he asked.

"I'm physically capable of it," she said. "But the mind, you see, once it has known pain and associated that pain with an event or action, it doesn't forget. If I go too fast, my instinct is to slow to a safer speed, which makes me lose the competitive edge. Fear is a rather powerful thing to conquer."

Rhystan had the sudden thought that she was no longer speaking of racing. Though her face remained composed, he could feel the thoughtful weight of her sidelong glance. "So you're afraid of taking another fall?"

"Aren't we all a bit fearful of pain, Your Grace? Falling or otherwise?"

"You've never been afraid of anything in your life."

He did not attempt to hide the depth of his esteem. Why would he? He'd always valued her mettle…her *spirit*. Sarani's gaze swung to his as she faltered, her horse veering sharply as her hands jerked on the reins.

Deviltry tugged at him. "Besides, you seem to be falling for me quite happily. Most women do, you know. It's inevitable."

The horse jolted to an ungraceful stop.

"Good gracious, your arrogance is astounding." Splotches of color skimmed her cheeks, but she kept her expression calm when she started moving again and regarded him haughtily over one shoulder. "I'm not 'most women,' Your Grace."

"No, you're not." He grinned, clicking at his horse to speed up to match her increased gait as she angled her horse away from him. Her cheeks were blazing now, making an indistinct rush of pleasure gather in his chest. God, she was lovely. "Are you blushing, my lady? My word, the boatswains would argue that London Town has made you soft, cabin boy."

She shot him an arch look. "We are not on your ship now, Duke."

"I'm well aware of that," he said. "Would that we were, however."

In truth, he'd give anything to feel the salty sea spray on his face, to stand in the path of a hurricane, or even outrace brigands in the Caribbean Sea. Anything was preferable to the tedium of the city. Balls, assemblies, dinners, and hours and hours of incessant discussion on etiquette and suitability. He was sick of it. Sick of pretending to be someone he was not. This duke whom everyone revered…that was not him. Even the women his mother insisted on foisting upon him were wearing him ragged. If he heard one more simpering giggle, he was going to strangle someone.

Rhystan glanced over at his riding companion. She most certainly was not like those women. Sarani did not simper or giggle.

She laughed with everything in her, full and raw and so sultry it made his bones melt. And she did not trifle. She always had something intelligent to say.

He recalled his mother's intervention in the study earlier and fought a wave of disgust. Her thoughtless words galled him, but he knew she wasn't alone in her sentiments. If the *ton* got wind of who Sarani really was, they wouldn't hesitate to treat her with veiled disdain or ridicule her behind closed doors in their drawing rooms as they had her mother after she'd left England. If there was one thing the aristocracy loved more than celebrating their own importance, it was slander.

And by association, his family would be smeared by the scandal.

The gossip in the wake of the Duke of Embry taking such a bride would ruin the dowager's standing in the eyes of the *ton*. They would never insult her directly, but invitations would dwindle, as would her influence. She would become the subject of gossip, something he knew she loathed. Ravenna, too. The Huntley name would lose its eternal luster.

Who gives a tinker's curse about the title?

He didn't, but others would, namely his peers. Not that he gave a shit about the *ton*… It was Ravenna he worried for. She needed to secure an excellent match and a husband who would look after her. He worried for his mother as well. For all her endless faults, she loved her children dearly and was steadfastly loyal to her family.

Rhystan shoved down his worries, determined to enjoy the few moments of peace and quiet. They were nearing the corner of Hyde Park. He rolled the knotted tension from his neck muscles. "Shall we have a race on Rotten Row? Last I heard it's been significantly widened and new railings installed."

"You wish to race?" Sarani asked, but her eyes glittered with excitement. "Are ladies allowed?"

He glanced down at his pocket watch. "It's early. Most of the toffs won't be out for the afternoon promenade for hours yet. And besides, a future duchess can do as she likes."

"I am not a future duchess," she said.

"A princess, then."

She laughed, the sound hollow. "Trust me, no one here sees me as that. They see me as a strange creature, likely raised by wolves in some remote, vulgar corner of the world, whom the gallant and brave Duke of Embry doubtless rescued from a ghastly life."

"Well, at least they got the 'gallant and brave' part right," he teased. "You did forget handsome though. The gallant, brave, and dashingly handsome Duke of Embry."

"One day, your head will explode with all that vanity, and that will be the end of you."

"Will you mourn me?"

She grinned. "I'll dance on your remains like the Goddess Kali did with her lover, Lord Shiva."

"I expect no less from you, my bloodthirsty princess." He reached over and grabbed her reins, enjoying the snap of temper in those brilliant eyes. "Though we are not lovers. *Yet*."

Her gorgeous skin bloomed. "Never, if I have anything to say about it."

"Never is a long time," he said, tracing a gloved finger over her delicate wrist. "You might change your mind."

Sarani snatched her hand away. "The sun will rise in the west before I come to your bed, Your Grace."

"Not even if I beg you for hours on my knees?"

He let the erotic slant of his thoughts show, his gaze sweeping her body with scorching intent. She gaped at him, chest rising and falling beneath the hunter-green bodice that brought out the emerald fleck in her eyes. "We are in public. You are unspeakable!"

"In public or in bed." His smile was wicked. "I am the robber of all speech."

"You're obsessed with the bedchamber," she shot back, her

voice husky and her expression wild. Damn but he loved teasing her. He wanted to watch that becoming blush spill down into her décolletage, then distill even lower, and he wanted to trace its path with his tongue. His groin ached with pure, self-inflicted torment.

"Aren't all men?"

She rolled her eyes, but her lips twitched as she fought to keep her natural inclination to spar battened. "Only the clearly deprived ones."

His smile was slow. "Are you offering to rescue me?"

"No!" She steered the mare away in a huff toward the start of Rotten Row. "Are we racing or is it only your tongue you intend to put to use?" She froze, her face as bright as a summer strawberry. "Don't you dare answer that!"

Rhystan had to laugh at her chagrined look as the sounds of a few choice foul oaths reached him. God, he'd missed their banter and her fire. Even on the ship, he'd look forward to the wordplay. She made him think, she made him laugh, and she made him forget that he was anything but a man. It was grounding.

"We need to decide on a prize for the winner," he said. "Something of value, otherwise neither of us will make any effort."

"I win simply for the thrill and to put you in your place, Your Grace."

He wound his hands into the reins of his stallion and patted the horse's sorrel-colored neck. "Alas, I require more of an incentive." He put his fingers to his chin and squinted into the distance as though deep in thought. "I claim a kiss when I win."

"*When* you win?" she asked.

"You are riding sidesaddle, you've admitted that you've lost your edge, and the part of you that desperately wants me to kiss you again will sabotage your competitive instincts quite thoroughly."

Sarani opened her mouth and shut it, incredulity filling her gaze. "You…you…"

"Yes, yes, I'm unspeakable. Saying it more won't make it any less true. Stop stalling. What do you choose as your prize?"

"It is truly a wonder that you aren't married with all that conceit."

He winked and leaned in. "You adore me."

She shook her head in wary disbelief as though he'd transformed into a stranger before her eyes. Rhystan supposed he had. He hadn't had this much fun in ages. Not since…well, five years ago.

Sarani narrowed her eyes at him. "Somehow I do not remember you being this vexing."

"In my defense, I was trying to impress you back then."

"And now?"

"Now I intend to trounce you soundly." He pasted on a determined expression. "I'll have you know, I take my kisses very seriously."

She rolled her plump lips between her teeth as though not to smile and studied him, resolve firming her jaw before she nodded. "If I win, you'll escort Ravenna to the next three balls of her choosing, including the one at Lady Windmere's."

Lady Windmere? He blinked, his brain cataloging the endless procession of eligible ladies who had been thrust upon him in the past week. A voice like razors on glass came to him, followed by roving hands better suited to a flash thief in St. Giles than a lady in Mayfair. The Duchess of Windmere was none other than the mother of Lady Penelope. The girl was tenacious and bold in an entirely unattractive way. How his own mother thought he would ever be inclined to marry a chit like that was beyond him. It was nearly enough to drain the lust from him.

He almost groaned and peered at Sarani, but her face gave nothing away. "That's three things. Do I get three kisses?"

"Stop stalling," she mocked. "Deal or no deal, Your Grace?" One slim, ebony brow arched, her horse prancing beneath her as amusement flashed in those autumn-colored eyes. God, she was beautiful. He wanted to lean over and claim that tart tongue right then.

Good thing he had no intention of losing. "Deal."

Seventeen

THE DUKE OF EMBRY SEEMED TO BE GOING A BIT GREEN IN THE gills. Sarani grinned. He looked like he'd eaten a bowlful of crow and was going to cast his accounts all over the ballroom. But the greenish tinge to his features was worth the look on his sister's face when they'd been announced together by the majordomo at the entrance to the Duchess of Windmere's midseason ball.

Lady Ravenna Huntley, accompanied by His Grace, the Duke of Embry.

Etiquette dictated that the duke be announced first, but Rhystan must have instructed the majordomo otherwise. Sarani had to admit it was a nice touch. Every eye in the room had turned to them, and even the grim dowager duchess—whom Sarani had arrived with earlier and, by some miracle, had not throttled in the carriage—had cracked a proud smile. Ravenna had not had her own coming-out ball after her presentation at court, given her brother's absence, and this was the next best thing: a public presentation at the most popular ball of the season.

As Sarani had hoped, within moments, every single dance on Ravenna's dance card had been claimed. Every bachelor in attendance longed for a connection, even through marriage, with the wealthy, elusive, and powerful Duke of Embry. As Sarani had also expected but wasn't sure she liked, the duke had not been able to escape the clutches of Lady Penelope all evening.

The girl was relentless. Though she had ignored Sarani after that first soiree, deeming her of no consequence, once word of their engagement got out, Sarani knew things would take a turn for the worse. She recognized the type—the entitled girl who felt everything was her due. Including men.

Watching Rhystan surrounded by twittering debutantes, Sarani attempted to hide her grin behind her fan. She'd beaten him soundly in the horse race down Rotten Row, despite the challenges he'd enumerated, the least of which had been her scorching desire to be kissed. What an arrogant rotter! The thought of it still heated her insides to mortifying levels.

Because she *had* wanted it. She'd wanted him to kiss her. Hard. Deep. Soundly.

She'd wanted so much more than a kiss.

The way he'd looked at her when he'd teased of going to his knees… Intimate, wicked visions of him doing exactly that had crowded her brain. Even now, her body tingled with desire, her nipples pebbling beneath her bodice at the mere thought of being seduced by such a fit, virile man. She'd had such scandalous thoughts before, of course, but years ago, when her chaste fantasies had been those of a young girl.

Now, they were much less chaste.

Memories of Rhystan lying half-naked on his cot when she'd first climbed aboard his ship burst into life in her head. They were quickly followed by flashes of him in his copper tub—large, wet, and glistening—and then him on his knees before her again… She lifted her fan, employing it briskly to ward off the sudden flare of heat. Oh, her thoughts were ungovernable!

Air, she needed air.

Hurrying toward the balcony along the border of the ballroom, Sarani slipped outside to the less-crowded terrace. The change in location didn't make her imaginings any less filthy, but the cool evening breeze helped.

She needed to stop thinking about *him*.

It wasn't as though she intended to have any husbandly prospects after she and the duke went their separate ways, and Sarani still had an assassin to contend with, though as the days went by, she was less and less sure that they had been followed on the high seas. Perhaps it had been a coincidence. Perhaps Vikram had given up and let her go.

"Pardon the intrusion, my lady," a quiet male voice said, a glass of champagne appearing before her. It was attached to a man she did not immediately recognize, though he was well heeled and undoubtedly titled. One had to have been invited to this particular ball.

Sarani was desperately parched, but she knew better than to accept drinks from strangers, even at exclusive parties, and he was breaching decorum in the worst way by approaching her without an introduction. She shot him a pointed look. "We have not been introduced, sir."

He gave a slow nod. "Forgive my trespass, then. I'm quite new to town, you see. New to all this, really. We rarely come to London for the season as my wife prefers the country."

Sarani stared at him, at a loss for words. "Is there something I can help you with, Lord…"

"Beckforth."

Heart in her throat, she turned to stare at him more fully, but nothing registered beyond the fact that he was about a decade older than she was and had a stern if handsome face.

He bowed. "The Earl of Beckforth at your service, my lady."

Good heavens. Her lungs squeezed behind her ribs. This man was her family. Only a distant cousin on her mother's side, but still. *Family.* And he had sought her out on the balcony, which meant he obviously knew who she was. But why?

She could barely formulate a reply as he offered her his card. "It would please me if you called upon me at Lockhart Manor sometime."

His manner wasn't overtly friendly, but it wasn't curt either. In fact, the whole exchange was remarkably bland, albeit unexpected, like a bolt out of the blue. With an awkward nod, he took his leave, and Sarani tucked the calling card into her reticule.

What were the odds that he would seek her out? And again… why?

Did he mean to expose her? Embrace her? Convince her to go away?

Her throat burned from a tight combination of thirst and confused emotions. She reached for a glass of champagne from a passing footman and downed it in one swallow, putting up a finger for him to wait. She replaced the empty glass with a new one, only to have it snatched from her fingers.

"Champagne is supposed to be sipped, not gulped," the duke of her fantasies said.

"I am not a child, Your Grace," Sarani tossed back. "And why aren't you inside the ballroom? Don't you have a wager to fulfill?"

"Do you enjoy being groped, my lady? Poked and prodded as though you were a stud bull on display for breeding?" he asked, his raspy voice doing all kinds of unnatural things to her unruly senses, and Sarani nearly let out a shocked laugh. His lips lowered to graze her ear as a firm hand gripped her elbow and steered her toward a hidden alcove behind a potted fern. "Because I assure you, it is quite tiresome. I am not a piece of meat."

Her suddenly agreeable tongue wanted to point out that he was indeed a *fine* piece of meat, but she buttoned her lips firmly. Sodding champagne—she'd never had much tolerance for the stuff. "Welcome to the ugly world of courting, Your Grace, and what we women have had to endure for centuries."

His large frame tensed beside her in the gloom. "Someone has touched you without permission?" His voice was almost a growl…and now the tingling sensation had turned into something more scorching.

"No." She laughed. "And besides, no one dared to touch me but you, even at the risk of the maharaja's wrath or my kukri."

Sarani almost sensed him smile and then felt him shift closer, though he did not touch her. She was grateful. If he did, she was likely to go up in a shower of indelicate sparks. "Do you have your blades on your person right now?"

"Why? Does that scare you?"

"No," he said, his breath feathering over her face. Gracious, he was close. So close that she was aware of every inch of him, even in the shadows. "But I don't wish to find myself on the business ends of them."

"Why would you—?"

But the rest of her words were blanketed by the warm pressure of his mouth bearing down upon hers. Every nerve in her body pulsed like lightning in a storm. Sarani couldn't help herself—her hands reached up between them to clutch the lapels of his tailcoat, dragging him closer. He'd looked so sinfully handsome tonight. She'd practically salivated when he'd been announced on arrival. Rhystan in full ducal dress was clearly her Achilles' heel.

And him naked… That might be the death of her.

Body on fire, she melted into his mouth. His lips were soft and firm as they explored the contours of hers, his tongue tracing the seam before plunging inside. Sarani moaned. She'd forgotten how good he tasted, how skilled he was at kissing, how right she felt in his arms. She didn't care if he had an ulterior motive. She just needed him.

His mouth dragged down her jaw, peppering small kisses along its edge. When he reached her sensitive throat and bit lightly, her knees nearly buckled. A finger traced the edge of her bodice and Sarani froze, reason returning in between the bouts of utter insanity. They were on a very public terrace at a very public ball.

"Rhystan…"

He licked at her skin, and her eyes nearly rolled back in her head, protests all but forgotten. *No, no, no.* She was saying something…something important. Sarani tried to get her mutinying brain under control, but that was hard when the dratted man was treating her body like it was his own personal banquet.

"People will see," she whispered.

"No, they won't," he murmured thickly against her collarbone, the sinful rasp of his voice making her skin leap.

"But—"

But nothing else came out as her words turned into gibberish as his fingers yanked at her bodice and his mouth closed around the aching bud of one taut nipple. Sensation rioted across her in hot rippling waves, arrowing down her belly, straight into her hot, yielding core. A low groan escaped him as he shifted to suck the other breast into his mouth.

"Your skin is like velvet," he rasped.

Grasping her hips, Rhystan sank to his knees—*heaven help her wicked thoughts*—gathering her hem and reaching down beneath her crinoline to trace her stockinged legs up over her calf, past the hem of her drawers, his fingers freezing on the leather straps of her kukri sheaths crossing each thigh. He lifted a brow, glancing up. "You are armed."

"A girl can't be too careful," she said.

"How do you retrieve them?"

"Pockets," she panted as his wandering hand left the straps and climbed higher. "Cleverly stitched holes, really."

With a growl at her words, he moved toward the slit in her drawers to caress her bare, trembling thighs. His knuckles grazed over her heat before she felt his finger slip between her slick folds. A groan tore from him. "So wet, so perfect. Is this all for me?"

"Rhystan…" she whispered, too far gone to be embarrassed about her arousal, her own hands winding into his hair.

This was madness. What they were doing was madness. And yet she did not want him to stop. She never wanted him to stop.

"I've wanted to touch you for fucking weeks," he muttered. The vulgar oath only made her burn hotter. "Teach that tart mouth a lesson, grasp this tempting arse." His hand left her briefly, reaching around to grab a handful of her derriere, and she squeaked. *Oh!* She saw his mouth curve into a dissolute grin before he returned his palm to her core. "Discover all of you."

When his fingers began to move again, aided and abetted by a disconcerting amount of wetness between her legs, Sarani nearly fainted. Sensation built and built, his free hand reaching up to pinch and roll her nipple while his clever fingers toyed with her damp flesh, until it almost became too much, blindingly bright, before shattering. A scream gathered in her throat, but then Rhystan was standing and his mouth was there, kissing her and swallowing her soft cries as her sated body settled into a boneless state against his.

They stood there, breathing hard, his forehead resting on hers.

"That's also been on the list of things I've wanted to do for weeks," he whispered.

She licked her swollen lips. "There's a list?"

"A rather long one, considering I started it five years ago." He brushed his mouth over hers. "All the debauched, wicked things I wanted to do to Princess Sarani Rao."

Gracious, her body twitched with need as if she hadn't just had the orgasm of her life. But as sanity replaced stupor, Sarani drew away and sucked in a horrified breath. It was a miracle no one had seen them or happened upon them. Though Rhystan was right. The alcove was concealed by an outcropping and the nearby plant, which had afforded them a modicum of privacy.

But still…

Sarani's body heated, her fantasies of the duke on his knees well and truly met. Thank the heavens she hadn't been *too* loud. A ferocious blush filled her cheeks, and she was glad for the darkness. Hastily, she put her bodice and skirts to rights, checking the intricate coiffure that Asha had insisted on, but thankfully that felt like it was still in place.

"We should go back inside," she said, jostling out of the nook and past his big body. "You will undoubtedly have been missed."

Rhystan's hand darted out to grasp her arm and tug her back in toward him. "Sarani, wait, I—"

But whatever he'd been about to say was cut off as his eyes went wide, a frown pinching his lips. She didn't dare look behind her, but she knew someone stood there. They'd been discovered, and while she was scandalously crushed against his chest, no less. Sarani bit her lip. At least it hadn't been while his hand had been up her skirts. Small mercies.

"Good God, Embry," a drunken male voice cawed loudly. "Leave some for the rest of us, will you?"

She stepped out of the duke's embrace only to get an eyeful of Lord Littleton...of course it had to be this season's loudest dandy. Her skin prickled as curious stares flocked to them. *Oh no, oh no, oh no.* Things could not possibly get worse. She was going to swoon.

A cool hand took hers, tethering her to his side. "Since when can't a man sneak a moment with his betrothed, Littleton?" Rhystan drawled.

"Betrothed? Congratulations, good man!"

Sarani's breath hitched as none other than the dowager duchess appeared at the balcony doors. Things could definitely get worse. Her gaze narrowed on them as if she could clearly see the cloud of sin around them. "Embry, our host has been looking for you."

"Oy, Dragon Duchess," Littleton brayed. "Looks like you're about to be replaced and put in the dower house, eh?"

The stark anger on her face was brief but ugly, and the sight of it made Sarani lift her chin in angry defiance. She gripped Rhystan's hand tighter and smiled at Littleton. "We've been keeping it a secret, but I suppose the cat's out of the bag now."

Rhystan sat back in the carriage, staring at Sarani and his sister, who had not stopped chattering about her first real ball. His mother had long since departed in a froth in her own coach, leaving Sarani to find her own way back. His carriage was stuffed with two young ladies, both of whom made his blood boil for vastly different reasons.

Ravenna because her high-pitched shrieking was about to do him in, and Sarani…well…he couldn't think about her without sporting a flagpole in his trousers. Hell, he was still half-hard after the interlude on the balcony. He'd always known she was responsive, but her soft moans…how wet she'd been…how sweetly her body had clenched around his fingers, had combined to demolish him.

His trousers instantly grew crowded. Discreetly, he attempted to adjust himself on the seat but caught Sarani's eye anyway. Her gaze darted away, dropping to her hands clasped in her lap, a violent blush spreading on her cheeks as she fixed her attention on his sister.

"You naughty, naughty, *naughty* wretches," Ravenna was saying. "I honestly cannot believe your antics. Being discovered in flagrante delicto on the balcony. Littleton would have spread it far and wide already. The man is a menace."

Sarani buried her face behind her hands, a laugh spilling out. "I'm so embarrassed."

"Why? You two are engaged."

"Yes, but your mother wished for your brother to wait to make an announcement so she could let the other prospects down gently."

Ravenna gave an indelicate snort. "You mean so she could push Penelope in your place." She giggled. "Lord, her expression was priceless when Littleton was braying the news that you're now the official winner of the Duchess Duels."

Rhystan almost snorted at the ridiculous designation.

"As if anyone could hold a candle to you." Ravenna rolled her eyes and threw herself back against the squabs. "And as if my brother could keep his eyes off you. He practically galloped out of the ballroom the minute you stepped out onto that balcony. It was a wonder that Mama did not see him leave and discover you earlier herself." Her gaze sparkled with mischief and panned between them. "Is it true what Littleton said that you were doing out there?"

"We were talking," Rhystan said.

Ravenna grinned. "Is that what they're calling it these days? I suppose you do use your tongue for both."

Sarani gasped with a smothered laugh, and he scowled, though the recollection of Sarani's sweet taste made his mouth water. He suddenly wanted to kiss her again. Kiss her elsewhere. See if she was as sweet *there* as her lips had been.

His sister cackled. "You are a dissembler, brother."

"Ravenna, enough," he snapped. "That is unseemly."

But of course his warning went unheeded. "My goodness, the gossip was afire. A duke ravaging a lady? The aloof Duke of Embry no less?" She pressed a hand to her mouth to hold back her giggles. "Poor Penelope. She and Lady Windmere were dead certain she was going to receive an offer from you. Though I warned her months ago that I suspected my brother's heart was elsewhere."

"Was she expecting an offer?" Sarani asked.

"Penelope intimated as much," Ravenna said. "She has already had seven offers from suitors. It's because she's an heiress of course. Her dowry is enormous, like her head."

Rhystan shook his head. "She could have all the money in England, but marrying that chit will drive any man to an early grave. Any other gentleman is welcome to her, but not me."

"Speaking of suitors," Sarani interjected, peering at Ravenna. "Any young men take your fancy tonight? I did not spot a single silly, smelly sir in tonight's mix."

"Not a one, no." Ravenna let out an aggrieved sigh. "They're all boring, full of their own importance, and lacking in ambition. They were all commendable dancers, though, and creditable punch fetchers. I was not thirsty for one second the entire evening."

Rhystan flattened his lips. "Courtship is not a joking matter, Ravenna. You need to secure a husband."

"Why?" his sister shot back. "So you can leave again? Go back to your exciting, shipboard life?"

He stared at her. That was exactly why. But hearing it stated so baldly and seeing the fleeting flash of hurt on her face made something tighten inside him.

"Ravenna—"

"I don't wish to marry anyone." She drew a deep breath. "Well, not right now. I want to travel and see the world as you have. Visit India, maybe where Sara grew up. I've talked to Asha—"

"You talked to Asha?" Sarani blurted out, her panicked gaze meeting Rhystan's.

Ravenna reached for her hand. "Please do not be cross with her, Sara dear. I practically forced her to tell me stories of you when you were younger, about where you grew up and some of your adventures. She misses her home, too." Oblivious to Sarani's brewing panic, Ravenna went on. "She told me that you grew up in a palace. How delightful! And your jaunts to the river and all the trophies you took for horse racing." She sighed. "It sounds much better than dreary, stuffy old London."

"It wasn't all roses," Sarani began haltingly. "Every place has its trials and thorns."

"I don't care. I want a bit of adventure before I become some man's property."

"And risk scandalizing the Huntley name?" Rhystan firmed his jaw. "No, I forbid it. You will secure an appropriate match and marry to your station as is your duty."

Two incredulous stares—one a wounded copper and the other a furious hazel—crashed into him. The bitter thought that he sounded exactly like his father slid through him before he quashed it. He also dimly recognized that he was the pot challenging the kettle, given that he was avoiding his own mother's trap as well as his obedience to duty with a fake betrothal to a lady whom most of the *ton* would deem unsuitable.

His thoughts were reflected in Sarani's eyes. There was injury there, too, along with a flicker of ferocity. Why would she be angry? Their engagement wasn't even real. She had no say in who Ravenna married or whether the match was sound. He leveled her with a cool expression. "Do you have something you wish to say?"

"Sometimes fathers or brothers don't know what's best."

He gaped in incredulous surprise. "You've certainly changed your tune from five years ago. Your father spoke, and you jumped."

"That's not fair and you know it." Her gaze flicked to Ravenna, but she was too caught up in her own anger to have noticed his slip. "You know very well what was required of me. I had no choice."

Rhystan shook his head and ground his jaw, well aware of what a hypocrite the situation made him. He'd expected Sarani to defy the wishes of her father while expecting Ravenna to keel over and do what she was told. The irony of the double standard did not escape him.

"This is the way things are done."

Her eyes flashed. "That doesn't make it right. Sometimes, things have to change."

"As you've changed, Lady Sara?" He couldn't keep the bitterness from his voice.

"This isn't about me, Your Grace. This is about your sister and you being here for her instead of out on the sea somewhere." Her voice hushed. "At least you have a family."

Narrowing his gaze, he pinned his lips in anger. How dare she judge him for his choices? "Ravenna will marry."

"So that's it?" his sister burst out. "You forbid me from living my life, and you'll hand me over to the first man who offers, like a purse of coin over a card table."

Rhystan hardened his heart at the break in her voice. "If he suits, yes."

"I wish to hell you'd stayed away," Ravenna whispered, her eyes brimming with tears.

"That makes two of us, then."

Eighteen

It'd been over a week since the news of their engagement had broken, and the scandal sheets had yet to stop writing about the standoffish duke and his mysterious fiancée who, rumor had it, he'd imported from a palace in India. Sarani snorted. As though she were a case of wine from Italy or France.

An imported burgundy…an imported bride.

The name Lockhart was now synonymous with intrigue, since the Earl of Beckforth hadn't claimed any connection. Apparently, when asked outright if she was a relation, he had refused to answer. Had he changed his mind about his invitation for her to call? Or was he respecting her privacy? In truth, Sarani didn't know what to believe. Deep down, it wouldn't surprise her if he regretted approaching her. Scandal wasn't for the fainthearted.

As a result, the wagers on who she was were now as high as the ones that had been placed on the now-defunct Duchess Duels. Since Sarani had not been one of the debutantes in the running, the entire pot had been lost. The caricaturists had had a field day with that as well—showing her wearing a dress made of banknotes while gentlemen shook their fists at her.

One of the more brazen caricatures depicted her at the feet of the duke. The artist had over-emphasized her features and dressed her in Eastern clothing, which had caused a swarm of hornets to erupt in her belly. It had been so close to the truth that she'd nearly brought up her breakfast, but Rhystan had assured her they were trying to sell gossip rags rather than anyone knowing the truth.

Her identity was still safe. For now.

Her thoughts drifted back to the scene in the carriage after the Windmere ball.

Ravenna had been inconsolable for days, spending her evenings with trays of French chocolates for company. Sarani had joined her while she'd berated her high-handed, intractable brute of a brother who—in her words—had a stick lodged so firmly up his arse that it was a wonder he could walk. Sarani had bitten her lip to keep from laughing. The description matched several she'd come up with in the last months of knowing the man.

Despite Ravenna not leaving her chamber in days, Sarani had finally managed to bribe her with a silk scarf she'd brought from Joor to get her to take a bath. So now Sarani sat with a book in hand on the armchair in Ravenna's chamber, waiting for her to finish.

"Why would he forbid me from seeing the world?" Ravenna groused, stalking from the bathroom, her hapless lady's maid following. "He's done it!"

"He's a man. They are expected to go on a grand tour."

"Why can't ladies do the same? Why should we be fashioned like good little puppets whose strings will be passed from one master to the next? Tied down, hearth-bound, and miserable."

Sarani did not have a reasonable answer. She'd always thought the same. If the boys could do it, so could she. Though England was new to her, she'd seen quite a bit of India on travels with her father, and he had not hesitated to take her along in spite of her sex. Odd that a country that was viewed as backward by England had more progressive views of women in positions of power. Her friend Manu had exceeded all expectations and surpassed all limits as the queen of Jhansi in her own right, riding into battle like the warrior she was, not in the least bit inhibited by the fact that she was a woman.

A wet-haired Ravenna peered at her. "What are you reading over there?"

"*Wuthering Heights*," Sarani said. "Do you know it?"

She scowled. "I'm all in favor of vengeance right now."

"It's more than just revenge," Sarani said. "It's about the darkest of passions, loss, and the balances of power. And in the end, perhaps it's about allowing ourselves what we deserve."

"Heathcliff is like Rhystan. Hard of heart, ruthless of mind, and empty of soul."

Sarani cast her a stern look. "Ravenna, your brother might be a cold and exacting man, but he's not soulless. And he loves you. He only wants what's best for you."

"By forcing me to marry?"

"By seeing you safe. I wish I had someone left to care enough to do the same." The hard words were out before she could stop them. "I have no one left in the world."

Besides a cousin who wants to murder me.

She didn't add that last part.

"I am sorry," Ravenna said, her soft voice contrite. "But you cannot understand what it's like to be forced into an unwanted position."

"I understand more than you know. Before my father died, he betrothed me to an odious man twice my age without my approval or consent."

Ravenna blinked. "Not to Rhystan?"

"I did not know the duke then…" The lie felt sour on her tongue, but then she froze, her eyes snapping to Ravenna, who wore a guilty look on her face. "What is that look?"

"Nothing." She wrung her hands, her cheeks going red. "It's not Asha's fault but she might have mentioned that you and my brother knew each other from when he was an officer. She slipped and called you Princess Sarani. And I heard Rhystan in the coach saying something about five years ago." She bit her lip as Sarani felt the bottom drop out from beneath her feet. "You're the girl, aren't you?"

Heaven help her, Sarani quailed on the inside. She placed the book carefully down on her lap and calmed her erratic breaths. Speculation wasn't the truth. "Which girl?"

"I overheard my parents arguing years ago about Rhystan and some letter my father had received from an admiral or some such overseas." Ravenna paused. "They spoke about a girl. An Indian princess with an English mother." Sarani's heart sank. "That's you, isn't it."

She drew a breath. "Ravenna…"

"Don't treat me like a birdwit. I know it's you. I've seen your likeness before, you know. Did you know my brother carries a miniature of you in a locket? I discovered it when he came back for the funeral. He was quite in his cups, you see, clutching it as though it was his most precious possession and cursing it in the same breath." She quirked her lips. "The girl was younger, of course, but I see the resemblance clearly now. I always knew she was special." She laughed. "I'd even told Penelope about it to prove that Rhystan was mad for someone else and she should set her sights elsewhere."

Sarani frowned. Why would the duke have kept a portrait of her? As a talisman? A reminder of his distaste?

"I won't tell anyone," Ravenna whispered. "It doesn't even matter to me who your parents are."

She swallowed, meeting the girl's eyes. "It does to me."

"Are you truly a princess?"

"I used to be."

A pleat forming between her brows, Ravenna stared at her. "How does one stop being a princess?"

"By burying her."

———

Rhystan raked a hand through his hair as he stared at Gideon over a pint at the small dockside tavern near where the *Belonging* had been dry-docked for repairs. He'd needed a drink after the day he'd had. A robbery, of all things. The servants had been in a flurry because no one had suspected the young chimney sweep, who claimed he'd been sent by the duke himself.

"So you're saying that someone broke into your house in Mayfair?" Gideon asked, thick dark brows rising.

"Stole a few loose banknotes, rifled through the study, but nothing of great value was taken." He frowned—for a robber, his study would have been a veritable treasure trove. "Either it was a terrible thief or they were there to scout the place."

"You suspect trouble?"

Rhystan took the last swallow of his whisky. "I don't know yet. Tell the men to keep an eye out here as well. Could be simple-minded thieves." He let out a breath. Or it could be something more. "Any more news on the ship that was following us?" he asked. He'd begun to doubt that the ship behind them had been anything but another trade ship following the same route.

"Nothing, but another ship put into port a week ago, resupplied, and left a day later," Gideon said with a frown. "An Indiaman vessel with not a drop of cargo and a handful of tight-lipped crew. Couldn't pry a word out of them. Red only found out that they'd come from Bombay after greasing some palms and checking with the customs docking logs."

"Any idea where they went?"

"I put a couple men on a clipper to follow them."

Rhystan blew out a breath. "Good man."

"How's the Duchess of Terror?" Gideon grinned. "Does she miss me? I reckon I could get her to soften up after a few pints. We almost had a moment at the funeral."

"She had you tossed out on your arse by the largest footmen we had," Rhystan said dryly. "And banned from ever returning to Huntley House."

"Best day of my life," Gideon said, raising his tankard.

Rhystan laughed and lifted his as well.

"And what of your bride-to-be?" Gideon asked slyly.

"She's well."

Gideon smirked. "So talkative. Cat got your tongue? Or

perhaps a saucy young lass with legs for days and a smile that could fell a man."

"Sod off, Gideon."

His quartermaster laughed heartily, though the amusement was only on his end. They drank in blessedly pleasant silence for a while. Rhystan was grateful Gideon hadn't pressed on the matter with Sarani. He could not spare her a single thought without hearing her soft moans, without recalling the sweet slick of her arousal on his fingers and itching to experience it again. If Gideon guessed how much she affected him, he'd never let him forget it. Rhystan drained his glass and ordered another round.

"Thirsty?" Gideon sent him a knowing look, and Rhystan shot him a crude gesture. The bastard only laughed, sliding over a ledger. "Business, then. One of the ships is due to head back to China on the tea route. The other is bound for Italy. Once the *Belonging* is ready, I'll begin preparing to leave for the West Indies in a few weeks." He eyed Rhystan. "Were you planning to be on any of those?"

The crew were getting restless, and now that two more of his fleet had put into port and unloaded their cargo, they were ready to head out to sea once more. Rhystan was more than ready to head out with them, but something held him back.

Not something…*someone.*

He studied the logs that Gideon had pushed across the table. They noted the recent custom duties for the three ships that had arrived as well as the names and voyages of his few dozen other ships currently at sea and in other ports. He couldn't see wrapping up his finances here anytime soon, and there was still the matter of seeing Ravenna settled. A few weeks should be more than enough time.

"Antigua. I need to see Chase." Courtland Chase had accomplished what many men hadn't—a life in the colonies that actually helped the locals. "The people who work for him have their own lands and businesses. I want to replicate that elsewhere."

"You already have," Gideon said loyally. "Those on your former lands are thriving and buying from the locals directly makes a difference."

"There's always room to do more."

Gideon nodded. "What about the princess?"

"If all goes as planned and there is no confirmed threat to her safety, the lady will be happily ensconced in a Cornish village somewhere, living the life she wants."

"And you?"

Rhystan frowned, well acquainted with his quartermaster's snide tone. "And me what?"

"What about you? Will you be living your best life when you leave the only woman you ever cared about behind?"

With a burst of annoyance, Rhystan slammed his tankard down, drawing stares from men at neighboring tables. Gideon did not so much as flinch, only raising a sardonic brow at the uncharacteristic display of temper. "It's what she wants. It's what we agreed."

"Agreements change."

"I am not in need of a wife," Rhystan snapped. "Least of all her."

"She's your match, Captain."

"You know who she is to me, Gideon. Those were the darkest days of my life."

Gideon studied him and then downed the rest of his ale with a quiet nod. "Aye. They were. I pulled you out of that opium house where you were slowly attempting to obliterate yourself. But it was not only because of her. You had many other demons you were trying to drown, your father being the worst of them." His voice gentled. "And let's be honest here. You didn't exactly fight for her either."

Rhystan crashed his fist into the table, nostrils flaring with fury as he leaped to his feet ready to send his friend to the floor. Anger that he'd kept buried for years burned through his veins like acid. "I was in hell, you bastard!"

"And you chose to put yourself there." In the next breath, all

Rhystan's fury died, and all he could do was stare at the ever-calm Gideon, who had not batted an eyelash. "I gave you an out, and you took it. At any point after you sobered up, you could have gone back to Joor."

"She was already married," he muttered.

No, she hadn't been. He'd only thought she'd married. Markham had lied, which Rhystan would have discovered if he had gone back for her. The truth hit him like a kick to the gut. Gideon was right. He could have gone back to Joor. He could have spoken to her, used his fucking name for something worthwhile. Done something, anything. He was only responsible for his own actions, and he'd chosen to do nothing.

"You're right," he said, sitting heavily. "Even so, I can't marry her."

"Why not?"

"This is London, Gideon. If the truth came out about who she is, it would most likely have an effect on Ravenna's chances of making the best possible match, simply by association. You know how narrow-minded the *ton* can be. The gossip will be interminable."

Gideon stared at him, and from the growing scowl on his face, Rhystan had the feeling that he'd just gone down a few pegs—a few dozen pegs—in his friend's estimation. "Since when does the captain I know care about gossip or polite society?"

"Since he became duke."

"That's never been you, lad. The man I know would never let a person's circumstances determine the sum of their worth." He stood and tossed a few coins down onto the wood. "Whoever that duke is isn't worth a scrap of the man you were. Don't lose sight of him, my friend, or you will truly have become your father."

———

After dinner at home, Asha's low notes on the *shehnai* soothed Sarani's soul. Ravenna, too, if her transported expression was any indication.

"I've never heard anything so hauntingly beautiful in my life. You're very good at that, Asha," she said, clapping with enthusiasm as the maid wrapped up a piece in the music room. "Would you teach me sometime?"

Asha glanced at Sarani, but it was up to her. Sarani gave a tiny shrug and a smile. "It would be my honor, Lady Ravenna. Here, why don't you hold it? Familiarize yourself with the feel of the wood and each sound."

Watching them, their heads bent together—one dark and the other auburn, so dissimilar in looks yet so unequivocally united in their love of music—Sarani couldn't help smiling. Though she missed Joor on occasion, London was starting to grow on her. And it was all because of Ravenna. She'd never had a sister, and Ravenna had turned out to be nothing like she'd expected.

The girl was unlike any of the other English debutantes she'd met. Ravenna had laughed when Sarani had told her that and said that she hadn't met anyone besides Penelope—arguably the worst of the bunch. The blond-haired girl who had seemed excited about the Indian princes was one of Ravenna's best friends, Lady Clara.

To Sarani's surprise, there'd been no more discussion of her origins or the scandal her parents had caused. She had expected Ravenna to treat her differently because she was not fully English, but it simply did not signify. Each day, Sarani kept waiting for the ax to fall, and every day, it didn't.

"Are you not concerned?" Sarani had blurted out once during breakfast, her voice guarded. "Given who I am?"

"A princess?" Ravenna had returned.

Sarani had grimaced. "A fraud."

"You are no more a fraud than Penelope, who pretends she is the most eligible heiress of all when the truth is she looks nothing like her father but rather one of her mother's old lovers. Evelyn Darkle's father was a cobbler's son who became a spice merchant worth a fortune. Or even Lord Beckforth, who I've discovered was rumored to be a pig farmer before he became earl." Sarani had digested that knowledge with surprise, her gaze darting to Ravenna, who had paused with a sad smile to bite into a piece of buttered toast. "Or even me. A duke's daughter without a dowry trying to decide her own fate. We're both misfits trying to find a place."

Sarani blinked. "You have a dowry."

"I did, once." Ravenna's lip curled. "You didn't think the gossip couldn't touch us, did you? Scandal is the one thing that unites every man, highborn or lowborn. Gossip doesn't care for rank, fortune, or beauty. If someone falls, the world will know. Mama could not keep our ruin from the creditors, and she was too proud to write to Rhystan. That was all part of her scheme, you see. Find an enormously rich, perfect heiress and all would be solved. Son would be rightfully settled as duke. Daughter would be married to a peer. Mother would live happily ever after. Never mind she had to sacrifice her last remaining son's happiness to do so."

Ravenna had broken off, a tear dripping down her cheek, and then she'd excused herself from breakfast. Until Asha had offered to play the instrument for a bit of cheer later that afternoon and Sarani had sought her out, Ravenna hadn't said a word. Sarani supposed that she'd kept those raw feelings inside for a very long time.

She clapped as Ravenna played a few notes, her smile stretching from ear to ear. They were so caught up in the accomplishment that none of them heard the door open until the warm voice echoed through the room, making the hair on Sarani's nape stand on end.

"What's this?" the duke asked.

Ravenna leaped to her feet, the *shehnai* tumbling from her lap, only to be caught by Asha at the last moment. "Nothing, Your Grace."

Rhystan flinched at his sister's cool address, though Sarani saw remorse blanket his expression. Likely, he knew how much he'd hurt her with his high-handedness. Ravenna understood what was expected of her...but like most intelligent, independent-thinking girls, she wanted to have some say in her own future, no matter how small.

"It did not sound like nothing," he said. "It sounds wonderful. Will you play it again for me, Ravenna?"

His sister brightened, relieved that she wasn't going to get a scolding or perhaps even understanding that he was extending an olive branch. "Do you truly wish me to? It's only the first measure of the song, but I'm certain that I can manage it now."

The duke nodded and moved to sit on the sofa beside Sarani. She held her breath, his very presence stealing the air from her shrinking lungs, every inch of her body acutely aware of every inch of his. Heavens, he smelled divine. Like salt and storm and pure male, as though he'd just stalked from the quarterdeck of his ship.

Sarani fought the urge to breathe him in and commanded her body to be still. It was a losing battle. She could hear each inhale, feel every rustle of his clothing. If she listened hard enough, she was certain she could hear his pounding heartbeat. Or was that hers?

Winding her fingers into her skirts, she'd just decided to make her excuses and flee the room—and his presence—when he spoke.

"I'm sorry for what happened in the carriage. This, being both brother and duke, is new to me."

Sarani peered up at him. "Ravenna only wants to be heard."

"I know."

The sultry notes of the *shehnai* wound between them like silken drapes, teasing her already frail senses. She had to depart before she did something truly untoward...like climbing into his lap and sealing her lips to his.

"I cannot stop thinking about you," he whispered.

She froze in place. "I beg your pardon."

"Since the ball, my nights have been torture."

Hers had, too, if she was being honest. Sleepless, restless… waking with the sheets bunched around her waist and her body drenched in sweat, she was plagued by dreams that bordered on indecency. She didn't dare think of any of them, or her face would give her scandalous thoughts away.

"Is that so?" she murmured, staring at Asha and Ravenna, who were lost in their own musical world and would not notice if the roof caved in over their heads.

As if determining the same, Rhystan leaned toward her ever so slightly, the side of his muscular arm brushing the sleeve of her dress, and Sarani swore that sparks arced between them. Her cheeks flamed. Ducking her head, she attempted to compose herself. Goodness, she wished she didn't blush so easily. Or that her body wasn't so… *weak* where he was concerned.

His ungloved hand came to rest beside her on the seat, and she lowered hers to rest beside his. Slowly, *slowly*, their small fingers touched, hot, bare skin sliding together. Sarani bit back a gasp as the barest graze of his finger ignited the ember of memory in her core that was impossible to ignore. Impossible to forget.

"I want you, Sarani," he rasped. "Will you come with me?"

The pure need in his words preceded the storm, now brewing inside of her.

A cyclone of desire and unfulfilled dreams.

And heaven help her, she wanted to steer the bow of her doomed ship right into it. She wanted to give herself over to it, to let it take her to destruction or completion. She did not care which. Sarani needed to keep just one part of him when everything shattered around them. Because it would…eventually.

Lies weren't meant to hold up forever.

For now, she wanted to embrace the fantasy. Even if it meant lying to herself.

She gave the only answer she could. "Yes."

Nineteen

She isn't bloody coming.

It wasn't his first thought. His first thoughts had been gilded in elation. In bliss. In brilliant, fiery-edged desire. But the possibility of her not showing up gutted him. She'd seemed so willing in the music room. She'd said *yes*. But it'd been nearly an hour of him having a bracingly cold bath and then pacing a hole in the Aubusson carpets of the drawing room, checking his pocket watch every time the long hand moved.

Maybe she'd run into Ravenna on the way or, God forbid, the duchess. Or perhaps she'd simply changed her mind. He could not—would not—blame her if she did. People were allowed to have second thoughts.

God, she truly wasn't coming.

The tentative footsteps in the hallway had his heart pounding and his blood heating.

It was scandalous in the extreme what they were doing. An engaged couple could step out together alone, but not at night. If either of them got caught, a swift trip to the altar would be the least of it. But he'd dismissed Fullerton for the evening, and he knew for a fact that his mother had already retired. All that left was Ravenna, and she'd been angling to push them together for a while now. Any servant who saw them leaving Huntley House would hold his or her tongue on pain of dismissal without a reference.

Rhystan cracked open the door of the salon, and she slid inside, the sultry scent of jasmine flowing in her wake and making his entire body clench with need. If he wasn't careful, he'd slam her to the door, rip the cloak and gown from her body, and take her against the walls right then and there.

"I thought you'd decided against joining me," he ground out, reaching for his hat. He was holding on to his discipline by the thinnest of threads.

"I considered it," she said, eyes wide as though she could sense his struggle, though she did not retreat. In fact, answering desire flashed in that dark green-gold gaze.

He groaned, nearly crushing the satin-edged brim of his hat. "Do you wish to go with me, Sarani?" he rumbled. "Because once we leave this house, I won't let you out of my sight, out of my reach, until I've made you mine—ruined you—in every way."

She shivered, but feral bright eyes lifted to his as she whispered, "Ruin me, then."

This woman.

Grabbing her hand, he led her down the stairs to where his coach was waiting. The door hadn't fully closed before he was upon her, his mouth crushing hers. God, her taste! Like sin and summer nights, like spice and sunshine. The blend, uniquely her, did him in. Sarani did not hold back either. Her fingers sifted into his hair, breasts smashing into his chest and erasing what little space there was between them, parting lips and legs to receive him. She'd never held back, not with him. Even as a girl, her kisses had been passionate, her response without artifice.

He wanted to see her come again, but this time not with his fingers.

"I'm sorry. I need to—" Rhystan tore his mouth from hers as he crashed to his haunches on the floor of the carriage, kissing along her neck and tugging at the fastenings on her cloak.

"Rhystan, what are you doing?"

He opened the upper garment, only to growl at the sight of the gauzy white fabric that molded to her slim legs and had no business being outside a lady's bedchamber. "What are you wearing?"

"A night rail."

Hell. He was so hard he nearly spent in his trousers. "A night rail?" he mumbled incoherently.

"Well, I *was* planning on going to bed." He could hear the smile in her voice. "And then I got a more interesting offer."

His hands moved, caressing the skin of her lower legs to the silken texture of her thighs. "What offer was that?"

"An offer from a man who once boasted to rob me of all speech."

He groaned. "Is that so?"

"Yes."

Gathering the soft fabric in one fist, he yanked her hem to her waist, another voracious sound bursting from him. Hell. She was going to kill him. No drawers. *Of course no drawers*, his asinine mind corroborated. *She's wearing a sodding night rail made of ribbons and dreams.*

He looked his fill, her beautiful skin made even more golden by the lamp in the carriage. "You are perfect." He skimmed up her inner thigh to graze her sex, the heart of her hidden by fine jet curls, making her whimper and her eyes grow hooded. "Your skin is like the smoothest silk, and here, you're so damp, so ready for me."

The scent of her was maddening. Intoxicating. Rhystan reached around to grasp her rounded hips with both hands, shifted her toward the end of the bench, and lowered his head. He couldn't wait a second more before sating his deepest desire. He licked up her entire length, his instant groan and her moan merging in the silence.

His eyes nearly rolled back in his head as the honeyed silk of her curled over his tongue. One taste wasn't enough. Nowhere near enough. Growling his pleasure, he clutched at her hips as she knotted her fingers in his hair, and he settled on the sweet bud that made her writhe against him.

Rhystan glanced up, the sight of her on the edge of coming

undone making him as hard as stone. Her face was flushed with dark color, her hooded eyes fastened on him and what he was doing. Fascination burned with the lust in her gaze, its brownish-green depths almost gold with desire.

"Shall I continue?" he whispered with another wicked lick.

Her cheeks bloomed, her eyes fluttering shut, her thick black lashes fanning her cheekbones. Her nod was jerky, even as her fisted fingers yanked him closer. Grinning, he continued his onslaught, his own body responding to her soft moans and sighs and threatening to tear through the fall of his trousers.

"Don't stop, please."

He didn't plan to, not until her beautiful body shattered on his tongue. The taste of her was like tangy, salted ocean breezes and redolent tropical nights spent in a hammock. Sweet with a hint of fire. Here was his mistress. His shrine.

His *queen*.

Settling himself between her legs, he lapped and sucked and drank from her delicious body until she was writhing beneath him, reveling in the soft cries leaving her lips that made him mad with desire. Rhystan slid a thick finger into her wet passage, watching as she shuddered with satisfaction, eyes popping wide with surprise.

When her legs started to tremble with tension, he redoubled his efforts, alternating long drags of his tongue with shorter licks at the apex of her sex. Inside her, he curled his finger toward him, and she cried out.

"Rhystan," she whispered.

One decadent swipe, and then she was there, hurtling over the edge into the paroxysm. She came like the evening tide, her body going still and then shuddering beneath him in small, intense waves, bursting on his tongue like the sweetest of fruit.

It was like watching a shooting star bursting through the night sky over an endless ocean. A force of nature. Fucking beautiful.

Rhystan wrung every drop of her release from her until she was limp against the squabs, eyes hazy with passion.

Putting her clothing to rights and fastening her cloak, he climbed back up her body and kissed her lips. "You are magnificent."

"What about you?" she asked, eyes darting to the painful bulge in his dove-gray trousers. Her cheeks turned dusky rose in the light, and his stare followed hers down. A wet spot had gathered on his fly. His arousal, not hers.

"That's what you do to me."

Blushing hotly, Sarani reached for him, palm curving around his nape. For a moment, she looked uncertain, unsure, gnawing that plump lower lip between her teeth and making him want to kiss her again. "Should I? You need to…"

His smile was wolfish. "Oh, I'll have my turn, don't worry. When we get to my residence, I plan to take you to bed and ravage you until you can't speak your own name."

———

Rhystan's filthy promises only made her want him more. She loved seeing the aloof, put-together duke stripped down to this raw, fundamental version of himself. He was savagery swathed in velvet, the jagged edge of danger tempered by decorum. A puzzling enigma that she was powerless to resist. She wanted him bare.

Sarani flushed. Did that make her a brazen hussy? She was a lady, but this man had always incited the devil in her. Twice now, he'd brought her to completion—first with his fingers at the ball and then with his mouth.

Oh, sweet heavenly stars, that mouth.

Even now, her body still quaked with tingling aftershocks. The fact that he had kissed her there had been utterly wicked. She'd opened her mouth to protest, but the only thing that had emerged when his hot, wet tongue had touched her body had been an unbecoming moan. And then her brain had ceased to function.

A part of her wanted to feel ashamed, mortified even, but she couldn't bring herself to care. For the first time in months, she felt alive. Sarani had no doubt that what she was doing was what no lady in her right, decent mind would do with a man, much less a duke. But happiness wasn't guaranteed. Life could be taken at the blink of an eye, with the slash of a blade. She'd already lost so much, and now she had a chance to keep one thing for herself.

She was aware of the absurdity. She would be losing the only thing she had left to lose—her precious virginity. Her calling card to respectability. A woman's innocence…so valued and yet a commodity to be traded to the highest, most titled bidder, even if it was against her wishes.

She wasn't naive. She knew that if she did this, if she let Rhystan into her body without the sanctity of marriage, in the eyes of society, she would be ruined. She did not care. If they had any inkling of who she was, this society would not welcome her anyway. Not truly. What did she need their approval for? And besides, Rhystan would be gone back to the sea soon, the agreement between them fulfilled.

This was for her.

Her choice, even if the consequences would see her fall entirely from grace.

The coach stopped and she met Rhystan's burning eyes. Goodness, he was so incredibly handsome. He made her want to leap across the carriage like a hussy and demand that he take her to the stars again. And again.

Something of her thoughts must have been evident in her eyes because a growling rumble broke from his chest. Sarani hadn't even taken a breath before she was swept into his powerful arms and ferried up the steps into his residence. He paused, letting her down to throw off his hat and coat, left her cloak in place for modesty's sake in light of what she wore beneath, and then she was scooped up once more.

Sarani didn't take in a full breath until they'd bypassed another flight of stairs and she heard the soft snick of a door closing. She had no time to push to her feet before she was tumbled gently onto a soft mattress. Rhystan stepped back to speak to someone at the door, presumably his valet, and dismissed him for the evening. Sarani blushed. She was sure the man would know that his master had a woman in his chamber. Despite surely turning a closed eye to their arrival, in her experience, there was very little that servants did not know.

She turned her attention back to the chamber. Several lamps lit the space and the counterpane on the bed had been turned down. A small fire burned in the grate to ward off the evening's slight chill. She'd met Harlowe briefly, and the man was efficient to a fault. No wonder he'd been on their heels ready to enter just before.

Her gaze took in the details of the tastefully appointed room— the huge bed she sat upon, the plush armchairs near the window, the intricately carved wardrobe and matching furniture. It was a handsome bedchamber. Rhystan's bedchamber. She hadn't seen it in the handful of hours she'd been at this residence when they'd first arrived in London, but she recognized the decor that matched the adjoining room.

For the lady of the house. The woman who would one day be his wife.

The one who wouldn't be her.

Her heart stuttered against her rib cage, and Sarani tamped down the emotion. She had known from the start that this was a pretense, and she'd tried to keep her heart guarded as well as she could. But this was Rhystan. In truth, she'd given her heart to him five years ago and she'd never gotten it back. Her body, in comparison, was inconsequential. Secondary.

"What are you thinking?" he asked, watching her. "Do you wish to return to Huntley House?"

He would do that, no questions asked, she knew.

"No, quite the contrary." She let her gaze wander over his face, from his disheveled hair to his glittering steel-blue eyes and that wicked masculine mouth that had pleasured her so skillfully. Her breath caught on a wave of molten desire and she let it show. Boldly, Sarani licked her lips, letting her stare drop. He'd discarded his boots and waistcoat, and the sight of him in shirtsleeves, untucked from his trousers and all rumpled with desire, did delicious things to her insides. "What I wish for is for you to take off the rest of those clothes."

His full lips parted. "Do you now?"

Sarani unfastened the ties of her cloak, seeing his eyes darken as the light in the bedroom revealed what the dim lamp in the carriage had not. The design of the night rail was truly outrageous. It wasn't anything she would ever choose for herself but had been included in the order for the full wardrobe she'd placed with a celebrated local modiste. Panels of sheer silk and organza, edged with lace, were held together with scraps of ivory ribbon. The thing was scandalous, barely covering her intimate parts.

And by barely covering, she meant not at all.

Rhystan stared, his throat working, hands arrested over the knot of his necktie. Sarani didn't dare glance down, knowing she would see the tops of her pale-brown nipples peeking through the lace. Fighting the heat that shot up her neck and into her cheeks, she jutted her chin. If she didn't faint from apprehension, soon he would see her in much less.

"You're staring," she whispered.

"I've never seen anything so beautiful in all my life."

The duke prowled toward her, the cravat dangling from one finger and falling carelessly to the floor. His shirt went next, over his head, joining its fallen comrade. Sarani gulped. Great goddess of fertility, he was pure, sinful, masculine perfection. He was a man who led by example, which meant he pulled his weight with his crew, hauling cargo and hoisting sails.

The result of hard outdoor labor was what she saw now. Acres of bronzed muscles spanned his broad chest, covered in a light patch of brownish-gold hair that arrowed down his hard stomach…where more stacked muscles vied for attention.

A shirtless Rhystan wasn't anything she hadn't seen before on the *Belonging*—she'd gawked enough from her perch on deck. But ogling from afar and knowing she was seconds away from running her fingers over all those mouthwatering ridges and valleys were two vastly different things. She swallowed hard as his fingers unbuttoned his trousers, letting them gap open to hang on his narrow hips as memories of his cabin swamped her.

Pausing, his eyes lifted, his gaze full of wickedness. "More?"

"Definitely more."

With a grin, he gave her what she wanted, shoving the fabric down until he was standing there like a proud warrior god. Nude, muscled, spectacular. All he was missing was a wreath of laurel leaves and a sword.

Well, she supposed he did have a sword of sorts. Her eyes dipped to view a very prominent, large, heart-palpitating weapon jutted from his groin. Her mouth dried as her gaze dashed away, a hand flying up to her throat. Sarani couldn't breathe because her damned lungs refused to work.

"Guh…"

And evidently, intelligent speech had deserted her as well.

Rhystan grinned and joined her on the bed. Despite her momentary panic—she was not uninformed in the ways of carnal joining, after all—Sarani gave in to her desires, letting her palms run over his thick arms. "No wonder you're so strong," she murmured. "You're as hard as rock."

"Lately, my natural state where you're concerned," he said with a pointed look down.

He was teasing her, but yes, *that* was hard, too. A sudden burst of nerves skittered through her. Was she really going to do this? Give him her maidenhead? Offer him her body without the vows of marriage in place?

Sarani almost laughed out loud. Given Rhystan wasn't wearing a stitch of clothing and she wasn't covered in much more, they were quite beyond the point of misgivings. But a lifetime of indoctrination regarding a woman's place and a woman's worth did not vanish so easily.

His fingers caressed her cheek, his gray-blue eyes the color of a brewing storm. "What is it? You don't have to do this."

"No, I want to do this. With you." She searched for the right words, wanting to articulate what she felt. "Right here and right now with nothing between us…no titles, no rules, no duty. Just you and me. A man and a woman making a choice to…" *Make love.*

It wasn't love. Sarani knew that.

She bit her lip, cheeks going hot. "Do what we're doing."

"Fucking," he said helpfully.

"Must you be so vulgar?"

He kissed her, biting her lower lip and tugging on the ties to her night rail. The garment loosened with shameless ease, pooling to her hips in a glimmer of silk and lace. "You like it."

"I do," she admitted on a moan as his clever mouth dipped to find her bare breast.

"You have the most beautiful nipples, Sarani." Goodness, she loved it when he called her by her real name and not Sara as she insisted. It made her think that his affection hadn't all been burned away by betrayal. "Your skin is like velvet, and I want to gobble you up." He tossed away the night rail and lowered her to the bed before turning his attention to her other breast. She whimpered as his teeth grazed the sensitive peak. "Tell me what you want."

"You," she said breathlessly.

His hands slid down to cup between her legs, and Sarani arched beneath him, a shock of hot need blooming beneath his palm. "You need to be more specific," he said, kissing up her throat. "I need to be certain."

His grinning mouth captured hers in a drugging kiss. Goodness, he was ruthless. She squirmed under him, knowing exactly what he wanted her to say and shying away from it. She couldn't possibly be so crude. "I...I want you to take me."

"Take you where? To the theater? The opera?"

"Brute!"

Sarani would have shoved him away if what he was doing with his tongue wasn't so heady. He was back to her breasts, alternating between her pebbled nipples, and as it was, she was hard-pressed not to have her eyes roll back in her head from the pleasure streaking through her.

"Tell me, Sarani, what do you want?" He pressed one finger between her slippery folds. "Do you want this?"

"Yes," she gasped, rolling her hips to increase the delicious friction.

He withdrew his finger, the cruel wretch, caging her against the mattress with his big, heavy body. "Then say it. Say the dirty, filthy, *vulgar* word."

"Fine. I want you to...fuck me. Happy?" Her cheeks flamed, but strangely, the crass demand made her feel powerful, especially when she saw the answering flare of his irises. That she could reduce the dominant, formidable man above her to a mass of want and desire made her feel bold. "I need you inside me, Rhystan. Now."

Her smug-faced lover rewarded her with a deep kiss and then positioned himself on top of her, his hips in the cradle of hers. "As my princess wishes."

"I'm not a princess."

Sarani stared at him, seeing nothing but hunger for her in those beautiful storm-ridden eyes. There was no judgment there, only need. A need that was deeply, fiercely reciprocated.

"No," he whispered, notching himself at her entrance. "You're a queen."

And then he slid into her body.

Sarani nearly screamed, clutching at his shoulders. The fit was distressingly tight, the friction almost impossible to bear as her untried body adjusted to his size.

"Sarani? Are you all right?" Rhystan's face was strained, a muscle flexing in his cheek.

"Yes," she said. "But go slowly. Are you in pain?"

He shook his head. "No. You feel so good. So tight."

Only when he was finally seated did she attempt to pull a breath into her lungs. The movement pushed her breasts into his chest, the rub of his hair against her sensitive nipples making pleasure spiral through her. She felt so full, so deliciously full of him as her body accommodated his alarming girth.

"Oh, my word," she blurted out. "That was rather not what I expected. Then again, it's simple mathematics—volume and displacement really. I should not have been surprised, given your dimensions."

"Dimensions?"

A smile stretched his lips, one brown brow arching with amusement. She was babbling like a lunatic, while he was still seated inside her.

"Size, then," she said, blushing. "Er, what's next?" She bit her lips, fighting for composure. She did not want to seem like an oblivious, incompetent henwit, even though she was technically incompetent. "I seem to recall a promise about not being able to speak my own name? Was that a euphemism?"

With a low laugh, Rhystan shifted his hips, drawing a gasp from her. "I always deliver on my promises. No speech, guaranteed."

He withdrew and slid back in, to her sublime delight, the erotic push and pull making her body crave deeper and faster contact. Instinctively, Sarani rolled her pelvis forward on the next thrust, ripping a growl from his chest as she lifted her hips to take him deep.

"Yes, love, like that."

His face was still scrunched, his eyes dilated with pleasure as his body worked. Every slow rock of his huge frame sent her spiraling higher and higher, climbing toward some invisible summit. "Rhystan, please... I need..."

"I know, sweetheart." He took her lips with his, a warm palm finding her breast and kneading. The sensation gathering within her was almost too much. Her skin felt like it was on fire, her very soul enflamed.

When she thought she couldn't take it anymore, her moans dissolving into incoherent sounds, Rhystan reached his hand between them and slid his hands to the top of her sex, circling a spot that made her body bend like a bow. One swipe of his fingers and she was shattering into a million pieces of light as her orgasm crested and broke.

A few short thrusts later, Rhystan followed her into bliss, a groan wrenching from his chest as he pulled from her body and spent his seed on the sheets between them. Sated and undone, Sarani exhaled, grateful that at least one of them had been thinking about the probability of conception.

Her heart gave a sad twinge. If circumstances had been different...he might have finished inside. Then, they would have cherished whatever came of their union. But those stars had never aligned and that future was not to be. They were merely lovers, not *in love*. They'd fucked, in his blunt words. They hadn't made love.

Love did not factor into anything between them. In the wake of such devastating pleasure, Sarani suddenly felt a beat of sorrow. She shook it off. She hadn't done it for love. There'd been very practical reasons, very rational reasons. Her virginity did not belong to the male sex to do with as they pleased. She'd wanted to experience carnal pleasure with a man she trusted with her body. And life was too short for regret.

Nothing to do with love whatsoever.

Twenty

IF HE COULD HAVE BOOTED THE MAN OUT ON HIS POMPOUS arse, Rhystan would have. Bloody fortune hunter. Viscount Marvelle was in debt up to his ears, and Rhystan had nearly laughed at the ludicrous offer of marriage for Ravenna.

How much is the chit's dowry? The duns are after me. I'll take her off your hands.

Marvelle was lucky he was leaving the residence with his legs in good working order. Rhystan wished he could say the same for his unraveling temper. He rubbed his temples. That was the sixth offer this week, all from known scoundrels. Titled gentlemen, but sodding wastrels. Once he'd reinstated Ravenna's considerable dowry, they'd come out of the woodwork.

Lord Belford, heir to a marquess, was a known gambler. Lord Penderton, an earl in his own right, was barely hanging on to his entailed estates. Mr. Lincoln Trent, son of a prominent barrister, had three by-blows living with him and was a known profligate. Rhystan respected the man's decision to acknowledge his progeny, but a man who fathered God knew how many children with different women was not the husband for his little sister.

None of them were sodding good enough.

Just like you.

The wayward thought struck him hard.

The truth was, who was he to talk? He'd ruined an innocent woman—a royal no less—because he needed to sate his lust. All because he wanted her. Rhystan raked a hand through his hair, stalking to the mantel where he poured himself a full tumbler of whisky.

"She consented," he muttered. "We both knew what we were doing."

Doesn't mean she wasn't innocent.

She'd been a virgin. Sarani had been so passionate, so responsive, but innate sensuality did not imply that she was experienced. Rhystan didn't know what he'd been expecting. She'd been engaged to Talbot for a few years. In hindsight, he'd made a stupid assumption. Sarani was *Sarani*.

Rhystan scowled. Hell, he was the worst kind of cad. Worse than Trent possibly.

He tipped up the whisky, feeling its contents burn a hot path to his stomach and waiting for the ease it would eventually bring. In the meantime, his thoughts remained on Sarani. In the aftermath, they'd lain together in his bed in a strange sort of comfortable quiet.

Neither of them had spoken until he'd risen to find a cloth, which he had used to wipe away the evidence of both her virginity and his prudence.

"Do you wish to return to Huntley House?" he'd asked. She'd stared at him, eyes unreadable, the barest flicker of something in them. Regret? Hurt? It had made his sudden awkward vulnerability become more acute. "Before it gets too late."

"I suppose I should return," she said, rising gracefully from the bed like the *apsara* he'd likened her to.

It'd been on the tip of his tongue to beg her to stay, but he'd held back. Once was enough. More than enough for them to get whatever it was between them out of their systems. Once would have to suffice. From then on out, abstinence would be in order.

As she'd dressed and retied her cloak, Sarani had glanced at the bed and then at the discarded cloth with pale-pink stains discoloring the pristine linen, her cheeks tinting. "Won't Harlowe…" She'd trailed off, embarrassed.

"I'll toss it in the grate. No one will know."

She'd nodded, pinning her lips. "Thank you."

Rhystan did not know how he'd had the presence of mind to withdraw, given his insensible state at the time, but she was inexperienced. He was not. Conception was not an outcome for either of them: him as a seafaring duke, her as an independent spinster. Their lives were meant to diverge at the end of their pact.

Sex did not change anything.

Until it does.

With a snarl at the logical voice in his head, he scrubbed a hand over his face, stopping himself from getting another drink. Whisky solved nothing.

"Your Grace?" Harlowe asked, knocking on the door to the study. "Her ladyship has sent a messenger inquiring whether you will attend the Van Dunne masquerade this evening."

Rhystan's eyes narrowed. "Which her ladyship? My sister, my mother, or my…or Lady Sara?"

"The second, Your Grace. She is adamant that she must receive a response."

Of course she was. Rhystan groaned. The last thing he needed was yet another ball, but a part of him knew he needed to come up with better suitors for his sister. And the truth was, he wanted to see Sarani again. In a safe place, surrounded by people, where he would not do anything untoward like drag her off to a deserted alcove to ravish her.

He'd done that already.

He truly was a dreadful excuse for a duke.

"Inform the duchess I will attend," he said.

Appearances had to be maintained. For Ravenna's sake, anyway.

Playing the wallflower on the fringes of the Van Dunne ball, Sarani did not feel any different. Not that she'd expected to—but she'd imagined that being ruined would feel somewhat salacious. That people would be able to see through the haze of immorality surrounding her.

Then again, she was wearing a mask. She huffed a laugh—not that the aristocracy didn't wear figurative masks every single day. Very few let their real selves be seen for fear of being hurt or ridiculed by their peers. For all their culture and confidence, fashion and fortunes, aristocrats were extraordinarily frail. Like almost everyone else, Sarani supposed.

Ravenna and Rhystan caught her eye as they twirled past. They made a stunning pair. Ravenna was radiant in a ball gown the colors of the sunset and a beautiful red-feathered mask, and Rhystan wore black. Without a mask. Sarani wondered if he'd done it to be contrary. Or perhaps he was one of those few who refused to hide who he was. She frowned, recalling his stony-faced demeanor in his bedchamber.

No, Rhystan's masks lay behind his eyes and appeared at will.

Few ever saw the real man.

"You won't have him, you know," a waspish voice taunted.

Sarani turned to see a lady in a buttercup-yellow gown with a Venetian-style mask hiding her identity, but those spiteful eyes were instantly recognizable. Lady Penelope, if Sarani were to hazard an educated guess. Given Sarani also wore a mask, she wondered how the woman had recognized her in the first place. Then again, she'd be standing with Ravenna, who was now dancing with her brother, the maskless duke. And from Penelope's tone, she'd been watching Sarani since their arrival.

She looked away. "Why is that?"

"You're a nobody," she said. "The dowager duchess won't stand for it. No one in the *ton* will stand for it."

"Good thing it's not up to her or anyone else," Sarani replied.

"You think you are above us, don't you?"

A bubble of laughter burned in Sarani's throat. It'd been quite some time since she'd felt above anyone. Practically her entire life, from childhood to adulthood, Sarani had felt as though she couldn't quite measure up, that something essential was missing that would elevate her…allow her to play with the other children, to marry a man who valued her, or to feel worthy of being loved. Even now, in pretense with Rhystan, she existed on the periphery. Good enough for some things. Not enough for others.

"All your airs and standoffishness," Penelope went on, "but secrets will always come out. Remember that, Lady Sara, when you look down your nose at the rest of us and covet that which does not belong to you."

"I did not covet anything that did not want to be coveted," Sarani said calmly, though the way Penelope had snarled "Lady" sent a wary shiver shooting up Sarani's spine. "And the duke is not a *that*, he's a *who*, and contrary to what you may think, he does have a mind of his own."

"No one denies me what is mine."

Sarani lifted her chin with as much haughtiness as she could muster. "Then it seems you've been rather spoiled, Lady Penelope. Please excuse me."

She strode away before the other woman could reply, her thoughts swirling. What had Lady Penelope meant by secrets having a way of coming out? If Sarani's biggest secret were to be exposed, the scandal would be unavoidable. Did Lady Penelope know something?

Sarani was so caught up in her own world that she nearly crashed into a small mountain. Or rather, a large duke.

"Your Grace, I beg your pardon," she murmured, her pulse already at war in her breast at his nearness. "I did not see you."

A pair of keen blue-gray eyes narrowed on her. "You are upset. Where were you running off to?"

She drew a strangled breath, though the sudden short supply of air had nothing to do with Penelope and everything to do with the man sucking the oxygen out of the room. Good gracious, why was the ballroom so bloody hot? Every hair on her body stood alarmingly on end, his very presence making her feel like she'd been touched by lightning.

"Nowhere. I just needed some air."

She swept past him to the narrow balcony beyond a pair of glass-paned French doors, acutely aware of what had happened last time they'd been on a terrace alone. But it was either that or faint. Thank goodness this one was well lit with no inviting alcoves to speak of. The duke followed, his huge frame propping against one marble column, and Sarani bit back a groan.

"What did Lady Penelope say to you?" he demanded.

Had he been watching her while dancing with Ravenna?

Sarani brought up her fan and stared at it before fanning herself vigorously. Dancing couples were beginning to stare at them whenever they twirled past the glass doors, not even hiding their interest. Rhystan was the sort of man who drew attention wherever he went, and she... Well, according to the scandal sheets, speculation was rife. The two of them arguing on a balcony would be too delicious for words.

"Nothing," Sarani said. "She was being her usual self."

"A brat?"

A puff of laughter escaped her lips. "Categorically."

"I've danced with several ladies of unimpeachable reputation, including Lady Pettigrew, who practically devoured me with her eyes, then with my sister, launching her off in the most respectable of ways, and now I wish to take a turn with you. Will you dance with me?"

Instant panic flooded her veins. Even standing an arm's length away from him, she was barely managing to restrain herself from dragging him to a deserted room, plastering her body to his, and begging him to ruin her again. She couldn't begin to imagine what feeling those large palms on her for the entirety of a dance would do. Already, she could feel the dampness between her legs and her nipples tightening in shameless arousal.

That would simply not do.

"I cannot, but thank you," she blurted out, bringing her fan up between them and fanning herself with brisk strokes.

He frowned at the lace device and then at her. "Why not?"

In response, her fan increased its speed, her brain failing to come up with an acceptable excuse that wasn't an outright lie. Her gaze fell on the elegant fan. "Did you know that there's a whole language to the lady's fan? For example, twirling it in one's left hand means we are being watched, which we are," she added for good measure. "Drawing it across one's eyes says 'I am sorry,' while resting it upon one's lips says the gentleman is not to be trusted."

A slow smile curved those very sinful lips as though he could see right through her. He leaned in, his next words low. "And fanning at such a speed means you are head over heels in love."

Both fingers and fan froze in midair, and then she snapped it shut.

"And snapping one's fan shut, dearest, means you're jealous." Rhystan grinned, his eyes sparkling with mischief. The playful look transformed his face, leaving her breathless at the glimpse of the boy she'd known. So he wasn't quite lost.

"No, it doesn't," she said and then frowned uncertainly. "Does it?"

"How should I know? I'm a man. We tend to say what we think."

Her eyes narrowed. "Unlike your sex, women have to communicate their desires in codes or be deemed indelicate and scandalous. It's all rather absurd, isn't it? That a woman should be afraid to speak her mind for fear of being shunned or ostracized and outraging high society."

"Absurd how?"

Gracious, he had a knack for riling her up. "That a female's opinion could create such world-destroying chaos."

"Women have been causing chaos since Eden."

Sarani snorted. "Good gracious, are you referring to the Bible?

How positively low you have sunk, Your Grace. At least base your arguments on something that wasn't written by a horde of ancient male historians."

"What of Darwin?" he asked.

"Well, we are discussing absurdity." She shook her head with disdain, warming to her subject and oblivious to their now avid audience in the ballroom, straining to hear their low but impassioned conversation. "The complexity of the human brain cannot possibly be determined by sex. My brain is no less effective than yours, and my parents proved that beyond the shade of a doubt with my unconventional education. Give us women a few decades, and chaos will be the least of what we can accomplish."

"I don't doubt that in the slightest, my lady."

Sarani searched his quiet reply for sarcasm, but there was none. She tapped her fan with a small grin. "We did invent an entire language around fans, after all."

A new voice cut between them.

"Tell me, my lady, regarding the language of fans, which I find mildly fascinating, what is the movement to say that one is engaged?"

Sarani turned, despite Rhystan's immediate glower and the impropriety of a strange gentleman interrupting their conversation, and felt the blood drain from her limbs. This particular gentleman did not require an introduction, because she knew him well, even with a half mask. She would never forget how her skin crawled whenever he looked at her, the way it did now.

An icy-cold sweat formed between her shoulder blades, dark spots threatening her vision as her legs shook beneath her dress. *No, no, no…* This could not be happening. But her memory was not playing tricks on her. The regent of Joor stood in this very ballroom, his familiar watery blue eyes swimming with anger and lust.

"Lord Talbot?" she whispered.

He bowed. "In the flesh. I've only recently discovered that my fiancée, whom I thought dead, is alive and has betrothed herself to another."

The weight of a thousand knives crashed down upon her. The depth of her predicament suddenly became clear. It wasn't Lord Talbot's return that struck fear into her heart. It was the fact that he knew who she was and who she was pretending to be.

He was judge, jury, and executioner.

"What do you want?" she asked.

"What I've been promised." His leer made her blood chill. "My bride."

Rhystan had not immediately recognized the masked man. Until Sarani had whispered his name, he'd been at a loss. He fought the urge to slam his fist into the earl's face. The fury coursing through him was impossible to control, the man's lecherous stare and the idea that he had any prior claim on her making him see red. Around them, people had stopped dancing and were colliding with one another in an effort to eavesdrop.

"The lady is spoken for," he gritted out.

"Why, Commander Huntley, no longer a boy, eh?" Talbot sneered. "And still chasing after these skirts, I see."

Rhystan's lips pulled back from his teeth in a smile that no sane person would mistake for friendly. "You will address me with the proper respect, Talbot. I am the Duke of Embry."

"Apologies, Duke. I've only just returned to England."

Rhystan knew without a doubt that the earl would have been aware of his altered circumstances after his father's death. The tragedy had been the news of London for months. The false ignorance was a deliberate slight, that Talbot still saw him as that weak, green lad of an officer. Well, he wasn't that boy anymore, nor was he the normal kind of duke.

He let his rage show in his eyes. "Walk. Away."

The earl's eyes widened. "What?"

"Do you really wish for me to elucidate?" His voice lowered to a snarl. "Walk the hell away, Talbot."

"Please, Your Grace," Sarani whispered, touching his sleeve. "Don't make a scene, for Ravenna's sake, if not mine. It's what he wants."

"Always so clever," Talbot said, his eyes pinning her. "We looked for you, you know, after your father's body was discovered. Such a pity." His sly tone indicated it was anything but, and Rhystan felt Sarani stiffen beside him. "It was speculated that you'd been taken, but the new maharaja insisted you were dead."

"The new maharaja," Sarani echoed.

"Your cousin Vikram." He rolled his eyes and gave a theatrical sigh. "Though who knows with you natives and your falsifying of heirs willy-nilly to keep it in the family." His voice lowered. "Then again, he isn't precisely the actual heir, is he, Princess Sarani?"

Sarani gasped, her eyes darting to the ballroom where people were craning their necks without shame, and she took a step closer to Rhystan without realizing it. He wanted to comfort her, reassure her that they could not hear, but he did not move a muscle, his stare narrowing on Talbot. He opened his mouth but Sarani spoke first.

"Why are you here, Lord Talbot?"

"Vice Admiral Markham… You remember your superior officer, don't you, Your Grace?" Talbot said. "Shall we say that I received the most interesting piece of correspondence requiring my immediate presence in London."

Rhystan's fists clenched at the mention of both Markham and a letter. The story of his life was apparently repeating itself. This time, he knew that the culprit had to be his own meddlesome mother. Who else would make those connections between the present and his past? He would wring her interfering neck. Right after he dealt with this conniving piece of shit.

The earl went on, oblivious to his impending fate. "It inquired about an English lady, but strangely enough, including a locket with a miniature resembling"—his calculating gaze slid to Sarani—"none other than you."

"A miniature?" Rhystan's heart pounded, remembering the robbery at his residence. The thief must have been commissioned to seek out only the locket.

But why? For what purpose? His gaze slid to Sarani's ashen countenance.

Unless someone *was* already here...looking for her.

Twenty-One

"I WISH TO LEAVE," SARANI SAID TO NO ONE IN PARTICULAR.

Her brain spun with a noxious concoction of fear, dread, and powerless rage. Who could have written to Markham? There was only one answer, truly. Rhystan's mother had the only motivation. She could not have wanted to be rid of Sarani so badly, could she?

Of course she could. The dowager duchess was ruthless, especially when it came to what she felt was best for her children. Sarani had seen that same protectiveness with Ravenna, though the duchess hid it behind a facade of detachment. She loved her children, but she had a strange way of showing it. But perhaps that was the English way of things.

Despite her roiling emotions and the nausea pooling in the pit of her stomach, Sarani did not blame the duchess. The past would have caught up to her sooner or later.

Right now, she needed to get away from Talbot, from Markham—that odious, bigoted brute had to be here somewhere—before she did something unforgiveable. Her kukri were burning a hole in their sheaths against her legs. She only had to slip her trembling fingers through the concealed slits at her hips, and they would be in her palms.

Not that she intended to murder a man in the middle of Mayfair.

She just needed not to feel powerless.

Sarani jutted her jaw, using the very people who had been staring unabashedly all evening. "Let me pass, Lord Talbot, or I swear to everything holy that you will regret it." She shot the earl a scathing glance. "Unless you don't give a fig for your reputation, that is, because I have no qualms making a scene to end all scenes."

"Wait." Rhystan's voice reached her, but she could not look at him now, or she would fall into his arms. And she needed to be strong. For herself.

Holding her head high, she swept past the curious onlookers toward the exit. She would call for a hackney if she had to. Her gaze scanned the crowd for Ravenna as she made her way over to the entrance salon to retrieve her cloak, but there was no sign of her. She glanced briefly at the duchess, who, like her son, had not deigned to wear a mask and whose face remained impassive. Then again, the untouchable dowager duchess would never lower herself to show emotion in public.

A body cut into Sarani's path, halting her progress.

"I told you," Penelope spit out viciously.

Sarani grimaced, stifling the urge to shove the girl aside. "Told me what?"

"That you would never have him," she said triumphantly. "Not when you were already engaged. Gracious, you do get around, don't you? Setting your sights on an earl, then a duke. Who's next, Prince Alfred? I'm glad I took the initiative to write that letter."

Her pretty face was marred with spite, but Sarani's brain was spinning at the boast. *Penelope* had written to Markham? How on earth had she made that connection? Or known about Rhystan's locket? But as quickly as she asked the question, she knew the answer.

It had to have been Ravenna, not knowing what Penelope would do, of course. Sarani had learned about the locket's existence from Ravenna as well, and come to think of it, she had mentioned saying something to Penelope herself. If one had the connections, which the Duke of Windmere, Penelope's father, would have, as well as the stolen miniature, getting information about Rhystan's former commission would have been easy.

Penelope let out an ugly laugh. "Such aspiration, Lady Sara, though one wonders whether you are even a lady at all."

"What are you talking about?"

Penelope winked and whispered, "I heard you're a bastard that poor Lady Lisbeth didn't even know who your father was."

Sarani truly didn't want to sink to her level, but she saw red. Tears smarted at the backs of her eyes. She was sick of being treated with such scorn. She let a slow, cold smile form on her lips and lifted a brow. "Why, you should know all about that, shouldn't you, Penelope?" The girl went pale, but Sarani didn't relent despite the sourness pooling in her belly. "Being born on the wrong side of the blanket, I mean."

"I..."

Sarani took a page from Rhystan's book. "Walk away, Penelope, before we both say something regrettable."

To Sarani's surprise, the girl did, hurtling backward like she couldn't get away fast enough. That was the thing about bullies—they did not like it much when the boot was on the other foot. Penelope might have been casting stones at Sarani's origins, but she'd forgotten about her own.

Sarani retrieved her cloak and was about to leave when she was stopped again. "Oh, for heaven's sake," she muttered. "How hard is it to leave this place?"

"Currying favor with your betters, I see," a voice sneered.

Vice Admiral Markham's bulk took up her vision in the foyer. Her eyes widened. Sarani would not have recognized him if not for the voice. Unlike Talbot, who had not changed in five years, Markham seemed rather worse for wear—he'd put on a stone or two and he looked like he had a rampant case of gout. He did not wear a uniform but was dressed in rumpled evening clothes that had seen better days. Her nose wrinkled. He also smelled like the inside of a chamber pot.

"Please excuse me," she said, unwilling to trade greetings with a man who had treated her like filth on the sole of his shoe.

"Leaving so soon?" he asked. "I shall have to find your betrothed, then. One of them, at least." He laughed as though he'd made the wittiest of jokes. "If Talbot had his preference, he would have swum here the minute I showed him that letter. Devil knows what he sees in you. But I'll tell you what I see." He swayed slightly. "Opportunity."

Sarani had had enough of men seeing her as a piece to be played at their whims—whether it was for money or her fortune or her body. Gritting her teeth, she hiked her skirts, darted past him, and fled down the stairs to the crowded streets. It wasn't that much of a walk to Huntley House—a few blocks at most. No one out here would harm her. The true danger was behind her in that ballroom, not on the streets of Mayfair.

Besides, she had her kukri and she had her wits. A brisk walk would clear her head. On her way past the line of stationary, luxurious coaches, she glimpsed a familiar face on the back of one of them, talking avidly to one of the coachmen.

"Tej!" she cried. "What are you doing here?"

Dressed in fancy livery, the boy smiled and sketched an elegant bow. "I was bored with my lessons so I'm pretending to be a tiger for His Grace this evening. Don't I look dapper?"

"You do." It was true. Tej looked happy and well fed, his small face glowing with health. The endearing plumpness of his cheeks made his young age even more apparent. "What kind of lessons?"

"Maths and reading." He wrinkled his nose in distaste. "I'm to start a fancy school soon as the duke's ward."

Sarani blinked her shock. "As the duke's *what*?"

"His ward. Like his charge. He says if I want to stay, I can. I just have to be willing to learn and make something of myself when I get older. He says I can apprentice to Mr. Longacre if I want." He screwed up his face. "He adores maths."

Unexpected warmth filtered through her chest. Rhystan was paying to send Tej to school? The boy was whip-smart, and Sarani had planned to do the same once she got settled, but things had been muddled of late. And now with Talbot and Markham in town, who knew what the future would entail?

Tej grinned. "May I offer you a ride, Princess?"

She could not deny him, not when he'd asked so prettily, his adorable face bright with childish enthusiasm. "Why, of course, gallant sir. Lead me to your chariot."

Rhystan stared at the calling card presented to him by his butler. What the hell did the disgraced Vice Admiral Markham want with him? He'd been caught corralling private wealth and had faced a court-martial that had had him cashiered and dismissed with disgrace. The bit of business he'd gotten into with illegal shipments of opium had been his end. That the man expected an audience now was entirely laughable.

In any other circumstance, Rhystan would have set the bastard out on his heels with a few choice words, but with Sarani's reputation hanging in the balance, he hesitated. A duke of his station was unassailable...but Markham knew exactly who Sarani was. As did Talbot.

The earl could be dealt with—Talbot was a coward at heart. Markham, however, was a political strategist who had gotten the maharaja's ear and been the right arm of the British Crown in Joor for years. Rhystan frowned. What was he doing here?

"Show him in," he said to Morton. "But make him cool his heels for a bit."

"As you wish, Your Grace."

Briefly, Rhystan's thoughts strayed to Sarani, who, his coachman had informed him, had been returned safely to Huntley House last night. He'd been prevented from chasing her by his sister, who demanded to know what he'd done to upset her, and then the duchess, who had had the gall to stare at him as if he'd done something unforgivable. By the time he'd arrived outside, his coach had just been returning, and instead of going back inside, he'd elected to go home.

His instructions followed to the letter, a quarter of an hour went by before the vice admiral was shown into the study. Rhystan collected his thoughts, trying to figure out the man's angle. He had to have one. They were not allies. In fact, Rhystan considered the man an enemy. But the timing of both Talbot's and Markham's arrivals in London stank of conspiracy.

"Markham," he said, not looking up from the papers on his desk. "Feel free to sit."

"Your Grace," the vice admiral said, settling himself into a chair opposite. "Your father's death was a loss to England."

"Thank you." Rhystan looked up, hiding his shock at the man's dissipated appearance. The years had not been kind. And fortune, too, he supposed. Not that he gave a whit. Markham could rot for all he cared. "What do you want?" he asked brusquely, dispensing with any pretense of pleasantries.

Markham's eyes narrowed. Despite his circumstances, shrewd intelligence glinted in that hawk-eyed gaze. "Money."

"I'm not a charity, Markham."

"This is not a charitable contribution," he said. "Consider it an…investment. Say in a future partner on the seas."

Brows high, Rhystan sat back in his seat and pretended ignorance. "You're in shipping?"

"A man has to eat."

Rhystan recognized that the words were those of a bitter man…a man who'd had his pride stripped and everything he valued taken away from him. Rhystan felt regret that it hadn't been him to be the one to punish the vile man. He would have relished seeing the pompous prick on his knees. Then again, wasn't he on his knees now? Begging for coin?

"I do not require partners for my fleet, and if I did, you would be the last man I would consider."

"Still holding grudges, eh?" His eyes panned to the mantel where an array of decanters and bottles stood. He licked his lips. "Won't you offer me a drink, Duke?"

"No." Rhystan clenched his jaw. "I do not consider it a grudge when I was stripped of all dignity, beaten to within an inch of my life, trussed, and tossed on a cart. The answer to your proposal is no. Now, get out."

"I took it upon myself to do you a favor," Markham spat out. "You needed to be taught a lesson. Fawning like a green lad over a gutter-blooded chit."

The slur to Sarani made his blood boil, but Rhystan stilled. "You took it upon yourself?"

Markham froze like a rabbit catching sight of a fox. "I wrote your father because I had to make an example of you. For the other men. And her, too; she had to know her place."

Rhystan's eyes narrowed, a thought striking him. "Did you mail my letters to the duke?"

The man had the decency to flush, though his eyes glittered with hateful defiance. "The ones complaining about the treatment of the locals and the unfairness of the treaties?" He guffawed before sneering. "No. I put those in the fire where they belonged."

Rhystan blinked. He could not control the flood of rage that saturated his veins, nor his sudden desire to pummel this man into the ground. "Did Embry tell you to discharge me or did you do that on your own?"

"The duke would have wanted the same even if he did not say so in his summons. I know your father, and he would not have stood for you sullying his good name with a native."

"Careful, Markham," he warned.

"Why?" the viscount asked. "Because she's your toffer now?"

Rhystan half rose out of his chair, his entire body bracing with fury at the audacity of the man. "Get the fuck out."

"Such foul temper, Your Grace." Markham grinned. "I see I've touched a nerve. In any case, Princess Sarani is the subject of our negotiation. You settle a healthy sum upon me, and in return, I'll take Talbot away and prevent him from pursuing her—and you— for breach of promise."

"Are you threatening me?" Rhystan asked in a silky voice.

Markham shook his head. "Only if you consider it that way. Think of it as incentive. I'm a businessman now, Your Grace."

An underhanded businessman if he was resorting to extortion, not that that was any change from what he'd been charged with or his unscrupulous dealings in the opium trade. Rhystan's eyes narrowed on the former vice admiral's stained coat and the pallor of his skin. He refused to be intimated by anyone, and yet he could not put his family or Sarani into such a position.

"And if I refuse?"

"Then the *Times* and the *ton* will have a lovely new scandal to froth over." Markham rose but dug into his pocket for a crumpled slip of paper. "That number will be sufficient for now. I'll give you a day or two to secure the funds, but make no mistake, Duke, a scandal will ensue if you don't comply."

Rhystan didn't deign to look at the paper lying between them on the desk. "What makes you think I won't have you thrown on a convoy bound for the Americas the minute you walk out of here?"

Markham tutted, his face smug. "Because I have taken measures to ensure my safety. A message with strict instructions to be delivered to the *Times* if I am not heard from within short order. Good day, Your Grace. I look forward to a lucrative business relationship."

After the piece of filth left, Rhystan clenched his fists, resisting the ferocious urge to flip the desk over. Calm, he needed to be calm. And he needed to think. There was no way he was going to pay a fortune—he glanced at the obscene number written on the paper. Blackmailers like Markham did not go away.

"Morton," he called out and wrote out two quick notes on pieces of parchment.

"Yes, Your Grace?" the butler asked.

"See that these get to Mr. Longacre and Gideon Ridley down at the Green Stag on the north bank of the Thames at once." He paused, eyes narrowing on his butler. Servants were excellent sources of information. "I need to know everything there is to know on that man who was just here, Markham. Any and every detail about his dismissal. Pay who you have to."

"Of course, Your Grace."

"And call for my carriage," he added. A little reconnaissance at his club wouldn't hurt.

———————

"How on earth anyone can imagine that using this racquet to hit a shuttlecock over a patch of lawn while sweating one's thighs off underneath all these layers is entertaining is utterly beyond me." Ravenna collapsed on the bench beside Sarani, her face flushed with exertion. She gulped down a glass of cool lemonade.

"Battledore and shuttlecock is wonderful exercise," Sarani said, lifting a brow after Ravenna's rather indelicate burp. It was a good thing that Asha was their chaperone, though they did not really need one in the privacy of their gardens. She had heard much worse from her own mistress, especially when she and Tej used to have contests to see who could belch the longest.

"Saying that word is unseemly, Ravenna," Clara, Ravenna's bosom friend, chided, walking over with her own racquet in hand after retrieving the feathered cork that had been trapped in a bush.

"Cock?" Ravenna asked. "Sara said it, too."

Clara blushed and then clapped a hand to her mouth. "No, the women's body part, and Lady Sara said *shuttlecock*, which is entirely different, as you well know."

Ravenna grinned. "Don't be a prude for Sara's sake. Besides, how is 'thighs' beyond the pale? Sara's been teaching me much worse words she learned on my brother's ship. She's one of us, truly."

Clara looked uncertain, and Sarani almost laughed. With friends like Penelope, no wonder the girl wasn't sure whether she would be summarily shunned for not exercising proper decorum.

"The East India Company officers in India used to call the game poona."

Clara plopped down beside them in a flurry of muslin skirts, eyes widening with interest. "What was it like? Living there?"

"Hot," Sarani said with a laugh, fanning herself. "But a different kind of heat than here. There were the same rules for the nobility in court of course—dresses, petticoats, and the like." She speared a glance at Ravenna, who was listening intently. Sarani was grateful that the girl had been true to her word and not mentioned her other royal half. "But in the villages, it was so vibrant. The women wore draped garments of woven silk and cotton in so many colors." She lowered her voice. "Some of them did not wear undergarments beneath the wrap. At least until English concepts of modesty demanded that they wear a blouse called a *choli*."

Ravenna's and Clara's eyes went wide, and then they both collapsed into giggles. "God, what I wouldn't give not to wear a corset!" Ravenna said. "Sounds divine!"

Ravenna glanced at Asha, who was sitting quietly nearby. "Do you have any of these types of wraps?"

The maid froze, eyes darting to her mistress, but Sarani grinned. "I might have saved one or two. Shall we dress you in one, then?"

Both girls squealed with delight. "Oh, yes, please!"

"Just don't let the duchess know or she will likely say that I'm corrupting you with my heathen ways."

They laughed again, and then Clara's eyes goggled as her laughter turned into awkward spluttering, her face going nearly puce while she fought for breath. The reason for her choking was quickly apparent as the duke strode down the garden path toward them.

As always, Sarani's chest squeezed at the sight of him. She had no idea how a man became more handsome with every passing day, but he did. Today he wore a navy coat that hugged his broad shoulders, a silver-stitched waistcoat, and gray striped trousers. His hair was windblown and his cheeks flushed as though he'd just been out on a bracing ride. He looked downright edible. Sarani flushed at her unruly thoughts and ducked her head.

Too late—Ravenna was already staring at her and grinning. "You're besotted with my brother, admit it!"

"I am not."

"You are, too. You went all calf-eyed the minute you saw him."

Sarani blushed. "You are being silly."

"Silly but right."

But the duke was already upon them before she could form a reply. Sarani's breath caught, her senses running amok as he came to a stop, bowing to them, those forceful eyes falling upon her like a tangible caress. "Ladies. No, no, please don't get up."

"Your Grace," Clara squeaked, while Sarani murmured the same.

"Brother, dearest, to what do we owe the pleasure?" Ravenna squinted up at her brother. "Do hurry up. You're interrupting a rather fabulous conversation about fashion. Sara's going to let us try on some of her clothing from India."

The duke's gaze fastened to her, and Sarani fought to keep from squirming. The last time he'd seen her wear anything like a sari had been at the river, and that garment had been partially transparent even over a chemise. She seemed to recall him clutching his coat to his lap as if he'd die without it, and at the time, she'd been confused. Now that they'd been intimate, she knew exactly what it signified.

Her face warmed. "It's all in good fun, Your Grace, I assure you."

Rhystan opened his mouth and shut it as if he, too, was reliving the same memory. Sarani closed her eyes to avoid looking at his groin. Because *that* would be unseemly.

"I need to speak with you," he said. "Alone."

Grinning widely, Ravenna bit her lip as though she had something to say, but at the sharp look on her brother's face, she curbed her tongue and grabbed Clara's hand. "Don't mind us, we'll be just over here, hitting feathered bits of cork and sweating like piglets."

Sarani bit back a laugh before standing to join Rhystan a few steps away. "What do you wish to speak to me about?"

"Markham has demanded money."

She faltered. She hadn't expected that. "How much?"

"An exorbitant amount," he said, raking a large hand through his hair in a frustrated motion that would account for how messy it'd looked earlier. "I've just come from my club. Markham was stripped of his property by Lord Canning himself and discharged with disgrace. He was accused of conduct unbecoming an officer under court-martial and found guilty by the viceroy for levying his own taxes on the locals and running a smuggling ring."

"Good heavens," Sarani whispered.

"He has a mountain of debt, which means he's desperate—at least enough to threaten a peer with extortion."

"Will you pay him?"

"No," Rhystan said, causing her heart to tumble to her feet. "Scum like him can't be stopped. He'll just keep coming back for more." He paused, seeing the distressed expression on her face. "Do you trust me, Sarani?"

They were the same words he'd said to her a lifetime ago in Joor.

Sarani stared at him, seeing nothing but sincerity in those steel-blue eyes. She sucked in a breath, searching them. He held her fate in his palm.

"I do."

Twenty-Two

THE FIRST PART OF HIS PLAN REQUIRED A BIT OF STALLING ON Rhystan's part. He accomplished that by having Longacre deliver an official letter from the bank to Markham's rented apartments, stating that the requested funds would take some time to gather. A week was the best he could stretch it to without making the man suspicious, but he was leaning on the fact that the disgraced vice admiral needed the money.

The second part required more finesse. Finesse because Rhystan wanted nothing more than to beat the man to a bloody pulp for daring to blackmail him. But he needed something on Markham—something that would make the bastard sweat. In the meantime, he'd directed Longacre to pay off Markham's creditors and consolidate his debt.

From what Gideon had dug up, the man had a reputation for being a swindler, and he had a number of enemies. Someone would want his pound of flesh, and Rhystan was prepared to supply it. Unless, of course, Markham agreed to stand down. The duke would deal with Talbot summarily, too, but that was for later.

An eye for a fucking eye.

He stared at Sarani, who had insisted on joining him at the Green Stag where he was meeting Gideon for an update on Markham's enemies. She caught his look across the wooden table and sent him a jaunty grin over her mug of ale.

Once more, she was dressed as a young man, in a pair of trousers, a tweed coat, a plain waistcoat, and a cap. All her glorious dark hair was tucked neatly away. She'd taken a kohl pencil to her upper lip to sketch in a thin mustache. It would fail any close inspection but passed muster at first glance, though the black shading did call attention to her indecently full lips. They were currently moist and glazed from the last sip of her ale. Which made him want to lick it off her.

Not the time and place, clearly.

Rhystan studied the woman in front of him. God, he wished they were back on the *Belonging*. He wanted to see the hint of those freckles across her nose pop in the sun, see that jet-black hair loosened and wild, watch her be unencumbered and happy and not have to answer to anyone but herself.

The rarest ruby among prosaic diamonds.

Everything about her sang to him. Her beauty, her wit, her sense of justice as well as mischief. As evident from the current sparkle in her eye, it was obvious that she loved the subterfuge. Or perhaps it was the feeling that being back near the docks brought. He had to admit, he felt the same, as though a garrote around his neck had been loosened.

"Where did you get the togs?" he asked.

"Borrowed them from Tej," she replied with a wink. "We're the same size, now that he's filled out a bit." She paused, observing him. "He told me that you were sending him to school."

"He deserves an education."

She stared into her mug. "Even for a humble houseboy?"

He gave a shrug. "Tej is smart. I'd rather not let a perfectly good mind go to waste. And besides, when he does take up a trade and becomes the best at what he does, I can hire him. So it's all in my own best interest."

The way she was looking at him was worth everything. She stared at him as though he'd gifted her the stars and the moon, her green-gold eyes limpid with gratitude and affection.

"It's a small thing," he said.

She shook her head. "It's no small thing! You've changed his life. You've given him an opportunity to make something of himself." She drew in a soft breath. "It means so much. I don't know what to say."

"You don't have to say anything. I did it for you."

Her eyes glittered. "Rhystan."

Sod it. He stood, nearly knocking over the chair in his haste. He wanted to yank her into his arms and throw her over his shoulder, but instead he gave a rough jerk of his head for her to follow him. Biting her lip in a way that made him harder than he already was, she nodded. He practically limped down the corridor leading to a backstreet.

Rhystan waited just inside the door, near what looked like a storeroom, his heart pounding a staccato in his chest until she walked by, the scent of her like a red rag to a turkey-cock. He hauled her to him and pressed her into the nook, filling his palms with her luscious bottom. He kicked the wooden slat shut behind them.

"Hell, Sarani, these trousers," he whispered, nuzzling into her fragrant neck. "They're criminal on your legs. On this arse."

"You like them?" she panted, arms going around his neck as she rubbed her body against his. It gratified him to see that the near-painful state of arousal was mutual.

"I like you in them."

With a moan, she kissed him, shoving up to her tiptoes and dragging her open mouth across his. He felt the swipe of her tongue and then the wicked nip of her teeth on his lower lip. He groaned at the bite of pain, pleasure following in its wake. And then it was a mass of lips, teeth, and tongues as they devoured each other, uncaring of the tiny room or the fact that they could be discovered at any moment.

"What are you doing to me?" he growled, one hand tugging her shirt out and slipping up inside to her warm skin.

Her breasts were bound with linen, but he still rubbed over her hardened nipples, pinching them lightly. He swallowed her moans with his mouth, his hand going to her falls. *Blast these buttons!* He tore them from their moorings, shoving them down to cup her sex with his palm.

"Bloody hell, you're soaked." His cock was hard enough to hammer steel. "I want you so badly."

"Yes," she gasped, her tongue sucking his, her own fingers tugging at his hair. "Now, please."

Rhystan didn't hesitate. He unbuttoned his own fly—not falls, thank his ingenious tailor—pulled his weeping cock out, lifted her up, and drove himself to the hilt. She was so wet that he glided in snugly, though she gasped at the intrusion and he groaned at the tightness.

"Rhystan," she said breathlessly.

He kissed her harder. "I love hearing my name on your lips."

She clenched her muscles, hooking her knees over his hips, hardly able to do more, impaled as she was on him. "Enough prevaricating, Your Grace. Hurry up and take me before someone barges in here."

God, this woman.

Rhystan did just that, grabbing handfuls of those perfect hips and driving into her. Sarani held on for dear life, arms winding around his neck. The position of her split legs wrapped around him made her gasp every time their bodies ground together, and soon, she was panting, her desire spiraling to the precipice.

"Rhystan!" she cried.

She bit his shoulder hard as her body convulsed around him, the undulation setting off his own release as he groaned and yanked himself from her. Supporting her limp body with one arm, he finished in his fist, barely able to keep them both upright.

"That was…" He couldn't even speak.

"Outstanding."

He couldn't have agreed more. There weren't many ladies who

would have been up for an impromptu tiff in a cobwebbed public nook in a tavern, but she had been as amorous as he. Smiling foolishly, they put themselves to rights, cleaning up with a handkerchief, tucking in shirttails, and buttoning up trousers. In all the passion, her braid had unraveled and unpinned from its moorings, so he helped her secure the silky mass.

"I've never felt hair like yours," he said, lifting a fragrant handful to his nose and inhaling deeply. The scent of jasmine invaded his senses.

"It's just hair," she replied self-consciously.

"Not yours. It's like liquid silk through my fingers." He deftly rebraided the sleek skeins into a thick braid, catching her astonished look. "I have a younger sister who forced me to comb her hair when we were little."

"Forced you?" Sarani asked grinning.

"Have you met Ravenna?" He sighed and expertly pinned her hair to her scalp, taking care not to scrape her skin before fixing the cap back in place. "The little hellion had me learn all the fashionable girls' styles one summer in the country when her maid quit because of newts in her bedclothes. Mother said that she would have to do without a maid since she chased Hettie away with her infernal pranks."

Sarani laughed, her eyes twinkling. "Ravenna is my kind of girl."

"She likes you, too."

He pulled her back by the arm, wiping away the remnants of her smudged mustache with his thumb. Her lips were swollen, plump, and dusky red. He couldn't resist kissing her one last time before they made their way back out to the main hall of the tavern.

Gideon, who was waiting, took one look at them and his brows shot upward. Sarani's cheeks flamed, but Rhystan couldn't help puffing his chest slightly. "Not a word," he told his friend.

"Wasn't going to say anything," the quartermaster drawled. "Good to see you looking so hale, Princess."

Her blush intensified. "And you, Gideon."

They resumed their seats, and Rhystan ordered a new round of drinks before looking expectantly to his quartermaster. "Find anything?"

"Yes. Finn Driscoll lost a fortune with him when Markham claimed the ships containing his cargo were sunk at sea. But rumor is Markham stripped the ships himself."

Rhystan had heard of Finn Driscoll. The Irish captain was as ruthless as he was cruel. "Good. Arrange a meeting. The quicker we muzzle Markham, the safer Sarani and my family will be."

He felt Sarani glance at him, and he felt a swift rush of guilt. He didn't make the rules of the beau monde, but the scandal if the truth got out would also hurt them, simply by association.

Like his mother, he would do what was necessary to protect his family name.

The hour was late. Sarani had excused herself from the musicale that evening, citing a megrim and retiring to her room, but she'd really just needed to think. Something Rhystan had said earlier in the tavern kept niggling at her—that he had to keep his family safe as well. While helping her had been part of their bargain, she hadn't really thought of the other consequences.

Like what being linked to her would do to Ravenna. Or even the duchess.

These aristocrats did not like their social laws bent, unless they were doing the bending. And she, by virtue of her mixed blood, was not one of them. There was only one thing for it: she had to leave for their sakes. Sarani's heart constricted. Tej would have to stay behind. She would not rob him of such a bright future. To Asha, she would give the choice.

A crashing noise from downstairs made her fly up from the armchair in her bedchamber. That had sounded like breaking glass.

Flashes of the glass she'd seen on the terrace of her own palace in Joor filled her mind. No, no, it was simply a servant dropping a goblet or a wineglass. But she couldn't shake the feeling that something was amiss. Snatching a shawl, she threw it over her shoulders and peeked outside. Her kukri were both strapped to her thighs in their usual sheaths—she hadn't yet disrobed for bed.

It was late, so only a single lamp burned in the corridor. As far as she knew, the dowager duchess and Ravenna had yet to return from the musicale. The hairs on her nape lifted as she crept down the dimly lit staircase. Her nerves coiled, tension filling her veins when hushed voices reached her ears. It had to be the servants, but she would check to make sure, just for peace of mind.

On soundless feet, she rounded the corner to the kitchen, which was also deserted. The dowager must have returned then—no servant would withdraw before she had. Peering into each of the rooms she passed and noting each one empty with no visible sign of broken glass, Sarani halted when low voices trailed from the vicinity of the drawing room.

She frowned and then picked up the pace as Her Grace's imperious voice cut through the silence. "What do you want?" she asked.

Sarani whirled, but the dowager duchess wasn't addressing her. Flanked by two footmen, she stood outlined by the glow of the light coming from the drawing room, still dressed for the evening. Someone replied, but Sarani could not make out the words.

"I've sent for the police," she said calmly. "If you don't want any trouble, then why have you broken in?"

Sarani inched forward, her blood chilling as the reply came. "I want only the princess."

"The who?" the dowager duchess asked.

"Princess Sarani Rao. Her cousin would like to have a word with her."

Everything in Sarani's body froze. Vikram had found her, and she had no doubt that the only words he meant to have would be at the point of a pistol or edge of a blade. But she could not allow the dowager or, heaven forbid, Ravenna to get caught in the cross-hairs of her cousin's quarrel with her. Sarani had only to hold off the uninvited guests until the police arrived.

"What's all the hubbub?" Ravenna asked, approaching from the opposite end of the foyer and peering into the room. "Who are you?"

Fear flicked across the older woman's face as she gestured for one of the footmen to safeguard her daughter. Sarani sucked in a deep breath, ready to announce her presence, when the dowager angled her head to look directly at her. Sarani could feel the panicked blast from those irises where she stood. Closing the distance between them, she opened her mouth to tell both of them that everything would be well, when an odd expression crossed the duchess's face. Shame? Dread? Both?

"She's here," the dowager duchess said.

"Mama," Ravenna cried as understanding flashed in her copper eyes. "What are you doing?"

The duchess firmed her lips. "Protecting this family."

"Sara *is* family," Ravenna said, yanking on the footman's grip. "Let me go, you lout!"

"She has brought this trouble to our doorstep."

"You can't just hand her over," Ravenna protested. "He'll hurt her."

"I'll do anything to keep you safe."

"*Mother*!" Ravenna screamed. "Stop this!"

Shaking her head, the duchess let out a ragged gasp. "I've already lost a husband and two sons. I will not lose you as well. I will protect you at any cost, even if it means you hate me for it."

"Please, Mama." Ravenna resorted to begging. "Rhystan will hate you for this, too."

"I will have to take that chance," the dowager replied.

Deep down, Sarani understood the protective instinct that was driving the dowager, but the justification didn't help much. Gritting her teeth, Sarani slid her hands into the false pockets sewn into her gown, reassuring herself that her blades were there and ready. A short, wiry man came into view then, one whom Sarani did not recognize. Though why would she? If he was Vikram's assassin, she wouldn't know him.

"Who are you?" she asked.

"I want only to talk," the man said.

She huffed a breath. "Is that why you've been following me? Did you murder my father?"

The gasps from the other end of the foyer were loud.

"No," he said, but Sarani was sure he was lying. He'd been paid to assassinate both of them, and he was here to finish the job. She had to think! This man would kill without blinking.

Suddenly, Ravenna broke free of the footman's hold and rushed forward, hurtling into the unsuspecting man. "Run, Sara!"

The duchess's scream was the only warning before the man spun and grabbed Ravenna by the hair, putting her under a deadly looking blade. Sarani's heart slammed into her throat as Ravenna's fearful eyes met hers.

"No one move," the assassin snarled to the duchess. "Tell them to stay back, or I'll slit her throat."

The dowager duchess let out a keening cry and lifted a hand, waving back the footmen and stalling the other servants who had been drawn to the noise. "Please…don't harm her."

Sarani growled. "She is the daughter of a duke and the sister of one, you fool. Spill one drop of her blood, and the entire might of the British Crown will be on your employer's head," she said, walking forward with slow, measured steps. "Trust me, Vikram does not want that kind of attention or retaliation."

The man's eyes narrowed. Sarani considered her options. She couldn't run, not without leaving Ravenna exposed. And who knew where the police were or if the duchess had had the wisdom to summon her son at the same time.

"I'll go with you," she said. "Just let her go."

"Sara, no!" Ravenna cried.

She nodded, hands wide, easing forward. "Yes. I couldn't forgive myself if anything happened to you because of me. Your mother is right. I brought this to your doorstep. It's my problem." Her gaze met the man's, and she reached out a hand. "Me for her. I'm the one you're here for. Do we have an agreement?"

Without hesitating, he shoved Ravenna to the side, and she scrambled away. Exhaling unhurriedly, Sarani braced herself and let her energy flow from her center as her weapons master had taught her. She would have seconds, if that, to extricate herself. From the look in his eyes, he intended to finish the business right here. Unlike Ravenna, she did not have a powerful duke on her side, and she doubted that any of these footmen would come to her aid.

The moment his fingers closed around her wrist, she moved, twisting one arm down and reaching into the slit in her gown with the other. One would think that her fingers would get tangled, but she'd practiced for hours until the act of getting the hilt in hand was second nature. She sliced her blade across his chest, leaving red in its wake, and leaped back at the same time.

"Get Her Grace and Lady Ravenna out of here!" she shouted to the gaping footmen.

As if they'd been in a trance watching her, they jolted into action. She didn't take her eyes off the assassin who had brought up a second razor-edged blade to his bleeding chest. She retrieved her second kukri from its sheath. They circled each other like predators in the water.

"That was devious," he said.

She scowled. "You expect me to offer you my neck meekly?"

"Your cousin wants to talk."

"And I'm the queen of England."

Snarling, he lunged forward, one blade coming precariously close to her shoulder as she shifted her weight onto her heels and brought up her left arm to block the blow. Within seconds, their blades spun and crashed, the noise echoing in the now-empty foyer. The man was skilled. Then again, if he was the man who had murdered her father, he would have to be.

She didn't have time to breathe before he came at her again, his knives whirring so quickly she had to work to keep track of them. Sarani danced around him a few times, observing his footwork and the way he held his weapons, searching for anything that she could use against him while keeping him off-balance with a basic attack strategy. It was a technique she'd learned fighting Rhystan.

As if she'd conjured him, she felt the duke's presence even before she laid eyes on him.

"Sarani!" The growl was male and guttural and tore through her like a tempest, but Sarani didn't dare take her stare off her foe. One mistake, and it would be over; she knew that much.

"Stay back, please," she told him.

She cleared her mind of everything but the man in front of her, lunging and parrying. Learning. The assassin was good, but there were flaws in his skill, like the roll to his back heel every time he struck left and then right in a certain sequence. It threw him off-balance the tiniest bit. Waiting for the right moment, Sarani propelled all her weight forward as they both fell, her kukri flashing in midair in a vicious six-strike series.

An incredulous look was punctuated by a gurgling scream, red blooming through his linen shirt on his abdomen and the cuff of his sleeve. The six weren't fatal cuts, but the one slashing through his wrist meant he would never wield a blade with such finesse again, and the one severing his Achilles tendon would ensure he couldn't walk. Or run.

Hitting the ground hard, Sarani rolled and vaulted to her feet, putting distance between them, feeling a solid wall of male enclosing her from behind. Rhystan's crisp masculine scent of salt and sea surrounded her.

The assassin wheezed from his crumpled position on the floor. "Finish it."

"I'm no murderer," she said. "I have no power in Joor, but you will be tried for your crimes on English soil. Feel free to write to my lily-livered cousin from prison that if he sends any more of you, I will come for him."

Sarani glanced up at the man holding her in his arms, blue-gray eyes scanning her body for injury. Movement flickered behind him as the police swarmed the foyer. She wiped her faithful blades on her skirts and returned them to their sheaths.

"Get me out of here, Rhystan."

Twenty-Three

WITH SHAKING FINGERS, RHYSTAN POURED HIMSELF A GLASS of whisky, but he could not even lift it to swallow. His nerves were shot to hell. When he'd been located at his club earlier that evening by the head of police himself, he had feared the worst, but nothing had prepared him for the sight of Sarani facing off against a man who even the untrained eye could see was a killer. He'd wanted to roar his rage, to tear the assassin apart with his bare hands, and only Sarani's voice had restrained him.

Stay back, please.

He'd heard the soft command, the utter steel in her tone, and obeyed. And then, he'd waited, heart in his throat, watching her. The seconds had turned into lifetimes, but the moment she'd felled the man, he'd shot forward to gather her into his arms and make sure she was unharmed. Of course she wasn't harmed—she was a warrior goddess, Durga incarnate.

After he'd taken her back to his house with strict instructions to Harlowe to see to her every need, he returned to Huntley House to take care of matters there with the police. The assassin had been taken into custody, the foyer scrubbed of blood, and servants sworn to secrecy. Ravenna was distraught, refusing to speak to their mother, who was her usual unemotional self, though strain was evident in her eyes. Both women had taken to their chambers.

He'd only just returned home and gone straight to his study to calm himself before checking on Sarani. Rhystan stared at the tumbler in his hand. He'd come so close to losing everything he held dear—his remaining family and the only woman he'd ever let himself care for. Maybe cared for still. *Hell.* With a frustrated growl, he flung the glass into the hearth.

"That was Venetian crystal, Your Grace." The low voice slid into his veins like honey. His gaze followed the sound to find Sarani curled up in a chair near the bookshelves that was thrown into shadows, observing him over the rim of the twin to the goblet he'd carelessly smashed.

"What are you doing?"

"Thinking." She held up her glass. "Imbibing."

Rhystan frowned. She was still dressed in the torn, blood-stained gown she'd had on earlier. His frown turned into a scowl. Hadn't he instructed his valet to tend to her? A soothing bath would have been the least of it. "Harlowe didn't run you a bath?"

Watching him, she let out a sigh. "Before you strip the hide off your very kind valet, I dismissed him."

He approached her cautiously. "Are you all right?"

"Not particularly," she said. "But this is helping. You really do have the finest whisky. Where's it from? Scotland?" He nodded, and she smiled, lifting the glass for a sip and then licking the bow of her top lip to collect the moisture there. The provocative swipe made his breath hitch. "Tastes like you."

Was she sotted?

"My lady—"

"Sarani," she whispered. "Call me by my name, Rhystan. I'm so sick of pretending to be someone I'm not." She made a wry smile. "If I'm being honest, you're the only one I've ever been able to be myself with. Then and now. As the princess and as the pretender. I'm so bloody tired of trying to fit in and follow all these ludicrous rules that make no sense. I don't belong here." She let out a sound that was painful. "I don't fit anywhere."

"You fit with me."

"You're a person, not a place."

Rhystan closed the gap between them and dropped to his

knees in front of the armchair. "Belonging isn't always defined by earthly margins." He tapped his heart and then his temple. "It can be here and here. Home is where you make it."

Her soft laugh rasped over his senses. "The Duke of Embry, so poetically mawkish... Who would have thought it?"

"Tell a soul and I'll deny it to the grave."

She stared at him, so much swirling in those glittering eyes that appeared dark in the dimness of the study, and took another sip before offering the tumbler to him. He took it and swallowed. It was strangely intimate, sharing her drink. Her hand lifted and reached forward, sifting into a lock of hair curling onto his brow. Rhystan fought the urge to lean into her palm like a cat.

"Thank you," she whispered.

"For what?"

"Helping me."

He frowned, something in her tone grating at him. Why did it sound like she was saying goodbye? "I didn't do anything. You dispatched that man on your own. And besides, it was part of our agreement, remember?"

Her face shuttered. "Ah, yes. I'm your pretend fiancée." She laughed, the sound hollow. "There's that word again. *Pretend.* It's so whimsical, isn't it? But all it is...is a blade hidden in silk, roses sheathed in thorns. A dangerous lie." She reached for the glass, wrapping her long fingers over his, and drained the remainder of its contents.

Then she leaned forward and kissed him, the scent of her invading his senses, the press of her lips making his thoughts unravel. "Sarani...what are you doing?"

She uncurled her slender, graceful body from the chair and stood, every inch a princess, ever still a warrior goddess, voice imperious. "I believe you said something about a bath, Your Grace."

Sarani's hands trembled as she disrobed, the sound of running water making her breaths shorten. Thank the goddess for the front-fastening ties of her gown, as it would have tested her mettle to have Rhystan undress her. She was on the edge of absconding as it was. But this had to be goodbye, and before she left, she wanted him to make love to her as herself. Not as anyone else.

She'd never staged a seduction before, but a bath was as good a place to start as any.

She would be naked, after all, and if she had anything to say about it, he would be, too.

A blush chased over her skin. Before she lost courage, she pushed open the connecting door to the bathing chamber and peeked around it. The room was empty, though steam rose from the filled bath, the scent of jasmine oil drifting toward her.

"Rhystan?" she called.

There was no answer, so she darted across the floor and stepped in, sinking into the deliciously hot water of the massive tub. It slid across her skin, the heat seeping into her aching muscles, and Sarani sighed with unbridled pleasure and closed her eyes. It was so large that she couldn't reach the other end with her toes and she had to stretch her arms wide to reach the sides. It was obvious that this bath was built for two. The thought made more heat drizzle through her.

"Good?"

Her eyes flew open to see the duke standing at the door to his chamber. Sarani's breath fizzled in her throat. His coat and waist-coat were gone as was his cravat, and his shirtsleeves were rolled up, exposing thick, muscular forearms. Her mouth dried as he walked toward her, sitting on the carved built-in mahogany bench at the end of the bath. He reached for a cloth and dipped it into the water.

"What are you doing?" she asked over her shoulder, watching as he wrung it out and rubbed a bit of soap on it.

He grinned, his eyes flashing. "Seeing to my duties as a good cabin boy and washing your back. May I?"

"I suppose I could get used to this." She nodded and bit back a groan when the cloth grazed her nape.

"Lean forward and put your arms around your knees."

Doing as he asked, Sarani sighed in contentment as he rubbed the cloth over her shoulders, leaving a rash of gooseflesh in its wake. His strong fingers massaged the soap into her skin with small, ever-expanding sweeps, and she couldn't hold back her moan when they dug deep into the tense muscles of her back. She was nearly purring like a kitten as his hands worked their way down her spine.

After a while, the only sounds were their combined breathing and the soft slosh of the water as he worked the knots out until Sarani was limp and boneless. At some point, he'd discarded the cloth, and it was skin to skin. His fingers caressed her sides, up her ribs, tantalizingly near the slope of her breasts beneath the water, and she shivered.

When he gently tugged back on her shoulders so that she was lying with her nape resting on the lip of the tub, his slippery hands moved down her clavicles in tiny circles. Each sensual dip brought them closer to her tautened breasts. Her nipples ached in anticipation of his touch, and when he finally slid his wet palms over them, Sarani couldn't swallow her whimper fast enough, arching into his touch and eyes finding his.

His gaze stormed into hers, blue fires lit in his smoldering irises. The blue had darkened almost entirely to slate gray with desire. "Do you have any idea how exquisite you are?"

Words failed her at the possessive look on his face. The slippery feeling of his hands on her skin was intensified as he rolled her nipples between his thumbs and forefingers until every inch of her was aflame with arousal. He didn't release her eyes, and Sarani felt the pressure start to build deep in her core, just from the combination of his touch and the intensity of his stare.

"Kiss me, Rhystan," she whispered.

He braced his arms on the sides of the tub and hovered over her, taking her lips in an inverted position. He sucked her lower lip into his mouth, his tongue grazing along the soft inside of it, the reverse feel so erotic that her entire body shuddered in response. Heat danced across her nerve endings as she parted her lips and invited him in, their tongues teasing and dueling for control. The sultry kiss threatened to incinerate both of them.

"I want you in here," she moaned into his mouth. "With me."

Rhystan licked along her swollen lip. "You wish me to bathe with you?"

"Among other things."

Sarani had no idea where her sudden boldness came from, but an answering groan ripped from his chest. He stood and pulled off his shirt, making her mouth water along with other needy parts of her. She would never tire of seeing him unclothed. He was magnificent—all sculpted, lean muscles and edible masculinity.

Shucking off the rest of his clothes, he stood there in all his ducal glory. His erect male part bobbed nearly at eye level, standing thick and firm, a drop of opaque liquid pearling at the end. Sarani didn't stop to think. She pulled herself to the side and licked it off. The taste of him was heady and potent. Encouraged by his groan, she rose to her knees, gripping the edge of the bath, and took the rounded crown of him into her mouth.

"Sarani!"

She peered up at him through her spiky, wet lashes. "You like this?"

"Yes." It was part gasp, part growl as she took him deeper. Emboldened at his reaction and how she'd felt when he'd licked her, she flicked her tongue on the underside of him, working her mouth up and down and adding more friction with one palm curled around his base.

She was just settling into a rhythm when he groaned and

pulled himself from her mouth. Water sloshed over the sides as he plucked her from the bath, but Rhystan didn't seem to care. He sat on the edge and hauled her toward him between his knees until she was flush against his large body, his arousal prodding her stomach. Water from her body dripped down his.

His gorgeous eyes were laced with desire, his thumb caressing the curve of her jaw. "Who are you?"

"A princess," she whispered. "But you may call me Sarani. In private."

Fraught with emotion, his gaze captured hers. She'd said it on purpose. It'd been the exact words she'd said to him when they'd met for the very first time. In a way, this was a glimpse into what could have been. And that was all she wanted to take with her when she left—one memory of what they might have been.

"I'm Rhystan," he replied huskily.

She kissed him then, fitting her mouth to his. "I want you."

"I am yours to command, Princess."

Sarani's eyes widened as he lifted a wicked brow with a slanted glance to their bodies. She blinked in confusion. Did he mean right *here*? Or for her to mount him as one would a horse? Or *both*? Some of the erotic sculptures she'd seen in various temples of couples threaded together came back to her, and she felt heat fill her cheeks.

Rhystan answered her unspoken questions when he took her lips in a hungry kiss and lifted her over him so that she was straddling his hips with hers. The intimacy of the position and the slickness of her wet body against his made her gasp. Her legs dangled into the hot bathwater behind him before she wrapped them around his waist.

"Here?" she asked.

"Here." His voice was as tight as hers, his fingers palming her breasts. "Ride, Sarani."

His filthy command went straight to her core. She moved then, lifting slightly to notch him at her entrance and then letting gravity do the work. They groaned in unison when she was fully seated, her muscles clenching around him. The upright position added to the heightened sensations, making her breath hitch as he stroked her on the inside.

He placed his large hands over her hips and eased her up before guiding her down again. The slow erotic slide nearly had her eyes rolling back in her head with pleasure.

"You feel so good."

"So do you, my *apsara*."

The endearment, his love, filled her with sorrow-tinged bliss, and she tucked it away deep inside her heart. He might not truly love her or be willing to make her his duchess, but at least she would always have this part of him and this memory. In this moment, he was hers forever. In this moment, she felt cherished. Maybe even a little loved.

Sarani closed her eyes and quickened her movements, letting the glorious sensations build inside her until they were nearly impossible to bear, until she could only whimper as her body repeatedly impaled itself on his, taking everything he could give.

"Rhystan…"

His hand slid between their writhing bodies, his thumb circling the pearl of her sex where everything coalesced, and then her vision went to white as everything detonated. Pleasure shivered through her veins as she clenched around him. With a growl, Rhystan sped up his thrusts until he, too, was on the brink of eruption before yanking himself from her and roaring his release.

Sarani collapsed onto him, breathing hard and listening to his pounding heartbeat as it slowed. Her skin grew chilled as the heat dissipated, but nothing short of a miracle would incite her to move.

Tonight, something profound had shifted between them. An understanding. A release of past hurts. An acknowledgment of what they'd been and what they were now.

Friends. Enemies. Shipmates. Lovers.

"What are you thinking?" he asked after he'd caught his breath, fingers trailing down her back.

Her smile felt bittersweet. "That I wish we could stay here forever…and that we probably both need a bath."

Rhystan gave a chuckle as he stood, scooping her up into those strong arms, and then stepped into the still warm water. He sighed, once she was propped against him, her back to his chest. "I know the situation isn't perfect. Once things are settled with Ravenna, I'll free you from our agreement and see you settled anywhere of your choosing." He paused, and Sarani's heart squeezed, predicting what was coming. "Perhaps we can still find a way to see each other? I could…visit you."

Like a paramour.

Sarani didn't answer. He didn't have to say the words, though they hung between them like a cloud. A tiny part of her screamed that she would do anything to see him, even for a few stolen moments, and even if she was hidden away like something to be ashamed of. But the rest of her railed. She could never be anyone's mistress…not even the man she loved.

She deserved more.

But Sarani understood all too well about the demands of duty and the bonds of family. She would never begrudge Ravenna, whom she adored, a good match. And the dowager duchess… Well, she'd lost nearly everything—a husband and two sons. Sarani did not blame her for wanting to protect the family she had left. If she were a mother, she'd do the same thing.

Logic did not make the thought of what she had to do hurt any less. She let out a breath. She would start fresh, store away her memories, and treasure the time she'd had. Sarani felt a tear trek down her cheek and was grateful for the humidity of the chamber and the bathwater to disguise it. How would she ever be able to leave?

How would her body survive without its heart?

Twenty-Four

"GOOD GRACIOUS, THIS IS THE WORST KIND OF CRUSH," Ravenna complained sotto voce. "I can barely move, and have you ever noticed how much it stinks? Underneath the oils and the perfumes, you'd think people would smell pleasant, but no, it's sweat and grime and goodness knows what else. Honestly, if I breathe in this putrid air much longer, I might die."

Rhystan frowned at his sister's diatribe, but Sarani hid her smile behind her fan. "Surely, you must love Eau de Smelly Sirs by now?" she teased and then winked at Ravenna.

His sister, the very soul of indiscretion, threw back her head and laughed, drawing the attention of many in the ballroom, including their mother. He resisted the urge to tug on his collar. Being in this sweltering ballroom was torture, but it had to be done for Ravenna's sake. The sooner she married, the quicker he could leave.

The hypocrisy weighed on him, but he shoved it down.

He cleared his throat. "Then be sure to set your attentions on the least smelly suitor. I wouldn't want my only sister to perish because of sensitive nostrils."

Both ladies stared at him in astonishment, Sarani pinning her lips to stop from grinning and Ravenna gaping, but their responses disappeared as his mother neared with her usual entourage. Lady Penelope, rather surprisingly, was on the arm of Lord Talbot. Rhystan did not miss the earl's lustful stare trailing over Sarani, and he fought a spike of anger. He frowned, scanning the crowd. Would Markham dare to show his face as well?

The bastard wouldn't be far off, and God knew that he'd been persistent in his efforts to gain another audience. He hadn't heard from Gideon about Finn Driscoll, but it was only a matter of time. And Markham was desperate enough not to risk the bird he thought he had well in hand.

Rhystan's gaze flicked to Sarani, but if she noticed her former betrothed with her archenemy on his arm, she did not show it. Her expression was unruffled, eyes displaying none of the sparkling humor from earlier. One wouldn't guess that she'd been in a knife fight with an assassin just a handful of days before. Princess on the surface, warrior beneath.

He hoped she would consider maintaining a friendship, but he knew it wasn't likely. She deserved better than a half-life with a duke who could not marry her. She deserved a chance at a loving husband, children, and a home full of laughter.

Not a man who didn't even know who he was.

"Embry," someone said, interrupting his thoughts.

Rhystan inclined his head to an old acquaintance, a Frenchman, who had approached with another gentleman. "Lord Marchand. Fishing for prospects on this side of the channel?"

The marquis grinned. "I cast my nets where I can, Your Grace."

Introductions were made, including the young buck who'd been angling to meet the Huntley heiress. He watched as Ravenna and Sarani were led off by Marchand and the hopeful suitor for the start of the next dance and suppressed his groan when his mother arrived at his side where he'd walked to stand in a quieter corner of the ballroom.

"Ravenna is in good spirits tonight," she said. "The gentleman she is dancing with is the son of an earl, and the one dancing with…"—she broke off, lip curling—"and the other is a French marquis."

It wasn't the time or the place, but Rhystan did not care. His blood boiled, but for civility's sake, he kept his voice low. "What is your problem with Sarani?"

"I beg your pardon?" She looked startled for a moment at the brusque question, but her mouth firmed at his expression, eyes going wintry. "She's…not a suitable match, Embry."

"Why?" He resisted the urge to rake his hands through his hair. "Tell me, Duchess, what in your judicious opinion makes her unsuitable?"

"She is not fit for a duke. Everyone here knows that but you."

Rhystan had had enough. "*Everyone here*? That woman has more nobility and integrity in her little finger than half the purported *blue-bloods* in this room, and if you think I give a fig for what any of these intolerant fops think, you're wrong."

"Embry!" His mother's eyes widened and darted around the room. "Control yourself. This is what I mean… Look at you, this behavior is not befitting a duke."

He let out a grim laugh. "Believe me, that has nothing to do with her. Roland and Richard were ducal material, not me."

She flattened her lips. "Your gallivanting all over the world and consorting with these colonials has made you forget who you are."

"On the contrary, Mother, they've made me see the duke I wish to become."

Their furious exchange was drawing notice, though no one dared approach. One word from the Dragon Duchess and they would no longer be welcomed in the *haute ton*'s illustrious circles. Rhystan frowned. Was that what she was afraid of? That she would lose all the precious influence she'd built?

Rhystan settled a cold glare on the duchess. "Did you wish it had been me to die instead? Then you would have been content with your perfect sons and their approved wives, though at the rate Roland was going, the ducal coffers would have been empty."

Pain broke in her eyes, and he felt the smallest slash of guilt. "No, I don't wish that. I want only the best for you, Rhystan. I always have. Your father, too."

"Don't you dare bring him into this."

He expected her to walk away. This was much too public for her tastes, but to his surprise, his mother turned to face him, her back to the crowd. "You were much too alike, the both of you. Headstrong, smart, rebellious. Until he died, he insisted on updates of your accomplishments. He was proud of you."

Stunned, Rhystan faltered. "He had a strange way of showing it."

"The duke was not a demonstrative man, but he loved you." She inhaled a deep breath, looking unsure of herself for the first time he could think of. "He did not send for you five years ago. I did. I sent the message with the ducal seal to the vice admiral after we received his letter."

He blinked. "Why would you do that?"

"To prevent you from making the same mistake as you are now with a woman who will tarnish the Huntley name. Then, you were only the son of a duke. Now, by fate's decree, you *are* a duke. Consider what this will do to your reputation, our standing in society. You need to marry a woman of consequence, one who matters."

"Like Lady Penelope?" he shot back. "Whose parentage is disputable?"

"That is gossip. In the eyes of the *ton*, she is the catch of the season."

He shook his head at the double standard. "Then the *ton* is bloody obtuse." His mother's mouth curled with displeasure at his crudeness, but Rhystan had had enough. "I will see the estates sorted out, and I will see Ravenna married. And when that is done, I will leave for good."

"And your fiancée?"

"You will have your wish, Mother," he said wearily. "Our agreement will be ended. Family bloodlines will be unsullied, and your precious reign will continue."

Sarani watched from the ballroom floor, barely taking in the conversation of her partner. He had a delightful French accent, but beyond that, she hadn't heard a word. She'd been much too interested, like most everyone else, in the discussion taking place between the dowager duchess and her son. While their faces were composed and their voices remained low, Sarani was so attuned to Rhystan that she could feel the tension rolling off him. It didn't surprise her when he gave his mother a curt bow and strode off in the direction of the terraced gardens.

"Thank you for the dance, Lord Marchand," she told the marquis when the polka ended and he escorted her toward the refreshments room.

"It was my pleasure…Princess Sarani," he replied softly. Sarani's feet rooted to the spot, her eyes darting to his. The marquis smiled. "I had the pleasure of visiting your father's court some time ago. We were introduced, though I'm certain you do not remember me. I was sorry to hear of his death. He was a good man."

"He was, thank you," she stammered, at a loss. A stranger had recognized her, a member of French nobility no less, and he did not regard her any differently or look at her as though she were an interloper. Even knowing exactly who she was, he'd asked her to dance. Sarani cleared her throat. "I apologize for the deception of my name. It was necessary for my safety."

"I understand," he said with a courtly bow. "If I can ever be of service, please do not hesitate. It is good to see you again, Princess. Now I must go and claim my dance with the lovely Lady Ravenna." He grinned. "Any suggestions?"

"Be yourself," Sarani said and then almost laughed at the irony.

After the marquis left, she surveyed the ballroom, looking to see if Rhystan had returned, but the duke was nowhere to be seen. Following his footsteps, she made her way out to the terrace. He was not there either. She paused at the top of the stairs leading down to the lawns framed in thick hedgerows. The idea of walking alone into the shadowy gardens to find him was unnerving. But he needed her; she could feel it.

She would have a quick look and then return to the ballroom. Walking briskly, she'd stepped past the first set of hedges when a hand latched on to her elbow, yanking her into a narrow arbor.

"Excuse me," she began and then stopped when she recognized her companion with a wave of nausea. "Lord Talbot, this is untoward."

The earl smiled. "Is it? Engaged couples have secret trysts all the time."

"We are not engaged."

"I beg to differ," he said, his body blocking the exit.

She gritted her teeth—she would barrel through him if she had to. "You can beg all you like," she said. "Agreements change all the time. You do not own me."

"Not yet," he said, stepping closer. "But I will have my way, one way or another."

Sarani did not move, squaring her shoulders and refusing to cower before this man's aggression. "Tell me something, did you ever see the fighting exhibitions at my father's court in Joor, Lord Talbot? The ones with the knives."

He stopped moving. "Yes. What of them?"

"Would you be surprised if I told you one of the masked fighters was me?"

She lifted bladeless palms and whirled them in a complicated but recognizable pattern for anyone who might have viewed the matches. Talbot's throat bobbed, eyes widening. Sarani grinned. In this public setting, she would use her faithful kukri blades only as a last resort. She was trying not to cause any further scandal, if she could help it.

She stepped forward until they were nearly nose to nose. "You are a gutless coward, accosting a woman in the dark."

His hands flew out to capture hers, his grip punishing. "I am a peer of England."

"Good for you," she said. In response, his fingers tightened painfully. Sarani hefted her knee, but her stupid crinoline frame was in the way, blocking the blow from connecting where it would hurt him the most.

"Do you think anyone will care about you?"

Rhystan would. Ravenna would. The French marquis would. And maybe there were others. There were always exceptions to every rule and people who might not be so close-minded or judgmental. She lifted her chin. "Yes."

"Vikram didn't," he drawled, squeezing the slender bones of her wrists. "He was all too willing to barter you like chattel for a crown. Why do you think he sent a man to find you? You were part of the agreement; no princess, no prince." Sarani inhaled, but the earl went on. "Eventually, I would have relieved him from his position and annexed your little state. But I have one thing to claim first...my bride."

"I will never be yours. Release me, Lord Talbot."

"I'd do as the lady says," a voice said from behind them.

The deadliness in Rhystan's words sent shivers down Sarani's spine. Talbot released her so quickly that she stumbled backward, nearly crashing into the duke. He moved to intercept the earl, but Sarani put a hand on his chest, stalling him. "He's not worth it."

His gaze burned with rage. "But *you* are."

The words filled her with both happiness and sadness. She knew he meant them, but words were empty unless they were backed by action. He could declare it in front of a snake like Talbot but not anyone else. Not the duchess. Not the *ton*.

She straightened her spine. "I am, and I know I am. Will you please escort me back inside, Your Grace?"

Rhystan nodded with reluctance, his fist clenched at his sides, but offered her his arm. As they walked back up the terrace, Sarani did not look back. That was her mistake, she supposed. Because she wasn't prepared for the wild-eyed earl who'd followed them, crashing into the ballroom like a bull gone mad.

"You stupid, worthless creature."

Music cut off, and voices went silent. Sarani's heart climbed into her throat, though there was nothing she could do but watch the train wreck of her life finally derail.

"She's nothing but a filthy mongrel, Embry!" Talbot shouted. "Daughter of a native and a disowned countess. Lady Lisbeth? Everyone knows what a harlot she was, running after that Indian like a bitch in heat. Even Beckforth wrote her out of his will."

Sarani whirled. "Don't you dare speak about my mother!"

"That's your future duchess?" Talbot sneered at the Duke of Embry. "Lady Mulatto?"

She glanced at the duke, whose face had gone rigid with fury. She recognized that deadly look—she'd seen it on the *Belonging*. A thousand men could not hold him back, much less Sarani. She did not even try. With one fist, he flattened the earl, knocking him out cold. Screams cut through the ballroom, chatter climbing to the rafters. Rhystan had silenced the man, but the damage had been done.

She caught the horrified eyes of the dowager duchess, the sympathetic ones of Ravenna, and the triumphant glare of Penelope. But mostly, people stared at her with disdain and mistrust, as though she were an impostor who would run off with the silver or contaminate them with some malodorous disease. The whispers grew around her—*native, duchess, scandal*—until nothing else could be heard.

There, the truth was out.

Everyone knew.

Twenty-Five

THE SCANDAL SHEETS THE NEXT DAY WERE FAR FROM KIND. Rhystan had expected it. They were calling him the Disgraced Duke, though Lord knew why he should be disgraced in any way, beyond engaging in fisticuffs in the middle of a ballroom to defend a lady's honor. As though that had never happened in the history of the aristocracy.

He was the one who had let Sarani down. In the aftermath of Talbot's announcement and Rhystan's own ungoverned reaction, he had called for their carriages and they'd left. His mother, predictably, had had a fit of the vapors and returned home to Huntley House. Ravenna, however, had insisted on staying with Sarani at his residence. They'd slept in Sarani's bedchamber, and he'd been grateful that Sarani had not been alone. He had no idea what she must be thinking or feeling, and it gutted him. He didn't want her to feel pain or be hurt in any way.

In the breakfast room, Rhystan stared down at the caricature in the newssheets with a grimace. This one rubbed him raw. It was one of him standing with his foot on top of a map of India with a pencil-shaded Sarani staring up at him with avarice in her eyes. Her features had been exaggerated—eyes lengthened, lips fattened, and curves emphasized—painting her as a foreign, title-hunting jezebel. It made him sick to his stomach. That was what Talbot had intended, perhaps. To shame her into running.

The one good thing out of this was the loss of Markham's leverage. Gideon had found Finn Driscoll, and once Rhystan had given the Irishman the vice admiral's marker, Markham had gone to ground. But it was only a matter of time before his crimes—and the new owner of his debt—caught up to him.

Rhystan's skin prickled with awareness moments before his sister and Sarani entered the room. God, she was beautiful. Even with an ashen cast to her skin and purple shadows under her eyes, she was lovely in a pale-green-and-white-striped dress, trimmed in gold ribbon.

"Good morning, Brother," Ravenna said without looking at him, her attention on the sideboard where steaming dishes let out mouthwatering smells. "Goodness, I could eat an elephant." She giggled. "Though I'm sure if Mama were here, she would scream that eating elephants is just not done."

Sarani's eyes met his. He saw her gaze skip to the folded news-sheets beside him, apprehension flickering in their green-brown depths. He wouldn't hide the news from her, should she choose to see them, but neither would he shove it in her face.

"Good morning, Your Grace," she said.

He smiled. So proper. "Good morning, Princess," he said, startling her. "If we're standing on formality, that is. Though I suppose it's 'Maharani' now."

"What does that mean?" Ravenna piped up, plopping down in a chair that a footman had pulled out for her and pointing to the seat opposite her, on his left, to Sarani.

"Queen," Rhystan said.

"I am not a queen," Sarani said. "My cousin is maharaja. I am… I don't have a title."

"But you were born a princess," Ravenna pointed out while gesturing at the footman to fill her plate. She glared at him when he stopped after a small scoop of eggs. "I'm a person, Camden, not a bird," she told him. "Keep going until it reaches the edges."

Rhystan saw Sarani biting back a grin. How close she and his sister become pleased him, but then Sarani had always had a knack for drawing people to her.

"So, as I was saying," Ravenna went on, buttering a piece of toast once her plate had been piled to heaping, "you were born royal, which means you don't just stop being royal, no matter what you concoct in that clever head of yours. One cannot run away from one's birthright. Ask my brother here, who has been running for years, only to discover—*sod it to purgatory*—that he's still a bloody duke."

"Ravenna!" Rhystan chided.

"What?" she asked innocently. "Do stop being a milksop, Brother dearest. Mother Dragon isn't here."

Rhystan blinked. Did his baby sister just call him a *milksop* in his own house? He opened his mouth to give her a piece of his mind but stopped as Morton came to the entrance of the breakfast room with a bow.

"Begging your pardon, Your Grace, but the dowager duchess has just arrived," his butler announced.

"Oh, hell on wheels," Ravenna squeaked, brushing the crumbs from her chin and shoving her overfull plate toward the waiting footman. "Camden, take this, for the love of all things holy, before she sees! She'll sack you for feeding me. Trust me, she's done it before."

The footman blanched and hurried to take the plate. Rhystan shook his head at Ravenna's antics, but he had to admit, his spine went a little straighter, too. It was appalling the effect his mother had on them. He had the sudden urge to pull off his cravat, muss his hair, and smear jam on his pristine shirt.

"Thank you, Morton. Instruct the footmen to set another place in case Her Grace decides to stay," he said instead and braced himself.

The dowager duchess swept into the room, elegantly appointed from head to toe. Besides being paler than usual, she had a fight in her eyes. By God, Rhystan had had enough and she hadn't even spoken. He opened his mouth to say so and stopped as she lifted an imperious hand.

"Allow me to apologize."

Rhystan swore he could hear half a dozen jaws hitting the floor—his, Sarani's, Ravenna's, the butler's, and even those of a couple of the footmen. A small part of his brain wondered if she might be ill or going mad. Either was possible.

Still, he wasn't going to allow his mother to lower herself in front of the servants. He waved a hand, and the footmen cleared the room, Morton closing the door, until it was only the four of them. His mother gave him a grateful look.

"I was wrong, Embry," she said haltingly. "About all of it. What you said there at the end about my reign made me think. You were right about me and the silly things I valued, and I asked myself, for a woman who has lost so much, would I be willing to lose the family I have left to preserve the status quo? To care for those who would cut my family down for sport without blinking? I'm ashamed to even think I put them first." She drew a shattered breath. "Because the answer is no. I don't wish to lose you." Her gaze slid to Ravenna. "Or you. You're all I have left, now that Elodie has remarried and taken my granddaughters to Northumberland." She walked to the table where Rhystan sat, calmly picked up the newssheets, and ripped them in half. "And no-goddamned-body vilifies my family and gets away with it."

Ravenna gasped, staring at their mother like she'd grown wings and a tail, her mouth ajar. Even he was shocked speechless.

The duchess sent them an arch glance. "What? You thought your straitlaced mother didn't know how to swear?"

Sarani, for her part, held her composure, though something like shock flashed in her eyes. She tensed when the duchess turned her gaze toward her as though uncertain of what to expect. "I was wrong to judge you so harshly. What you did for Ravenna when that man had her in his grasp…" She choked up, a hand coming to her throat. "I made a horrible mistake. I was so afraid for her, so afraid I'd lose her, too, and I admit my reaction was cowardly in the extreme."

"Your Grace," Sarani began, but his mother held up a palm.

"Please, before you say anything, I have something more to say. I know it's asking quite a bit, but I hope you have it in your heart to forgive me. My very smart son has the right of it. A person should be judged by their conduct and character, not by the color of their skin or their place of birth. I was wrong."

A stunned Sarani looked like she was considering her reply before she spoke. Rhystan would back her up no matter what, but he waited. "Thank you for saying that, Your Grace," she said softly. "It's hard when those who are different from others have to *earn* respect instead of it being afforded as a basic courtesy, but I can't fault you for owning up to what you did. It takes great strength of character…and if I hope to honor my own mother's and father's teachings, it would behoove me to be equally gracious. We all make mistakes. What matters is that we learn from them."

God, Rhystan wanted to take her into his arms and kiss her. She was in a word…*queenly*.

The duchess bowed her head. "I intend to. I truly am sorry."

"Then I accept your apology."

His mother let out a ragged breath. "So that's it," she said, her gaze drifting to Rhystan. "That's what I came to say."

She stood there, uncertain, and suddenly looking rather old and frail. He let out a breath. It took both courage and humility to admit when one was wrong, reinforcing his thought that the duchess was one of the strongest women he knew.

He stood and pulled her into his arms. "Thank you, Mother."

"Oh, *oh*, dear boy," she whispered, hugged him back, and then pulled away, dabbing at her eyes. "That's quite enough. Wouldn't want the servants eavesdropping outside that door to think I've gone soft now."

Ravenna's cheeks were wet, and even Sarani had a suspicious sheen to her eyes.

"Would you like to stay for breakfast?" Rhystan asked.

The dowager duchess smiled. "I would like nothing more."

Sarani's heart had swelled for both Rhystan and Ravenna. What had happened at breakfast had been a step toward them reconnecting as a family and the only thing she had ever wanted for him. For someone who had no family left, she knew how important it was to hold on to the loved ones you had. Her Grace's astonishing confession, while heartwarming, didn't change anything for her, however. She still had to leave.

"There, Princess, those trunks are packed," Asha said, neatly stacking a few hatboxes to the side. Most of the fancier clothes would be donated to a local orphan asylum, where the residents could take what they needed and sell the rest. A sleepy seaside village in Cornwall did not require formal ballgowns. And now that Sarani's banker in Bombay had been able to transfer the rest of her inheritance to London, she had no immediate need of money. Once the dust settled with Talbot, she intended to return to Joor. Something would have to be done about Vikram.

"Thank you, Asha."

Tej pouted, sitting on one of the trunks. "I don't understand why you have to leave. Everyone is talking about the duchess saying she was sorry."

It amazed Sarani what got out through perfectly solid, closed doors. Then again, she wasn't surprised. The duchess's declaration had floored them all.

"I am grateful," she said. "But that's not the reason I'm leaving."

"Then why?"

Because the duke does not love me.

That was part of it. It had everything to do with the letter he'd written her years ago and her place in his world. They'd both made mistakes, and though he'd written those sentiments in anger and apologized, that didn't make them any less true. The truth was, a union like theirs was destined to be doomed, and if he did not love her, nothing on earth would save it.

Her heart squeezed. "Because I must stand on my own two feet, and I don't belong here. Regardless of the duchess's changed feelings toward me, she wants only to protect her family. The scandal will die down if I am gone, and soon the fact that the Duke of Embry was engaged to a woman of my petrifying ilk will be forgotten."

"What about Lady Ravenna?"

"She's promised to write and to help you write letters as well." Sarani grinned and chucked him in the arm. "I expect to hear wonderful things about your excellent marks and your new school."

Ravenna had not taken well to the fact that she was leaving. Sarani had sworn her to secrecy. She would tell Rhystan herself when she was ready…when her heart and mind were both prepared. In truth, if he asked again whether she would be his paramour, Sarani wasn't sure she would have the strength to say no.

She had to stay the course and do what was right.

Even if it felt like dying.

"Don't pack that one," Sarani told her maid, pointing to a heavy, magenta-colored gown with intricate gold embroidery. "I'll wear it for the ball tonight. Go out fighting, as the pugilists say."

Asha's dark eyes widened. The dress had not been acquired here in London. In fact, it'd been designed in Joor as a coronation gown, and Sarani had not wanted to leave it behind. It had cost a small fortune. If worse had come to worst, she'd planned to sell it. But for now, she'd wear it with pride.

It was undeniably the most magnificent gown she'd ever owned. Part European, part Indian, the dress had seemed to bridge both her halves. A fitted bodice with heavily embroidered, scalloped edges curved down toward her waist where a heavily embroidered stomacher adorned with gold flowers, connected the top with the bottom.

The lower half of the gown was even more extravagant than the top. The full skirts were sewn with hundreds of elaborate flowers, studded with tiny pearls and diamonds, and paired with a cream-colored gold-stitched underlay, visible only at the hem. The design was elegant but bold in both color and style.

A perfect amalgamation of Eastern traditions with Western flair.

And if she wanted to make a statement, which she did, this would be the gown to wear. It was a statement that she would be seen, no matter who wanted to render her invisible. It was a statement that she mattered.

That she was there, not to stay, but there nonetheless.

———————

God knew why his mother wanted to throw a ball of all things. Rhystan sighed. Half of the ton had accepted the invitation out of morbid curiosity. The other half had been too afraid to decline, given her influence, which apparently had not waned as much.

Rhystan had not seen Sarani since she'd returned to Huntley House. It was to stave off any more salacious gossip, she'd said, especially now that the scandal sheets had painted her as a greedy fortune hunter with the most eligible duke in London in her grasp. Not that they knew that she had more money than most of the *ton* combined.

He shouldn't have been surprised that she'd laughed off the awful caricatures.

"If only my eyes were that large," she'd joked. "Or other parts of me."

Rhystan had grinned. "Other parts of you are perfect as they are."

Not that he'd seen any of said parts since the bathing chamber, a cherished memory that had gotten him through a number of lonely nights since. Neither of them had spoken about what would happen next. His ship was leaving in a week or so, and he knew that she was still set on finding a quiet cottage somewhere. Who was he to take away her choices?

The ballroom at Huntley House was enormous and it was already crowded, even though it was early in the hour. The sharks were out for blood, while other smaller fish circled in the hope of scraps. Rhystan couldn't believe that Sarani had agreed to this, but she understood what the duchess was trying to do. His mother wanted to show the peerage that the Huntleys were a united force. He knew it was her way of making amends.

"Your Grace," someone said to his right, where he stood in the shadows of a pillar. "Lord Beckforth, at your service." Rhystan tensed, but the man's expression was not hostile. "Princess Sarani's cousin," he added helpfully when Rhystan kept frowning.

"You know who she is?"

The earl nodded. "I was informed of the gossip from the previous assembly with Talbot, and of course, took it upon myself to research my relative Lisbeth, who we were told had died shortly after leaving England. I did not know that she had married. Nor that it was to an Indian prince. I was only ten when she was removed from the family annals by my granduncle, the then earl. We were only told never to speak of her and that she had disgraced the family name by running off with a colonial laborer."

"Not a laborer," Rhystan said. "A prince who worshipped the ground she walked on and showered her with every affection. And then gave her a daughter they both adored. Until her death a decade ago, your aunt was loved."

"Thank you for that. I'm glad she had a happy life, at least."

Rhystan cleared his throat, not adding that it was likely Lady Lisbeth had been poisoned because of deeply ingrained prejudices, much like those Sarani faced. "And your cousin?"

"Whenever she is ready, I wish to get to know her," he said.

"And I wish for my wife and children to know her as well. We are family, after all."

"Why didn't you say anything to the newssheets when asked about being possible relations?"

The earl inclined his head. "It was not my place, and I wanted to respect her privacy."

An unfamiliar emotion expanded and thickened in Rhystan's chest. It was gratitude mixed with a growing esteem. "And now, do you not care what everyone will think?"

Beckforth smiled. "The thing about scandal, Your Grace, is that it only hurts you if you choose to let it, and in the grand scheme of things, it's just noise, fleeting and irrelevant. My family has been touched by more than its fair share. I am the grandson of a pig farmer on my mother's side. We were poor as dirt, but we were loved, and when I became earl, others shunned us because of that. I vowed never to let anything get in the way of family. Or love."

Rhystan was silent for a moment, suspecting that last part was meant for him, but then he nodded. "I will pass on the message. Thank you, Beckforth."

After the earl took his leave, Rhystan considered what he'd said. As much as his peers pretended they were better than everyone else, they weren't. They had the same flaws and the same fears. All that separated them from their common-born brothers were chance and circumstance of birth.

He was a duke, but he'd made his own fortune, carved his own path. Sarani was a princess, but she'd defied all odds of her sex to educate and arm herself. She was no wilting flower, no tame English rose. And the truth was, he didn't want her to be. He wanted her exactly as she was: vibrant, singular, and so sublimely beautiful she made his heart hurt. Rhystan kept glancing to the staircase, waiting for her to walk down the steps.

"Hiding, Rhyssie?" Ravenna asked, poking him in the side.

"Trying to," he replied. He glanced at her, struck by how

splendid she looked in an aquamarine gown. Her auburn hair was piled into high coils, and her coppery eyes glowed. "Are you partial to a rich French marquis by the name of Marchand?"

She scowled. "I'm not partial to anyone. I told you, I don't want to marry yet."

"Ravenna—"

"Yes, yes, I know." She tossed her head, but not before he saw a flash of misery in her eyes. "I'm wrecking your plans because you want to run away again. I am aware."

He drew in a breath. "That's just it, Ravenna, I've just now decided I'm not leaving. At least not for a while. Gideon can manage the fleet for now."

"You're not going?"

"No," he said. "I've responsibilities here, and you and Mother are here. I want to have Elodie visit with the girls and get to know my nieces." He paused, drinking in her radiant smile. "But we're still finding you a husband."

The smile disappeared behind thunderclouds. "I've told you that…"

But Rhystan wasn't listening. At the tingling sensation along his spine, his eyes lifted and connected with a pair of the most beautiful eyes he'd ever seen. Even in the thronged ballroom, she'd found him instantly, and then the breath lodged in his throat, his heart beating so fast he could scarcely countenance it.

"Oh, *my*," Ravenna whispered, her gaze following his. "She's a vision."

That was the least of what she was.

Sarani Rao was a goddess in the flesh, and now everyone would know it.

Twenty-Six

THIS WAS IT. NO TURNING BACK.

"Her Highness, Princess Sarani Rao," the majordomo for the evening said, giving Sarani a conspiratorial wink. She'd come to know and was quite fond of Her Grace's staff. Fullerton, in his role of butler, was one of her particular favorites.

But as hundreds of eyes fastened to where she stood at the top of the staircase, Sarani's already jumbled nerves weaved into knots. She wasn't ready for this. She *wasn't*! It was a bad idea to make a statement. Any statement at all. These people would eat her alive. Heaven knew friends of Talbot and Markham would be here, ready to draw blood with their eyes and their words.

They hated based on an ideal, and that was the most ignorant kind of hate.

She reminded herself of Asha's advice. "Sticks and stones," she murmured and took the first step down. At the bottom, the Duke of Embry stood waiting, and she almost stumbled as he took her hand and kissed her knuckles. Gorgeous in his tailored evening wear, his brilliant ocean-blue gaze glittered with pride and smoldering desire.

His voice was low, only for her ears. "Woman, you're killing me." And then louder, "Princess, your beauty casts everyone in the shade."

"Thank you, Your Grace," she said with an elegant curtsy, though she felt her body respond as he devoured her with his eyes. Only Rhystan had ever looked at her that way, as though he could hardly keep his hands off her. She would miss that.

"May I escort you to my mother?" he asked.

Basking in his admiration, Sarani accepted and took his arm. She kept her head high, but she could feel the contempt and wariness from many of the guests, scrutinizing her distinctive gown and studying her face, looking for signs of her other half—the lesser half.

Her dual heritage would be evident in her choice of gown and in the gold bangles on her wrist, the extravagantly embroidered veil falling from her crown, and the heavy kohl lining her eyes. But her skin was as beautiful as theirs, the blood beneath her skin just as red.

When they reached the dowager duchess, she gave her a small smile as Sarani made a curtsy worthy of the queen's court. "Your Grace," Sarani said.

"Your Highness," the dowager greeted her in return. "That's a rather intriguing choice of dress."

Sarani almost fell over at the use of her title and then bit her lip at the fastidious survey of her gown. Despite their recent truce, she'd expected nothing less. "It was designed in Joor where I grew up."

The dowager duchess gave the tiniest of smiles, the light in her eyes reminding Sarani of her son's. "It's extraordinary, and I have to say, it suits you remarkably well."

That was a resounding stamp of approval if ever there was one. "Thank you, Your Grace."

The strains of a waltz echoed through the ballroom as the musicians tuned their instruments. "Dance with me?" Rhystan said.

Sarani bit her lip and nodded. All eyes were on them as the duke escorted her into the set. Sarani's entire body felt wooden, but she followed his expert lead. Normally, she felt deliciously light in his arms, but for some reason, she felt only hollow.

This was the last time they would dance.

The last time he would hold her.

Her eyes stung.

"What is the matter?" he asked, ever in tune with her emotions. "You looked sad for a moment there."

"Nothing," she said. "I'm happy."

"Fibber."

She smiled as he spun her through a turn that she almost bungled with a double step. He didn't push any more, but she could see the small pleat between his brows as if he could sense the maelstrom of feelings barreling through her. It took all her poise to keep from bursting into tears.

"You're a disgrace."

The ugly accusation came out of nowhere. Sarani wasn't sure whether it was directed to her or to the duke, but he came to an abrupt stop, nearly colliding with some of the other dancers. They, too, stumbled to a halt and the music petered out.

"Who said that?" he demanded. When no one answered, he raised his voice. "Show yourself."

A sneering Markham stepped forward. At the violent, hateful look on his face, Sarani's entire body braced for attack. Now that the truth of her identity was public knowledge, he was an embittered man with nothing to lose.

"I did." His eyes scraped down her person. "You can dress her in pretty clothes, but it doesn't change who she is. And you're a disgrace to the entire aristocracy bringing that…creature here and parading her as one of our own."

"She is one of your own, you inbred imbecile," Rhystan shot back. "Her mother was a countess with more patrician blood in her veins than you have in yours."

"Her father was a blackie."

"He was an Indian prince," Rhystan corrected with a glare. "Do you plan to make a salient point anytime soon, Markham?"

"She does not belong here."

A few bodies turned away from her toward the vice admiral,

hands opening fans to block her from view, and Sarani felt her stomach churn.

The duke seethed. "This is my house, and I say she has more right to be here than you do. You were not invited. I warned you once, Markham, show her some respect."

The man spluttered, his face going red. "I'm better than that… than that…"

"Careful, sir," Rhystan warned. "You are treading in dangerous territory, insulting a duke's guest in his own home. One would think you had a wish to meet with pistols at dawn."

"Dueling is illegal."

"We both know that peers are beyond the law, especially if it's a matter of honor. If I call you out, yours would be in question, wouldn't it?"

Sarani felt her belly quail at the threat. Goodness, no. He could not mean to fight Markham on her behalf. Her gaze scanned the room for Ravenna or even the duchess. The dowager duchess would not allow it, would she? But when Sarani found her, the duchess's face was as implacable and as merciless as her son's.

Sarani found her voice and stepped forward. "Stop this."

Markham's mouth twisted. "How dare you command me, girl."

Rhystan opened his mouth, but Sarani forestalled him with one hand. She did not make a reply to the vice admiral but instead scanned the ballroom. Almost everyone was staring at her, expressions varying from curiosity to contempt. None of it signified, but she wanted to take in each and every face.

She did not control anyone else's actions, only her own.

Her cold gaze returned to Markham, the man who had taken so much from her, stripped her of her very dignity as if it'd been his right to do so. "I am not a girl. I am a princess of Joor, and you will address me as Your Highness."

She exhaled and surveyed the guests. "My father was an Indian prince, and my mother was a countess of English and Scottish birth." She held her chin high. "My parents met and fell in love. I never knew anything but love from them. However, what I received from most of the outside world was just the opposite and much like what I see here: scorn, derision, and fear. I am not ashamed of who I am."

She turned to Rhystan with a soft smile and then caught the duchess's gaze and finally touched on Ravenna. "I thank the Duke of Embry and his family for taking me in when I had no one to turn to. They offered me safety when I needed it most." She took in a clipped breath, knowing the next part would be the hardest. "However, I am no longer engaged to the duke. The purpose of our engagement was to keep me safe from the man who murdered my father." Amid the loud gasps and whispers, she felt Rhystan tense at her side. "But now that the assassin is in the hands of the police, I think it's best to release the duke from our betrothal."

She narrowed her eyes at Markham for so long that he shifted in his scuffed boots, his face turning puce. "The truth, sir, is that you are the disgrace, not the duke. Not just for maligning me or for taking it upon yourself to punish someone for being different but for being so small-minded that you cannot see past your own ignorance. I pity you. The world is a big, big place, and you are but one measly, inconsequential prick." Sarani smiled. "I mean speck."

"How dare you insult me?" he fumed.

"I dare because I have a brain in my head and a tongue capable of articulating my thoughts. I am not afraid of you, Markham." She smiled a shark's smile. "However, if you want me to make it truly simple for your tiny little brain to comprehend, I dare because I outrank you."

Markham's face turned the color of an overripe tomato, and he lunged forward as if to strike her, but before he could get close, he was restrained by several large footmen. Sarani blinked as Her Grace's voice cut through the noise. "Fullerton, this man is trespassing and is unwelcome in this house."

As the butler and footmen dragged a kicking and screaming Markham out, Rhystan disappeared for a moment but then
returned with a satisfied smile on his face. Sarani shot him a ques-
tioning look. His grin widened. "We'll see how *he* likes being
knocked out, thrown on a wagon, and shipped to Australia."

"Can you do that?"

"He threatened and blackmailed a peer. It's the least of what he
deserves."

Sarani opened her mouth to reply and then gaped in surprise
when the duchess stepped up beside her and took her hand. She
nearly keeled over in shock. Her Grace's face was so hard it seemed
made of marble as she addressed the now-silent throng. "If any of
you are of the same opinion as that loathsome man, feel free to
join him."

When Ravenna came to stand on one side of her mother and
Rhystan stepped up to Sarani's other side, Sarani reeled at the
absolute declaration of support by one of the most powerful families in England. In defense of *her*.

She couldn't breathe, her throat was so clogged with emotion.

When all was said and done, a good number of the guests left.
They'd come for the scandal and gotten one, and they were simply
too set in their ways to change.

Among those who remained, Sarani recognized the French
marquis and then froze in recognition of another. She went mute,
her body shaking, as the man approached.

"Lord Beckforth," she said. "You're here."

The earl smiled. "Does that surprise you?"

"I thought all Englishmen were like Talbot and Markham. And
that you would want nothing to do with the half-blooded daughter
of your disowned aunt."

He laughed, and for a moment, she saw traces of her mother in
his smile. The familiar sight of it made her eyes burn.

"I would like to invite you to dinner, if that's not too forward.

I'd love for my family to meet you and for you to get to know us. You are welcome to stay at Lockhart Manor for however long you like."

Sarani's heart soared. "I would love to meet them. Thank you, Lord Beckforth."

"Henry," he said. "My name, dear cousin, is Henry."

———————

Rhystan dimly registered Beckforth talking with Sarani. All he could hear replaying in his head was her voice calling off their engagement. It gutted him, left him in a state of strange inertia. He felt untethered as though his ship was unmoored in the middle of the ocean with no engine, no sail, and no rudder. She was all those things to him.

The truth hit him with the force of a snapped mast.

Because he fucking loved her.

"No," he said to no one in particular, shaking his head. "*No*."

"I beg your pardon, Your Grace," Sarani said, glancing up at him. "Are you well?"

He took hold of her elbow. "No, I'm not well at all. Please excuse us, Beckforth. I have something to say to my fiancée."

Sarani's expression was confused, considering she'd just declared to the entire ballroom that the engagement was over. The earl shot him a perceptive grin and nodded, making himself scarce.

"Your Grace, what are you doing?" she asked.

"Setting the record straight," he said, gaining conviction by the second.

"What do you mean?"

Huge apprehensive hazel eyes stared into his, and he squeezed her hand in reassurance. It was more for him, however. He wanted to scream it, get it out before it burned a hole in his chest. Shout it to the rooftops so that there was no doubt in anyone's mind that she was his.

"I love you."

She stared at him in shock.

"I have loved you from the very first day I set eyes upon you. Things beyond our control drove us apart, but then we were given another chance. I won't lose you again."

"You love me?" she whispered.

"You are the only woman for me," he said. "You are my match in every way, and whether we make our home here or on the seas or in Joor or a quiet seaside village somewhere, I need you by my side." Rhystan swiped at the tear that rolled down her cheek and clasped her hands. "If you'll have me, I mean."

The entire ballroom went quiet. Again. Those who had stayed, hoping for something more, were about to be rewarded. Because she was either going to say no, whereupon the scandal sheets would be rife with caricatures cataloging his epic rejection, or she would say yes, and a ducal wedding would be the toast of the season.

"What about the dukedom? And the scandal?" Her eyes were wide and achingly transparent, so many emotions running through them. "People will talk, Rhystan. You saw how many of them left tonight."

"I don't care about any of them," he said. "'A moment of happiness, you and I sitting on the verandah, apparently two, but one in soul, you and I.'" He sank to a knee, right there in the middle of the ballroom. Whispers rose in a crescendo around them. "'The stars will be watching us, and we will show them what it is to be a thin crescent moon. You and I unselfed will be together, indifferent to idle speculation, you and I.'"

Her throat worked, tears gathering at the powerful, poetic words. "Rumi?"

He nodded. "He called it 'A Moment of Happiness,' but I insist on a lifetime of it. Marry me, Sarani, and make me the happiest of men."

"What about Ravenna?" Sarani asked, her beautiful face filled with worry.

"What about her? She's thrilled beyond belief."

Sarani shook her head. "No, I meant, her marriage prospects."

"If any suitor thinks she's not worthy of an offer of marriage because of my wife's heritage, then he can go sod himself with a pointy stick."

"Your Grace!"

He shrugged. It was true. If a bigot like that refused his sister, then she was better off without him. He'd prefer Ravenna marry a poor man who loved her for *her* than a wealthy, titled fop with hate in his heart and ignorance in his brain. If he could get the headstrong chit to marry at all, that was.

He sucked in a shallow breath, his voice lowering. "So what do you say, my love? Shall we jump on this ship and sail it to parts unknown?"

Sarani gazed at him, cheeks damp with tears. Were they happy ones? The love of his life dropped to her knees with him, cupped his face in her palms, and kissed him. People gasped, and his sister might have given a scream of joy, but Rhystan did not pay it any mind. The only thing that consumed him was Sarani. When she broke away, he suddenly felt uncertain.

"Is that a yes?" he asked.

Her gaze searched his, for forever it seemed, but he waited because in the end, it was her choice. He'd chosen her, but she also had to choose him.

"I realized something important a while ago," she told him. "You see, I was so worried about losing my heart to you, but the truth was, I couldn't lose it. Do you know why?"

"Why?"

"Because you've had it in your keeping all along." She stared at him with aching sweetness, her fingers cradling his jaw. "Five years ago, I gave it to you gladly. My heart is yours. I've always been yours. So yes, duke of mine, I'll marry you."

The ballroom erupted in cheers, and Rhystan lifted his future bride into his arms with a ragged laugh and inhaled her sweet scent. "Minx. I thought you were going to say no for a moment there."

"How could a girl resist a proposal from the man of her dreams who quotes Rumi?"

He gathered her close, loving the feel of her in his arms, right where she belonged. "Because he's a gorgeous, manly, virile, rich duke?"

Sarani rolled her eyes. "One day, your head will pop and it will be your own fault. For your information, it's in spite of the duke-dom." She put a tender palm over his heart. "I fell in love with the man underneath it all."

The musicians began a celebratory waltz, and he moved them to the center of the floor. It felt like they had crossed an entire ocean in between their last dance and this one. And perhaps they had in a symbolic sense.

Rhystan knew times ahead could be difficult, that there would be those who might look down their noses at such a match, but a wise soon-to-be-relative had recently told him that scandal was just noise. They would weather those storms together.

With a shout of joy, he spun her around, and she laughed, the uninhibited sound making him want to kiss her again. But the kiss he had in mind wasn't one for the ballroom.

"Why are you looking at me like that?" she asked when her toes touched the floor again.

"Because I want to kiss you."

Answering flames flared in her eyes. "Then kiss me."

He gave a husky laugh. "If I kiss you now, Sarani dearest, I won't stop, and the day the duke ravished his beautiful bride and tossed her skirts over her head in a ballroom in Mayfair will be fodder for the gossip rags until the end of time."

"I expect those drawings will be quite scandalous," she said, blushing. "Maybe they will make your shoulders twice as broad and your muscles twice as large, though I'm sure certain parts of you won't require any…padding."

Certain parts of him went as hard as stone.

"Fuck," he groaned and dragged her toward him to disguise his erection.

"You say that word far too much for a toplofty duke," she teased. "It's vulgar and common, Your Grace, and offending to a lady's delicate sensibilities."

"Then you should stop provoking me." He shunted his hips into her belly, eliciting a gasp from her. "And the only thing delicate about you is the most succulent pair of silky brown nip—"

Cheeks flaming, she shoved her fingers against his mouth. "You are wicked, Your Grace."

"Categorically."

Desire lit her eyes, the gold flecks in them burning like hot embers, and Rhystan couldn't help wondering if she was as wet as he was hard. His mouth watered with the urge to strip her bare, until she was clothed in nothing but her beautiful, luminous skin.

Wasn't this dance over yet? He had new plans to drag her to an empty room and see for himself. Preferably with his tongue. He was so caught up in his fantasy that he didn't realize she had spoken until her laughter reached his ears.

"Having fun?" Sarani asked with an altogether wanton, knowing smile. Her eyes had gone dark and her cheeks were warm, too, as though she'd been imagining similar things. To his utter alarm, he felt his face flush, and his beautiful fiancée's smile widened. "I sincerely hope you'll share *those* thoughts with me later."

"Count on it," he said. "Because I promise to spend the rest of my life making up for those lost five years." He grinned, so enormously happy, it felt like he would burst. "To think, we could have had half a dozen little Rhystans running around by now."

"Half a dozen?"

"I should warn you that I'm not planning to let you out of my bed anytime soon."

His future duchess laughed, eyes bright with love, and wrapped her arms around him. "I can absolutely live with that."

Epilogue

HER GRACE, SARANI HUNTLEY, THE NINTH DUCHESS OF Embry, lay naked and sated in her husband's arms listening to the sounds of the waves crashing against the shore. He'd bought her the country estate in Hastings as a wedding present two years before, and though they split a lot of their time between London and the ducal ancestral seat in Kettering, they made the effort to spend time alone in their little slice of paradise, enjoying each other's company and being themselves.

The first years of marriage had been bliss, and apart from the occasional brush with bigotry, they'd kept themselves insulated from harmful gossip. People did talk and social invitations were fewer, but none of that mattered much to them.

Lord Talbot had squawked like a chicken for weeks but had quieted when Gideon paid him a short visit. Apparently, all he'd had to do was mention that Talbot's old chum Markham had ended up in Australia, and the craven earl had changed his tune. Rhystan hadn't quite forgiven him for leaving bruises on her wrists, though, and after a few months, the earl had suffered a sudden reversal of fortune that had left him destitute. Word had it that he'd gone back East in search of employment.

As far as Joor, her snake of a cousin had gone missing some six months after he'd stolen her father's throne—Sarani suspected that Talbot might have had a hand in that—and another heir had been named prince. From what she could discern, the new prince was both kind and capable, but she'd still insisted on a trip to Joor to see for herself; she'd had enough of half-truths and lies. The people seemed content with him, and the truth was, apart from making sure her people were in good hands, Sarani felt her efforts were better served in London, where she could make a difference.

Going back home had hit hard, especially with her father not being there, but it had also been a chance for her to say her good-byes to him properly. She was touched to see that a statue had been commissioned to be built in the palace in his memory. Asha, her dearest friend, had chosen to stay in Joor with her family, but Sarani had made sure that she would never have to work again. Sarani would miss her, but at least she still had Tej, who would no doubt be an excellent man-of-business one day.

Rhystan, for his part, had taken to being duke like he was made for it, supporting efforts in the House of Lords to improve the conditions of the people in India and humanizing popular opinion in Britain, hitherto shaped by biased reports. He championed bills that stood against the injustices brought on by colonialism, not just in the east but also in the West Indies, and fought for fair practices in trade and commerce. Unlike most peers, he listened to her ideas and saw them to fruition in chambers, which pleased Sarani to no end. It was satisfying having a hand in changing the tide. She might not wear the wig and the robes, but she was determined to be part of the solution.

Forming close ties with other like-minded women in London, she attended functions organized by the India Office, including events for visiting Indian dignitaries during the season. She had even started a charitable organization for those who had resettled in Britain and needed assistance. Her work kept her busy, but she loved every moment of it.

Rhystan still sailed, but only on occasion. The bulk of his fleet was managed by Gideon.

"A penny for your thoughts, Duchess?"

Sarani smiled at her husband. "Only a penny? My thoughts are worth at least a sovereign."

"Is that so?" Rhystan scrunched up his nose. "Sounds rather dear to me. Just a month ago, they were half that."

She turned in his arms and propped herself up on her elbows, chin to her hands. "Would you like me to explain how inflation works?"

Rhystan groaned. "I love it when you use big words."

"You love it when I don't use words at all."

The sheet at his hips tented magnificently. "That's true, too."

Sarani laughed. Oh, she loved this man to distraction. And he worshipped her, body and soul.

After their wedding, the gossip rags had gotten tired of writing about how besotted the Duke of Embry was with his wife. They'd fixated on the duke's younger sister, whose refusal to marry had become almost comically legendary. Rhystan had been at the end of his rope, but Sarani had convinced him to give her time. At nearly one and twenty, Ravenna was hardly on the shelf. She was simply particular about what she wanted. Like her brother.

Sarani dragged a fingernail down her husband's damp chest. "So about those thoughts you were interested in…"

His eyes narrowed. "Do I still need to pay a pound?"

"It's worth it, I promise."

"Very well, you drive a hard bargain."

She stuck out her tongue. "You didn't even haggle, Your Grace. Haven't I taught you anything? Haggling is ninety percent of the fun."

Rhystan grinned and rolled them over so that he was braced above her. She gasped at the deliciously hard pressure between her thighs. Her blood went molten. She was wrung out and sore from his attentions overnight and again that morning, and suddenly, she wanted more.

With a wicked grin, he tilted his hips, making her whimper. "Three pounds, then."

"I think you're missing the point of haggling, my lord duke," she said and wrapped her legs around him, pinning his hardness to her softness. Two could play at his game.

He groaned. "Five pounds!"

Sarani laughed as she tugged his head down to hers, slanting her mouth across his and nibbling on his full lower lip. "You are absurd."

"Absurdly in love with you," he said. "Now, tell me these thoughts of yours before I'm forced to increase my offer."

"I'm with child."

Rhystan stilled, his glowing eyes capturing hers. So many colors swam in them—blue, green, gray—much like the ocean lit by the sun with a storm in the distance. He didn't say a word, but his mouth trembled slightly. Sarani pinned her lips, uncertainty suddenly blanketing her.

They'd talked about children, but with his work in Parliament and the scandal broth surrounding their unconventional, highly publicized marriage, they'd decided to wait. Rhystan had been careful and she'd timed her courses, but a handful of times a couple of months ago, they'd been so consumed by passion that no precautionary measures had been taken.

"Rhystan?"

"We're going to have a baby?" he whispered.

"I know we didn't plan on it, but does the thought please you?"

"Does it please me?" Her duke's smile was slow and lit his eyes with love and joy as he slid down her body to place a kiss on her bare abdomen. He peered up at her, steel-blue gaze shining. "You undo me, Your Grace. I am delighted." He kissed her skin again. "And you, little one, I cannot wait to meet you."

Sarani felt a tear slip down her cheek, watching this powerful man place tender kisses on her belly, cherishing the tiny being they had created. Rhystan rubbed his cheek against her and then crept back up her body to gather her into his arms.

"I hope our child has your eyes," she whispered. "And your huge heart."

"If it's a boy, he better get my *huge* heart!"

She chucked him in the shoulder, giggling at his awful innuendo. "You are a ridiculous man."

"You adore me," he said, kissing her again.

"Someone has to."

He placed a sweet kiss on her lips and then peppered over the sun spots covering her nose. "I hope our child has your smile and your courage. And most of all, I hope they have beautiful skin like yours and freckles like these."

Daily walks on the shore had turned her skin golden brown and made her spattering of freckles stand out. Sarani hadn't cared—he loved her skin and her in it. And she knew beyond a shadow of a doubt that any child of theirs, regardless of what they looked like, would be beloved as well.

"I love you, Rhystan."

"It cannot possibly be as much as I love you, my duchess." Blue-gray eyes full of joy and love held hers. "Thank you, *my love*."

She stroked her fingers over his jaw. "For what?"

"For loving me. For choosing me." He placed a hand on her heart and then the small curve of her stomach and pressed his forehead against hers. "For giving me everything a man could ever hope for." He let out a choked breath. "And for saving me."

"Saving you?"

He gave a solemn nod, his eyes so full of love that her throat went tight. "You did, even when I didn't know I needed saving, you were there. You will forever be my port in the storm. My safe harbor. My *home*. Always."

Keep reading for a sneak peek at

RULES
FOR
HEIRESSES

Coming October 2021 from Sourcebooks Casablanca

One

LADY RAVENNA HUNTLEY, UNWED SISTER TO THE DUKE OF Embry, was in the biggest pickle of her life, and that was saying a lot, considering she'd been a fugitive on one of her brother's ships across the Atlantic. Now, she was about to lose a substantial fortune playing vingt-et-un while disguised as a man...unless she did something she'd never considered before.

Unless she *cheated*.

This win was a matter of survival. She was almost out of money, barring her last pair of earbobs. Notwithstanding her previous exploits, her brother would have her hide if his precious sister ended up getting thrown into the stocks on an island in the British West Indies.

But she wasn't a cheater and never had been. Ravenna could understand how desperate times made people consider unpalatable options because at the moment, she truly *was* out of options. She hadn't fully thought through her plan. Yet again.

She *could* win if she bluffed her way through it, but if she lost… Well, better not think of that. Why was it so bloody sweltering? It felt as though sweat was pouring down her back in rivers. She eyed the men gathering around the table in the gaming hell at fashionable Starlight Hotel and Club, and tugged at her collar.

Jump first and think later had served her marginally well over the past six months.

Not now, naturally.

Her overwarm skin itched beneath the scratchy fabric of her clothing. Men's fashion, while practical, chafed unbearably especially when sweat was involved. And right now, she was boiling like a hog farmer on a blistering day. A part of her—a sad, whimsical, miniscule part of her—missed the silks and the satins of her gowns, but those times were behind her. These days, she went by Mr. Raven Hunt, young nob and ne'er-do-well who enjoyed a spot of gambling…especially when finding his amiable, charming self in need of quick, easy coin.

Though said coin at the moment was neither quick nor easy.

She'd lost count of the cards ages ago…because of *him*.

Ravenna gulped, her heart kicking against her ribs, currently restrained beneath a starched band of linen. Despite its functional purpose of keeping her identity as a female hidden, the stiff, restrictive layer made it quite hard to breathe. And at the moment, she needed to capably inhale, exhale, and focus, mostly because of the inscrutable gentleman across the felted table who watched her with hard, piercing eyes.

Mr. Chase. Shipping magnate. Undisputed local sovereign.

Ruthless, cold, powerful.

Her one remaining adversary.

His sinful looks didn't help. Lips, luscious and wicked to a fault, were framed by a square jawline covered in a dusting of dark shadow, and an aquiline nose was drawn between high-bladed cheekbones. A pair of thick slashes for brows sat over an onyx gaze that was so mercurial it was impossible to read. His eyes reminded her of a churning ocean at midnight, lightning flashing over its surface. Those storm-dark eyes were a study in temptation alone—she'd only ever seen such intensity in one person before. She shook off the unwelcome near miss of a memory. It had been a very long time ago, and that boy was gone.

This *man* certainly was striking. Possibly even the most attractive man she'd ever seen.

Forget his bloody looks, you twit!

Ravenna shook herself hard, hoping to knock some sense into her own head. What were the odds that *he* would be at *her* table, over *this* pot? As far as she knew, Mr. Chase wasn't known to frequent the exclusive gaming rooms of the Starlight Hotel. On occasion, he'd have dinner at the exclusive restaurant there, a beautiful woman on his arm, but Ravenna had only glimpsed him from a distance. It would be impossible to live on an island and *not* know who wielded the most influence here or the man who ran most of the trading ports in the islands. But powerful people made for powerful enemies, and she'd hoped to avoid him and escape his notice.

No such luck, however.

He did not resemble a soft, displaced Englishman in the least. Ravenna narrowed her eyes and fought the urge to yank on her sweltering, suffocating collar. While he didn't seem to be an expert gambler, she could tell he wasn't used to losing. She frowned. Had he *meant* to play poorly early on so she wouldn't suspect him… and then lure her into this final snare? Or was she reading into things?

Blast, her own sharp instincts were failing her.

She peeked at her excellent hand—possibly a winning hand— unless her opponent held a natural. The last round had seen all of the other players overdrawn, except for the dratted Mr. Chase who claimed he was content with his two cards. Ravenna eyed them and ground her jaw in frustration. She was so close. She *needed* the money for lodgings and food, or even passage back to England. And besides, Mr. Chase didn't need it. He was richer than Midas, or so the rumor mill said.

A bead of sweat rolled down her skin, beneath the linen drawn mercilessly across her breasts. She wished she'd left an hour ago, her pockets well lined and heavy. But no. Greed, overconfidence, and plain stupidity had taken over.

And she might as well admit it: smitten lady parts.

Not just because Mr. Chase was beyond a shade of a doubt unnervingly gorgeous, but because her shocking attraction to him—to *any* man—was something she had never, ever experienced. His arrival had thrown her off her game.

Ravenna didn't fancy gentlemen; she didn't fancy *anyone*.

In London, suitor after suitor had been foisted upon her—rich, titled, handsome fellows—and she'd felt nothing. Even when offers had been made, Ravenna had found a way to thwart them.

After all, she'd been engaged twice and almost compromised into a third betrothal.

The first had been arranged in her infancy, but that betrothal had been squashed by her father when her future groom had taken off for parts unknown without so much as a by-your-leave. Ravenna didn't know what could possibly have made Cordy do such a thing, but she hadn't cared.

She'd been glad to be rid of the pesky nuisance!

Over the years, the two of them had been occasional friends but mostly enemies, having childhood adventures between their adjoining country estates in Kettering. He had been obnoxious and arrogant, and had thrown it in her face that when they were married, she would have to do everything he said. He'd sported a blackened eye for weeks after that declaration. One day, Cordy disappeared, sent off to school, she'd been told, and much later on, she'd been saddened to learn from his brother that he'd perished from illness.

Betrothal number two had been a momentary blip in sanity. After her brother Rhystan's love match, Ravenna had felt the first stirrings of indecision. Didn't she *want* a family of her own? She would have to wed…eventually. Perhaps she could attract the ideal sort of gentleman: old, bored, perhaps on his deathbed, and willing to let her live her life. Lord Thatcher had ticked all the boxes—widower, older, quiet—and after he'd proposed, she convinced herself she *might* have been content. But in the end, Ravenna couldn't go through with it.

Her third and final *almost* engagement, though it could hardly even be called that, had caused her to flee London on her brother's ship. Ever since her come-out, the Marquess of Dalwood had been persistent in a way that had made her skin crawl. She'd barely escaped his slimy clutches.

"Are you going to play, lad?" The low, lazy drawl drizzled through her chaotic thoughts like thick, smoky honey.

She peeked up at Mr. Chase through her lashes and grunted a noncommittal response. Drat, he was stunning…stunning in the way she imagined a fallen angel would be. A sultry, terrible, beautiful angel meant to lure poor innocent souls into doing sinful things. Her skin heated with what could only be a surge of primitive lust. Ravenna opened her mouth, not even sure what was going to come out—a breathy *Take me now* or a much smarter *I withdraw*.

"What's it to be then?" Mr. Chase asked, idly tapping his long, elegant, and shockingly tanned fingers against his cards in a repeated sequence that made her stare. His little finger tapped followed by the ring finger, then the middle, ending with his index finger. Those hands looked familiar and strange at the same time. Ravenna felt she might be hallucinating. His voice recalled her with a snap. "I haven't got all night."

"A man has to think."

"I could have sailed to England in the time it takes you to think."

"You can forfeit if you're in a hurry," she grumbled. The other gentlemen at the table had long since backed out, and now it was down to the two of them. He reminded her of a proud, terrifying dragon sitting atop his treasure, daring anyone to come take it. And here she was…daring to do just that.

"Why would I when I have the winning hand?" he drawled.

"I'm sure you think you do, especially as quite a bit of money is at stake," Ravenna remarked, keeping her naturally husky tones low. A man like him missed nothing, and while her disguise of a young, rich, well-born chap had served to fool many, she had the feeling it would not trick him so easily. She had the advantage as dealer, but if she took one more card, she could easily overdraw and lose. Twenty was solid and she doubted he had a natural. Those two cards under his drumming fingertips taunted her.

Mr. Chase peered at her. "What are you called?"

Hiding her sudden dread, Ravenna sketched a cheerful bow from her seated position, hand tipping the brim of her hat. "Mr. Raven Hunt, at your service. Seventh son to a seventh son seeking his fortune, friendship, and a fine adventure." She cringed. That was a smidge too dramatic, but she held on to her charming grin as though it were a shield.

Eventually, one side of his full lips curled up at the corner into a half smirk. "You're barely wet behind the ears. What's a whelp like you doing here?"

"I'm old enough to seek my own way."

"Is that what you're doing?" She was still contemplating how to respond when he leaned back in his chair. "I make it my business to know everyone who comes onto my island."

"Is that a fact, *Your High-Handedness*?" she shot back.

"Careful, puppy." His lips tugged into a full smile, though it didn't make her feel any better. This one was a downright threat.

Ravenna bristled. No one, not even Rhystan, had ever spoken to her with such condescension. Who did he think he was?

A duke's heir, her brain interjected. If local gossip was to be believed anyhow. But the rumor mill on the island was unreliable at best. He had money, certainly—the cut of his clothing revealed that—but Mr. Chase didn't carry himself like elitist British nobility. Notwithstanding the delicious layer of scruff covering that hard jaw, his attitude was relaxed and unconcerned as though he didn't *need* an English title to flaunt his power. No, that came from within…from someone who had earned his place in the world and reveled in it.

Even now, a muscle in his cheek jaw flexed with careless ease, a hint that there was a good chance he held nothing. Besides, she had three of the aces and the last had already passed. *Hadn't it?* Yes, she was quite certain. There was no way he had a natural. Even if he had twenty, she would still win as ties paid the dealer.

With a grand flourish, Ravenna set down her cards. She shot him a wink. "What do you know, old man, you just got trounced by a pup."

―――――――――

Courtland Chase sat back in his chair.

Old man? The lad had balls, he'd give him that. Word of the boy's winning streak had filtered up to him, mostly from grumbling members. This was his hotel and his club, and he made it his business to know what went on. At first, he thought the boy a cheat, but his skill with the cards was extraordinary. Closer scrutiny revealed that the lad didn't *need* to cheat to win; he simply kept track of the cards that had been dealt. It was bloody genius.

But that didn't mean the boy hadn't practiced some clever sleight of hand. Nine cards adding up to twenty was incredibly lucky. Or extremely resourceful.

A fascinated Courtland had kept a watchful eye on the young

man from afar for a few weeks, the boy's natural baby-faced charm making him a popular addition to aristocratic circles. There was something uncannily familiar about that stubborn jaw—the arrogant tilt of that head—but Courtland couldn't figure out what it was.

The lad was so young he barely had any hair on his pallid chin, but aside from his skill, something about him had rubbed at Courtland. It wasn't anything more than a feeling that something was out of place, but his instincts had never served him wrong. The boy was hiding something. Not that many of the gents here didn't—half of them had run from responsibility or duty in England.

Technically, Courtland himself had been shipped *off*, but what was in the past was in the past. This was his life now and this was his domain.

Which brought him back to his current predicament.

Disappointment warred with admiration. Courtland didn't know how, but the more he thought about it, the more it was evident that the boy had probably cheated. He had to set an example or thieves would run roughshod all over him. *No one* had that kind of luck.

Courtland set his cards down—without disclosing them—and steepled his fingers over his chest. "We don't abide cheaters at the Starlight."

"I'm not a cheater."

Courtland's brows rose in challenge. "Aren't you?"

"No."

"Nine cards and not overdrawing is more than sheer skill."

"Sore loser?" a confident Hunt shot back. "I wouldn't have countenanced it."

Courtland blinked. What an odd choice of phrase. It tickled at his memory. Not that the local aristocrats didn't speak the Queen's English, but it wasn't as common a saying on the island. It was a pretentious expression, typically wielded by some censorious tongue in a London drawing room. His own stepmother had been fond of it.

A boy like you, better than my Stinson? I couldn't countenance it.

Swallowing hard, he shrugged off the old anger and rush of unworthiness. His birth mother had been born a free woman of mixed heritage. His father, a duke's spare, had loved and married her and, when she died in childbirth, brought his infant son back to England to be raised in his family home. When Courtland was barely a few months old, his father had remarried—most likely to secure him a mother—but it became apparent by the time he was five that his new stepmother didn't care to raise another woman's child.

Who his own mother had been didn't signify...until it did.

Until Courtland was deemed a *hindrance* to the new marchioness's ambition.

His stepmother hadn't been able to do much while his father was alive, but once his father died, she'd made it her mission to get rid of Courtland. It was obvious she wanted the dukedom for her own son, born shortly after him, though Courtland couldn't imagine how she intended to accomplish that, short of murder. Primogeniture was a devil of a thing.

She resented that he was heir, as the firstborn male, and despised him for it.

Her son too.

At home, his younger half brother made life intolerable, and when they were away at Harrow, life became unbearable. He fought and was bloodied every day by his so-called peers, including Stinson, whom Courtland suspected was behind a lot of the hostility and certainly relished his older brother's torture. He'd fought back. Who wouldn't? Eventually, they'd kicked him out at sixteen, citing rebelliousness and belligerence.

The marchioness—by way of Stinson—offered him passage anywhere he wanted and enough money to live on and support a small retinue. He was young, but he did not return to London or to the ancestral seat in Kettering. He boarded a train to Europe instead. He'd then apprenticed to a Spanish railway industrialist and paid his own way to finish his education at the Central University of Madrid.

Blessed with a keen mind, he invested heavily in shipping and trade, and eventually migrated to the West Indies to see if he could find any of his maternal family. When he had arrived, it'd been a shock to his system. A *wonderful* life-changing shock—one he'd sensed in the air he'd breathed into his lungs and felt to the marrow of his bones. *This* was home. The British gentry had welcomed him with open arms, but they'd always been swayed by pretty faces and prettier fortunes. The islanders had taken longer—thirty years of abolition hadn't shaken the shadows of the past—but he'd been determined to earn their trust. And he had.

Now, Courtland belonged here. He'd built his fortune and reinvested in local infrastructure. The Starlight was his kingdom, and here, he reigned. This bold boy who threatened his rule needed to know his place.

"I never lose," he told the cocky Mr. Hunt.

"Everyone loses sometimes" came the quick answer. "Get used to it."

Courtland smirked. "Not me."

"'Pride goeth before destruction, and a haughty spirit before a fall.'"

An unexpected chuckle burst out of him. "Let me guess, you forgot to mention you're the seventh son of a vicar?"

From beneath the wild sprigs of auburn curls poking askew from beneath the boy's hat, sharp eyes the color of polished pennies narrowed on him. They shone with intelligence and suspicion. Good, the boy wasn't foolish. "Something like that. I'll just collect my winnings and be off, then."

Hunt stood and pulled his coat tight, his fingers darting up to the inside of his waistcoat. Courtland noted the garment was well stitched, though the edges along the coat cuffs had seen some wear. Courtland suddenly felt sure there might be a card hidden in one of those sleeves. "Wait," he commanded in a deadly soft voice.

The young man froze. Courtland could care less about the money, but the principle mattered. His gaze glanced to the crowd standing a few feet away and those seated at the table. If he didn't act and Hunt had indeed cheated, it would encourage others, and that, he could not permit.

He nodded to one of the men behind him and the porter stepped up to the boy, grabbing him by his arms. Hunt tried to pull away without success. "Unhand me at once, sir!"

"Remove your coat," Courtland ordered.

"What? No!" The boy's coppery eyes rounded with panic. "What kind of establishment is this? I'll have you know I will seek out the owner of the Starlight and have you thrown bodily from this hotel. How dare you, sir? You cannot do this."

"You're in luck, *puppy*. I'm the owner so feel free to state your grievance at any time. Now, remove that coat."

"This is an outrage," the boy insisted, his thin shoulders rising up and down.

His mouth opened and closed, a rivulet of sweat trickling from his temple to the hairless apple of his cheek. He was a baby. Courtland wouldn't put him at more than seventeen, if that. The thin brown mustache over his lip seemed out of place on his face, and it also seemed to be traveling of its own accord and curling away at the corner. The more the youth struggled, the more it shifted. Courtland's gaze narrowed on the brown stubble along the lad's sloping downy jaw where sweat mixed in with the chin hairs.

What in the hell? Was that *ink*?

"Remove your coat or Rawley here will do it for you. Or break your arms if you don't cease struggling."

His man of affairs and second cousin, Rawley was a large,

brown-skinned man with a razor-sharp wit and a quick brain that outmatched many. Blessed with both brain and brawn, Courtland had hired him years before, and now, he trusted him with his life.

"No, wait," Hunt pleaded. "Please."

Someone in the crowd jeered. "If you have nothing to hide, take it off."

In the next moment, Rawley yanked the coat off the boy's shoulders, buttons popping. A high-pitched yelp tore from the boy as the plain waistcoat went next, leaving him standing there in a linen shirt, hastily knotted cravat, and trousers. His narrow frame shook, shoulders hunching forward, arms crossed over his middle.

"Please, cease this," he begged in a plaintive whisper. "You don't understand."

Courtland hesitated at the hushed desperation in the boy's voice. It wasn't in him to publicly shame someone this young who might have made a mistake and could learn a valuable lesson, and besides, he liked the boy's spirit. However, before he could order Rawley to take him to his private office, his burly factotum, Fawkes, shoved through the crowd. He was closely followed by a perspiring, balding, well-heeled man.

"What is it, Fawkes?"

"Mr. Chase. An urgent messenger has arrived." The man was fairly bursting with news, and a dribble of unease slid down Courtland's spine. "From London. From—"

"Your Grace," the unknown man said in a loud voice, and every muscle in Courtland's body solidified to stone. "I'm Mr. Bingham, the private solicitor of the late duke, your grandfather, His Grace, the Duke of Ashvale, God rest his soul. As your grandfather's eldest heir, you've now been named duke. However, the will is being contested, claiming you are deceased, though clearly, my eyes attest that you are not."

Thunder roared in Courtland's ears. This was not bloody happening.

For all intents and purposes Lord Courtland Chase, the rightful Marquess of Borne, *was* dead. But the damage was done. Amid the chatter now soaring to the rooftop, he opened his mouth to say what Bingham could do with the title and the rest of his message, but was thwarted by the young thief who now seemed to have lost half his mustache and was gawking at him with wide, incredulous eyes that burned with an unnaturally disturbing degree of emotion. Not shock or wonder or even awe like everyone else in the room, but...*recognition.*

"Cordy?" the boy whispered.

Courtland hadn't heard that name in well over a decade, but it was a like a punch to the chest, more powerful, deadly even, than the wallop about him being duke. No one had ever called him Cordy...no one except...

His jaw hardened, confusion pouring through him. "Who the *fuck* are you?"

Two

RAVENNA FORGOT THAT SHE'D BEEN ACCUSED OF CHEATING and almost stripped down to the altogether in front of a crowd in a popular local hotel and club. Not even the whispers of *Your Grace* and the *Duke of Ashvale* could take away from the fact that her childhood friend and nemesis, her once-upon-a-time betrothed, whom she hadn't seen in eleven years and also thought long dead, was standing in front of her.

Hale, healthy, and cold as a winter ocean.

And so obviously *alive.*

No wonder he'd seemed so familiar. Ravenna blinked her shock away. His family had mourned him. Stinson, Cordy's younger half brother, had been devastated and inconsolable after his death, even taking to burning down the woodland fort she and Cordy had built. Ravenna had let him, guessing it was due to his inconsolable grief. A breath shivered out of her tight lungs. If Cordy was alive and living here of all places, why wouldn't he have let his family know?

"Answer me, damn you!" he demanded in a growl. "Where did you hear that name?"

The snarl shook her out of her memories. *Blast it.* If she admitted to knowing him, he might know who *she* was. And well, she wasn't exactly dressed as Lady Ravenna Huntley at the moment. Revealing herself as the daughter of a duke and an unmarried female in the midst of a gaming room full of men would be the pinnacle of stupidity, not that her decisions leading her here hadn't been foolishly reckless. It didn't matter that she wasn't in England;

the scandal would be swift and inevitable. She had to deflect somehow, until she could run.

Piercing dark eyes held her prisoner, but Rawley, the enormous and handsome brute who had several stone of muscle on her, had released her arms. This was it! Her moment to escape. Her nemesis must have seen what she meant to do in the sudden tension of her body because he snarled a denial and lunged across the table for her.

For once, her small stature helped as she snatched up her fallen coat—it had her winnings in it, after all—and shoved through the dense crowd. She could hear a predator's frustrated roar, and even as she reveled in her almost victory, a part of her quailed at the savage sound.

Luck was finally back on her side. She let out a soft whoop. Thankfully, everyone in attendance wanted to congratulate the new duke, which gave her plenty of opportunity to slip away. She'd lost her hat and she was certain half her face paint was now a sweaty mess. Oh, well, it was probably about time for the fantastic Mr. Hunt to abscond to another island anyway. She'd danced with the devil, nearly gotten caught, and the near discovery of her identity had tested her every nerve.

Lengthening her strides toward the exit without breaking into a run that would draw attention, Ravenna could taste the sweet, fresh tropical air on her tongue, just beyond the wide paneled doors of the hotel. It was a far cry from the smog and foul scents of London, and one she'd grown to love.

"Not so fast, you little scamp," a gravelly voice breathed into her ear, a huge hand encircling her upper arm in an unbreakable grip. Ravenna gasped, though it wasn't pain that forced the air from her lungs.

Horrifyingly, the rush of hot breath against her skin and the sultry tenor of his words sent heat flooding through her body and her knees went rubbery.

What on earth was wrong with her? He was going to strangle her and she was falling to pieces. Her breath was short, her stomach was weak, and her heart was racing like a horse on the last leg of a race. This wasn't a swoon, was it? She'd never swooned a day in her life!

A powerful frame steered her into a receiving room off the foyer and manhandled her into a chair. The salon wasn't empty, but Ravenna had much worse to worry about, like the incensed male looming over her whose face could be carved from granite. His mouth, that she'd thought so full and supple before, was a flat, furious line. His stormy eyes were unforgiving.

She goggled that *this* man was Cordy. It was unfathomable! For one, he was huge. Cordy had been rangy but scrawny with nary a muscle in sight. Built like a Roman gladiator, this man looked nothing like the rangy boy he'd been. His complexion was a much richer brown now, after being exposed to the hot sun of the islands. Ravenna had the sudden, inexplicable urge to run her hands over him.

A muscle flexed in that lean, stubbled-dusted cheek, his intense gaze not veering once from her. "I'll ask you once, brat, who are you?" The ruthless snap of his voice raked across her mind, reminding her that his good looks weren't the problem. The fact that he was going to toss her into jail was. She had to get out of this mess somehow! "Speak or I'll make you regret disobeying me."

This was *not* good.

"I was a friend…of Lord Richard in Kettering," she blurted out, fear of discovery making her quiver. Was that too close to the truth? Richard was her second oldest brother who died years ago in a fire along with her father and eldest brother. *Blast!* Richard had been a bit of a loner, preferring his books to actual people.

Mr. Chase—*no, the Duke of Ashvale*—would see right through her falsehood and ferret out her identity in an instant.

"Richard Huntley?" he said. His dark gaze scoured her, fingers still clamped over her arms, though not cruelly. Ravenna forced herself not to fidget or break eye contact. She needed him to believe her.

"I saw you once at Embry Hall," she rushed out, panic overtaking her explanation. "His sister called you 'Cordy' and he said you were the duke's grandson."

"His sister."

Her body quivered. Gracious, was that a question or some kind of proclamation? Ravenna almost swore aloud and clamped her mouth shut, well aware of the obvious relation between her fake male name and her real one. It wasn't much of a stretch to connect Raven and Ravenna. Deuce it, how could she have been so stupid? The real question was: would *he* notice? The Cordy she'd known might have been lacking in muscle as a boy, but he'd never lacked for acuity. She doubted that would have changed as an adult.

"Your Grace," a harried-looking man with his hair and spectacles askew burst through the door and interrupted them. "It's madness in there. Bingham is waiting."

Rawley, the large man from before, entered the room with a nod. "I'm afraid you can't hide much longer, old friend. The gossip is like a bushfire...already rampant and impossible to contain." His gaze came to rest on Ravenna. "I can ferry this one to the stocks."

The man who clearly did not want to be duke ran a palm over his face and nodded to his man. "Very well. Escort Bingham to the library adjoining the office first. I'll be along shortly." He then turned brutally cold eyes on her. "It doesn't matter who you are or how you know me. Cheaters are a disgrace, and the piper must be paid. I have to make an example of you, young buck, and I reckon you'd much rather a harmless night in the stalls than the loss of a finger."

"Take it," Ravenna blurted out, though her body trembled almost violently. A paltry finger was much less of a price to pay than being unmasked as a lady of quality or being thrown into a filthy jail.

"You jest," he said with a long-suffering look.

"I do not. Take. My. Finger."

"No."

"Then let me go. You cannot accuse me of thievery without proof." In response, Ashvale skimmed up her forearms as if attempting to feel beneath her sleeves for evidence. "I didn't cheat, *Your Grace.*"

She spat the title with a mouthful of mockery, enjoying the tightening of his face and the ashen cast to his sun-kissed skin. A part of her wondered why he was so against being duke. It was his birthright, and one of privilege and power. No gentleman of sound mind would refuse a coronet, and yet, he seemed to loathe the very idea.

"I don't require proof. I'm judge, jury, and executioner here." He released her arm and handed her over to his man who had returned. "Rawley."

"No, wait, please," she said in alarm, her fingers catching on his coat. "You can't. I can't go there. Anything else. I'll do whatever you want me to here in the club, scrub pots and clean carpets, but not the jail."

"It won't kill you, boy," Rawley muttered. "It's a damn sight better than losing a body part."

Ravenna ground her jaw. If he only knew that she was in danger of losing much more than that if her secret was discovered by a bunch of criminals who wouldn't care that she was nobility. Or female. She suppressed a shudder. "I'm begging you. Please."

When the duke made to leave, Ravenna panicked, yanking her arm from Rawley and heaving herself between him and the door. Hushed gasps from their avid onlookers reached her ears, but she had no choice. She would not survive a single hour in the local jail. Her reputation might turn to tatters, but she wasn't about to give up the last of her dignity.

"Grow a pair of ballocks, Hunt," the newly minted duke growled.

Her voice lowered. "I can't." She peered up at him, though she kept her chin tilted down. There was still a chance she could salvage everything by not giving away *exactly* who she was, at least in public. "I'm female."

The whispered confession seemed to stump him for a second, but then his face hardened. "Being female doesn't win you leniency."

Gracious, he truly was without a heart, but enough was enough. Ravenna drew up her shoulders, channeled her mother's hauteur that had been drilled into her since birth, and met his burning gaze. "You are making a grave mistake, Your Grace," she told him in clipped British accents that left no doubt that she was female and of unquestionable high birth. "Either release me at once, or you will not like the consequences, I assure you."

A menacing growl ripped from his throat. "Don't threaten me."

She'd never met such an autocratic man in all her life. One would imagine he was made of fire and brimstone with a clockwork heart beating in his chest. A chill settled over her—this was it, the point of no return. She should have known her freedom or anonymity wasn't going to last. She had one last hope.

"Then in that case, I doubt the Duke of Embry would appreciate you sending his sister to jail, regardless of any error in judgment on your part."

"Embry's *sister*?" he echoed, dark eyes glinting.

He studied her, his face giving away nothing as the chatter in the salon around them grew, the whispers of her identity a delicious on-dit. Scandal tended to have its own decibel level, after all. Ravenna breathed out. "What a delightful surprise to see you alive and well, Cordy."

The little hoyden from the neighboring estate in Kettering had grown up into a spitfire. Wearing men's clothing and cheating at cards in *his* hotel. What were the odds?

Lady Ravenna Huntley.

Courtland didn't doubt who she said she was. When he'd thought her a young gent, something about her face and swagger had struck a vague chord of recognition in him, and when she'd claimed to know him via Richard Huntley, it had clicked. He'd assumed her to be a cousin or some such. But now, as he took in her heart-shaped face, huge eyes, and trembling lips, he saw distinct signs of the girl he once knew. Though she wasn't a girl anymore—she was grown. In spite of her clever disguise, that much was obvious. His lip curled in irritation. What the devil had she been *thinking*?

As if she could sense his thoughts, her chin lifted and she met his gaze with defiance.

"Does Embry know you're here?" he demanded.

"What do you think?" Her tongue was as cutting as he remembered.

"I think he should put you over his knee."

She rolled her eyes. "My brother is not a barbarian."

"Then perhaps the task should fall to me."

A furious copper gaze slammed into his. "Touch me and you will be the one missing a finger, I promise you. I've learned a few things since we were children."

His brow dipped. He didn't doubt that, considering she was *here*, and not tucked away in a ducal residence somewhere in England, being waited on hand and foot like the gently reared lady she was. What the hell *was* she doing here? And come to think of it, did she have a lick of sense left in that idiot head of hers? She had just announced her identity in a public drawing room while scandalously dressed in men's clothing. And yes, it was a far step away from London, but oceans didn't stop gossip.

Swearing under his breath, he shrugged out of his own coat, draped it over her shoulders, and shepherded her from the room to his personal offices, which he should have done from the start.

Then his own ill-timed ducal news as well as her revelation would have occurred behind private, closed doors. Too late for any of that.

Bloody hell.

"Drink?" he asked.

"No, thank you."

In silence, he poured two fingers of imported French brandy into a tumbler and took a healthy sip. Coppery irises of the same changing hues as the brandy met his. Had her eyes always been that color? He'd remembered them being brown. Her shorn hair was a surprise, the close-cropped curls lying flat beneath the copious pomade. As a girl, her long hair had been braided tight to her scalp and gingery-red—to the point where her brothers had called her *gingersnap* mercilessly—and not such a dark auburn.

It was no wonder he hadn't recognized her outright, though some instinct deep within him had sensed…*something.*

"Why?" he asked.

"Why what?"

Thick russet lashes lifted and he questioned how he'd ever thought she was male. Even with smudges of dark ink on her chin and cheeks, she was comely. *Too* much so. Courtland shrugged. The now defunct mustache, obviously fake, had been a damned convincing touch.

But now, he couldn't stop thinking of her as a woman— scrutinizing each of her features—including those copper-bright eyes and the rosy pout that he *hadn't* noticed before. The meddlesome, nosy little Lady Ravenna had grown up to be a beauty, one whom gentlemanly suitors in London drawing rooms would have been fawning over.

Speaking of, why wasn't she married? *Was* she married? He was only two years older than she was, so she should be three-and-twenty or thereabouts. Long past marrying age.

"Why are you here?" he asked, enunciating each word.

"My grand tour?" she replied. "A pleasure trip?"

He couldn't help noticing that the huskiness in her voice stayed that way. Put together with the fact that she was female, the raspy just-waking-up-after-hours-and-hours-of-sex sound of it shaping the word *pleasure* arrowed straight to his groin. Scowling at the reaction, he moved behind his desk. "Women don't do grand tours."

"Hence my ingenious disguise," she said. "At least until today."

"You would have been found out eventually. Be glad it was by me and not someone else." He cringed to think that he'd nearly sent her to a public jail. "So I take it Embry doesn't know you're here then."

Courtland wasn't close with the duke though they were close in age. The sons of the Duke of Embry had all gone to Eton when he'd been fighting for his life at Harrow. Even in Antigua, however, he'd learned about the tragic fire that had made the youngest Huntley duke, and then the news had come four years ago about the duke's shocking nuptials with an Anglo-Indian princess. *Good for them*, he remembered thinking.

If only the marchioness and his own brother had been that accepting, the path his life had taken might have been vastly different, though the final destination had turned out to be inevitable. While his grandfather had written steadily over the years, always knowing exactly where he was—first in Spain, and then Antigua—they hadn't cared.

Courtland had received all of the letters, but had refused to read them. He'd instructed Rawley to dispose of them. If he was being summoned to Ashvale Park, he didn't want to know. He had no intention of going back to England.

Without Courtland's presence, his ambitious stepbrother would no doubt have led a charge to prove he was the Duke of Ashvale's true heir. Courtland wondered idly if his stepmother had tried to have him declared dead through the courts. He wondered what his grandfather might have had to say about that.

Scowling as fresh feelings of bitterness rose, Courtland stalked forward to refill Ravenna's glass and then his, lifting a brow and waiting for her answer. Her brother would never have condoned this, that much he knew.

"Stop dithering around and answer me—what does Embry believe?"

"He thinks I'm in Scotland with Clara."

"Clara?"

"A recently married dear friend. She wed a Scottish earl."

Courtland frowned. "How is Embry not worried?"

"I wrote several letters in advance, which she will mail out at monthly intervals, and swore Clara to secrecy as long as I was in good health." She lifted her glass and sipped. "Which as you can see I am. No need to trouble my brother."

"And this Clara considers you a friend?" He didn't hide his sardonic tone.

Her eyes narrowed on him. "The best kind."

"Forgive me if I've been out of London society too long, but friends don't force friends to lie on their behalf. Much less lie to a respected and rather formidable peer of the realm."

Ravenna tossed her head. "What Embry doesn't know won't hurt him, and besides, he's just had a new baby and deserves every joy. If he knew where I was, he'd be frantic with worry instead of focusing on his own happiness."

"For good reason, you daft girl!"

"Because I'm female?" she shot back. "Why should men have all the adventure and women be forced to sit at home tending the hearth? We are *not* possessions or brainless biddable toys designed for male consumption."

He almost choked on his drink at the images her provocative words produced, but the hostility beneath was clear. "Because it's not safe or smart for a woman to be traveling on her own."

"I know how to use a pistol, Cordy," she said. "I was a better shot than you, remember? Or perhaps you choose not to remember how many times I bested you just to preserve your insufferably delicate male pride."

He didn't remember her being this...caustic. Silent laughter rippled through him. Who was he fooling? She'd always been a hothead.

"We were children then," he said. "And my name is Courtland, not Cordy."

"Apparently, it's *Ashvale* now," she reminded him.

Yes, it was, apparently. He was going to have to deal with that complication as soon as possible, too. "How did you get here anyway?"

"I took one of Embry's clippers." She lifted an ungloved hand to sift through the pressed strands of her shorn mane. "Hacked off my hair and disguised myself as a boatswain. Learned a lot over the last few years from my brother and his old quartermaster so it was easy. Kept my head down, did the work, and no one was the wiser."

Courtland balked in horror—she'd spent close to five weeks on a ship full of male sailors? His hands fisted at his sides at her rashness. "Why not an ocean liner?"

"Too easily tracked. I didn't need luxury, I needed to disappear."

"Why?"

Her lip curled. "None of your deuced business."

"If you were mine, I'd definitely put you over my knee." Courtland regretted the words as soon as he said them. The thought of her lying across his lap, her pert bottom bared to his gaze, was not something he wanted to envision, not while she already had him on edge. She busied herself with her gloves, but he could see color flare into her pale cheeks.

"Good thing I'm not then."

Not yet. Courtland had no idea where that thought came from, nor did he want to know. He had no time for a smart-mouthed, self-centered heiress who knew no better than to traipse willy-nilly around the world with no regard for her own welfare. When he thought of the misfortunes that could have befallen her, his anger surged again. "You got lucky, you know. How could you have been so foolish? Things could have been so much worse."

"But they weren't."

He was going to throttle her. "They *could* have been."

"Let's agree to disagree. Are you going to send word to Embry?"

Controlling his temper, Courtland shook his head. "I won't have to."

He heard her sharp exhale. They both knew what his answer meant. Lady Ravenna would be disgraced just from being in the West Indies on her own without a chaperone. If word got out about her travels on a ship with a bunch of rough-and-tumble sailors, her reputation would take an unrecoverable thrashing.

But that was none of his business. Her virtue, or lack of it, wasn't anyone's concern, but he more than anybody knew the exacting nature of the *ton*'s rules. Upon her return, they would slice her to ribbons. Any hope for a suitable match would be lost. Courtland felt an expected stroke of pity for what she would face, even if she'd brought the storm upon herself.

They fell into tense silence.

"What would it take for you to forget you ever saw me?" she asked after a while.

Courtland blinked—she couldn't possibly be asking what he thought she was. "I couldn't in good conscience do that."

"Yet you were willing to throw me in jail an hour ago."

"You weren't *you*!" He glared at her.

She cleared her throat. "Look, I'm serious. You know what awaits me if I'm sent back to London. What will it take? Money? You are welcome to whatever I have. My body? Though I don't know what good it'll do—it's as frigid as they come, or so I've been told."

He ignored the bolt of pure lust at her wicked offer, even as her cheeks flamed. "I'll protect you."

"How? Trust me, you can't."

"Bloody hell, woman, I can't let you go off on your own." He pinched the bridge of his nose, closed his eyes, and sighed. "Embry would pulverize my bones to meal. My father would turn in his grave if he knew I abandoned an innocent girl to her own foolish devices."

"I'm not innocent or foolish."

"Your actions prove otherwise," he said.

"Then I'm sorry for this."

A noise that sounded uncannily like a cocking gun made his eyelids snap open. He was right—a loaded pocket pistol was pointed right at his face.

Author's Note

Hello, readers. I hope you enjoyed Sarani and Rhystan's story! When I started this book, I knew I wanted to write a story that would incorporate some of my background (I'm a biracial West Indian-American woman, and have been in an interracial marriage for twenty years), but the journey I went on for this novel was more than I'd hoped for. The questions of identity and self-worth are themes that every woman struggles with—especially in areas of friendship, family, and romance. My heroine, Sarani, who changes her name to fit in when she travels to England, embodies that struggle. I changed my name when I went to college because my first name was difficult to pronounce. It stuck, and later on, I found myself torn between the two vastly different identities I had constructed. It took quite a long time for me to bridge the two. What I've found, however, is that the creation of separate personas isn't isolated to cultural or racial differences. Many women have different faces they share with the world. We become who the world needs us to be at any given time, whether that is at home, at work, in relationships, or even with our own families, and sometimes, it's hard to reconcile those facets of ourselves.

Lakshmi Bai, the Rani of Jhansi, also known as Manu, whom I mention in this novel as a friend of the heroine and who inspired me so much, was an actual Indian queen in the nineteenth century. Born in 1835, she lived in the princely state of Jhansi (inspiration for the fictional princely state of Joor) and was a fierce leader in the Indian Rebellion in 1857, fighting against British rule in India until her death in 1858. She was raised as a trained fighter, horsewoman, and independent thinker. When the maharaja she married

(Gangadhar Rao) died, she became regent to their adopted son. However, the boy was not recognized as a true successor, and under the doctrine of lapse, the princely state was annexed to the British Crown. At a mere twenty-two years of age, Lakshmi Bai refused to surrender to the injustice and even pleaded her case to a court in London. As regent of Jhansi, she was at the forefront of the Indian Mutiny, and despite her bravery, she was killed in combat. In Solapur, Maharashtra, there's a statue of her riding into battle with her son strapped to her back, sword raised and daunt-less, which is just inspirational.

That said, colonialism was a very fraught period in history, and in no way do I want to make light of some of the terrible and unforgivable atrocities that occurred during this time. Having been born in a colonial country (Trinidad and Tobago got its inde-pendence from Britain in 1962) and having grown up on one of those sugar, cocoa, and coffee plantations that was taken over and farmed by locals and descendants of former indentured laborers, I have an intimate idea of the harm that was caused by colonization. My family might have risen out of the ashes of a violent, oppressed past, but we survived and it's part of my history.

Writing this book also showed me that there are so many facets to a diaspora. One POC's experience will not reflect another's. My experience as a woman of West Indian descent will not be the same as someone who was born or raised in the United States, England, India, or elsewhere. I saw this when working through nine sensitiv-ity reads during revisions (three Indian-Americans, two Muslim-Americans, two British-Indians, one West Indian-American, and one African-American) and each reader had a different but equally relevant worldview. This means that as a writer, I might not be the perfect representation for some South Asian readers or other members of a diasporic community. I can only write from my own experience and through the knowledge of my own sphere of existence. History might be shared, but cultural identity is vastly intersectional, and I hope that more diverse voices will be called to the publishing table to represent the amazingly rich narratives in the world.

As a result, I cover some hard ground in this story. Parts of it had to be raw because history is raw. *But*, you say, *historical romance is fantasy*. I mean…you aren't wrong. There are nine million dukes, everyone has great hygiene and health, the aristocracy miraculously got their wealth in a non-oppressive way, and people had sex without care for pregnancy or protection. Suspension of disbelief is part of the canon of historical romance. That said, I felt it would be a disservice to my biracial heroine to be disingenuous about some of the ingrained behaviors of the period. Being a character of color would simply be window dressing if she acted and behaved like everyone else. While I could have taken a less problematic route, sanitizing history wasn't my goal. That was a creative choice…to go a touch less fantasy for the sake of the story. I truly hope it made for a deeper reading experience.

In my research, one of the really cool things I discovered was how many women of color there actually were in British high society, even though it's not very well known or documented. Sarah Forbes Bonetta, a displaced West African princess brought to England, was raised and educated at the queen's decree, and praised by Victoria herself as being "sharp and intelligent." In the 1860s, she was also said to be an accomplished member of Brighton society who was fluent in both English and French. Her first born daughter was named after Victoria (Victoria Davies) and was the queen's goddaughter. Later on, in the 1880s, Princess Sophia Duleep Singh, a Sikh princess, was a court favorite of her godmother, Queen Victoria. After her father's death, she was granted a residence by the queen at the Hampton Court Palace and presented to British society as a debutante, along with her two sisters. She was also popular on the aristocratic scene, and loved riding, cycling, dogs, and traveling. Faced with prejudice and bias on account of both her gender and race, she went on to become a women's rights activist in the 1900s and fought against inequality both in England and India.

While *The Princess Stakes* is a work of fiction, I wanted to write a story that showcased not just what it meant to be a woman of color in historical times, but also what it meant to fall in love in a period that wasn't all ballrooms and ballgowns (though I do hope you love the dresses—I definitely did—I'm head-over-heels in love with the gorgeous gown on the cover)! *The Princess Stakes* is first and foremost a romance, but it is also an exploration into my characters, drilling down to the core of who they truly are. I wanted to strip down the hero and heroine to their fundamental layers—to the raw essence that connected them as people and, hopefully, to show that differences are meant to be celebrated and valued. After all, love is love, and it's certainly worth fighting for.

Thanks for reading!

Xo, Amalie

Acknowledgments

First and foremost, thank you to my brilliant editor, Deb Werksman. What a journey this has been, and you've had my back every single step of the way, editorially and otherwise. I cannot thank you enough for taking a chance on me and this book. I've wanted to work with you for years, and I'm so glad that I finally got a chance to do so…it has been everything I hoped for and more.

To my hands-down super star agent, Thao Le, what can I say except you are a freaking force of nature. Honestly, you're everything a literary agent should be: smart, professional, forward-looking, fierce, compassionate, and a devoted advocate. Thank you so much for going over and beyond for me. I'm truly lucky to have you.

Thanks to the entire production, design, sales, and publicity teams at Sourcebooks Casablanca for your tireless efforts behind the scenes—I'm grateful for all you do! A special shout-out to Stefani Sloma and Molly Waxman. There aren't enough words for how incredibly awesome you both are. Thank you.

To the women who keep me sane on this publishing roller coaster and are forced to read my scrappy first drafts, Katie McGarry, Wendy Higgins, Angie Frazier, Aliza Mann, Sienna Snow, Sage Spelling, MK Schiller, Shaila Patel, Vonetta Young, Damaris Doll, Kerrigan Byrne, Lisa Brown Roberts, Jenna Lincoln, Jen Fisher, Stacy Reid, Ausma Zehanat Khan, Jodi Picoult, and Brigid Kemmerer, I'd legit be curled up in a fetal position if it weren't for you. Thanks for being there and never letting me down.

Thanks also to everyone who reached out when I really needed it. Too numerous to name here, you know who you are.

To all the readers, reviewers, booksellers, librarians, and friends who support me and spread the word about my books, I have so much gratitude for you. Thank you for being patient with me on this particular book.

Last but not least, to my family...my beautiful children (who are English, Scottish, French, Indian, Middle Eastern, Chinese, Australian-Trinidadian-Americans)—Connor, Noah, and Olivia—you make me so proud to be your mom. I love seeing you embrace all sides of your very diverse heritage. And finally, to my forever love and wonderful husband, Cameron, I couldn't do any of this without you. Thank you for accepting me as I am and loving me so well all these many years.

About the Author

Amalie Howard is a *USA Today* and *Publishers Weekly* bestselling author, most notably of *The Beast of Beswick*, "a smart, sexy, deliciously feminist romance," and one of *O-The Oprah Magazine*'s Top 24 Best Historicals to Read. She is the co-author of the #1 bestsellers in regency romance and Scottish historical romance, *My Rogue, My Ruin* and *What A Scot Wants*, and has also penned several young adult novels, critically acclaimed by *Kirkus*, *Publishers Weekly*, *VOYA*, *School Library Journal*, and *Booklist*, including *Waterfell*, *The Almost Girl*, and *Alpha Goddess*, a Kid's INDIE NEXT selection. Of Indo-Caribbean descent, she has written articles on multicultural fiction for *The Portland Book Review* and *Ravishly* magazine. She currently resides in Colorado with her husband and three children. Visit her at amaliehoward.com.